Sense & Sensibility

Also by Joanna Trollope

Sense
&
Sensibility

JOANNA
TROLLOPE

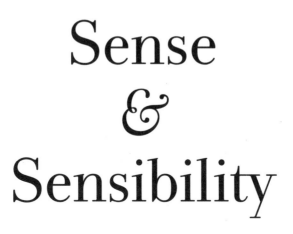

HarperCollins*Publishers*

HarperCollins*Publishers*
77–85 Fulham Palace Road,
Hammersmith, London W6 8JB

www.harpercollins.co.uk

Published by HarperCollins*Publishers* 2013

3

A catalogue record for this book
is available from the British Library

ISBN: 978 0 00 746176 9

Set in Andrade
Typographic design by Lindsay Nash

Printed and bound in Great Britain by
Clays Ltd, St Ives plc

MIX
Paper from
responsible sources
FSC **FSC™ C007454**
www.fsc.org

FSC™ is a non-profit international organisation established to promote
the responsible management of the world's forests. Products carrying the
FSC label are independently certified to assure consumers that they come
from forests that are managed to meet the social, economic and
ecological needs of present and future generations,
and other controlled sources.

Find out more about HarperCollins and the environment at
www.harpercollins.co.uk/green

For Louise and Antonia

Volume I

1

From their windows – their high, generous Georgian windows – the view was, they all agreed, spectacular. It was a remarkable view of Sussex parkland, designed and largely planted two hundred years before to give the fortunate occupants of Norland Park the very best of what nature could offer when tamed by the civilising hand of man. There were gently undulating sweeps of green; there were romantic but manageable stretches of water; there were magnificent stands of ancient trees under which sheep and deer decoratively grazed. Add to all that the occasional architectural punctuation of graceful lengths of park railing and the prospect was, to the Dashwood family, gathered sombrely in their kitchen, gazing out, perfection.

'And now,' their mother said, flinging an arm out theatrically in the direction of the open kitchen window, 'we have to leave all this. This – this *paradise*.' She paused, and then she added, in a lower voice but with distinct emphasis, 'Because of *her*.'

All three daughters watched her, in silence. Even Marianne, the middle one, who had inherited in full her mother's propensity for drama and impulsiveness, said nothing. It was clear to all of them, from long practice, that their mother had not finished. While they waited, they switched their collective gaze to the scrubbed top of the kitchen table, to the spongeware jug of artless garden flowers, randomly arranged, to their chipped and pretty tea mugs. They were quite still, scarcely breathing, three girls waiting for the next maternal tirade.

Belle Dashwood continued to gaze longingly at the view. It had been the girls' father – their recently, appallingly, dead father – who had called their mother Belle. He said, in his emotional, gallant way, that, as a name, Belle was the perfect fit for its owner, and in any case, Isabella, though distinguished, was far too much of a mouthful for daily use.

And so Isabella, more than twenty years ago, had become Belle. And in time, quietly and unobtrusively, she had morphed into Belle Dashwood, as the wife (apparently) of Henry Dash-wood, and (more certainly) the mother of Elinor and Marianne and Margaret. They were a lovely family, everyone remarked upon it: that open-hearted man; his pretty, artistic wife; those adorable girls of theirs. Their charm and looks made them universally popular, so that when Henry had had a fairy-tale stroke of luck, and was summoned, with Belle and the girls, to share the great house of a childless old bachelor uncle to whom Henry was the only heir, the world had rejoiced. To be transported from their happy but anxiously threadbare exist-ence to live at Norland Park, with its endless bedrooms and acres, seemed to most of their friends only a delightful instance of the possibility of magic, an example of the occasional value of building castles in the air.

Old Henry Dashwood, uncle to young Henry, was himself part of that nostalgic and romantic belief in the power of dreams. He had been much beloved, a kind of self-appointed squire to the whole district, generous to the local community and prepared to open the doors of Norland to all manner of charitable events. He had lived at Norland all his life, looked after by a spinster sister, and it was only after she died that he realised the house needed more human life in it than he could possibly provide by himself. And that realisation was swiftly followed by a second one, a recollection of the existence and circumstance of his likeable if not particularly high-achieving heir, his nephew Henry, only child of his younger and long-dead sister, who was now, by all accounts, living on the kind of breadline that old Henry was certain that no Dashwood should ever be reduced to. So young Henry was summoned for an audience, and arrived at Norland with a very appealing companion in tow, and also, to old Henry's particular joy, two little girls and a baby. The family stood in the great hall at Norland and gazed about them in awe and wonder, and old Henry was overcome by the impulse to spread his arms out and to exclaim, there and then, that they were welcome to stay, to come and live with him, to make Norland their home for ever.

'I will rejoice', he said, his voice unsteady with emotion, 'to see life and noise back at the Park.' He had glanced, damp-eyed, at the children. 'And to see your little gumboots kicked off by the front door. My dears. My very dears.'

Elinor, watching her mother now, swallowed. It didn't do to let her mother get too worked up about anything, just as it didn't do to let Marianne get over-excited, either. Belle didn't suffer from the asthma which had killed Elinor's father, young Henry, and which made Marianne so dramatically, alarmingly fragile, but it was never a good thing, all the same, to let Belle run on down any vehement track, in case she flew out of control, as she often did, and it all ended in tears. Literal tears. Elinor sometimes wondered how much time and energy the whole Dashwood family had wasted in crying. She cleared her throat, as undramatically as she could, to remind her mother that they were still waiting.

Belle gave a little start. She withdrew her gaze from the sight of the huge shadow of the house inching its way across the expanse of turf beyond the window and sighed. Then she said, almost dreamily, 'I came here, you know, with Daddy.'

'Yes,' Elinor said, trying not to sound impatient, 'we know. We came too.'

Belle turned her head sharply and glared at her oldest daughter, almost accusingly.

'We came to Norland', she said, 'because we were *asked*. Daddy and I came here, with you all, to look after Uncle Henry.' She stopped and then she said, more gently, 'Darling Uncle Henry.'

There was another silence, broken only by Belle repeating softly, as if to herself, 'Darling Uncle Henry.'

'He wasn't actually *that* darling,' Elinor said reasonably. 'He didn't leave you the house. Did he. Or enough money to live on.'

Belle put her chin up slightly.

'He wanted to leave both to Daddy. If Daddy hadn't—' She broke off again.

'Died?' Margaret said helpfully.

Her older sisters turned on her.

'Honestly, Mags—'

'Shut up, shut up, shut the f—'

'Marianne!' Belle said warningly.

Tears immediately sprang to Marianne's eyes. Elinor clamped an arm round her shoulders and held her hard. It must be so awful, she often thought, to take everything to heart so, as Marianne did; to react to every single thing that happened as if you were obliged to respond on behalf of the whole feeling world. Holding her sister tight, to steady her, she took a breath.

'Well,' she said, in as level a voice as she could manage, 'we have to face what we have to face. Don't we. Dad is dead, and he didn't get the house either. Did he. *Darling* Uncle Henry didn't leave him Norland or any money or anything. He got completely seduced by being a great-uncle to a little boy in old age. So he left everything to them. He left it all to John.'

Marianne was quivering rather less. Elinor relaxed her hold and concentrated instead on her mother. She said again, a little louder, 'He's left Norland Park to John.'

Belle turned to look at her. She said reprovingly, 'Darling, he had to.'

'No, he didn't.'

'He did. Houses like Norland go to heirs with sons. They always have. It's called primogeniture. Daddy had Norland for his lifetime.'

Elinor dropped her arm from her sister's shoulders.

'We're not the royal family, Ma,' she said. 'There isn't a *succession* or anything.'

Margaret had been fiddling, as usual, with her iPod, disentangling the earpiece flex from the complicated knot she was constantly, absently, tying it in. Now she looked up, as if she had just realised something.

'I expect,' she said brightly, 'that Dad couldn't leave you anything much because he hadn't married you, had he?'

Marianne gave a little scream.

'Don't say that!'

'Well, it's true.'

Belle closed her eyes.

'*Please . . .*'

Elinor looked at her youngest sister.

'Just because you know something, Mags, or even think it, doesn't necessarily mean that you have to say it.'

Margaret shrugged. It was her 'whatever' shrug. She and her school friends did it perpetually, and when they were asked not to, they held up their splayed fingers in a 'w', to demonstrate the 'whatever' shape instead.

Marianne was crying again. She was the only person Elinor had ever encountered who could cry and still look ravishing. Her nose never seemed to swell or redden, and she appeared able just to let huge tears slide slowly down her face in a way that one ex-boyfriend had said wistfully simply made him want to lick them off her jawline.

'Please don't,' Elinor said despairingly.

Marianne said, almost desperately, between sobs, 'I adore this place . . .'

Elinor looked about her. The kitchen was not only almost painfully familiar to her, but also represented the essence of their life at Norland, its great size and elegant Georgian proportions rendered welcoming and warm by Belle's gift for bohemian homemaking, her eye for colour and fabric and the most beguiling degree of shabbiness. That room had seen every family meal, every storm and tantrum, every celebration and party, almost every line of homework. Uncle Henry had spent hours in the patchwork-covered armchair, a whisky tumbler in his hand, egging the girls on to divert and outrage him. Their father had spent as many hours in the carver chair at the head of the huge scrubbed table, drawing and reading and always available for interruption or consolation or diversion. To be without this room, and all its memories and capacities, seemed violently and abruptly unendurable. She said, tensely, to her sister, 'We all do.'

Marianne gave a wild and theatrical gesture. She cried, 'I feel as if – as if I'd been born here!'

Elinor repeated, steadily, 'We all do.'

Marianne clenched both fists and beat them lightly against her collarbone.

'No, I feel it *here*. I feel I *belong* at Norland. I might not be able to play away from Norland. I might never be able to play the guitar—'

'Course you will!'

'Darling,' Belle said, looking at Marianne. Her voice was unsteady. 'Darling...'

Elinor said wearily, as a precaution to Margaret, 'Don't you start too.'

Margaret shrugged again, but she didn't look tearful. She looked, instead, mildly rebellious; but at thirteen, she often looked like that.

Elinor sighed. She was very tired. She'd been tired for weeks, it seemed, months, tired with the grief of old Uncle Henry dying and then the worse grief, and shock, of Daddy, rushed into hospital after what had at first appeared just a familiar kind of asthma attack, the kind that his blue inhaler usually sorted. But not this time. This time had been terrible, terrifying, seeing him fighting for breath as if someone were holding a pillow over his face, and then the ambulance dash to the hospital, with them all driving behind him, sick with fear, and then a bit of relief in Accident and Emergency, and a bit more in a private room where he could gasp out that he needed John to come, he needed to see his son John, and then after John's visit, another attack when none of them were there, an attack by himself in that plastic, anonymous room among all the tubes and monitors and heart machines, and the hospital ringing Norland at two in the morning to say that he hadn't made it, that they couldn't help his worn-out heart any more, that he was dead.

They'd all convened in the kitchen then, too, after a last necessary, pointless visit to the hospital. In the dawn, all four of them grey with misery and shock and fatigue, had huddled round the table with mugs of tea clasped in their hands, like lifelines. And it was then that Belle had chosen to remind them, using the sort of faraway voice she used when reading fairy tales aloud, how she and Daddy had run away together, away from his first marriage – well, if facing facts, as Elinor preferred to do, his only marriage – and how, after too many struggling and penurious years, Uncle Henry had taken them in. Uncle Henry was, Belle said, an old romantic at heart, an old romantic who had never married because the girl he wanted wouldn't have him, but who loved to see someone else's adventure turn out to have a happy ending.

'He said to me,' Belle told them, turning her mug slowly in her hands, 'Norland was so huge and so empty that it reproached him every day. He said he didn't give tuppence for whether we were married or not. He said marriage was just a silly old convention to keep society tidy. And he told me that he loved seeing people do things he'd never quite had the nerve to do himself.'

Was it nerve, Elinor had thought, trying to comprehend

what her mother was saying through the fog of her own shock and sorrow, to live with someone for years and never actually get round to marrying them – or was it carelessness? Was it an adventure not to leave a responsible will that would secure the future of the person you'd had three daughters with – or was it feckless? And was it really romantic to risk being the true beneficiary of a wealthy but deeply conventional old uncle by remaining unmarried – or just plain stupid? Anyway, whatever Dad had done, or not done, would Uncle Henry always have left everything to John in the end, simply because John had had a son and not daughters?

She was still angry with Dad, even now, even though she missed him every hour of every day. No, she wasn't angry precisely, she was furious. Plain furious. But it had to be a silent fury because Ma couldn't or wouldn't hear a word against Dad, any more than she would accept responsibility for never giving a moment's thought to the possibility of her own future without him. He had been an asthmatic, after all! The blue inhalers were as much a part of the Dashwood family as the members of it were. He was never going to make old bones, and he was living in a place and a manner that was entirely dependent on the charity and whim of an old man who liked his fantasies to be daring but his facts, his realities, to be orthodox.

Of course Belle would not allow for any mistakes having been made, either on her part or on Dad's. She even insisted for weeks after Dad died, that he and John, his only child and son by that long-ago marriage, had had a death-bed reconciliation in Haywards Heath Hospital, and that they had both wept, and John had promised faithfully that he'd look after his stepmother and the girls.

'He promised,' Belle said, over and over, 'we can stay at Norland for ever. And he'll keep his word. Of course he will. He's Daddy's son, after all.'

And Daddy, Elinor thought, not without a hint of bitterness, is not only safely dead and thus unanswerable, but was perfect. Perfect.

But what had actually happened? Well, what had happened was that they had reckoned without John's wife, hadn't they? In the unbearable aftermath of Dad's death, they had almost forgotten about Fanny. Elinor glanced now across the kitchen to the huge old Welsh dresser, which bore all their everyday mugs and plates, and also holiday postcards from friends and family photographs. There was a framed photograph of Fanny up there, in a girlish white broderie anglaise dress, holding Harry, when he was a baby. Elinor noticed that the photograph had been turned to face the wall, with its back to the room. Despite the distress of the day, Elinor couldn't help an inward smile. What a brilliant little gesture! Who had done it? Margaret, probably, now sitting at the table with her earphones in and her gaze unfocused. Elinor stretched a foot under the table and gave her sister a little nudge of congratulation.

When John had first brought Fanny to meet them, Elinor had thought that nobody so tiny could represent any kind of force. How wrong she'd been! Fanny had turned out to be a pure concentration of self-interest. She was, apparently, just like her equally tiny mother: hard as nails and entirely devoted to status and money. Especially money. Fanny was mad about money. She'd come to her marriage to John with some money of her own, and she had very clear ideas about how to spend it. She had, in fact, very clear ideas about most things – and a will of iron.

Fanny had wanted a man and a big house with land and lots of money to run it and a child, preferably a boy. And she had got them. All of them. And nothing, absolutely nothing, was going to stand in the way of her keeping them and consolidating them. Nothing.

It was outrageous, really, how soon after Dad's death that Fanny came bowling up the drive in her top-of-the-range four-by-four Land Cruiser with Harry in his car seat and the Romanian nanny and the kind of household luggage you only bring if you want to make it very, very plain who's the boss round here now. She brought a bunch of garage forecourt flowers – they even had a sticker on the cellophane wrapping saying 20 per cent more for free – for Belle and then she said would they mind awfully just staying in the kitchen wing for a few hours as she had her London interior designer coming and he charged so much for every hour that she really wanted to be able to concentrate on him.

So they'd taken Harry and the nanny, who had blue varnished nails and a leopard-print miniskirt stretched over her considerable hips, into the kitchen, and tried to give them lunch, but the nanny said she was dieting, and would only have a smoke, instead, and Harry glanced at the food on the plate and then put his thumb in, and closed his eyes in disgust. It was three hours before Fanny, her eyes alight with paint-effect visions, had blown into the kitchen and announced, without any preliminary and as if it would be unquestionably welcome news, that she and John would be moving in in a fortnight.

And they had. So silly, Fanny said firmly, as if no one could possibly disagree with her, so silly to go on paying rent in London when Norland was simply standing waiting for them.

She seemed entirely oblivious to the effect that she was having, and to the utter disregard she displayed for what she was doing to the family for whom Norland had been more home than house for all their childhood years. Her ruthless determination to obliterate the past life of the house and to impose her own expensive and impersonal taste upon it instead was breathtaking. Out with the battered painted furniture, the French armoires, the cascading and faded curtains in ancient brocades, and in with polished granite and stainless steel and state-of-the-art wet rooms. Out with objects of sentimental value and worn Persian rugs and speckled mirrors in dimly gilded frames, and in with modern sculptured 'pieces' and stripped-back floors and vast flat television screens over every beautiful Georgian fireplace.

It was all happening too, it seemed to Belle and her daughters, with an indecent and brutal haste. Fanny arrived with John and Harry and the nanny, and an army of East European workmen, and took over all the best rooms, all the rooms that had once been Uncle Henry's, and the house resounded to the din of sawing and hammering and drilling. Luckily, Elinor supposed, it was summer, so all the windows and doors could be opened to let out the inevitable dust and the builders' smells of raw wood and plaster, but the open windows also meant that nothing audible could be concealed, especially not those things which Elinor grew to suspect Fanny of absolutely intending to be overheard.

They'd heard her, all the last few weeks, talking John out of any generous impulse he might have harboured towards his stepmother and half-sisters. Fanny might be tiny but her voice seemed to carry for miles, even when she was whispering. Usually, they could hear her issuing instructions ('She never says please,' Margaret pointed out, 'does she?') but if she wanted to get something out of John, she wheedled.

They could hear her, plainly, in their kitchen from the room she had commandeered as a temporary sitting room – drawing room, she called it – working on John. She was probably on his knee a lot of the time, doing her sex-kitten thing, running her little pointed fingers through his hair and somehow indicating that he would have to forgo a lot of bedroom treats if she didn't get her way.

'They can't need *that* much, Johnnie darling. They really can't! I mean, I know Mags is still at school – frightfully expensive, her private school, and really such a waste of money when there's a perfectly adequate state secondary, in Lewes, which is free – but Elinor's nearly qualified and Marianne jolly well ought to be. And Belle could easily go back to work, teaching art, like she used to.'

'She hasn't for yonks,' John said doubtfully. 'Not for as long as I can remember. Dad liked her at home ...'

'Well, darling, we can't always have what we like, can we? And she's had years, years, of just wafting about Norland being all daffy and artistic and irresponsible.'

There was a murmur, and then John said, without much conviction, 'I promised Dad—'

'Sweetness,' Fanny said, 'listen. Listen to me. What about your promises to me? What about Harry? I know you love this place, I know what it means to you even if you've never lived here and you *know* I'll help you restore it and keep it up. I promised you, didn't I? I promised when I married you. But it's going to cost a fortune. It really is. The thing is, Johnnie, that good interior designers don't come cheap and we agreed, didn't we, that we were going to go for gold and not cut corners because that's what a house like this *deserves*?'

'Well,' John had said uneasily, 'I suppose ...'

'Poppet,' said Fanny, 'just think about *us*. Think about you and me and Harry. And Norland. Norland is our *home*.'

There'd been a long pause then.

'They're snogging,' Margaret said disgustedly. 'She's sitting on his lap and they're *snogging*.'

It worked, though, the snogging; Elinor had to give Fanny credit for gaining her ends. The house, their beloved home which had acquired the inimitable patina of all houses which have quietly and organically evolved alongside the generations of the family which has inhabited them, was being wrenched into a different and modish incarnation, a sleek and showy new version of itself which Belle declared, contemptuously, to resemble nothing so much as a five-star hotel.

'And that's not a compliment. Anyone can *pay* to stay in a hotel. But you *stay* in a hotel. You don't live in one. Fanny is behaving like some ghastly sort of *developer*. She's taking all this darling old house's character away.'

'But', Elinor said quietly, 'that's what Fanny wants. She wants a sort of showcase. And she'll get it. We heard her. She's got John just where she wants him. And, because of him, she's got Norland. She can do what she likes with it. And she will.'

An uneasy forced bonhomie hung over the house for days afterwards until yesterday, when John had come into their kitchen rather defiantly and put a bottle of supermarket white wine down on the table with the kind of flourish only champagne would have merited and announced that actually, as it turned out, all things being considered, and after much thought and discussion and many sleepless nights, especially on Fanny's part, her being so sensitive and affectionate a person, they had come to the conclusion that they – he, Fanny, Harry and the live-in nanny – were going to need Norland to themselves.

There'd been a stunned silence. Then Margaret said loudly, 'All fifteen bedrooms?'

John had nodded gravely.

'Oh yes.'

'But why – how—'

'Fanny has ideas of running Norland as a business, you see. An upmarket bed and breakfast. Or something. To help pay for the upkeep, which will be' – he rolled his eyes to the ceiling – 'unending. Paying to keep Norland going will need a bottomless pit of money.'

Belle gazed at him, her eyes enormous.

'But what about us?'

'I'll help you find somewhere.'

'Near?'

'It has to be near!' Marianne cried, almost gasping. 'It has to, it has to, I can't live away from here, I can't—'

Elinor took her sister's nearest hand and gripped it.

'A cottage,' John suggested.

'A cottage!'

'There are some adorable Sussex cottages.'

'But they'll need paying for,' Belle said despairingly, 'and I haven't a bean.'

John looked at her. He seemed a little more collected.

'Yes, you have.'

'No,' Belle said. 'No.' She felt for a chairback and held on to it. 'We were *going* to have plans. To make some money to pay for living here. We had schemes for the house and estate, maybe using it as a wedding venue or something, after Uncle Henry died, but there wasn't time, there was only a year, before – before ...'

Elinor moved to stand beside her mother.

'There's the legacies,' John said.

Belle flapped a hand, as though swatting away a fly.

'Oh, those ...'

'Two hundred thousand pounds is not nothing, my dear Belle. Two hundred thousand is a considerable sum of money.'

'For four women! For four women to live on forever! Four women without even a roof over their heads?'

John looked stricken for a moment and then rallied. He indicated the bottle on the table.

'I brought you some wine.'

Margaret inspected the bottle. She said to no one in particular, 'I don't expect we'll even *cook* with that.'

'Shush,' Elinor said, automatically.

Belle surveyed her stepson.

'You promised your father.'

John looked back at her.

'I promised I'd look after you. I will. I'll help you find a house to rent.'

'Too kind,' Marianne said fiercely.

'The interest on—'

'Interest rates are hopeless, John.'

'I'm amazed you know about such things.'

'And I'm amazed at your blithe breaking of sacred promises.'

Elinor put a hand on her mother's arm. She said to her brother, 'Please.' Then she said, in a lower tone, 'We'll find a way.'

John looked relieved.

'That's more like it. Good girl.'

Marianne shouted suddenly, 'You are really wicked, do you hear me? Wicked! What's the word, what is it, the Shakespeare word? It's – it's – yes, John, yes, you are *perfidious*.'

There was a brief, horrified silence. Belle put a hand out towards Marianne and Elinor was afraid they'd put their arms round each other, as they often did, for solidarity, in extravagant reaction.

She said to John, 'I think you had better go.'

He nodded thankfully, and took a step back.

'She'll be looking for you,' Margaret said. 'Has she got a dog whistle she can blow to get you to come running?'

Marianne stopped looking tragic and gave a snort of laughter. So, a second later, did Belle. John glanced at them both and then looked past them at the Welsh dresser where all the plates were displayed, the pretty, scallop-edged plates that Henry and Belle had collected from Provençal holidays over the years, and lovingly brought back, two or three at a time.

John moved towards the door. With his hand on the handle, he turned and briefly indicated the dresser.

'Fanny adores those plates, you know.'

And now, only a day later, here they were, grouped round the table yet again, exhausted by a further calamity, by rage at Fanny's malevolence and John's feebleness, terrified at the prospect of a future in which they did not even know where they were going to lay their heads, let alone how they were going to pay for the privilege of laying them anywhere.

'I will of course be qualified in a year,' Elinor said.

Belle gave her a tired smile.

'Darling, what use will that be? You draw beautifully but how many architects are unemployed right now?'

'Thank you, Ma.'

Marianne put a hand on Elinor's.

'She's right. You do draw beautifully.'

Elinor tried to smile at her sister. She said, bravely,

'She's also right that there are no jobs for architects, especially newly qualified ones.' She looked at her mother. 'Could you get a teaching job again?'

Belle flung her hands wide.

'Darling, it's been forever!'

'This is extreme, Ma.'

Marianne said to Margaret, 'You'll have to go to state school.'

Margaret's face froze.

'I won't.'

'You will.'

'Mags, you may just have to—'

'I won't!' Margaret shouted.

She ripped her earphones out of her ears and stamped to the window, standing there with her back to the room and her shoulders hunched. Then her shoulders abruptly relaxed.

'Hey!' she said, in quite a different voice.

Elinor half rose.

'Hey what?'

Margaret didn't turn. Instead she leaned out of the window and began to wave furiously.

'Edward!' she shouted. 'Edward!' And then she turned back long enough to say, unnecessarily, over her shoulder, 'Edward's coming!'

2

However detestable Fanny had made herself since she arrived at Norland, all the Dashwoods were agreed that she had one redeeming attribute, which was the possession of her brother Edward.

He had arrived at the Park soon after his sister moved in, and everyone had initially assumed that this tallish, darkish, diffident young man – so unlike his dangerous little dynamo of a sister – had come to admire the place and the situation that had fallen so magnificently into Fanny's lap. But after only a day or so, it became plain to the Dashwoods that the perpetual, slightly needy presence of Edward in their kitchen was certainly because he liked it there, and felt comfortable, but also because he had nowhere much else to go, and nothing much else to occupy himself with. He was even, it appeared, perfectly prepared to confess to being at a directionless loose end.

'I'm a bit of a failure, I'm afraid,' he said quite soon after his arrival. He was sitting on the edge of the kitchen table, his hair flopping in his eyes, pushing runner beans through a slicer, as instructed by Belle.

'Oh no,' Belle said at once, and warmly, 'I'm sure you aren't.

I'm sure you're just not very good at self-promotion.'

Edward stopped slicing to extract a large, mottled pink bean that had jammed the blades. He said, slightly challengingly, 'Well, I was thrown out of Eton.'

'*Were* you?' they all said.

Margaret took one earphone out. She said, with real interest, 'What did you do?'

'I was lookout for some up-to-no-good people.'

'What people? *Real* bad guys?'

'Other boys.'

Margaret leaned closer. She said, conspiratorially, '*Druggies?*'

Edward grinned at his beans.

'Sort of.'

'Did you take any?'

'Shut up, Mags,' Elinor said from the far side of the room.

Edward looked up at her for a moment, with a look she would have interpreted as pure gratitude if she thought she'd done anything to be thanked for, and then he said, 'No, Mags. I didn't even have the guts to join in. I was lookout for the others, and I messed up that, too, big time, and we were all expelled. Mum has never forgiven me. Not to this day.'

Belle patted his hand.

'I'm sure she has.'

Edward said, 'You don't know my mother.'

'I think', said Marianne from the window seat where she was curled up, reading, 'that it's brilliant to be expelled. Especially from anywhere as utterly *conventional* as Eton.'

'But maybe,' Elinor said quietly, 'it isn't very convenient.'

Edward looked at her intently again. He said, 'I was sent to a crammer instead. In disgrace. In Plymouth.'

'My goodness,' Belle said, 'that *was* drastic. Plymouth!'

Margaret put her earphone back in. The conversation had gone back to boring.

Elinor said encouragingly, 'So you got all your A levels and things?'

'Sort of,' Edward said. 'Not very well. I did a lot of – messing around. I wish I hadn't. I wish I'd paid more attention. I'd really apply myself to it now, but it's too late.'

'It's never too late!' Belle declared.

Edward put the bean slicer down. He said, again to Elinor, as if she would understand him better than anyone, 'Mum wants me to go and work for an MP.'

'*Does* she?'

'Or do a law degree and read for the Bar. She wants me to do something – something . . .'

'Showy,' Elinor said.

He smiled at her again.

'Exactly.'

'When what you *want* to do,' Belle said, picking up the slicer again and putting it back gently into his hand, 'is really . . .?'

Edward selected another bean.

'I want to do community work of some kind. I know it sounds a bit wet, but I don't want houses and cars and money and all the stuff my family seems so keen on. My brother Robert seems to be able to get away with anything just because he isn't the eldest. My mother – well, it's weird. Robert's a kind of upmarket party planner, huge rich parties in London, the sort of thing I hate, and my mother turns a completely blind eye to that hardly being a career of *distinction*. But when it comes to me, she goes on and on about visibility and money and power. She doesn't even seem to *look* at the kind of person I am. I just want to do something quiet and sort of – sort of . . .'

'Helpful?' Elinor said.

Edward got off the table and turned so that he could look at her with pure undiluted appreciation.

'*Yes*,' he said with emphasis.

Later that night, jostling in front of the bathroom mirror with their toothbrushes and dental floss, Marianne said to Elinor, 'He likes you.'

Elinor spat a mouthful of toothpaste foam into the basin.

'No, he doesn't. He just likes being around us all, because Ma's cosy with him and we don't pick on him and tell him to smarten up and sharpen up all the time, like Fanny does.'

Marianne took a length of floss out of her mouth.

'Ellie, he likes us all. But he likes you in particular.'

Elinor didn't reply. She began to brush her hair vigorously, upside down, to forestall further conversation.

Marianne reangled the floss across her lower jaw. Round it she said indistinctly, 'D'you like him?'

'Can't hear you.'

'Yes, you can. Do you, Elinor Dashwood, picky spinster of this parish for whom no man so far seems to be remotely good enough, fancy this very appealing basket case called Edward Ferrars?'

Elinor stood upright and pushed the hair off her face.

'No.'

'Liar.'

There was a pause.

'Well, a bit,' Elinor said.

Marianne leaned forward and peered into the mirror.

'He's perfect for you, Ellie. You're such a missionary, you'd have to have someone to rescue. Ed is ripe for rescue. And he's the sweetest guy.'

'I'm not interested. The last thing I want right now is anyone else who needs sorting.'

'Bollocks,' Marianne said.

'It's not—'

'He couldn't take his eyes off you tonight. You only had to say the dullest thing and he was all over you, like a Labrador puppy.'

'Stop it.'

'But it's lovely, Ellie! It's lovely, in the midst of everything that's so awful, to have Edward thinking you're wonderful.'

Elinor began to smooth her hair back into a ponytail, severely.

'It's all wrong, M. It's all wrong at the moment with all this uncertainty and worrying about money, and where we'll go and everything. It's all wrong to be thinking about whether I like Edward.'

Marianne turned to her sister, suddenly grinning.

'Tell you what . . .'

'What?'

'Wouldn't it just *completely* piss off Fanny if you and Ed got together?'

The next day, Edward borrowed Fanny's car and asked Elinor to go to Brighton with him.

'Does she know?' Elinor said.

He smiled at her. He had beautiful teeth, she noticed, even if nobody could exactly call him handsome.

'Does who know what?'

'Does – does Fanny know you are going to Brighton?'

'Oh yes,' Edward said easily, 'I've got a huge list of things to pick up for her: bath taps and theatre tickets and wallpaper samples from—'

'I didn't mean that,' Elinor said. 'I meant, does Fanny know you were going to ask me to go with you?'

'No,' Edward said. 'And she needn't. I have her great bus for the day, I have her shopping list, and nothing else is any of her business.'

Elinor looked doubtful.

'He's absolutely right,' Belle said. 'She'll never know and it won't affect her, knowing or not knowing.'

'But—'

'Get in, darling.'

'Yes, get in.'

'Come on,' Edward said, opening the passenger door and smiling again. 'Come on. Please. *Please*. We'll have fish and chips on the beach. Don't make me go alone.'

'I should be working...' Elinor said faintly.

She glanced at Edward. He bent slightly and, with the hand not holding the door, gave her a small, decisive shove into the passenger seat. Then he closed the door firmly behind her. He was beaming broadly, and went back round to the driver's side at a run.

'Look at that,' Marianne said approvingly. 'Who's the dog with two tails?'

'Both wagging.'

The car lurched off at speed, in a spray of gravel.

'He's a dear,' Belle said.

'You'd like anyone who liked Ellie.'

'I would. Of course I would. But he's a dear in his own right.'

'And rich. The Ferrarses are stinking—'

'I don't', Belle said, putting her arm round Marianne, 'give a stuff about that. Any more than you do. If he's a dear boy and he likes Ellie and she likes him, that is more than good enough for me. And for you too, I bet.'

Marianne said seriously, watching the car speeding down the faraway sweep of the drive, 'He wouldn't be good enough for me.'

'Darling!'

Marianne leaned into her mother's embrace.

'Ma, you know he wouldn't do for me. I'm not looking for a nice guy; I'm looking for *the* guy. I don't want someone who thinks I'm clever to play the guitar like I do, I want someone who knows why I play so well, who understands what I'm playing, like I do, who understands me for what I am and values that. Values me.' She paused and straightened a little. Then she said, 'Ma, I'd rather have nothing ever than just anything. Much rather.'

Belle was laughing.

'Darling, don't despair. You only left school a year ago, you're hardly—'

Marianne stepped sideways so that Belle's arm slipped from her waist.

'I mean it,' she said fiercely. 'I *mean* it. I don't want just a man, Ma. I want a *soulmate*. And if I can't have one, I'd rather have nobody. See?'

Belle was silent. She was looking into the middle distance now, plainly not really seeing anything.

'Ma?' Marianne said.

Belle shook her head very slightly. Marianne moved closer again.

'Ma, are you thinking about Daddy?'

Belle gave a small sigh.

'If you are – and you are, aren't you? – then you'll know what I'm talking about,' Marianne said. 'If I didn't get this belief in having, one day, a love of my life from you, who did I get it from?'

Belle turned very slightly and gave Marianne a misty smile.

'Touché, darling,' she said.

From her bedroom windows – three bays looking south and two facing west – Fanny could see across the immense lawn to the walled vegetable garden, whose glasshouses were so badly in need of repair, never mind the state of the beds themselves, or the unpruned fruit trees and general neglect visible everywhere. And there, in the decayed soft-fruit cage, with its sagging wire and crooked posts, she could see Belle, in one of her arty smock things and jeans, picking raspberries.

Of course, in a way, Belle was perfectly entitled to pick Norland raspberries. The canes themselves probably dated from Uncle Henry's time, and in their well-meaning, amateur way, Belle and Henry had tried to look after the garden all the years they had lived at Norland. But the fact was that Norland now belonged to John. And because of John, to Fanny. Which meant that everything about it and pertaining to it was not only Fanny's responsibility now, but her possession. Staring out of the window at her husband's (by courtesy, only) stepmother, it came to Fanny quite forcibly that Belle was, without asking, picking Fanny's raspberries.

It took her three minutes to cross her bedroom, traverse the landing, descend the stairs, march down the black and white floored hall to the garden door and make her way at speed across the lawn to the kitchen garden. She let the door in the wall to the kitchen garden close behind her with enough of a slam to alert Belle to the fact that she had arrived, and with a purpose.

Belle looked up, slightly dazedly. She had been thinking about something quite else, mentally arranging the furniture in a cottage she had seen, for rent, near Barcombe Cross, which she had thought might be a distinct possibility even though Elinor insisted that they couldn't possibly afford it, and she had been picking almost mechanically while she dreamed.

'Good morning,' Fanny said.

Belle managed a smile.

'Good morning, Fanny.'

Fanny stepped into the fruit cage through a torn gap in the netting. She was wearing patent-leather ballet slippers with gold discs on the toes. She looked round her.

'This is in an awful state.'

Belle said mildly, 'The raspberries don't seem to mind. Look at this crop!'

She held her bowl out. Fanny gave a small dismissive sniff.

'You've got a huge amount.'

'We grew them, Fanny.'

'All the same . . .'

'I'd be happy to pick some for you, Fanny. I offered some to Harry — I thought he might like to pick them with me, but he said he didn't like raspberries.'

Fanny said carefully, 'We are very — selective in the fruit we give Harry.'

Belle resumed her picking.

'Bananas,' she said, over her shoulder. 'Only bananas, we hear. Can that be good for him, not even to eat apples?'

There was short, highly charged pause. Then Fanny said, 'Isn't Elinor helping you?'

'You can see that she isn't.'

'Because she isn't here,' Fanny said.

Belle said nothing. Fanny threaded her way through the raspberry canes until she was once again in Belle's sightline.

'Elinor isn't here,' Fanny said clearly, 'because she is in my car, isn't she, being driven by my brother, on her way to Brighton.'

'And if she is?'

'I wouldn't want you to think I hadn't noticed. I wouldn't want you to think I don't know. I wasn't asked. I saw them. I saw them drive away.'

Belle said defiantly, 'Edward invited her!'

Fanny leaned forward to pick a large, ripe raspberry very precisely out of Belle's bowl.

'He may have done. But she had no business accepting.'

Belle stepped back so that the bowl of raspberries was just out of Fanny's reach.

'I beg your pardon!' she said indignantly.

Fanny looked at the raspberry in her fingers and then she looked at Belle.

'Don't get any ideas,' she said.

'But—'

'Look,' Fanny said. 'Look. My father came from nowhere and ended up somewhere very successful, *all* through his own efforts. He was ambitious, quite rightly, and he was ambitious for his children, too. He'd be thrilled about Norland. But he wouldn't be thrilled at all about his eldest son being – being ensnared by his son-in-law's illegitimate half-sister with not a bean to her name. Any more than my mother would be, if she knew.' Fanny paused, and then she said, 'Any more than I am.'

Belle stared at her.

'I cannot *believe* this, Fanny.'

Fanny waved the hand holding the raspberry.

'It doesn't matter what you can or can't believe, Belle. It doesn't matter a jot. All that matters is that when Elinor gets back from her jaunt in *my* car with *my* brother, you have just two words to say to her. Two words. Hands off. Do you get it, Belle? Hands off Edward.'

And then she dropped the raspberry on to the earth, and ground it down under her patent-leather toecap.

Edward held out a crumple of white paper.

'Have another chip.'

Elinor was lying on her back on Edward's battered cotton jacket, which he had spread for her on the shingle. She waved a hand.

'Couldn't.'

'Just one.'

'Not even that. They were delicious. The fish was perfect. Thank you for holding back on the vinegar.'

Edward put another chip in his mouth.

'I have a thing for vinegar.'

Elinor snorted faintly.

'I mean,' Edward said, laughing too, 'I mean vinegar in *vinegar*. Not in people.'

'No names then.'

He lay down beside her, slightly turned towards her. He said comfortably, 'We know who we mean, don't we? And you haven't even met my mother.'

Elinor stretched both arms up and laced her fingers together against the high blue arc of the sky.

'Talking of mothers—'

'Did you know,' Edward said, interrupting, 'that when you talk, the end of your nose moves up and down very slightly? It's adorable.'

Elinor suppressed a smile. She lowered her arms.

'Talking of mothers,' she said again.

'Oh, OK then. Mothers. What about them?'

'Mine is so sweet, really—'

'Oh, I know.'

'—but she's driving me insane. Insane. Almost every day she goes off to look at some house or other. She must be on every agent's books in East Sussex.'

Edward put out a tentative finger and touched the end of Elinor's nose. He said, 'But that's good. That's positive.'

Elinor tried to ignore his finger.

'Yes, of course it is, in theory. But she's looking at stuff we can't begin to afford. They may technically be cottages but they've got five bedrooms and three bathrooms and one even has a swimming pool in a conservatory thing. I *ask* you.'

'But—'

Elinor turned her head to look at him, dislodging his finger.

'Ed, we can't actually even afford a garden shed. But she won't listen.'

'They don't.'

'You mean mothers?'

'Mothers,' Edward said with emphasis. 'They do *not* listen.'

'You mean yours won't listen to you either?'

Edward rolled on his back.

'Nobody listens.'

'Oh, come on.'

He said, 'I applied to Amnesty International and they said I wasn't qualified for anything they had on offer. Same with Oxfam. And the only reason for having anything to do with the law is that Human Rights Watch might – *might* – give me a hearing with the right bits of paper in my hand.'

Elinor waited a moment, and then she said, 'What are you good at, do you think?'

Edward picked a pebble out of the shingle beside him and looked at it. Then he said, in quite a different, more confident tone of voice, 'Organising things. I don't mean how many cases of champagne will two hundred people drink, like Robert. I mean quite – serious things. I can get things done. Actually.'

'Like today.'

'Well ...'

'Today,' Elinor said, 'you drove well, you parked without fuss, you got the bathroom people to find the right taps, you were firm with that useless girl at the box office over Fanny's tickets, you insisted on the right wallpaper books, you knew just where to get the best fish and chips and exactly where to be on the beach to get out of the wind.'

'Well – yes. Only very small things ...'

'But significant. And – and symptomatic.'

Edward raised himself on one elbow and looked at her.

'Thank you, Elinor.'

She grinned at him.

'My pleasure.'

He looked suddenly sober. He said, in a more serious voice, 'I'm going to miss you.'

'Why? Where are you going?'

He glanced away. Then he raised the arm holding the pebble and threw it towards the wall at the back of the beach.

'I'm not going, I'm being chucked out.'

'Chucked out? By whom?'

'By Fanny.'

Elinor sat up slowly.

'Oh.'

'Yes. Oh.'

'You know why?'

'Yes,' Edward said, looking straight at her. 'And so do you.'

Elinor stared at her raised knees. She said, 'Where'll you go?'

'Devon, I should think.'

'Why Devon?'

'I know people there. I was there at the crammer, remember? I can always hang out there. In fact, I can ask, in Devon, if there's anywhere for you to rent, shall I? It's bound to be cheaper, in Devon.'

Elinor said sadly, 'We can't go to Devon.'

'Why not?'

'It's too far. Margaret's school, Marianne going up to the Royal College of Music, me finishing my training . . .'

'OK then,' Edward said, 'but I'll still ask. You never know.'

'Thank you.'

'Ellie?'

'Yes?'

'Will you miss me?'

She didn't look at him.

'I don't know.'

He moved slightly, so that he was kneeling beside her.

'Please try to.'

'OK.'

'Ellie . . .'

She said nothing. He leaned forward and put his hand on her knees.

'Ellie, even though I probably taste of grease and vinegar, would it be OK if I did what I've wanted to do ever since I first saw you, and kissed you?'

And now, weeks later, here he was, back at Norland and getting out of the kind of car that Fanny would hate to see on her gravel sweep: an elderly Ford Sierra with a peeling speed stripe painted down its dilapidated side.

Margaret waved wildly from the kitchen window.

'Edward! Edward!'

He looked up and waved back, his face breaking into a smile. Then he ducked back into the car to turn off some deafening music, and came loping across the drive and then the grass to where Margaret was leaning and waving.

'Cool car!' she shouted.

'Not bad, for two hundred and fifty quid!'

She put her arms out so that she could loop them round his neck and he could then pull her out of the window on to the grass. He set her on her feet. She said, 'Has Fanny seen you?'

'No,' Edward said, 'I thought she could see the car first.'

'Good thinking, buster.'

'Mags,' Edward said, 'where's everyone?'

Margaret jerked her head towards the kitchen behind her.

'In there. Having a major meltdown about moving.'

'Moving! Have you found somewhere?'

'No,' Margaret said. 'Only hopeless places we can't afford.'

'Then . . .'

Margaret looked past him at the offending car.

'Fanny's throwing us out,' she said.

'Oh my God,' Edward said.

He stepped past Margaret and thrust his head in at the open window.

'Ta-dah!' he said.

'Oh Edward!'

'Oh Ed!'

'Hi there.'

He put a leg over the sill and ducked into the room. Belle and Marianne rushed to embrace him.

'Thank goodness!'

'Oh, perfect timing, perfect, we were just despairing . . .'

He put his arms round them both and looked at Elinor.

'Hi, Ellie.'

She nodded in his direction. 'Hello, Edward.'

'Don't I get a hug?'

Belle and Marianne sprang backwards.

'Oh, of course you should!'

'Ellie, oh, Ellie, don't be so *prissy*.'

Edward moved forward and put his arms round Elinor. She stood still in his embrace.

'Hello, you,' he whispered.

She nodded again.

'Hello.'

Belle said, 'This is so lovely, you can't think, we so needed a distraction. Come on, kettle on, cake tin out.'

Edward dropped his arms. He turned.

'Yes please, to cake!'

Marianne came to put her arm through his.

'You look horribly well. What have you been up to?'

He grinned down at her.

'Loafing about. Sailing a bit.'

'Sailing!'

'I'm a good sailor.'

Margaret came scrambling through the window. She said, 'Fanny's seen your car.'

'She hasn't!'

'She has. She's kind of prowling round it. Perhaps she'll think it belongs to one of the workmen.'

Edward said to Belle, 'Will you hide me?'

'No, darling,' Belle said sadly. 'We're in enough trouble as it is. We're about to be homeless. Can you imagine? It's the twenty-first century and we aren't penniless but four educated women like us are about to be—'

Edward said, abruptly, cutting across her, 'You needn't be.'

'What?'

Even Elinor dropped her apparent lack of interest and looked intently at him.

'What, Edward?'

He glanced at Elinor. He said, 'I – I mentioned I might ask about, while I was in Devon. If anyone knew anywhere for rent. Going cheap. And, well, it happens that – well, someone I know down there is sort of related to someone who's related to you. So I told them about you. I told them what had happened.'

He looked at Belle. She was staring at him, and so were all three of her daughters. Edward said, 'I think there might be a house down there for you. It belongs to someone who's some kind of relation, even. Or at least someone who knows about you.' He paused and then he said, 'It's – it's a sort of grapevine thing, you know? But I think there really is a house there, if you'd like it?'

3

Sir John Middleton liked to describe himself as a dinosaur. In fact, he said, he was a double dinosaur.

'These days,' he'd say, to anyone who would listen, 'it's out of the Ark to inherit a house, never mind a bloody great pile like Barton. And as for being a baronet – I ask you! The definition of antediluvian, or what? There isn't even a procedure for renouncing your title if you're a baronet, would you believe? I am stuck with it. Stuck. Sir John M., Bart., to my dying day. Hah!'

His father, another Sir John, had been born in the house, which he left, without a penny to run it, to his son. It was a handsome William and Mary house in Devon, set in dramatic wooded country above the River Exe, to the north of Exeter, and the household, in young Sir John's childhood, had grown used to the corridors being scattered with buckets placed strategically under leaks in various ceilings, and to draughts and damp and extremely intermittent hot water, provided by an ancient boiler in the basement which devoured industrial quantities of coal to very little consistent effect.

Sir John's father had minded none of these things. He had been a boy at the outbreak of the Second World War, and was absolutely indifferent to bad weather, bad food and chilblains. He inherited just enough money to continue living at Barton Park in increasing discomfort, but still able to indulge to the full his passion for field sports. He shot and fished anything that moved or swam, preferred his gun room and game larder to any other parts of his house and, after his wife unsurprisingly left him for a property developer in Bristol, spent any available cash on trips to slaughter snipe in Spain or sharks in the Caribbean. When he died – as he would devoutly have wished to do – big-game hunting on a private estate in Kenya, he left his son the run-down wreck of Barton Park, the title and a locked cabinet of beautifully kept, perfectly matched pairs of Purdey shotguns.

Sir John the younger was entranced to inherit the Purdeys. He had also inherited his father's passion for field sports – indeed all his local friends were distinguished by having subscriptions to the *Shooting Times* and freezers full of braces of pheasant that their wives were sick of cooking – but he had also profited from the childhood and adolescent years spent living with his property-developer stepfather, in Bristol.

It had been made plain to Sir John, from a young age, that the luxury of making choices in life simply did not exist without money. Money was not an evil, Charlie Croft said to his stepson, it was the oil that greased the practical wheels of life. It was foolish to the point of silliness to think you could do without it, and it was asinine to fear it. Money was there to be harnessed, to work for you.

'And if you want to keep that old barrack going that your dad left you – and I', Charlie Croft said, 'would pull it down in a heartbeat and build some practical, properly insulated executive houses there, if I had my way, because it's a cracker of a site

– then you'll have to make it earn its keep.' He'd eyed his stepson.

'Furthermore,' he went on, 'I'll be very interested to see how you do it.'

For most of his twenties, Sir John had had little success in making Barton Park work for itself. After a short commission in the Army, in his father's footsteps, he camped in a set of three rooms situated just above the antediluvian boiler, and commuted to a day job in Exeter, as managing director of a small company on an industrial estate making specialist pumps for desalination plants. The company had only hired him, he was well aware, because his title was useful in attracting the attention of overseas customers, who might initially be impressed by it. He actually performed quite competently, spent the winter weekends blasting the Purdeys into the skies, and hosted parties for which he became locally famous, to which everyone came dressed for the Arctic and played uproarious, childish, upper-class games that involved stampeding through the echoing rooms of Barton Park and lighting fires all over the house as randomly and recklessly as squatters.

Then, when even he, with his sociable and sanguine temperament, was beginning to despair of moving Project Barton Park even a millimetre forward, he had a stroke of luck. Panting down a passage at one of his own parties in the course of an eccentric treasure hunt, he came across a figure huddled, shivering and sniffing, on one of Barton Park's deep windowsills. The figure turned out to be a girl, a very pretty girl called Mary Jennings, who had come to the party because of a man who had invited her and then abandoned her for someone altogether heartier, and who was cold and miserable and had no idea where she was, or how to find her way back to Exeter and a train to London.

He had helped her off the windowsill, discovered that under the old blanket she had wrapped herself in – 'Good God, you can't have that thing anywhere near you, you really can't, it's what my dogs sleep on!' – she was wearing an enchanting but wholly inappropriate little chiffon dress embroidered with spangles, and borne her off to the least disordered of the rooms above the boiler, where he had given her a glass of brandy and also the most reputable of his ancient but quality cashmere jerseys.

Mary Jennings turned out to be, in old-fashioned parlance, an heiress. She was heiress to a company founded by her father, a country-clothing company which had had immense success in the 1960s and 70s with members of organisations like the Country Landowners' Association, so that when Mr Jennings died, he was able to leave his widow not just a penthouse flat in London, but also a considerable capital sum to be shared between her and his two daughters. Mary Jennings had come down to Exeter because of the man who had abandoned her, and she stayed because of the man who rescued her. Mary Jennings of Portman Square became Lady Middleton of Barton Park, and West Country Clothing relocated from its factory in Honiton – originally chosen by Mr Jennings for the relative cheapness of its labour costs – to the stable blocks and outbuildings that Sir John had almost despaired of finding a use for.

Sir John himself turned out to be an admirable entrepreneur. His mother-in-law, who shared his joviality and enjoyment of company, was delighted to allow him to modernise the company. He hired a new designer, researched modern methods of weatherproof and thornproof fabrics, and produced catalogues full of colour and energy, using his friends and their dogs and children as models. The turnover of the company doubled in three years, and tripled in five. Barton Park acquired a new roof and a central heating system that was a model of modern technology. Sir John and Lady Middleton themselves produced four babies in the same five years, and embarked upon a lifestyle that Sir John said he would make no apologies for.

'My friends,' he told an interviewer from the Exeter *Express & Echo*, 'call me the Robber Baron. Because of our pricing. But *I* call our pricing aspirational, and it works. Ask the Germans. They love us. So do the Japanese. Just take a look at our order books.'

He had been in his office that morning, his office converted out of an old carriage house and ablaze with ingenious and theatrical modern lighting, when his mother-in-law came to find him. He was fond of his mother-in-law to a point when he almost prided himself on that affection, and genuinely welcomed the amount of time she cheerfully spent at Barton Park. She liked the same things in life that he liked, she had given him a free hand with the company, and had provided him with a good-looking wife who never interfered in the business or objected to his boisterous pleasures as long as her children's welfare was paramount and nobody questioned the amount of money she spent on them, the house, or on her own wardrobe.

'Frightful,' Abigail Jennings said, blowing into the office in a plump whirl of capes and scarves. 'Frightful wind this morning. Awful portent of autumn, even for me with all my very own insulation.' She regarded her son-in-law. 'You look very jolly, Jonno.'

Sir John looked down at his terracotta cords and emerald sweater. He said, gesturing at himself, 'Bit bright? Bit brash?'

'Not a bit of it. You look splendid. All this creeping about in black and grey that girls do in London. Ghastly. Funereal. Jonno dear. Have you got a moment?'

Sir John glanced at his computer screen.

'I've got a conference call with Hamburg and Osaka in fifteen minutes.'

'I'll be ten.'

He beamed at her.

'Sit yourself down.'

Abigail wedged herself into one of the contemporary Danish armchairs that Mary had chosen for the office and unravelled a scarf or two. She said emphatically, 'Something extraordinary...'

'What?'

'I was in Exeter yesterday, Jonno. Giving lunch to that goddaughter of Mary's father's. And her sister. Sweet pair. So grateful. Lucy and Nancy Steele; their mother was—'

'Abigail, I only have ten minutes.'

'Sorry, dear, sorry. The trouble about my age is that one thing constantly reminds me of another and then that thing of a further thing—'

'Abi,' Sir John said warningly.

Abigail leaned forward a little over her bosoms and stomachs.

'Jonno. Do you have relations in Sussex?'

Sir John looked startled.

'No. Yes. Yes, I think I do. Cousins of Dad's. Well, mine too, I suppose. Near Lewes. Another idiotic great monster like Barton or something.'

Abigail held up a plump hand winking with diamonds.

'Dashwood, dear. They're called Dashwood. Lucy and Nancy had heard about them from a boyfriend of theirs or something

– I couldn't quite work out who, you know what these girls are like. But it's a terrible story, truly awful!'

'Could you possibly tell it quickly?'

'Of course.' Abigail laid her hand on the edge of Sir John's immense, sustainably sourced modern oak desk. 'There are four of them, the mother and three girls, two grown up, one at school. And because of various deaths, including the girls' father, and some antediluvian inheritance laws, this poor family finds itself out on its ear with very little money and nowhere to go. *Nowhere.*'

Sir John drew a rough circle on the pad on the desk in front of him and added a moustache and a smile. He said, doubtfully, sensing another appeal to his good nature coming up, 'Perhaps they could rent?'

'Don't behave like everyone else, Jonno,' Abigail said firmly. 'These are four members of your family, shocked by the death of their father and husband and being thrown out of a way of life which is the only one they know. And you are not exactly short of property, dear, now are you?'

There was a small silence, and then Sir John said, 'D'you know, I think I remember Henry Dashwood. Nice fellow. A bit head in the clouds but decent. Hopeless shot. He came for a hens-only day, one January, forever ago. It's his widow and daughters, you mean?'

'It is.'

Sir John added ears to his circle. He said with sudden resolution, 'Abigail, you were quite right to come to me. Quite right.' He beamed at her again. 'I have an idea. I'll set about it the moment I've dealt with the distributors. I do have an idea! I do!'

* * *

It was Elinor who saw his car arrive. She had been looking out for it because she didn't want Fanny snaffling him and dragging him into her lair in order to subtly dissuade him from making whatever kind of offer he'd driven all the way from Devon to make. Even if he was quite a forceful man – and he'd sounded pretty forceful in a cheerful kind of way, on the telephone – you never could quite count on anyone to be proof against Fanny if she wanted to bend you to her will.

So when Sir John's green Range Rover slid to a halt in the drive, Elinor raced from the kitchen to the front door to greet him and to thank him most earnestly for insisting on coming to see them, but also to indicate to him, somehow, that the startling renovations instituted by the new mistress of Norland Park – whose costly designer mood boards were propped prominently around the entrance hall – was not to be perceived in any way as indicative of any of the rest of the Dashwood family's own tastes, wishes or manners. It was Elinor's aim, flinging open both the leaves of the great front door, to get Sir John through the hall and along to their own unreconstructed sitting room as fast as she could. Only when he was safely ensconced by the fire that Belle had lit especially, alongside the jug of Michaelmas daisies that had been cut from the borders on a day when Fanny was in London, would she quite relax. Sir John looked, Elinor thought, like one of the good-hearted characters from a Dickens novel: broad and healthy, with a ready smile and clothes in optimistic colours. He kissed her warmly, and fraternally, collected a laptop and a bottle of champagne from the boot of the car, and followed her into the house, talking all the way.

'Of course I remember your dad. Lovely man. Useless with

a gun. I say, this is elegant. Look at this floor! We aren't quite as formal as this at Barton, though Mary would love us to be, but of course, the house is earlier. You'll love our library. I am very proud of our library. God in heaven, will you look at that staircase! I suppose you lot slid down the bannisters when you were little. Lethal, when you think about it, with a marble floor waiting at the bottom. Mary's put seagrass over foam rubber in our hall so the ankle-biters don't smash their skulls. I say they should take their chance, but she won't have it. As I'm a relation, dear girl, I'm free to tell you that you're really attractive. I mean that. And I hear that your sisters—'

'Are much prettier,' Elinor said quickly.

'Can't be. Simply can't be. I never saw your mother but your dad implied that she was a corker.'

'She still is,' Elinor said. She opened the door to the sitting room and stood back for him to enter. 'See for yourself.'

Belle and Marianne and Margaret all rose from the chairs where they had been waiting, and smiled at him.

'Golly,' Sir John said. 'Golly. Have all my Christmases come at once? Or what? Aren't you all gorgeous?'

'Look,' Sir John said later, expansive with tea and three of the scones that Belle had made that morning, 'look, I said to Mary, family's family, and we've been bloody lucky.'

He was settled deep in the armchair that Henry used to use, his tea mug in one hand.

'Bloody lucky,' he repeated. 'We are able to live in a great place, employ local people, educate the nippers, have good holidays and a very respectable standard of life. And, I said to Mary, what's Belle got? No home, no money, Henry dead and those girls. Listen, I said to Mary, blood's thicker than water. I'd never forgive myself for watching my old pa's cousins struggling while I book a chalet for Christmas in Méribel. No *thank* you, I said to Mary. Not my way.'

He took a final swallow from his tea mug and reached to park it on the nearest side table.

'And here we come to the crunch. I can't neglect you and your situation while Barton Cottage stands empty. I just can't. And we can use you girls in the business, I'm sure we can.' He winked at Marianne. 'You'd be fantastic in the catalogue.'

'I hate being photographed,' Marianne said distantly, 'I believe those people who think that the camera steals your soul.'

Elinor gave a little gasp.

'Oh, M, really—'

'Listen to her!' Sir John said, roaring with laughter. 'Just *listen*. Don't you love it?'

He beckoned to Margaret.

'Pass me my laptop, there's a good girl.'

She came slowly across the room and handed the laptop to him. And then she stood beside him and waited while he fussed over the keys. She said, wearily, 'Shall I help you?'

He grinned at the screen.

'Cheeky monkey.'

'It'd be quicker.'

'There it is!' Sir John shouted suddenly. 'There they are! Pictures!'

Margaret bent.

'How's that!' Sir John exclaimed. 'A slide show! A slide show of your new home! Barton Cottage. It's a charmer. You'll love it.'

Slowly, the four of them formed a semicircle behind the

armchair. Sir John made a tremendous show of clicking and flicking until a photograph of an uncompromisingly small modern house on a slope, backed by trees, filled the screen.

'But,' Marianne cried in disappointment, 'it's new!'

'I've just built it,' Sir John said with satisfaction. 'Planning was a complete nightmare but I battled through. I was going to use it as a holiday let.'

'It's – lovely,' Belle said faintly.

'Perfect spot,' Sir John said, 'amazing views, new bathroom, kitchen, utility, the works.' He glanced at Marianne. 'You wanted roses round the door?'

'And maybe thatch ...'

'Marianne, honestly! So ungrateful.'

'No, she isn't,' Sir John said. 'Just honest. And it's a come-down after this place. I can see that.' He looked back at the screen. It now showed an astonishing view down a wooded valley, dramatic and startlingly green.

'Well?'

Belle deliberately avoided looking at her daughters. She said, in a rush, 'We'd love it.'

'Ma—'

'No,' she said. She wouldn't look at them. She looked instead at the next picture, of a steep hill rushing up towards a cloud-dappled sky. 'We'd love it. It looks charming. Such a – setting.'

Elinor cleared her throat. She said to Sir John, 'Where is Barton exactly?'

He beamed at her.

'Near Exeter.'

'Exeter ...'

'What's Exeter?' Margaret said.

'It's a place, darling. A lovely historic place in Devon.'

'Between Dartmoor and Exmoor,' Sir John said proudly.

Marianne said tragically, 'I don't really know where Devon *is*.'

'It's gorgeous,' Belle said emphatically. '*Gorgeous*. Next to Cornwall.'

All three girls gazed at her.

'Cornwall!'

'Not as far ...'

Elinor said, trying not to sound pleading, 'I have just one more year to go at—'

'And my music!' Marianne cried. 'What about my music?'

Margaret had her fingers in her ears and her eyes shut.

'Don't anyone *dare* say I have to change schools.'

Belle smiled at Sir John.

'Elinor's studying architecture. She draws beautifully.'

He smiled back at her.

'I remember Henry saying you did, too. You'll be in your element at Barton, drawing and painting away.'

'I did figures, mostly, but I'm sure I could—'

'And Elinor', Marianne said loudly, 'draws buildings. Where can she study *buildings* in *Devon*?'

'Darling. Don't, darling. Don't be rude.'

John Middleton beamed again at Marianne.

'She's not rude. She's refreshing. I like refreshing. My kids will adore her; they love anyone out of the ordinary. Four of them. Enough energy to power your average city, between them.' He closed his laptop and looked up at Belle. 'Well,' he said, 'Well. Can I take it that you and the girls will come and live at Barton Cottage for what I promise you will be a very modest rent?'

Margaret took her fingers out of her ears and opened her eyes. She flung her arms wide in a gesture of despair.

'What about all my *friends?*' she said.

'I wonder', Belle said from the doorway, 'if I could trouble you for a moment?'

Both Fanny and John Dashwood, who were watching the evening news on television with glasses in their hands, gave a little jump in their chairs.

'Belle!' John Dashwood said, with surprise rather than pleasure.

He leaned forward and reduced the volume on the television, although he didn't turn it off altogether. Fanny remained where she was, holding her wine glass. John stood up slowly.

'Have a drink,' he said automatically, gesturing vaguely towards the bottle plainly visible on a silver tray on the coffee table in front of them.

'I'm sure', Fanny said, 'that she won't be staying that long.'

Belle smiled at her. She advanced into the room far enough to give herself authority, but not so far that she couldn't make a quick escape.

'Quite right, Fanny. I will be two minutes. We had a visitor this afternoon.'

Fanny continued to regard her wine glass. She said to it, 'I wondered when you would see fit to mention that to me.'

Belle smiled broadly at John.

'Would it be an awful nuisance to turn the television off?'

John glanced at Fanny. She made an impatient little gesture of dismissal. He picked up the remote again and aimed it at the screen.

'Thank you,' Belle said. She was determined to keep smiling. She folded her hands lightly in front of her. 'The thing is, that we won't be *troubling* you here at Norland much longer. We've been offered a house. By a relation of mine.'

John looked truly startled.

'Good heavens.'

Fanny said smoothly, 'But not too far from here, I hope?'

'Actually . . .' Belle said, and stopped, savouring the moment.

'Actually what?'

'We are going to Devon,' Belle said with satisfaction.

'Devon!'

'Near Exeter. A house on an estate which is, I gather, just a fraction larger than this one. It belongs to my cousin. My cousin Sir John Middleton.'

John said, almost inaudibly, '*My* cousin, I believe. A Dashwood cousin.'

Belle took no notice. She looked directly, smilingly, at Fanny.

'So we'll be out of your hair by the end of the month. As soon as we can sort a school for Margaret and all that.'

'But I was going to help you find a house!' John said aggrievedly.

'So sweet of you, but in the end the house came to us.'

'So lucky,' Fanny said.

'Oh, I agree. *So* lucky.'

'It's too bad,' John exclaimed.

'What is?'

'It's too bad of you to make all these arrangements without consulting me.'

'But you didn't want me to consult you,' Belle said.

Fanny said clearly, 'Sweetness, you've given them all

somewhere to live all summer, rent free, and the run of the kitchen gardens, after all.'

John glanced at her. He said with relief, 'So I have.'

'There we are,' Belle said brightly. 'All settled. You let us stay on in our own home for a while and now we've found another one to go to! Perfect. I've taken Barton Cottage for a year and, of course, it would be lovely to see you there whenever you are down that way.'

Fanny looked out of the window.

'I never go to Devon,' she said.

Belle paused in the doorway.

'No,' she said, 'I thought not. But maybe you'll break the habit of a lifetime. It's odd, really, that you never went to see Edward all the time he was in Plymouth, don't you think?'

Fanny's head snapped back round.

'Edward! Why mention Edward?'

Belle was almost out of the door.

'Oh, Edward,' she said airily. 'Dear Edward. So affectionate. He's going to come to Barton. I made a special point of asking him to come and see us in the cottage. And he said he'd love to.'

And then she reached for the handle and closed the door behind her with a small but triumphant bang.

4

'Marianne,' Elinor said, 'will you *please* put that guitar down and come and help us?'

Marianne was in her favourite playing chair by the window in her bedroom, her right foot on a small pile of books – a French dictionary and two volumes of Shakespeare's history plays came to just the right height – and the guitar resting comfortably across her thigh. She was playing a song of Taylor Swift's that she had played a good deal since Dad died, even though – or maybe even because – everyone had told her that a player at her level could surely express themselves better with something more serious. It was called 'Teardrops on My Guitar', and to Elinor's mind, it was mawkish.

'Oh, M, *please*.'

Marianne played determinedly on to the end of a verse. She said, when she'd finished, 'I know you hate that song.'

'I don't *hate* it ...'

'It isn't much of a song. I know that. It isn't hard to play. But it suits me. It suits how I feel.'

Elinor said, 'We're packing books. You can't imagine how many books there are.'

'I thought the cottage was furnished?'

'It is. But not with books and pictures and things. We could get through it so much more quickly if you just came and helped a bit.'

Marianne raised her head to look out of the window. She folded both arms embracingly around her guitar. She said, 'Can you imagine being away from here?'

Elinor said tiredly, 'We've been through all that.'

'Look at those trees. Look at them. And the lake. I've done all my practice by this window, looking out at that view. I've played the guitar in this room for *ten* years, Ellie, ten years.' She looked down at the guitar. 'Dad gave me my guitar in this room.'

'I remember.'

'When I got grade five.'

'Yes.'

'He did all the research, and everything. I remember him saying it had to have a cedar top and rosewood sides and an ebony finger-board, a proper, classical, Spanish guitar. He was so excited.'

Elinor came further into the room. She said soothingly, 'It's coming with us, M, you'll have your guitar.'

Marianne said suddenly, 'Fanny—' and stopped.

'Fanny? What about her?'

Marianne looked at her.

'Yesterday. Fanny asked me what the guitar had cost.'

'She didn't! What did you say to her?'

'I told her,' Marianne said, 'I said I couldn't remember exactly, I thought maybe a bit more than a thousand, and she said who paid for it.'

'The cheek!' Elinor exclaimed.

'Well, I was caught on the hop, wasn't I, because she then said did Dad pay for it, and I said it was a joint present for getting grade five from Dad and Uncle Henry, and she said, Well, that really means it belongs to Norland, doesn't it, if Uncle Henry paid for some of it, and not you.'

Elinor sat down abruptly on the end of Marianne's bed.

She said, 'You couldn't make Fanny up, could you?'

Marianne laid her cheek on the guitar's rosewood flank.

'I put it under my bed last night. I'm not letting it out of my sight.'

'And you still want to stay here? Even if it meant living with Fanny?'

Marianne lifted her head and then stood up, adjusting the guitar so that she was holding it by the neck.

She said, 'It's the place, Ellie. It's the trees and the light and the way it makes me feel. I just can't imagine anywhere else feeling like home. I'm terrified that nowhere else ever *will* be home. Even with Fanny, I just – just belong, at Norland.'

Elinor sighed. Marianne had not only inherited their father's asthma, but also his propensity for depression. It was something they all had learned to accept, and to live with: the mood swings and the proclivity for inertia and despair. Elinor thought about what lay ahead, about the enormity of this move to such a completely unknown environment and society and wondered, slightly desperately, if she could manage to accommodate a bout of Marianne's depression as well as their mother's volatility and Margaret's appalled reaction at having to leave behind every single person she had ever known or been at school with in her whole, whole life.

'Please,' Elinor said again. 'Please don't give up before we've even got there.'

'I'll try,' Marianne said in a small voice.

'I can't manage all of you hating this idea—'

'Ma doesn't. It was Ma who bounced us all into this.'

'Ma's on a high at the moment because she got one across Fanny. It won't last.'

Marianne looked at her sister.

'I'll try,' she said again, 'I really will.'

'There'll be other trees—'

'Don't.'

'And valleys. And jolly Sir John.'

Marianne gave a tiny shudder.

'Suppose they're the only people we know?'

'They won't be.'

'Maybe', Marianne said, 'Edward will come.'

Elinor said nothing. She got off the bed and made purposefully for the door.

'Ellie?'

'Yes.'

'Have you heard from Edward?'

There was a tiny pause.

'He hasn't rung,' Elinor said.

'Have you seen him on Facebook?'

In the doorway, Elinor turned.

'I haven't looked,' she said.

Marianne bent to lay her guitar down on her bed, like a child.

'He likes you, Ellie.'

There was another little pause.

'I – know he does.'

'I mean,' Marianne said, 'he really *likes* you. Seriously.'

'But he's caught—'

'It's pathetic, these days, to be still under your mother's thumb. Like he is.'

Elinor said quite fiercely, 'She neglected him. And spoiled the others. She isn't at all fair.'

Marianne came and stood close to her sister.

'Oh, good,' she said. 'Standing up for Edward. Good sign.'

Elinor looked at her sister with sudden directness.

'I can't think about that.'

'Can't you?'

'No,' Elinor said. 'Today I am thinking about packing up books so I don't have to think about giving up my degree.'

Marianne looked stricken.

'Oh, Ellie, I didn't think . . .'

'No. Nobody does. I know I'd only got a year to go, but I had to ring my year co-ordinator and tell him I wouldn't be back this term.' She broke off, and then she said, 'We were going to concentrate on surveying this term. And model-making. I was, he said, possibly the best at technical drawing in my year. He said – oh God, it doesn't matter what he said.'

Marianne put her arms round her sister.

'Oh, *Ellie*.'

'It's OK.'

'It isn't, it isn't, it's so unfair.'

'Maybe', Elinor said, standing still in Marianne's embrace, 'I can pick it up again later.'

'In Exeter? Could you join a course in Exeter?'

'I don't know.'

'Have you told Ma?

Elinor sighed.

'Sort of. I don't want to burden her.'

'Please think about telling her properly. Please think about finishing your course in Exeter.'

Elinor sighed. She gave Marianne a quick hug, and detached herself.

'I'll try. In due course, I'll try. Right now ... Right now I can't think about anything except getting us all settled in Devon without losing our minds or our money.' She paused and then she said, '*Please* come and help with these books?'

Sir John sent the handyman from Barton Park to Norland, with Sir John's own Range Rover, to drive the Dashwoods down to Devon. He also organised a removal company from Exeter to come and collect their books and pictures, and their china and glass, and Belle had the exquisite satisfaction of seeing the Provençal plates disappearing into paper-filled boxes, and in then labelling those boxes with a bold black marker pen so that Fanny, monitoring the whole packing-up procedure, could not fail to observe the china's departure.

John Dashwood was very uneasy around the whole process. When he returned each day from the notional job of running the Ferrarses' commercial property empire – he was regarded as an inevitable and unwelcome nuisance by the man who actually did the work – he hovered in Belle's sitting room or kitchen, mournfully reciting the expenses that made Norland such an exhausting drain upon his wallet and energies, and pointing out how lucky Belle was to be exchanging life at Norland for one of such carefree simplicity and frugality in Devon. Only once did Belle grow so exasperated by his perpetual litany of complaints that she was driven to point out quite sharply that the promise of generosity made in that room at Haywards Heath Hospital had never actually been adhered to. John Dashwood had been deeply wounded by her accusation that he had been other than both honourable and generous, and said so.

'It's too bad of you, Belle. It really is. You and the girls have had absolutely the run of the house and garden since Henry died, the complete run. It's been really inconvenient for Fanny, having you here and having to put all her decorating plans on hold, but of course she's been angelic about that. As she has about everything. I sometimes wonder, Belle, if Henry didn't spoil you, I really do. You don't seem to have the first idea about recognising or acknowledging generosity. I'm really quite shocked. I just hope poor old John Middleton knows what he's in for, trying to help someone who appears not to have the first idea of even how to say thank you.' He'd peered at her, cradling his whisky and soda.

'Just a "thank you, John" would be nice. Don't you think? It's all I'm asking, after everything you've been given. Just a thank you, Belle.'

It was a relief, in the end, to see Sir John's car. Belle climbed in beside young Thomas, the handyman, who had put on his new jeans in honour of this important commission from his employer, and the girls got into the back seat behind her, Margaret clutching her iPod, her childhood Nintendo DS and her pocketbook laptop, as if they represented her only frail remaining link to civilised or social life as she knew it. Behind the girls Thomas stacked their suitcases and, on top of that, Marianne's guitar case, which she had held in her arms all the time she was saying goodbye to John and Fanny. Fanny had been holding Harry's hand, as if he were a trump card that she needed to flourish at the final moment of victory. In the hand not gripped by his mother, Harry was clutching a giant American-style cookie which seemed to absorb too much of his attention for there to be any to spare for his cousins' departure. Elinor had knelt in front of him, and smiled.

'Bye, bye, Harry.'

He regarded her, chewing. She leaned forward and kissed his cheek.

'You smell of biscuit.'

He frowned.

'It's a *cookie*,' he said reprovingly, and wedged it in his mouth again.

'Poor little boy,' Elinor said, later, in the car.

'Is he?'

'Course he is. Having Fanny for a mother . . .'

Belle turned in her seat. She said, rolling her eyes slightly in the direction of Thomas, 'Let's not talk about Fanny.'

'She didn't wave,' Marianne said. She gazed out of the window, as if devouring what she saw as it sped past her.

'No.'

'She turned her face so that I kind of got her ear when I kissed her.'

'Yuck, having to kiss her at all . . .'

'She was pretty well smirking!'

'She's horrible.'

'She's *over*,' Belle said firmly. 'Over.' Then she turned and smiled brightly at Thomas, who was driving with elaborate professionalism, and exclaimed, almost theatrically, 'And *we* are starting a *new* life, in *Devon*!'

* * *

In the bright, small kitchen at Barton Cottage, with its immediate view of a rotary washing line planted in a square of paving,
Elinor surveyed the unpacked boxes. She had said that she
would sort the kitchen not just out of altruism, but also so that
she could have time to herself, time to try and retrieve her mind
and spirit, neither of which had yet made the journey with her
body, from Norland to Barton.

It had been quite a good journey for the first few hours.
Everyone was slightly hysterical with the immediate relief of
escaping the pressure of living in a house with other people
who so openly wanted them gone, but then Marianne had
gone suddenly very quiet and then very pale and when Elinor,
trained by long practice to be alert to her sister's symptoms,
asked if she was OK, she had begun to wheeze and gasp alarmingly, and Belle had ordered Thomas, in a voice urgent with
panic, to stop the car.

They had tumbled out on to the verge of the A31 somewhere
west of Southampton, and Elinor had been intensely grateful
to Thomas, who quietly established himself beside Marianne as
they all crouched on the tired grass by a litter bin in a parking
place, and supported her while Elinor held her blue inhaler to
her mouth and talked to her steadily and quietly, as she had so
often done before.

'Poor darling,' Belle said, over and over. 'Poor darling. It'll be
the stress of leaving Norland.'

'Or the dogs, miss,' Thomas said matter-of-factly.

'What dogs? There aren't any dogs.'

'In the car,' Thomas said. He was watching Marianne with a
practical eye that was infinitely comforting to Elinor. 'Sir John's
dogs is always in the car. Doesn't matter how often we hoover it,

we never get all the hairs out. My nan had asthma. Couldn't even have a budgie in the house, never mind dogs and cats.'

'Sorry,' Marianne said, between breaths. 'Sorry.'

'Never be sorry ...'

'Just say, a bit earlier, next time.'

'It won't be an omen, will it?'

Margaret said, 'We did omens at school and the Greeks thought—'

'Shut up, Mags.'

'But—'

'We'll put you in the front seat,' Thomas said to Marianne, 'with the window open.'

She nodded. Elinor looked at him. He was wearing the expression of fierce protectiveness that so many men seemed to adopt round Marianne. Solicitously, with Elinor's assistance, he lifted Marianne to her feet.

'Thank you,' Elinor said.

He began to guide Marianne back to the car, his arm round her shoulders.

'Nothing to thank me for,' he said, and his voice was proud.

The rest of the journey had passed almost in silence. Thomas drove soberly and steadily, with Marianne leaning her head back in the seat beside him, her face turned towards the open window, her inhaler on her lap. Behind them, Elinor gripped Margaret's hand and Belle sat with her eyes closed (in a way that suggested crowding memories rather than repose) as Hampshire gave way to Dorset, and Dorset, in its turn and after seemingly endless hours, to Devon.

It was only in the last five miles or so, as the countryside grew increasingly beautiful and spectacular, that they began to rouse themselves from the aftermath of shock and exclaim at what they were passing.

'Oh, look.'

'This is amazing!'

'Gosh, Thomas, is Barton going to be this good?'

It was. They left the road and turned in between stone gate-posts crowned with urns that heralded a series of drives curving away around a smooth hillside crowned with trees. There were freshly painted signs planted alongside the drives, indicating the directions to the main house, to the offices, to visitors' parking and, with a right-angled arrow, to Barton Cottage. And there, after a further few minutes, it was, as raw and new looking as it had been on Sir John's laptop, but set on a pleasing slope, with woods climbing up behind it, and the forked valleys falling away dramatically in front. They had gasped when they saw it, as much for its astonishing situation as for its uncompromising banality of design.

Thomas had looked at it with satisfaction.

'We never thought he'd get planning permission,' he said. 'We all bet he wouldn't. But he managed to prove there'd been a shepherd's cottage up there once, so there'd been a residence. If he wants something, he doesn't give up. That's Sir John.'

Sir John had left wine and a note of welcome in the kitchen, and a basket of logs by the sitting-room fireplace. Someone had also put milk and bread and eggs in the fridge, and a bowl of apples on the new yellow-wood kitchen table, and Margaret reported, after inspecting the bathroom, that there was also a full roll of toilet paper and a new shower curtain, printed with goldfish. Elinor could not think why, confronted both with the kindness of almost strangers, and a practical little house in a magnificent place, she should feel like doing nothing so much as taking herself off somewhere private and quiet, to cry. But she did – and there was no immediate opportunity, what with Marianne needing to be assisted into the house, and Belle and Margaret exclaiming at the advantages (Margaret) and disadvantages (Belle) of their new home, to indulge herself. The luxury of being alone and able to look at and begin to arrange her thoughts would have, as it so often did, to wait.

And now, here was her chance, by herself in the kitchen, with unpacked boxes of saucepans and plates. It was comical, really, the way she'd ended up with unpacking all the practical stuff, while the others, ably and eagerly assisted by Thomas, decided where the pictures should hang and which window gave on to the right prospect to be conducive to guitar practice. Margaret had found a tree outside where she could get five whole signal bars on her mobile phone, if she climbed up into the lowest branches, and Thomas had immediately said that he would make her a tree house, just as he had agreed with Belle that the cottage could be easily improved by extending the main sitting room into a conservatory on the southern side. He had said he would bring brochures. Elinor had said quietly, 'What about me?'

Belle went on looking at the space where the conservatory might stand.

'What about you, darling?'

'Well,' Elinor said, 'most architects get their first break designing extensions for family houses. Even Richard Rogers—'

Belle gave her a quick glance.

'But you're not qualified, darling.'

'I nearly am. I'm qualified *enough*.'

Belle smiled, but not at Elinor.

'I don't think so, darling. I'd be happier with professionals who do thousands of conservatories a year.'

Elinor closed her eyes and counted slowly to ten. Then she opened them and said, in as level a voice as she could manage, 'There's another thing.'

Belle was gazing at the view again.

'Oh?'

'Yes,' Elinor said, more firmly. '*Yes*. What about the *money?*'

She put two frying pans down on the kitchen table, now, beside three mugs and a handful of wooden spoons, which had been wrapped, in the universal manner of removal men, as solicitously in new white paper as if they had been Meissen shepherdesses. Money was haunting her. Money to buy and run a car – how else was Margaret to get to her new school in Exeter? Money to pay the rent, money for electricity and water, money to pay for food and clothes and even tiny amounts of fun, when all they had in the world was, when invested, going to produce under seven hundred pounds a month, or less than two hundred pounds a week. Which was, she calculated, bang-ing Belle's battered old stockpot down beside the frying pans, not quite thirty pounds a day. For four women with laughable earning power, one of whom is still at school, one is unused to work, and one is both physically unfit and as yet unqualified to work. Which leaves me! Me, Elinor Dashwood, who has been living in the cloud cuckoo land of Norland and idiotic, imprac-tical dreams of architecture. She straightened up and looked round the kitchen. The prospect – bright new units overlaid with a chaos of unarranged shabby old possessions – was sobering. It was also, if she didn't keep the tightest of grip on herself, frightening. She was not equipped for this. None of them were.

They had fled to Devon on an impulse, reacting against the grief and rejection they had been through, surrendering to the first hand held out to them without considering the true extent or consequences of that surrender.

Elinor closed her eyes. She mustn't panic. She mustn't. There would be a way to make this work; there had to be. Perhaps she could appeal to Sir John, perhaps he had already guessed, perhaps he . . . Her eye was caught by a movement outside the kitchen window. It was Thomas carrying planks of wood towards Margaret's communications tree. Already! They had been in the cottage one night and a tree house was under way. Elinor seized a saucepan lid out of the open box in front of her and flung it wildly in frustration across the kitchen. Who was going to *pay* for a tree house, please?

'Wonderful,' Sir John said. He was standing holding open the immense front door to Barton Park and beaming at them all. 'Come in, come in. I wanted you for supper last night, you know, but Mary wouldn't let me. Said you'd be exhausted. Probably right. Usually is.' He plunged forward, bent on heartily kissing all of them. 'She's upstairs now with the rug rats. Bedtime. Complete mayhem, every night, goes on for hours. And then they trickle down all evening under one transparent pretext or another. Nil discipline. Nil. Bless them. Fantastic children.'

Belle said, emerging from his embrace, 'Don't you get involved?'

'With bedtime? No fear. I do *Tintin* on Saturdays with the boys. I'm a wholly *un*reconstructed male, I'm happy to say. Now then.' He swung round, closing the door and gesturing lavishly with his free hand. 'What do you think of my old gaff?'

The girls gazed about them in silence. The hall was huge, larger than Norland, with niches for statues and an elaborate plaster frieze of gilded swags. It was as grandly chilly and unlike Norland in spirit or appearance as it possibly could have been. It resembled some kind of museum, a public space dedicated to the formal past. Elinor saw Marianne give an involuntary little shiver.

'Frightful, isn't it?' Sir John said jovially. 'Tarted up for a visit from Queen Victoria, all this marble nonsense. It's an idiotic house. Dining room seats thirty-six. Thirty-six!'

Margaret stopped swivelling her head in amazement. She said, 'Well, why do you live here, then?'

Sir John gave a gust of laughter.

'It's in my bones. Inheritance and all that. Can't live with it or without it.'

Marianne said tightly, 'We know about all that.'

'Course you do. Course you do. Just consider yourselves lucky to be well out of it, tucked up in the cottage with all mod cons. Now come on in and have a drink.' He paused in the doorway to an immense, bright room full of sofas and said, conspiratorially, 'And meet the mother-in-law.'

'Well,' Abigail Jennings said, rising from one of the sofas in a flurry of scarves and small dogs, 'if it isn't the famous Dashwood girls!' She flung her arms wide and laughed merrily. 'Jonno said you were all gorgeous and he isn't wrong! He's wrong about most things, bless him, being only a man and therefore by definition in the wrong, but he said you were gorgeous and you are. My goodness, you are.' She turned to a tall, lean man beside her and dug her elbow playfully into his ribs. 'Don't you think so, Bill?'

The tall man smiled, but said nothing. The girls stood in a row, just inside the door, with Belle slightly ahead of them, and looked at the floor.

'Can't stand this,' Marianne said to Elinor between clenched teeth.

'Sh.'

'She's fat,' Margaret hissed vengefully, 'as well as obviously being a sick bitch—'

'Mags!'

'I didn't *want* to come out to supper, I wanted to watch—'

Elinor lifted her head.

'Sorry.'

The tall man was looking at her sympathetically. Then his gaze shifted to Marianne, and Elinor saw something familiar happen, a startled arrested something that had everything to do with the arrangement of Marianne's extraordinary features, and nothing whatsoever to do with her current expression of pure mulishness.

Sir John was pulling his mother-in-law forward like a prize exhibit, the dogs yapping round their feet.

'Belle. Meet Abigail, my monster-in-law. Bane of my life, who, as you see, I adore. Mrs Jennings to you, girls. She's pretty well a fixture here, I can tell you. The nippers adore her too. When she's here, the gin goes down like bath water.' He put an arm affectionately round Abigail's shoulders. 'Isn't that true, Abi?'

'If you left any, it would be!' Abigail cried.

She extricated herself and came forward to kiss them all warmly.

'Belle, welcome, dear. And girls. Lovely girls. Now, let me

get you sorted. Elinor, you must be Elinor. And Marianne of the famous guitar? Oh, it *is* famous, dear, it is. Bill over there plays it, too. We know all about guitars at Barton – you'll see! And this is Margaret. Don't scowl, dear, I'm not a witch. Far too fat for any self-respecting broomstick. Now, Jonno, aren't you going to introduce Bill?'

Sir John flung out an arm in the direction of the tall man, who had stood quietly by the immense marble fireplace without moving or uttering a word since they came in.

'Meet my old mucker, girls. Belle, this is William Brandon. Late of the Light Dragoons. My regiment. My old dad's regiment.' He glanced at the tall man with sudden seriousness. 'We were in Bosnia together, Bill and me. Weren't we?' He turned back to Belle. 'And then he stayed in, and rose to command the regiment and now he devotes himself to good works, God help us, and comes here for a bit of normality and a decent claret. It's his second home, eh Bill?' He gestured to the tall man to come forward. 'Come on, Bill, come on. That's better. Now then, this is Colonel Brandon, Belle.'

She held out her hand, smiling. William Brandon stepped forward and took it, bowing a little.

'Welcome to Devon.'

'He's so old,' Marianne muttered to Elinor.

'No, he isn't, he looks—'

'They're all old. Old and old-fashioned and—'

'Boring,' Margaret said.

Mrs Jennings turned towards them. She looked at Margaret. She was laughing again.

'What wouldn't bore you, dear? Boys?'

Margaret went scarlet. Marianne put an arm round her.

'Come on now,' Abigail said. 'There must be boys in your lives!'

Marianne stared at her.

'None,' she said.

'One!' Margaret blurted out.

'Oh? Oh?'

'Shut up, Mags.'

Colonel Brandon stepped forward and put a restraining hand on Abigail's arm. He said to everyone else, soothingly, 'How about I get everyone a drink?'

Belle looked at him gratefully.

'I'd love one. And – and you play the guitar?'

'Badly.'

'Brilliantly!' Sir John shouted. 'He's a complete pain in the arse!'

'Would you play later?' Colonel Brandon asked Marianne.

She didn't look at him. She said, unhelpfully, 'I didn't bring my guitar.'

'We could fetch it!' Abigail said.

'Another time, perhaps?' Colonel Brandon said.

Marianne gave a ghost of a smile. 'Yes, please, another time.'

'Too bad,' Abigail said. 'Too bad. We were looking forward to a party. Weren't we, Jonno? No boys, no music . . .'

Sir John moved round the group so that he could put an arm round Margaret.

'We'll soon remedy that, won't we?' He bent, beaming, so that his nose was almost touching hers. 'Won't we? We can start by christening your tree house!'

Margaret pulled her head back as far as Sir John's embrace would allow.

'How d'you know about that?'

He laid a finger of his free hand against his nose.

'Nothing at Barton escapes me. Nothing.' He winked at his mother-in-law and they both went off into peals of laughter. 'Does it?'

'I can't do this,' Marianne said later.

She was sitting on the end of her mother's bed, in the muddle of half-unpacked boxes, nursing a mug of peppermint tea.

Belle put down her book.

'It was rather awful.'

'It was *very* awful. All that canned laughter. All the jokes. None of them funny—'

'They're so good-hearted. And well meaning, Marianne.'

'It's fatal to be well meaning.'

Belle laughed.

'But, darling, it's where kindness comes from.'

Marianne took a swallow of tea.

'I don't think her ladyship is kind.'

'Oh, I don't know. She was perfectly nice to us.'

Marianne looked up. She said, 'She wasn't interested in us. She just went through the motions. She only got a bit animated when the children came down.'

'So sweet.'

'Were they?'

'Oh, M,' Belle said, 'of course they were sweet, like Harry is sweet. It's not their fault if they are hopelessly mothered!'

Marianne sighed.

'It's just depressing', she said, 'to spend a whole evening with people who are *all* so – utterly uncongenial.'

'Bill Brandon wasn't, was he? I thought he was charming.'

'Of course you did, Ma. He'd be perfect for you. Right age, nice manners, even reads—'

'Stop it. He's much younger than me!'

Marianne tweaked her mother's toes under the duvet.

'No one is younger than you, Ma.'

Belle ignored her. She leaned forward.

'Darling.'

'What?'

Belle lowered her voice.

'Any – sign of Edward?'

Marianne shook her head.

'Don't think so.'

'Has she said anything?'

'No.'

'Have you asked her?'

'Ma,' Marianne said, reprovingly, 'I wouldn't. Would I?'

'But it's so odd.'

'He *is* odd.'

'I thought . . .'

'I know.'

'D'you think Fanny's stopping him?'

Marianne got slowly to her feet.

'I doubt it. He's quite stubborn in his quiet way.'

'Well?'

Marianne looked down at her.

'We can't do anything, Ma.'

'Couldn't you text him?'

'No, Ma, I could not.'

Belle picked up her book again.

'Your sister is a mystery to me. It breaks my heart to leave

Norland but not, apparently, hers. We are completely thrown by arriving here and finding ourselves miles from anywhere and she just goes on putting the herbs and spices in alphabetical order as if nothing is any different except the layout of the cupboards. And now Edward. Does she really not care about Edward?'

Marianne looked down at her mug again.

'She's made up her mind about missing him, like she's made up her mind about giving up her course. She won't let herself despair about things she can't have, and doesn't waste her energies longing for things like I do. She thinks before she feels, Ma, you know she does. I expect she does sort of miss Ed, in her way.'

'Her way?'

Marianne moved towards the door. She said, decisively, 'But her way isn't *my* way. Any more than those stupid people tonight were my kind of people. I want – I want...'

She stopped. Belle let a beat fall, and then she said, 'What do you want, darling?'

Marianne put her hand on the doorknob, and turned to face her mother.

'I want to be over*whelmed*,' she said.

5

The following morning Sir John, blithely oblivious to any reservations his guests might have had about their evening at Barton Park, sent Thomas in the Range Rover to collect them all for a tour of his offices and design studio. Margaret, in particular, was appalled.

'I'm not looking at pictures of those gross clothes!'

'And I', Marianne said, loudly enough for Thomas not to mistake her distaste, 'am not modelling them either, thank you very much.'

Thomas, who was leaning against a kitchen counter with the tea Belle had made him, said imperturbably, 'I don't think you have an option.'

They all stared at him.

'You mean we *have* to?'

'Yup,' Thomas said. He grinned at Margaret. 'He's the boss round here. Lady M. and Mrs J. make a fair bit of noise but they end up doing what they're told.' He took a gulp of tea. 'We all do.'

'So,' Marianne said, twisting her hair up into a knot and then letting it cascade over her shoulders, 'he's kind of *bought* us?'

Thomas shrugged.

'There isn't a bad bone in his body. But he likes people around him; he likes people to like what he likes. And he likes the business. We all like what we're good at.'

Belle looked at Margaret.

'Find some shoes, darling.'

'But I—'

'*Shoes*,' Belle said. 'And perhaps brush your hair?'

Elinor said, trying to be truthful while not betraying the acuteness of their situation to Thomas, 'We could do with some – well, work, couldn't we?'

Belle glanced at her.

'What do you mean?'

'I mean . . .' Elinor said, fidgeting with the buttons on her cardigan, 'I mean, if the design studio could use you in some way, and Marianne and Margaret were sort of – of needed for the catalogue, it would be kind – kind of helpful?'

Belle turned to look at her fully.

'To whom?'

Elinor stood a little straighter.

'Us.'

'In what way exactly?'

Elinor observed that Thomas was deliberately concentrating on his tea. She said, quietly, 'Money, Ma.'

'Why', Belle said, almost petulantly, 'is that all you can ever think about?'

'Because', Elinor said, in the same low voice, 'someone has to.'

'But we've got—'

'It's not *enough*. Not for four people in a cottage in the middle of nowhere, one of whom has to start school on Wednesday.'

Margaret reappeared wearing grubby trainers with the laces undone. She said, loudly, 'I don't want to go to school.'

Thomas put his mug down with decision. He said to her, firmly, 'It's the law.'

'Thank you,' Elinor said.

Belle looked at Marianne. She said, with forced gaiety, 'It looks like we're outnumbered, darling!'

'If you mean', Elinor said with sudden exasperation, 'that you think you don't have to make an effort to contribute, then you're quite right. You're outnumbered. *Everyone* has to do their bit.'

There was a brief pause, and then Marianne, apparently examining the ends of a handful of her hair for split ends, said to Elinor, 'And what bit are *you* going to do?'

For a moment Elinor thought she might lose all control. But then she caught Thomas's eye and registered a quick glance of sympathy, if not understanding. She swallowed, and let her hand drop from her cardigan buttons.

'Actually,' she said, 'I was going to ask Sir John about work of some kind anyway. So I can do it, can't I, this morning.'

'Oh, good,' Marianne said. There was the faintest edge of sarcasm to her voice. She let her hair fall again and smiled at Thomas. 'Let's get it over with, then, shall we?'

'It was my dream, of course,' Sir John said, 'to keep everything being manufactured in Devon. I started off that way, you know, got all the machines moved from Honiton, stayed up half the night mugging up labour laws, but I couldn't do it. Couldn't get the margins. Labour costs in the UK are just too high. So the machines – completely outdated now, of course – moulder in the old stables, and we outsource everything to North Portugal. Modern factory on an industrial estate. Not an oil painting as a place, but they do the business. Excellent quality—' He broke off and looked at Margaret. He said abruptly, 'You bored?'

Margaret nodded energetically. Sir John beamed at her. He seemed entirely unoffended.

'You're a baggage, Miss Margaret Dashwood.'

'Perhaps,' Belle said hastily, 'these aren't quite the clothes that someone of Margaret's age—'

Sir John put an arm round Belle's shoulders. He said, interrupting, 'We're coming to something that's for every age. You'll be bowled over by my design studio. Computerised drawing boards, technology to ascertain every average body shape and size...'

He began to guide her towards a doorway through which a high-ceilinged, brilliantly lit room was visible, talking all the time. Margaret trailed in his wake, sighing and scuffing her shoes, and Marianne followed, equally slowly and at an eloquently disdainful distance. Elinor watched them disappear into the studio ahead of her and felt, with mounting alarm, that it was going to be extremely hard, if not impossible, to persuade Sir John to give her any time or attention. He had already jovially dismissed their anxiety about getting Margaret to school by declaring that Thomas would drive her as far as the bus that would take her into Exeter, and, having done that, clearly felt he had more than done his duty by his new tenants for the moment. How could she, Elinor, buttonhole him further and explain to him in a way that neither dented their dignity nor diminished their plight that they were sorely in need of opportunities to make some money? How did you manage to make it look as if you weren't, somehow, just begging?

There were steps behind her. Elinor turned to see Colonel Brandon approaching from the stairwell that led up to the studio level. The night before, he had been dressed in an unexceptionable tidy country uniform of dark trousers and formal sweater. This morning, he was in a daytime, olive-green version of the same and his shoes, Elinor could not help noticing, were properly polished.

He smiled at her. He said, 'Had enough of thornproof waistcoats and poachers' pockets?'

She smiled back, gratefully.

'It's very impressive. I'm – I'm just a bit preoccupied this morning. I'm sure it's just moving – the change and everything.'

Bill Brandon put his hands in his trouser pockets.

'Especially if you're the practical one.'

'Well – yes.'

'Which you are.'

Elinor flushed slightly. She looked at the toe of her Converse boot and kicked it against the floor. She said, reluctantly, 'A bit.'

'We're so useful, we practical people. We hold it altogether. But we're seen as killjoys, somehow. Most unfair.'

She glanced at him. He looked so together and trim, the open collar of his checked shirt well ironed, his hands relaxedly in the pockets of his trousers. She indicated her jeans, and the cardigan that had once been her father's.

'Sorry to be so scruffy.'

'You girls', Bill Brandon said gallantly, 'could wear absolutely anything to great effect. Your sister ...'

'Oh, I know.'

'Is she in there?'

'Yes. With the others.'

'And why aren't you?'

Elinor sighed. She slid her own hands into the pockets of her cardigan and hunched her shoulders.

'I rather – wanted to see Sir John.'

'Jonno?'

'Yes. By – by himself.'

Bill Brandon looked carefully at her. He said, 'Is everything all right?'

Elinor said nothing. She pushed the knitted pockets as far down as they would go and stared at her feet.

'Elinor. What is it?'

'It's – nothing.'

'Look,' he said. 'Look, we don't know each other very well yet, but I'm sure we will because I'm here all the time – it's such a contrast to Delaford.'

'Delaford?'

'Yes. It's – where I live. Or, rather, where I have a flat. It's a – well, it's a place I started when I came out of the Army. I wanted to help some of my soldiers who'd got into a bit of trouble with drink and drugs and what have you. The result of what they'd been through, you know, coping mechanisms and all that, never mind not being able to adjust to life outside the Army. And I wanted – well, it's another story, but I wanted to help addicts in general, really, I wanted—'

'Addicts?' Elinor said, startled.

He nodded.

'Yes,' he said. 'Mostly drugs, but some alcoholics.'

'So that's what Sir John meant about your good works!'

'Jonno's been wonderful. So supportive, so generous. Our best patron.'

'That's wonderful,' Elinor said seriously. 'Really wonderful. What you do.'

'Not really.'

'We should have asked you, last night, we should have—'

'No,' Bill Brandon said, 'you shouldn't. I don't talk about it much. It's better to do something rather than talk about it. Don't you think?'

Elinor relaxed her shoulders a little.

'If you know what to do, it is.'

He moved slightly closer to her.

'Which is where I came in, I think. What is the matter?'

She looked up at him. He was wearing an expression of the greatest kindness. She said, 'I'm – just a bit worried. That's all.'

'About moving here?'

'Not – in itself...'

'Money?' he said.

She let out a breath.

'How did you know?'

'Just a guess.'

'Yes,' she said. 'Money. We're none of us really fit to work but we've got to. At least I have. And I was going to ask Sir John—' She stopped. Then she said, sadly, 'I don't really know what I was going to ask him. For help, I suppose. Unspecified help. Hopeless, really.'

'Not hopeless.'

'He's so busy, he does so much already.'

Bill Brandon looked towards the studio again. And then he looked back at Elinor.

'He does do a lot, you're quite right. He's a mover and shaker by nature. So why don't you ask someone who isn't trying to run a business as well as a wife and four children and a sizeable estate in dire economic times? Why don't you ask me?'

Back at the cottage, Marianne said she felt restless. She said, gazing out of the sitting-room window at the dramatic fall of land below them, 'We can unpack any time, can't we? Look at that blue sky.'

Elinor, coming into the room with a stepladder in order to help her mother hang their own curtains, said, 'And those clouds.'

'They're nothing. They're blowing away. Anyway, what does getting wet matter? We always got wet at Norland.'

Belle was pulling lengths of battered old damask out of a box to replace Sir John's brightly patterned ready-made curtains. She said to Marianne, 'What are you suggesting, darling?'

'A walk.'

'A *walk*,' Margaret said in tones of disgust.

'Yes,' Marianne said, 'a walk. And you're coming with me.'

'I hate walks.'

'Why d'you want to walk?' Belle said.

'I want to see the old house Sir John talked about. The old house in the valley where the old lady lives who never goes out. She sounds like Miss Havisham.'

'I don't', Margaret said, 'want to see anything.'

Belle regarded the damask. It had once been deep burgundy red. It was now, faded by the sun, irregularly striped with the colour of weak tea. But anything was better than bright blue cotton printed with stylised sunflowers. She said, absently, 'Lovely, darling.'

'But I—' began Margaret.

Belle raised her head.

'I don't want Marianne walking alone. Not after the other day. And certainly not till we know our way about.'

From the top of the ladder Elinor said, 'The house is called Allenham. The old lady is Mrs Smith.'

No one took any notice.

'We're going,' Marianne said to Margaret.

'You're going,' Belle said to Margaret.

Margaret looked up at Elinor on her ladder.

'Why can't *you* go?'

'Because,' Elinor said.

'I *always* have to do what I don't want,' Margaret said.

Belle dropped the curtains and put an arm round her.

'I promise', she said, 'that you'll get to an age where nobody tells you what to do any more. One day you can do exactly as you like.'

Elinor leaned forward to unhook the sunflower curtains.

'I wish,' she said softly, to no one in particular.

From the cottage, a path ran steeply up through the woods behind it, crossed a narrow, sunken lane, and gave on to a high, open ridge from which it was possible to see down, as if one were a passing bird, into all the interconnected valleys below. Once up there, Margaret, who had complained loudly all the way through the trees, became infected by the wind and the height, and went whirling, screaming, along the ridge, her arms held out and her hair streaming like tattered banners round her head.

Marianne followed more slowly, reluctantly entranced by what lay below her. There was Barton Park and its outbuildings, as neat and miniature as doll's-house furniture, set among scattered small blobs of trees and connected by the regular pale curves of drives, with green spaces in between dotted with cotton-wool balls of sheep and black and white dominoes of cows. Smoke rose from chimneys here and there, and the postman's red van crept along a drive like a little bright toy. And then, there, in the next valley, clinging to the hillside below a great hanger of trees, was the fairy-tale house of Allenham, built of soft, rosy brick, with twisted Tudor chimneys and narrow, glittering windows. Its gardens – famous, Sir John said, for being laid out to a particular design in 1640 and never substantially changed – were a distinct formal pattern, visible clearly from this height, of tall dark hedges and lower greener hedges, punctuated only by a few fountains standing dry and still in their pale stone basins. It was a different period to Norland, it was in a different situation to Norland, but something about the romance of that old, quiet house in its valley caught nostalgically at Marianne's throat and made her abruptly feel tears rising.

'She's an old dear, Mrs Smith,' Sir John had said. 'She's been a widow forever. Old Smith's family made money in the north, and he brought it down here and bought that house. Spent a fortune on it. Lovely old boy. Took up local history. Too bad they never had children, and now she's there alone, mouldering away, looked after by all these agency girls from God knows where. Heaven knows what they make of it, these Filippinos. If you'd grown up in Manila, you'd think you'd landed on the moon, arriving at Allenham, wouldn't you?'

Margaret came panting up. Marianne pointed down to the house.

'Look.'

'Bit creepy,' Margaret said. She had taken her fleece off and tied it round her waist.

'It's fantastic,' Marianne said.

Margaret squinted up at the sky.

'It's going to rain.'

'It doesn't matter.'

'You haven't even got a sweater.'

'I don't mind. What's rain?'

A large drop fell, on cue, on to Margaret's hand. She held it out. 'This,' she said.

Marianne glanced behind her. From the south-west and the direction of the sea, an immense pile of gun-metal clouds was moving purposefully towards them. She said, 'It's only *rain*, Mags.'

'No,' Margaret said, and her voice was suddenly urgent. She pointed, following Marianne's gaze, at the moment that a dramatic gash of lightning split the clouds and a crash of thunder echoed round the hills.

'Help!' Marianne said in a different tone.

Margaret unwrapped her fleece and thrust it at her sister. 'Take this.'

'No.'

'Take it. *Take* it. I haven't got asthma.'

As Marianne struggled into the fleece, the rain abruptly began in earnest. Pulling her sister behind her, Margaret began to retrace their steps at a stumbling run, with the rain bouncing off the turf beside them.

'Slower,' Marianne pleaded.

'No,' Margaret shouted. 'No. We've got to get back, we've got to get home!'

'I can't—'

'You can! You can! You must.'

They floundered on along the ridge, the turf increasingly slippery under their feet, their hands increasingly slippery in one another's.

'Oh please,' Margaret kept shouting. 'Oh, please, *run.*'

'I can't, I can't go faster, I can't see . . .'

Ahead of them, the hedge that bordered the lane grew dimly visible through the sheets of rain.

'Nearly there!' Margaret cried. Her hair was plastered to her face and needed perpetually pushing aside with her free hand. 'Not far!'

Marianne gave a little choked scream and then her hand slid from Margaret's and she subsided on the earth, heaving and gasping.

Margaret collapsed beside her.

'Marianne? Marianne? Are you OK?'

Marianne couldn't speak. She sat where she had fallen, crouched on the sodden grass, her hands pressed to her chest, battling for breath.

Margaret began to scrabble in her sister's pocket.

'Your inhaler, your inhaler.'

Marianne shook her head, jerkily.

'What d'you mean? You haven't *got* it? You came without your *inhaler?*'

Ashen and fighting, Marianne managed a brief nod.

'Oh my *God,*' Margaret said. She could feel panic rising in her like hysteria. She mustn't, she mustn't. What would Ma do, what would Ellie do, she must think, *think*, she must – she stood up.

'Listen!' she shouted above the rain. 'Listen! I'm going to race down to the cottage to get your inhaler and Ma and Ellie. Don't *move*. D'you hear me? Don't move, just do *little* breaths, don't panic. OK? OK?'

Marianne lifted one hand weakly from her chest in acknowledgement and Margaret set off towards the hedge and the lane at a speed she did not know she was capable of. As she plunged through the hedge she was aware of a car coming down the lane with its headlights on, a car coming fast, too fast, and even in the midst of her fervour about Marianne it occurred to her that the situation would not be improved if she managed to get herself run over, in addition. So she slithered down the bank and flattened herself against it to allow the car to roar by.

But it didn't. The driver obviously saw her sprawled against the bank below the hedge and screeched to a halt, spraying her with muddy water and grit. The passenger window opposite her slid down and a man's voice said, impatiently, 'You OK?'

Margaret scrambled up. The sight of another human, and an adult, was almost too welcome to be borne. She clutched at the gleaming car and thrust her dripping head into the interior.

'Oh please, oh please, it's my sister!'

The driver of the car was a young man, a dark young man. Even in acute distress, with her vision partially obscured by her wet hair, Margaret could see that on the scale of hotness, he registered fairly close to a full ten. He was – amazing. He said, slightly less irritably, 'What about your sister?'

'She's up there,' Margaret said wildly, close to tears, 'up in the field. She's having an asthma attack.'

'Ye gods,' the young man said, in quite a different tone.

He switched off the engine and was out of the car in a

flash, not bothering to take the key but scrambling nimbly up the bank towards the hedge almost before Margaret had time to register that he had moved at all. She began to follow him, clumsily, calling out, 'She hasn't got her inhaler. She forgot her inhaler.'

'Where is it?' he yelled.

'At home.'

'Where's home?'

'Down there. Barton Cottage.'

He paused for a second, halfway through the hedge.

'I know Barton Cottage,' he said. 'I'll bring her. Get home and tell them I'll bring her.'

'You can't—'

He had pushed through the hedge by now. He shouted down at Margaret, 'Do as you're bloody told!' and then he vanished from her sight.

'I've known Barton all my life,' the young man said.

He was standing by the fireplace in the cottage, towelling his hair with an old beach towel Elinor had fetched from a box on the landing. Marianne was on the sofa with her inhaler and a little faint colour in her cheeks. She and her mother and her sisters were gazing in disbelief at the young man by the fireplace.

'I just about come from round here. In fact, I'm staying in a house a couple of miles away, called Allenham. It belongs to my aunt. She's pretty well immobile now, but I've come all my life, every school holidays. It's a bit tricky to get away and come much, now, but I do when I can. She's an old sweetie.'

Belle swallowed. It had not crossed her mind to send Margaret upstairs to find dry clothes. Nothing at all practical had

crossed her mind since the mounting anxiety about Marianne
had begun with the change in the weather, followed by Margaret's distracted, sobbing arrival home, bursting with some
incoherent story about an asthma attack and a man bringing
Marianne in a car, and then the almost immediate roar of a
sports car outside and a perfectly strange and godlike young
man appearing at the front door with Marianne in his arms, as
pale as a ghost but still breathing. Still breathing. Belle stared
and stared at the young man. Even if he hadn't looked as he
looked, he would have been a hero to her: rescuing Marianne,
bringing her home as respectfully as if she had been – had been
a single flower. A lily. A butterfly. A broken butterfly. He had
been almost *tender*.

'I – I don't know how to thank you,' Belle said, 'I just...'

The young man stopped rubbing. His hair was thick and dark
and glossy. He grinned.

'Then don't.'

'But you can't imagine how we feel, what you have done for
us.'

He glanced at Marianne. He raised one dark eyebrow, very
slightly.

'Oh, I can.'

Margaret peered at her sister. If she hadn't been so pale,
Margaret would have said she was blushing.

'Do you have a name?'

He smiled. He dropped the towel casually on to the hearth
and ran his hands through his hair. Even in wet jeans, he looked
magnificent.

'I'm John.'

Margaret said, almost shyly, 'We know lots of Johns.'

'Ah,' he said. He winked at her. 'But I am John Willoughby. And everyone calls me Wills.'

'May we?' Belle said.

'I'd be offended if you didn't.'

'And *we* are—'

'I know who you are.'

'You do?'

'Everyone round here knows everyone else's business. Aunt Jane told me. She said there were new people in the new cottage and – well, I won't tell you what she said until I know you better.'

Marianne put her inhaler down. She said, hoarsely, 'I'm afraid that wasn't a very good introduction.'

He looked suddenly sober.

'Not from my point of view.'

She tried a little laugh and choked on it. Indistinctly, she said, 'Rescuing damsels in distress ...'

He said quietly, 'One hell of a damsel.'

She tilted her head back slightly. Even bedraggled from the rain and battered by the attack, her hair matted in damp clumps, Elinor marvelled at her sister's looks. A quick glance towards the fireplace indicated that she was not the only one marvelling. John Willoughby was wearing the expression familiar to Elinor for most of Marianne's life, the expression she had seen on Bill Brandon's face only that morning. And the fragility that asthma gave her, coupled with the natural intensity of her personality, plainly only magnified her appeal.

Marianne said, in a stronger voice, 'We were looking at your aunt's house. We were up there, looking down ...'

'Were you?'

'It's wonderful. So wonderful. So ancient and *knowing*, somehow. It made me want to cry.'

There was a brief powerful pause.

'Did it?' he said.

'Yes.'

'D'you know, it has that effect on me, too. I've always adored Allenham. When I was little, I never wanted to leave.'

'I can imagine.'

'Can you? Have you ever lived anywhere like Allenham?'

'Oh yes,' Marianne said. She pushed herself a little more upright. Her skin was brightening. 'I lived in the most amazing house. In Sussex. I grew up there.'

'We *all* did!' Margaret said indignantly.

'I wish I had grown up at Allenham,' Wills said, ignoring her.

Margaret looked out of the window. She said, determinedly, 'Is your car a Ferrari?'

'No,' he said, still looking at Marianne.

'What is it then?'

'It's an Aston Martin.'

'Wow,' Margaret said. 'I never saw one before.'

Wills looked down at his wet clothes.

'I ought to go. I'm sopping.'

'Please come back again,' Belle said. 'Please.'

Marianne said nothing. Elinor watched Wills watching her.

'I'd love to.' He bent towards Marianne, half laughing. 'Please, no more running in the rain. I might not be there to rescue you.'

She smiled at him with a smile Elinor would have described, if Marianne were not still holding her blue inhaler, as languorous.

'I'll try not to.'

'Because', he said, 'I couldn't stand anyone else to rescue you.'

Margaret gave a little gasp and put her hand over her mouth. Elinor said to her, quickly, 'Why don't you go ahead and change?'

'Yes,' Belle said, as if waking from some kind of dream. 'Yes. Darling, go and change. And Elinor, do put the kettle on.'

Wills held up a hand.

'Not for me. Thank you. Aunt Jane's expecting me.' He gave an almost imperceptible smirk. 'The obligations of the heir ...'

'Oh my God,' Marianne exclaimed. 'Are *you* the heir to *Allenham?*'

He nodded.

'So fortunate,' Belle said dazedly.

Marianne's eyes were shining.

'So *romantic*,' she said.

He nodded.

'That's what I think.'

He came right up to the sofa. He said, looking down at Marianne, 'I'll come and check on you tomorrow.'

She looked straight back up at him.

'Yes.'

'Take care of yourself.'

'Oh, we will,' Belle said with fervour.

Wills smiled at her.

'This cottage feels great already.'

'Oh! Oh, it's so *ordinary* ...'

'Depends entirely upon the inhabitants, you know.'

Margaret said, dawdling in front of him, 'Can I have a go in your car sometime?'

'Of course.' He looked round at them. 'I'm here for a bit longer. We can rip up some of Jonno's miles of drives.'

'Yes, *please!*'

'On one condition.'

'Anything, anything!'

'No more thank yous,' Wills said.

And then he was gone. A slam of the front door, of his car door, the roar of the engine and he was gone, leaving the atmosphere behind him as charged and alive as if it had been full of fireworks. They looked at each other in the strangely complicated silence that he had left behind him. Then Marianne put her hands over her glowing face. From behind them, she said, 'Don't anyone say anything. Nothing. Not one word.'

'Oh, he's such a dish, isn't he?' Mary Middleton said without much emphasis.

She was standing in her enormous recently fitted kitchen, spooning fruit purée into her youngest, a little boy with his father's ripe apple complexion, who was wedged into an immense and expensive-looking high chair.

'Amazing,' Belle said. She had been given a cup of coffee from a dedicated espresso machine. 'I'm not sure I've ever seen a better-looking man.'

Mary bent until her face was level with her baby's. She said, in a diddums voice, 'Don't talk like that in front of Mr Gorgeous!'

Belle sighed. She had never much liked babies, even if she had adored her own, especially when they grew into articulate children. She said, 'Does he come down here often?'

Mary straightened and began to swoop another spoonful of purée down towards the baby, as if it were a descending aeroplane.

'Well, enough to keep the seat hot, if you know what I mean.
Do look at this face, watching the spoon. Open mouth, poppetty,
big big mouth for Mumma. Jane Smith is a dear, and she adores
that boy. But he's spoiled, if you ask me.'

Belle looked into her coffee cup. The coffee had a creamy
foam on top. It looked, it had to be said, extremely authentic.

'We thought he was charming.'

'Oh, charming all right.'

'What does John think?'

'Jonno?' Mary said. She scraped the spoon along the baby's
chin. 'Oh, he just thinks he's good fun. You know. Good shot, fun
at parties, all that. He knows how to behave, I'll grant him that.
And, of course, he's very ornamental. Though not', she said,
bending again, 'half as ornamental as some scrumptious people.'

The baby blew a few appreciative bubbles.

'And', Belle said, still looking at her coffee, 'he's, well, he's
going to inherit Allenham?'

Mary dropped a kiss on her son's head and began to untie
his bib. To Belle's eye, she looked in remarkably good shape
for someone who had had four babies so close together, and
her clothes and hair seemed to owe more to Bond Street than
to Barton.

'That's what we gather,' Mary said. 'Jane's got no children
of her own, and this is her only sister's boy, her younger sister.
She – I mean Wills's mother – died years ago, of a brain tumour
or something, poor thing – and his father was useless, by all
accounts, lives abroad, one of those old-fashioned playboy
wastes of space. Up you come, poppetty. Ooh, what a heavy boy!
So lucky old Wills stands to get everything and of course she
dotes on him. Not that she's a pushover, mind you. She's very

strict about some things.' She put her mouth into the baby's neck. 'Just like your mummy.'

Belle said slowly, 'He came up to the cottage this morning...'

'Oh!' Mary said, settling on a bar stool next to Belle with the baby on her knee. 'Don't touch that cup! Hot, hot, hot! We know all about this morning. Poor old Bill. He spent hours finding all the best late roses to take up to Marianne and then there was Wills with a handful of nothing from the nearest ditch, and she didn't even look at the roses!' She smiled down at her son. 'What a naughty girl, baby, what a naughty, naughty girl. And then we get Bill back here looking utterly down in the mouth, and he won't stay, will he, but says he's got to get back to Delaford and off he goes at a million miles an hour, gravel sprayed *all* over the edges. And they'd only just been trimmed.'

'Come on,' Belle said. 'He *is* Marianne's age—'

'Who? Wills? Oh, I know. But Bill is such a darling. He's adorable with my little lot, so sweet. It's so sad he hasn't any of his own. Officially, that is.'

The baby had found a teaspoon under Belle's saucer, which he was now banging randomly about and shouting. Mary made no attempt to quell him.

Flinching slightly, Belle said, 'He seems awfully nice. Bill Brandon, I mean.'

'What a noisy person! What a noisy, noisy boy! Oh, he's lovely. You can't believe no one's snapped him up, can you? There was supposed to be somebody he'd adored once who wouldn't have him or went off the rails or something, but he's frightfully private, I've never heard him say anything himself. No, not on Mumma's hand. Poor Mumma's hand! And there's a daughter somewhere—'

'A daughter!'

Mary took the spoon out of the baby's right hand and put it in his left. He instantly transferred it back again and resumed banging.

'Well, I don't know. He's never mentioned her, so it may be just a rumour. Such a waste, if so; he's so good with children. Not that that's very hard, is it, my pumpkin? He'd be a fantastic husband, so loyal. And I think, personally, he'd love to be in love again.'

Belle drained her coffee.

'Then he'd be at complete odds with my Marianne. And me for that matter. We believe in the love of a life, you see.'

Mary kissed the baby.

'Well, I've got that, haven't I, four times over!'

Belle waited a moment. She said, 'I rather meant men.'

Mary smiled at her.

'Bill would say that Marianne is young yet. And he loves a young mind. That's why he adores the children so.'

Belle put her coffee cup down.

'Well,' she said, smiling back in a way that was not entirely natural, 'there's young and young, isn't there? And to my mind, the young man who brought Marianne home and wouldn't be thanked is pretty close to perfection.'

'And to hers too?'

'Her what?'

'Is John Willoughby, in Marianne's mind, pretty close to perfection?'

Belle got off her stool with less grace than she had intended. She extended a finger to the baby, who regarded it and turned away.

'I think', she said in a tone designed to discourage any disagreement, 'that the feeling between Marianne and John Willoughby is mutual.'

'After two days!' Mary cried.

Belle took a step away.

'Sometimes,' she said loftily, 'it is only a matter of *recognition*. Time means nothing. Nothing at all.'

6

'I 've known Bill Brandon for years,' Peter Austen said. He had a neat grey beard and was wearing an equally neat open-necked denim shirt. 'He's been – well, wonderful to my family.' He cleared his throat and looked briefly at the smooth white expanse of his desktop. Then he smiled again at Elinor. 'You probably know what he does. At Delaford.'

'Yes, a little, he doesn't really ...'

'No,' Peter Austen said. 'He doesn't talk about it. But he's helped a lot of us, and saved more than a few. My boy, for one.'

Elinor also looked at the desktop. It was amazing to see so much white surface with so little on it. Even for an architect.

'I'm sorry,' she said politely.

'Yes, well ...' He cleared his throat again. 'So, any friend of Bill's ...'

'I hardly know him,' Elinor said quickly. 'I mean, we only met a week or so ago, but he said you might be able to help?'

'I always,' Peter said, 'I always like to do anything I can. For Bill.'

Elinor looked round the room. It was on the first floor of a new building on the river estuary, and the light flooding in from the windows and skylights gave it an unearthly brightness.

She said, awkwardly, 'I feel really shy about all of this, about asking . . .'

'Those who don't ask, don't get, you know. Especially when we need help.'

Elinor looked ruefully at him.

'Which I do.'

He smiled again.

'I know. Bill told me. And I took the precaution of ringing your college tutor before we met.'

'Oh my goodness!'

He gestured towards the white wall behind him, on which hung huge high-resolution coloured photographs of various dramatic-looking buildings.

'We are very lucky, Elinor. May I call you Elinor? We are still busy, even in these parlous times. We are diversified, you see. Community projects, education projects, commercial projects, conservation work, private houses: you name it; we do it. All over the county. I've even had the diocesan people approach me about the cathedral. We pride ourselves on a healthy team profile of all ages and nationalities.' He gave his beard a quick appreciative stroke. 'I'm probably the oldest director and the only one with a B.Sc. Hons and no RIBA qualification, but I have a way with the planning authorities that has proved pretty useful over the years.'

Elinor swallowed. It was hard to tell what was coming, even if the general geniality was hopeful. She said, trying to sound simultaneously modest and confident, 'I was only a year away from—'

'I know.'

'I loved it,' Elinor said with sudden release, remembering. 'I really *loved* it.'

'Your tutor thought very highly of you.'

'Did he? Oh, *did* he?'

Peter Austen leaned forward, resting on his forearms. He linked his hands.

'But you need the money.'

Elinor swallowed again.

'Yes. Did Colonel ...'

'He did. Not in so many words. But he did.'

'The thing is', Elinor said, 'that I don't know if I'm employable. I don't know if I'd be of any use. I mean, I'd work like anything, and I wouldn't mind what I did, but I don't know if—' She stopped and looked shyly at him. 'Sorry,' she said, 'I haven't done anything like this before. I've never asked—'

'And what did I say about asking?'

She relaxed a little.

'OK.'

'I'll be honest with you,' Peter Austen said. 'I can't offer you much but I can offer you something. We were looking for someone to assist our chief designer, someone with graphic abilities even if they don't have much of a grasp of building technology yet. And from our point of view, you seem good, and you're cheap. I'm willing to give you a trial. I'm willing to give you three months working with Tony, and see how we all get on. How does that strike you?'

Elinor sat up straight and gazed at him. The light in the room around her seemed suddenly to swell into utter brilliance.

'It strikes me', she said, 'as completely – completely *wonderful.*'

* * *

'Fifteen hundred a *month?*' Belle said. She was ladling out portions of chicken casserole.

Marianne, at the far end of the table, was reading a volume of Pablo Neruda's love poems. Without looking up, she said, 'Won't that work out at below the minimum wage?'

Elinor took a plate of casserole from her mother and passed it to Margaret. She said, steadily, 'It's a job. I have a *job.*'

'But to work five days a week for—'

'It'll pay our rent. And some of the bills.'

'What bills?' Belle said vaguely.

Margaret looked at her plate.

'Do I *have* to eat the carrots?'

Elinor nodded patiently.

'Electricity, gas for the cooker – that's the tank by the washing line – and water rates.'

'But artistically—'

'I am a *graphic* artist, Ma.'

Belle sighed.

'Well, darling, if it's what you want ...'

'I do.'

'I'm sure Jonno—'

'Ma, I have a job in my own profession. It's not well paid but I'll be learning. He was a nice man. And he thinks the world of Bill Brandon.'

Marianne, her eyes still on her book, gave a faint snort.

'And,' Elinor said, 'I can meet Margaret after school and we can come home together.'

Margaret was carefully lining her carrots up around the rim of her plate. She said, 'Suppose I want to see my friends after school and not my *sister?*'

Elinor reached across to put a baked potato on her plate.

'I thought you hated your new school.'

'I do. But I might not hate all the *people*.'

'I see.'

Marianne raised her eyes from her book.

'Good on you, Ellie,' she said unexpectedly.

'Goodness. Thank you.'

'She's right,' Marianne said to Belle. 'She's got a job. She's *doing* something for us all.'

Margaret jabbed a knife into her potato. She said to Marianne, 'Well, I suppose *you* can't really, can you?'

Marianne let a brief pause fall, and then she said nonchalantly, 'Well, actually, I can. As it happens.'

Belle stopped ladling. She looked at Marianne, the spoon suspended.

'What do you mean, darling?'

Marianne let go of the book and stretched her arms lazily above her head. She said carelessly, 'I saw Wills today.'

'Oh, we know . . .'

'You amaze me!'

'What a surprise, darling.'

'And he said—' Marianne stopped.

'What? What did he say?'

'And he said,' Marianne repeated, her head thrown back, gazing at her raised hands, 'he said – that he was going to give me a car.'

Margaret dropped her knife with a clatter.

'Wow!'

'A car!'

'M,' Elinor said earnestly, leaning forward, 'he can't. You

can't—'

Marianne lowered her arms and regarded her sister.

'Why can't we?'

'You can't drive,' Margaret said.

'I can learn.'

'You can't accept a car from Wills,' Elinor said.

Belle put the spoon down.

'So romantic,' she said, 'but he shouldn't. Really, he shouldn't.'

Margaret picked up her knife again and reached for the butter.

'What kind of car?'

'An Alfa Romeo Spider,' Marianne said airily. 'Series 4. A design classic.'

Margaret jumped to her feet.

'I'm going to look it up. I bet it's worth megabucks.'

'Sit down, darling!' Belle said sharply. Then she looked at Marianne. 'It's very sweet of him . . .'

Marianne smiled to herself. She said, 'Typical, really, the grand gesture but something that we really need, too. It was his twenty-first present from Aunt Jane. So sweet! It's been on blocks in the garage at Allenham for ages, ever since he got the Aston. He says it's perfect for me.'

Belle glanced at Elinor. Then she said to Marianne, 'Dear one . . .'

'He's so wonderful,' Marianne said.

'Yes, darling. Yes, he is. But before Elinor says it, I have to put a bit of a dampener on things and say we can't afford it.'

Marianne's head jerked up.

'What's to afford? He's *giving* me a car!'

'We'd have to insure it,' Elinor said. 'And tax it and fuel it. And you would need driving lessons.'

'Thomas will teach me!'

'No,' Belle said, quietly but firmly.

'But we need a car!'

'A sensible, dull car,' Elinor said. 'Not a sports car that only fits two people and no luggage.'

'You are just so *sad*,' Margaret said crossly.

Marianne bit her lip. She looked at her mother and her older sister. She said quietly, to Elinor, 'What would it cost?'

Elinor reached along the table to take her hand.

'Don't know. But maybe a couple of thousand. A year, I mean.'

Marianne squeezed her sister's hand briefly and let it go.

'Well,' she said, 'I can't have it then, can I?'

'No. Sorry, babe.'

Marianne sat up straighter.

'If we can't afford it...'

'And', Belle said unwisely, 'it might be a bit *much*, you know. As a present, I mean. It's the kind of thing you get given when – well, when you get *engaged*, or something.'

Marianne stood up slowly, ignoring her supper, and picked up her phone, holding it hard against her. She moved towards the door and, as she left the room, she turned long enough to say, almost triumphantly, 'Well, what would *you* know, anyway, about that?'

Margaret could see, from the line of light visible under her door, that Marianne was not yet asleep. She herself had been doing what was strictly forbidden after bedtime, which was going online, with her laptop under the duvet, and looking up all the random things that suggested themselves to her, so seductively beyond the confines of her own circumstances. Tonight, fired up and fed up with her family's attitude to Wills's glittering offer – much enhanced, in Margaret's eyes, by the forceful glamour of his personality – she had found a website which gave valuations for, it said, cars for the connoisseurs.

She tapped with one fingernail on Marianne's door. Marianne called, 'Ellie?'

Margaret pushed the door open far enough to reveal her face. 'It's me.'

Marianne was sitting up in bed with her phone, her thumbs poised, mid text. She said sternly, 'Mags, you should be asleep.'

Margaret eeled into the room and settled on Marianne's bed. 'Who are you texting?'

'Guess.'

'Why don't you ring him?'

'I do.'

'Does he ring you?'

'He can't, staying with Aunt Jane.'

'Yes, he can – he can go somewhere.'

'Mags,' Marianne said loftily, 'he's very respectful of Aunt Jane and what he owes her and how he has to give her his company and attention. So it's better for me to text him while he's at Allenham.'

Margaret craned to see the screen on Marianne's phone. 'That's more like an essay than a text.'

Marianne laid the phone face down on her duvet.

'Why, exactly, did you come in?' she said.

Margaret wriggled a little. 'That car . . .'

'What car?'

'The one you can't have.'

Marianne tried to look indifferent.

'What of it?'

Margaret leaned forward.

'It's worth over seven thousand pounds!'

'How do you know?'

'I looked it up. It said about seven thousand five hundred if it has good documented history. That's amazing.'

Marianne made a series of little pleats in the duvet cover. She said, sadly, 'I've told him I can't have it.'

'Have you? When?'

'Tonight. I rang him after supper. He said that it was mine whenever I wanted it and it would just wait at Allenham until I was ready.'

Margaret said, 'Was he cross?'

'No. Of course not. Why should he be cross? He's never cross.'

Margaret watched her sister's pleating hand.

'You're pretty gone on him, aren't you?'

Marianne said nothing. She leaned forward a little more and something swung out of the neck of her pyjamas. They were pyjamas Margaret coveted, patterned in plaid, with rosebuds.

'What's that?'

'What's what?'

'Round your neck. That shiny thing.'

Marianne stopped pleating and put a hand to her collar.

'It's nothing.'

'Show me,' Margaret demanded.

'You're not to tell Ma ...'

'I won't!'

Marianne held something out between forefinger and thumb. It was a ring, three linked bands of different coloured gold, threaded on a chain.

'It's a ring,' Margaret said accusingly.

'I know, muppet.'

'Well,' Margaret said, pushing her hair behind her ears, 'a ring looks a bit weddingy, to me.'

Marianne put the ring against her lips.

'He's got one, too.'

'Wills? Wills has got a ring like this?'

'He got them for both of us. His is bigger, of course.'

Margaret sniffed slightly.

'You *have* got it badly, haven't you?'

'He's wonderful,' Marianne said. 'He's Mr Wonderful. Don't tell Ma and Ellie about the ring. I mean it.'

Margaret sighed.

'Ellie isn't speaking to me much, anyway.'

'Isn't she?'

'Not since I let out about Ed and her.'

'Oh, Mags.'

'Well,' Margaret said aggrievedly, 'I was being nagged and nagged, wasn't I, by Mrs J. and everyone, about boyfriends and stuff, and I can't exactly diss Mrs J., can I, however much I'd like to, so after a bit I just said I couldn't talk about it but there *was* someone and Mrs J. gave one of her gross cackles and said to Ellie, Who, who, and Ellie looked at me like she wished I was dead and I said I couldn't say but his name began with an F and then Jonno started teasing Ellie and I thought she might hit him and then thank goodness all those dire kids came in and started screaming so I was saved. Sort of. Except Ellie had a go at me afterwards and Ma heard her and said what was going on and Ellie said, Well, someone, meaning me, ate a whole bowl of stupid for breakfast, didn't they. And she's still cross.'

Marianne smiled at her sister.

'She's private, Mags.'

'Aren't you?'

Marianne held her ring away from her, on its chain, so that she could admire it.

'I don't need to be, Mags. I'm proud of how I feel.'

Margaret got off the bed.

'I'd be proud to drive an Alfa Romeo Spider, I would.'

'One day.'

'What?'

Marianne lay back on her pillows and tucked the ring out of sight into the jacket of her pyjamas.

'One day, there'll be all kinds of things. Marvellous things. Happy, glorious things in beautiful places.'

'Like', Margaret said, 'no more picnic outings with all the Middletons and those kids.'

Marianne stared at her.

'What are you talking about?'

Margaret made a face.

'Didn't they tell you? We've all got to go, on Saturday. Jonno wants to have a barbecue, in a wood somewhere, last outing of summer or something, all of us with sausages and stuff. Bill's taking us; it's a wood belonging to someone he knows.' Margaret grinned at her sister. 'Your lucky day, M. Bill'll want you to sit next to him.'

Marianne gave a little groan. Then she touched the ring under her pyjamas.

'I'll ask Wills.'

'Yay!'

Marianne winked at her sister.

'I'll ask Wills to come too, and he can drive me.'

Margaret waited a moment, and then she said, carefully, 'If I don't tell anyone about the ring, can I come in the Aston with you two?'

Across the meagre landing, Belle heard Marianne's door close and the scamper of Margaret's feet going back to her own bedroom. If you could call it a bedroom, really. It was more like a large cupboard, just big enough for a bed and a chair, but at least it gave Margaret privacy, the privacy which she had claimed as being as much her right as her sisters'.

'Why shouldn't I have a bedroom of my own? You've all got bedrooms of your own.'

'But we haven't got tree houses,' Marianne had pointed out. 'You have a tree house, and we only have bedrooms. There are three proper – well, sort of proper – bedrooms, and one cupboard. So, as you have a tree house, you should have the cupboard.' She had paused. 'Unless, of course, you'd like to share the tree house?'

There'd been a short silence in which Margaret wrestled with her painful sense of being outmanoeuvred. And then, glaring, she'd given in. But Belle could never hear her door slam on the cupboard without a pang.

'I just wish', she said in a whisper to the photograph of Henry with which she had futile conversations most nights, 'that you were here to help me make it better. For little Margaret. For the big ones too. Except that that's mad thinking. Because if you were here, we wouldn't *be* here, in the first place.'

She had him, as usual, propped against her knees in bed, holding him by his silver frame. He looked very young in the picture, very carefree, in an open-necked shirt against a summer Norland garden. There were secateurs in his trouser pocket, just visible.

'Look,' she said to him, slightly louder, 'you really do need to help me. Some sign. Just some little teeny sign that I'm not letting Marianne just be swept away like someone in a canoe over rapids. It's all happened so fast, this gorgeous boy and the drama of her being caught in a storm without her inhaler, and two seconds later, they seem to be at a point where he's offering her a *car*, for heaven's sake, and she seems to think it was the most natural thing in the world to be offered it as well as to accept it. I know you'll laugh at me, darling, but she seems to have even less idea of reason or restraint than I did, and although he is heart-stopping to look at, and seems a model of charm, I can't help but have a twinge of anxiety about the whole thing. It's happened so suddenly. I mean, we didn't even know he existed ten minutes ago, and I just have this little nag inside me that she's riding for a fall, and she's going to get hurt—'

There was a sound from the landing. Belle stopped talking, laid Henry down on her duvet, and climbed out of bed. She padded over to the door and opened it cautiously. The landing was dark and ringed by closed doors. Silence reigned. She shut her door again and got back into bed. She looked down at Henry. He smiled up cheerfully at her from his supine position on her duvet.

'And I've got something to confess to you, darling. I did an awful thing, even if most mothers would do the same in my place. Henry, I snooped on her phone. She was washing her hair, and I went into her room and had a look at the texts on her phone – and it was, even by my standards, unbelievable. I couldn't believe how many. There was actually nothing at all in her sent box except these completely passionate texts to him. I know you'd say I shouldn't have looked in the first place. You'd say that the Marianne apple didn't fall far from the Belle tree, wouldn't you?' she said to him. 'You'd say that if anyone ought to have faith in Marianne surrendering to her heart in a flash, like this, it should be me. Wouldn't you? And you'd be laughing, and teasing me a bit. And I know I'd deserve it. I do. But all the same . . .'

She stopped, picked Henry up and put him back on her bedside table. Then she said, to the empty, shadowy room, 'I expect it's being a lone parent that's making me think like this. You're bound to be more anxious if there's no one to tell you not to be daft, aren't you?' She glanced back at Henry. 'So I'll try not to be daft, darling, I really will. The last thing you'd want me to do is to mistrust a lovely, pure, energetic welling up of true passion. So I won't. I'll believe in her just as − as you always did. Didn't you?'

Sir John said that they would take two cars to the barbecue, and that Wills could bring Marianne and Margaret in what he called the Nonsense.

'What is the point of a car in which you can't get a dog and a gun and a brace of nippers? I ask you.'

'The point', Wills said behind his hand to Marianne, 'is that I don't have to take J Middleton or his brood or his gloomy friends anywhere, ever.'

They were standing on the drive below the great front steps to Barton Park. A portable barbecue and a vast number of cool boxes were being loaded into the back of Jonno and Bill

Brandon's Range Rovers, and various squeals were emerging
from the front hall of the house where all the little Middletons
were being inserted by their mother and an exhausted-looking
Estonian nanny into outdoor clothes and boots. The Dashwood girls, who had been instructed to bring nothing but their
looks and their company, were standing by Wills's car, or, in
Marianne's case, lounging gracefully along the bonnet. Belle,
who had complained of a sore throat at breakfast, had been
persuaded by Elinor to stay at home.

'Perfect timing, Ma.'

'It is rather, I know. But this sort of outing is far more fun
for you girls.'

'Or not.'

'Well, Marianne will love it.'

Elinor gave her mother a quick kiss.

'Marianne would love watching paint dry, if Wills was watching it with her.'

'Darling,' Belle said, 'can I ask you something? Do you know
if Wills has got a job or anything?'

Elinor grinned.

'Ma, you old matchmaker!'

'Well, I can't help noticing, can I?'

'That he doesn't seem to be in any hurry to get back to whatever he does, and that he and Marianne—'

'Yes,' Belle said.

She was wearing the misty expression that usually heralded
another reference to Dad. To forestall her, Elinor said quickly,

'I think he's in property, or something.'

'Property?'

'Yes. I think he's a sort of search agent. Looks for flats and houses in London, for foreigners. As investments. All very high end.'

Belle said carefully, 'It sounds a bit – venal.'

'Well, yes,' Elinor said, laughing. 'Yes. He likes the good things, does Wills. Look at that car! A fantasy of a good thing.'

'What d'you mean?'

'I mean', Elinor said, 'that it's probably leased. Not many people can *buy* a car like that.'

'Oh,' Belle said faintly, and then, 'do you think Marianne knows?'

Elinor sighed.

'Marianne is deaf to anything anyone says about Wills, if it isn't praise. He's kind of mesmerised her. She can't think about another thing.' She glanced at her mother. 'Ma, I'd better go.'

Wills, indeed, was in high spirits at Barton. He was making no attempt whatever to disguise the fact that he wouldn't have had anything to do with an uproarious Middleton family outing if it wasn't for Marianne. He had made loud fraternal remarks to Margaret about tolerating her company for the outward journey in the Aston, but definitely not for the return, and had also, to Elinor's dismay, made fun of Bill Brandon, who was patiently loading picnic chairs and rugs into the back of his car, as instructed, with every appearance of indulgence towards his host.

'God knows why he bothered to return,' Wills said, lounging beside Marianne. 'He went back to Delaford last week and I can't think why he doesn't stay there. He must be far more at home among all those fruitcakes than he is anywhere else.'

Marianne laughed. She was by now leaning against him quite shamelessly.

'Stop it,' she said, not meaning it. 'Stop it! He's not a fruit-cake. He's just very, very dull.'

Wills glanced down at her head, only an inch below his shoulder. He said, comfortably, 'He's King of the Bleeding Obvious.'

'He's OK,' Elinor said.

Marianne grimaced up at Wills.

'Her *patron*, you see. He found her a job.'

'How wonderfully *good* of him.'

'He *is* good,' Elinor said.

'But good', said Wills, 'is so boring.'

'People really like him,' Elinor said.

'But not people I give a toss about. Not exceptional people. Just – just *worthy* people.'

Elinor said, trying to sound light-hearted, 'You're being pretty unfair.'

'No, he's not,' Marianne said. 'It's just that *you* feel you owe Bill something. Look at him. Look at him now, on his mobile. He can't even talk on a mobile without looking weird.'

'The hero of Herzegovina.'

'The Balkan bulldog.'

'And master of the monosyllable.'

'Stop it,' Elinor said. '*Stop* it—'

'Oh, look,' Margaret said suddenly. 'Look! He's running! What's happened? What's happened?'

Wills slipped an arm around Marianne.

'Well,' he said, 'whatever it is, at least he looks vaguely alive, at last.'

And they laughed together. Elinor watched Bill Brandon reach Sir John, put a hand on his arm to get his attention, and then have to persist as Sir John, far more intent upon the arranging of everything in the back of his car, failed to respond. Then she saw Bill Brandon grasp Sir John's shoulders and turn him forcibly and say something very earnestly to him, his face very close to Sir John's. Sir John's hearty countenance abruptly altered from one of irritation at being interrupted to one of real concern. He put an arm up and grasped Bill Brandon's sleeve, and then, with the other hand, patted his shoulder. It looked like reassurance.

'It's something serious,' Elinor said.

'Bill Brandon only knows how to do serious. Serious is his default mode.'

'No,' Elinor said. 'No. Really serious. You can see.'

'Then don't look,' Wills said fondly to Marianne, his arm firmly round her. 'It might be catching.'

Bill Brandon was now climbing into the driver's seat of his car while Sir John and Thomas, with much show of speed and importance, unloaded all the things that had, only moments before, been so carefully loaded in.

'Go and see, Ellie,' Marianne said lazily, heavy against Wills.

'No. No, I can't. Everyone looks really upset.'

'I'll go,' Margaret said. She glanced at Wills. 'Don't you dare go without me,' she added, and then she dashed across the gravel, towards Sir John.

'Perhaps,' Wills said, his voice as light as ever, 'there's been a mutiny at Delaford?'

Marianne gave a little giggle. Elinor shot her a look of reproof. 'Well, if there *has* been . . .'

Sir John was saying something gravely to Margaret. He wasn't smiling. He gestured at all the rugs and folding chairs dumped on the drive, and then he raised one arm and beckoned to Elinor, calling out, 'Picnic's off! Some bloody crisis, poor fellow! Crying shame, really it is. Come here while I decide what to do instead!'

Elinor glanced at Marianne.

She said, 'Go on, Ellie. He's summoning you.'

Elinor began to cross the drive towards him. The moment she was no more than two metres away, Wills slid his arm down Marianne's back and said, in a stage whisper, 'Jump in.'

'What?'

'Jump in. Get in the car. Ghastly outing off, wonderful reprieve and alternative on.'

Marianne stood slowly upright. She was smiling delightedly at him.

'What alternative?'

He came swiftly round the car and opened the passenger door.

'Hop in. Like I said. Quickly!'

She still paused in front of him. He was looking down at her with the mixture of intensity and merriment that made her feel she could never refuse him anything.

'Wills? What—'

He leaned forward and brushed his mouth across hers. And then he said, his face only an inch away,

'We're going to Allenham. And we are going *alone*.'

'Now,' Abigail Jennings said to Elinor, 'I am not one for gossip, and I don't want to upset your mother . . .'

Elinor looked down at her right arm, which was in Mrs Jennings's firm grasp. She had seized it as they all assembled in Sir John's library ('The question *is*,' Marianne had said of it, 'not does he read, but *can* he?') at the end of a fretful and unsatisfactory day which had never regained its impetus after Bill Brandon's sudden departure. Elinor had tried to return home with Margaret, but Sir John, baulked of his original barbecue plans, had insisted that they all stay on right through the day, until supper at Barton Park, as if eventual success could be wrenched from the day through sheer force of will.

Elinor was very tired. The day had required enormous effort to fend off roguish assumptions about what Wills and Marianne might be up to, and to restrain Margaret's fury at being deprived of a ride in Wills's car and then offered a dank picnic in Sir John's own woods, standing on wet leaves under gently dripping trees, by way of a substitute. She would have given anything not to be faced with an evening of determined jollity, but Marianne's glaring absence had left her with no courteous option.

She tried to disengage her arm.

'Please ...'

Abigail Jennings was smiling, but her grip was firm.

'Where do you suppose your sister is?'

Elinor said wearily, 'I have no idea.'

'You must do.'

Elinor gave her arm another half-hearted tug.

'None.'

'Hasn't she texted you, at least?'

Elinor looked down at her arm.

'Please let me go.'

Mrs Jennings leaned closer. There was no one else in the library – Margaret had been inveigled upstairs to play table football with the two older children – but that didn't stop her almost whispering, with a vehemence Elinor tried not to see as triumph, 'They're at Allenham!'

'Who are?'

'Don't be silly, dear. Don't play dumb with me. Your sister and Wills have been at Allenham all day!'

Elinor tried not to show the dislike she felt.

'Why shouldn't they be there?'

Mrs Jennings let go of Elinor's arm at last.

'No reason, dear. If they'd done it openly.'

Elinor took a small step away.

'What d'you mean?'

'I mean', Mrs Jennings said, 'that Jane Smith doesn't know that they've been.'

Elinor looked at her with real distaste.

'Nonsense,' she said.

Mrs Jennings smiled.

'No, dear. Not nonsense at all.'

'How do you know?'

'Well, dear. Jonno knows everything that goes on round here, and I know nearly everything. Mary knows what she wants to know – so wise of her, I always think. But Nina, who looks after the children here, is a friend of Thandie, who is looking after Jane Smith just now, and Nina had a text from Thandie this afternoon to say that she caught your sister and Wills upstairs at Allenham and Wills made her promise not to tell his aunt that they'd been. Poor Jane's so deaf now that she wouldn't hear a brass band playing in the same room, bless her.'

Elinor stared at her.

'Caught them?'

Mrs Jennings laughed.

'Well, they wouldn't have been playing cards, dear, would they?'

Elinor stepped back.

'It doesn't sound like Marianne, like the kind of thing she'd do.'

'Doesn't it, dear?' With a boy like Wills? They're all mad about Wills. Thandie'll never say a word if he's asked her not to. But your mother . . .'

'What about my mother?'

'It might worry her.'

Elinor took a further step away. She said, unhappily, 'Please don't mention this.'

'Oh, I won't, dear.'

'I'm going to find Margaret.'

'Oh, don't do that, dear. Jonno was so hoping—'

'We should get back,' Elinor said with decision.

Mrs Jennings nodded. Her expression sobered.

'Maybe you should.'

'Yes.'

'Tell you what, though . . .'

Elinor paused.

'What?'

Mrs Jennings gave her a sudden conspiratorial smile.

'Allenham's a lovely house. But so dated. Modernised, it would be a dream. A dream. And I know Mary would be happy to help – she's so good at houses. Wouldn't that be fun?'

'Don't *lecture* me,' Marianne said indignantly.

Elinor moved to close the kitchen door. Margaret was already asleep upstairs, and Belle was in the bathroom with the radio on.

'I'm not.'

'You're so *priggish*,' Marianne said. 'You're such a prude. Just because you only let Edward kiss you if he's brushed his teeth.'

'It's not that.'

'Not what? Not what? Say it, Ellie, *say* it. Say, "You, Marianne, should not have sex with Wills in the house that's going to be his anyway, one day." Just *say* it.'

Elinor said angrily, 'Stop showing off. I don't *care* about the sex.'

'Oh, don't you? Don't you? We've been down here for weeks and not a word from Ed, not a flicker, nothing. And I meet someone really special and you don't mind at all, do you, you don't mind that he adores me like I adore him, and that he's going to inherit this amazing house and that we had this incredible—'

'No, I don't!' Elinor shouted.

The comforting rumble of the radio from the floor above stopped abruptly.

Elinor leaned towards her sister. In a furious whisper she said, 'I don't give a stuff what you and Wills do or where you do it. I don't envy you being almost off your head about someone. I really don't. What I object to is that you did it behind his aunt's back, and he knows she's deaf. I object to the fact that you *sneaked*.'

The kitchen door opened. Belle stood there wearing an old towelling robe of Henry's, with her hair scooped up on top of her head in a pink plastic clip.

'Not fighting, I hope,' she said severely.

Marianne shrugged.

'No.'

Elinor said, looking at Marianne, 'I was defending Bill Brandon.'

'Good for you, darling.'

Marianne didn't look at her sister. She said, 'I said it must have been a crisis about this mystery daughter. And Ellie said it would be something at Delaford, someone broken out or something...'

'Enough', Belle enquired, 'to raise your voices?'

Elinor said, 'It's been a long day.'

Belle advanced into the room.

'*Has* he really got a mystery daughter?'

'I don't know. Maybe it's just gossip.'

Belle looked at Marianne.

'What does Wills say? Wills knows everything about everyone round here.'

Marianne leaned against the kitchen table.

'Wills thinks Bill Brandon is a joke.'

'That's not very kind.'

'But it's accurate.'

'My darling,' Belle said directly to Marianne, 'is there anything you want to tell me about today?'

Marianne looked up at her mother. Her eyes were shining.

'Nothing, thank you, Ma. But everything is good. No, that's not accurate. Everything is *wonderful*.' She came round the table and stood in front of her mother. 'Ma,' she said, 'isn't it just fantastic? It feels so right. I've never felt anything so *right* before.' She looked round the kitchen. 'D'you know what he said today? He said that although he knew Allenham was historic and amazing and all that, he really loved this cottage. He said he hoped you'd never change it, even all the awful Middletonisms. He said he just loved it and that he'd been happier in the last few weeks than he'd ever been in his life.' She clasped her arms around herself in a close embrace, and closed her eyes. 'He said that, Ma. He said he'd never, ever felt like this before and he's coming over tomorrow to say it all over again.'

And then she opened her eyes and went off into a peal of laughter.

'Tomorrow!' she said, 'If I can wait that long!'

7

It was difficult to persuade Margaret to leave Marianne on her own at Barton Cottage the next morning.

'But he *promised* I could go in his car. And he didn't take me yesterday because of all that hoo-ha with Bill and everything, so he will today. He *promised!*'

'I don't think it was actually a promise.'

'It was! It was! I told everyone at school I knew someone with an Aston Martin.'

Marianne stopped brushing her hair long enough to say, '*No*, Mags.'

Margaret stuck her lower lip out.

'Why d'you have to see him so specially today, anyway? You see him all the time, *all* the time, so what's so—'

Belle said firmly, 'He asked to see her today. He made an appointment.'

'What d'you mean? He isn't a *dentist*, or something.'

'Maybe', Belle said, 'he wants to say something very particular.'

'Well, he could say that anywhere. He could—'

'Mags!'

'You', Belle said to Margaret, 'are coming to church with

Elinor and me.'

Margaret looked appalled.

'*Church!*'

'Harvest festival, darling. Barton Church, small community, joining, all that sort of thing.'

'Why doesn't Marianne have to come, then?'

Belle smiled across at her middle daughter.

'I expect she'll tell us why when we get back. Elinor?'

'Yes, Ma.'

'Do you think perhaps not jeans, for our first appearance at Barton Church?'

Kneeling in church, Elinor tried to focus on the things she had to be thankful for. Margaret might insist she hated her new school, but she was at least going every day and was not, as far as Elinor knew, playing truant. They had a roof over their heads in a lovely place with a landlord who might be slightly trying as a personality but who was unquestionably large-hearted. Her mother, though strangely unfocused without Fanny to battle with, was not visibly unhappy and from Monday week she, Elinor, would be employed, however modestly, in a structured and congenial company whose very occupation was as close to her heart as she could have hoped for.

It was unwise, she thought, shifting slightly on her unevenly stuffed hassock, to think too much about hearts. Marianne's, always loftily removed from all the optimistic boys who had been in hot pursuit of her throughout her teenage years, appeared to have been given away, and gladly, eagerly, to a complete stranger in a matter of days. Elinor couldn't but acknowledge that Wills scored incredibly highly on both looks and charm, and she was in no doubt that he was as besotted as Marianne, but something in her held back being able to rejoice fully with her mother and sister. She supposed, a little sadly, that her temperament just wasn't designed to believe that nothing mattered in the world besides romantic love. Try as she might, she couldn't convince herself that the world was well lost for love, or that a penniless life in a garret meant bliss as long as love was there as a substitute for warmth or food. Sometimes over the years she had looked at Marianne and envied her ability to abandon herself almost ecstatically to music, or place, or literature or – as so intensely in the present case – to love. It must be extraordinary, Elinor thought, to be able to surrender oneself so completely, not just because it would feel so exhilarating but also because it meant that one was – oh, how unlike me, Elinor thought regretfully – able to trust. Marianne could trust. She trusted her instincts; she trusted those dear to her; she trusted her emotions and her passions. She drank deep, you could see that; she squeezed every drop of living out of all the elements that mattered to her. It made her careless sometimes, of course it did, but it was a wonderfully rich and rapt way to be.

And I, Elinor said silently to herself, am not rich or rapt in the very slightest. So, although I can see that Wills is really beautiful, and delightful, I also kind of mistrust all that beauty, all those high spirits, and think unjust, quelling thoughts about where does his money come from and why doesn't he need to get back to work and why does he beguile us with questions instead of telling us anything about himself? We know nothing, really. It's all hearsay, sort of fairy-tale inheritance stuff that belongs in a novel, not the real world. And suppose he just really fancies Marianne, and it isn't real love? Suppose it's just sex? I wouldn't blame him, I wouldn't blame either of them, but Marianne, being so absolutely wholehearted, can't separate love and sex and she might get hurt. Which I, for all my dreary cautiousness and prudence, could not bear. She's never fallen this hard, not ever. And there's just a little cold part of me that doesn't have any faith in what's going on.

Which is probably a bigger cold part than I want to admit, and pretty off-putting to the world in general, because Ed hasn't been in touch since we got here. Nothing. Not a text or a call or an email. Nothing. And I am not contacting him. I am absolutely not. In fact, I have deleted his number from my phone and I have defriended him on Facebook, because although I don't really want to do either, I have to take charge of the things I can take charge of, and removing myself from contact with him is one of those things, however pathetic. I've got to protect myself. Or, to be truthful, I have got to be able to tell myself that I'm at least trying to. I may have felt more comfortable with him than I ever have with anyone, but I am not laying myself open to any more pain or disappointment than comes my way any more. If he's dumped me – and I'm not sure, if I'm honest, that we ever really got to the level you could be dumped *from* – then he just has, and I'd better get over it. If he's met someone else, then he has. I'm not going to cry over him – or at least, I'm not going to cry except in strict, strict privacy – and I'm not going to waste time and energy thinking about him. I'm not. I get fed up with the number of times he *occurs* to me, every day, but I won't encourage it. I will get on with what there is to get on with, one foot in front of another—'How much longer?' Margaret hissed beside her.

Elinor didn't look at her. She kept her eyes closed.

'Two more prayers,' she whispered. 'One more hymn.'

Margaret leaned closer.

'I bet when we get back, they'll have gone off somewhere and I won't get a ride in his car today *either*.' She paused and then muttered vehemently, 'It's not *fair*.'

The Aston was, surprisingly, still outside the cottage when they got back, walking across the park from the church with Belle cajoling Margaret to admire the view, and the weather, and the prospect of a roast chicken for lunch. Margaret was immediately excited to see the car, and began to run towards it, squealing, so that Elinor, impelled by some instinct that she couldn't immediately identify, began to run too, catching at Margaret's sleeve.

'Stop, Mags, stop!'

'Why? Why should I?'

Elinor dragged her sister to a halt.

'Don't, Mags.'

'But he *promised*!'

Elinor glanced up at the cottage. It looked exactly as usual except that there was a distinct and unwelcome air, to Elinor's perception, of something not being quite right. She held on to Margaret's sleeve.

'Just wait.'

'Why? Why?'

'I don't know. Just – just let me go in first.'

'You are so mean!'

Elinor turned as Belle came up. Belle said, 'What's the matter?'

'Nothing, maybe . . .'

Belle looked at the cottage.

'We should make a noise, so that they—'

'No,' Elinor said. She let go of Margaret. 'No. I'll just go in first. Quietly.'

'Darling, what's all the drama?'

'It may be nothing,' Elinor said.

She walked towards the front door, leaving her mother and sister standing by the car. Margaret laid a reverent hand on the bonnet. She said, in surprise, 'It's still warm!'

Belle was watching Elinor.

'So he hasn't been here long.'

Elinor put her key into the lock and turned it. As the door opened and Elinor went in, Belle saw, quite plainly, Marianne dash sobbing out of the sitting room and rush towards the stairs and then the door swung shut behind Elinor and left Belle and Margaret standing there, beside the car.

'I can't explain,' Wills said.

To his credit, he looked as stricken as Marianne had. He was standing on the hearthrug, on the very spot he had stood after rescuing Marianne from the thunderstorm, but this time he looked almost cowed, Elinor thought, beaten. His hair looked lank and his face was suddenly the face of someone both older and sadder.

From the doorway, Elinor repeated, slightly louder, 'What's happened?'

Wills made a limp gesture with one hand, as if whatever it was had been both incomprehensible and also impossible to avoid or repair.

'Just – something.'

'What, Wills, *what?* What did you say to Marianne?'

Elinor heard the front door open again behind her.

'That – that I've got to go back to London.'

'Why? Why have you, on a Sunday, all of a sudden?'

'I just have to.'

Elinor sensed Belle and Margaret coming up right behind her.

'Did you have a row?' she demanded.

He shrugged.

'Did you?'

Belle put a tentative hand on Elinor's arm.

'Darling...'

Elinor shrugged her off.

'Did you have a row, Wills? Did you upset your aunt?'

He sighed.

'I'll take it as a yes,' Elinor said. 'Was it about Marianne? Was it about yesterday?'

He raised his head slowly and looked at them all.

'No,' he said.

'Is that the truth?'

'Yes!' he said, almost shouting. 'It has nothing to do with Marianne!'

Belle pushed past her daughters. She crossed to the fireplace and put a hand on Wills's sleeve.

'Stay here, dear Wills, you'd be so welcome.'

He gazed down at her, his eyes full of tragedy.

'I can't.'

'Of course you can! You can have Mags's room.'

'I've got to go back to London.'

Margaret said, in amazement, 'Are you being *sent?*'

He attempted a lopsided grin.

'Sort of.'

'But she can't.'

'She can.'

'Because', Elinor asked pitilessly, 'she pays the bills?'

He looked immediately uncomfortable. He said, hesitantly, 'This isn't about that.'

'Then what?'

He seemed to pull himself together. He said, 'I can't tell you. I can't tell Marianne. But none of this, none of it, has anything to do with her. She's—' He stopped and then he said, 'I'm really sorry but I've got to go.'

Belle was still touching him. She said earnestly, looking up at him, 'Till when?'

He paused and firmly disengaged himself. And then he said bitterly, to no one in particular, 'I wish I knew.'

'Please eat something,' Belle said pleadingly.

Marianne had her elbows on the table, planted either side of her untouched plate, and her head in her hands.

'Can't.'

'Just a mouthful, darling, just a—'

'Can I have her roast potatoes?' Margaret said.

Elinor, who wasn't hungry either, put a piece of unwanted chicken in her mouth and chewed. Marianne pushed her plate towards Margaret.

'Can I?' Margaret said eagerly, spearing potatoes.

Elinor swallowed her chicken. She said quietly to Marianne, 'What did he actually say to you?'

Marianne shook her head and put her hands over her eyes.

'M, he must have said *something*. He must have said why he couldn't—'

Marianne sprang up suddenly and fled from the room. They heard her feet thudding up the stairs and then the slam of her bedroom door.

'You told me', Margaret said through a mouthful of potato, 'not to ask her anything, so I didn't, and then you go and do it.'

'It must be Jane Smith,' Belle said to Elinor, ignoring Margaret. 'She must disapprove.'

'Why should she?'

'Well, we've got no money.'

'Ma,' Elinor said angrily, banging her knife and fork down, 'this isn't 1810, for God's sake. Money doesn't dictate relationships.'

'It does for some people. Look at Fanny.'

'He loves her,' Elinor said, as if her mother hadn't spoken. 'He's as crazy about her as she is about him.'

'He'll be back. I know he will. He'll ring Marianne. He's probably rung her already.'

'Then why', Margaret said, 'does she keep crying?'

Elinor pushed her chair back.

'I'm going to talk to her.'

Belle sighed.

'Be gentle.'

Elinor paused for a second; then she bit back whatever had occurred to her to say and went out of the kitchen and up the stairs to the landing. She tapped on Marianne's door.

'M?'

'Go away.'

Elinor tried the handle. The door was locked.

'Please let me in.'

'No.'

'I want to talk.'

'Talking won't help. *Nothing* will help.'

Elinor waited a moment, her cheek almost against the door, and then she said, 'Has he rung?'

Silence.

'Have you rung him?'

Silence.

'Or texted?'

There was a stifled something from the far side of the door.

'Oh, Marianne,' Elinor said, 'please let me in. Please.'

She could hear a faint shuffling as if Marianne was approaching the door.

'M?'

From behind the door, Marianne said hoarsely, 'You can't help. No one can. Aunt Jane threw him out just like Fanny did Edward. You ought to understand, if anyone can. You *ought*.'

Elinor waited a moment and then she said, as quietly as she could, 'M. Is it −over?'

There was a long, long silence and then Marianne hissed through the keyhole, 'Don't say that. Don't say that. *Ever.*'

'My dear,' Abigail Jennings said, 'has she stopped crying?'

Belle was making coffee. She had not been at all pleased to see her visitor, especially as she had neither Elinor nor Margaret at home to shield her. She nodded towards the huge jug of mop-headed chrysanthemums that Abigail had brought with her.

'Lovely flowers.'

'You look, my dear, as if you need a stiff drink rather than flowers. It's exhausting living with a broken heart. I remember it all too well with my own girls. Mary was a terrific weeper but luckily Charlotte was more like me and always thought there'd be a better bet somewhere else every time it happened. Mind you, I thought she'd do the dumping when it came to Tommy Palmer. But no. He has no manners whatsoever but she seems to find him funny. No accounting for taste, that's for sure. Except when it comes to Wills — he seems to be to the taste of every living thing with a pulse.' She looked at Belle with concern. 'Your poor girl.'

Belle said carefully, 'It would help if we knew why.'

Abigail raised her plump hands and let them crash on to the table, making the mugs Belle had just put down dance.

'Money, dear.'

'No, he—'

'Sorry, dear, but it'll be money. He'll have asked Jane for another handout and she'll have given him a flea in his ear. That car...'

'Beautiful.'

'Tens of thousands it would cost, dear. Tens. Even to lease it. He has champagne tastes, that boy.'

'But', Belle said, feeling that even if Abigail wasn't the right person it was a relief to have someone to talk to, 'why be so melodramatic, if it was just about money? Why rush off leaving Marianne in pieces like this if—'

'Pride, dear. Men like that don't care to be dependent. He'd want Marianne to think he'd earned it.'

'*Hasn't* he?'

Abigail gave a cackle of laughter.

'He wouldn't know hard work, dear, if it jumped up and bit him on the bottom!'

Belle began to pour the coffee.

'They were so adorable together.'

Abigail leaned forward, folding her arms under the cushiony shelf of her bosom.

'Well, luckily, dear, marriage bells aren't the only answer for girls these days, are they? And Marianne's only just out of school, for goodness' sake.'

Belle said abstractly, 'I was only eighteen when I met their father.'

'You were an exception, dear. The modern way is to be like your Elinor, with a career and no time wasted mooning over this F boy. Jonno and I have been killing ourselves over that. The F-word boy, we call him!' She looked round. 'Where is Marianne?'

Belle pushed a mug of coffee across the table.

'She's gone for a walk. She walks all the time, poor darling, wearing herself out. I make her take her phone and her inhaler but I can't help her sleep.'

'And Elinor?'

Belle looked a little startled, as if she'd temporarily forgotten about Elinor.

'Oh, she's at work.'

'Sensible girl. Does she like it?'

'I think so,' Belle said uncertainly. 'I mean, she's only just started, so it's a bit early to know.'

Abigail took a swallow of coffee.

'He's a naughty boy, Wills, a very naughty boy. And the sooner Marianne gets over her infatuation, the—'

'It's not an infatuation!' Belle said indignantly.

Abigail stared at her. Belle leaned towards her, across the table.

'Don't you', she said, in a different and more emotional tone of voice, 'believe in love at first sight?'

Abigail went on staring. Then she picked up her coffee mug again.

'Sorry, dear,' she said, 'but no. I do not.'

On the hill above Allenham, where the fateful thunderstorm had begun, Marianne sat on the damp grass, hugging her knees. Below her, the old house lay quietly in hazy autumn sunshine, on its hillside, a plume of bluish smoke rising softly out of one of the marvellous twisted Elizabethan chimneypots, the only other sign of life being the miniature figure of one of Jane Smith's gardeners raking up leaves. She couldn't hear him from where she sat, but she could watch him, with avidity. He was raking across the sweep of grass below the window behind which she had had the most wonderful afternoon of her life, in a four-poster bed whose hangings, Wills said, had been embroidered in 1720. She had put a hand out to touch them, reverently, and he had captured her hand in his at once and said that she wasn't to give a flicker of her attention to anyone or anything but him, or he'd be jealous.

He'd been gorgeously, blissfully jealous of everything that day. She'd wanted to examine every painting and rug, to exclaim over panelling and marquetry and plasterwork, to run her hands over velvet chair seats and polished chests, but he'd stopped her, laughing, pulling her to him, taking her face in his hands, touching her, kissing her, pushing her down into that welter of linen pillows and silky quilts on the great bed until she capitulated completely and let him take her over. Her eyes filled now thinking about it, thinking about him. It had been the ultimate in truth and beauty, to surrender to someone like that when it was someone that you were meant – *meant*, as she and Wills were – to belong to.

'Don't contact me,' he'd said to her on that Sunday, kneeling on the hearthrug in front of her, clutching her to him, his cheek pressed to her belly. 'Don't do anything until I'm in touch again, *anything.*'

She'd had her hands in his hair. She said shakily, 'But how am I to know—'

'Trust me,' he said. She could hear that his teeth were clenched. '*Trust* me.'

'Of course.'

He lifted his face. He said, 'You do, don't you?'

She nodded vehemently.

'You've got to,' he said. 'You've *got* to. You're the only person in my life who I trust and who trusts me. The *only* one.'

Even in her shock and misery, she had felt a jolt of happiness then, a little flash of recognition and self-justification. He'd be in touch. He'd be back. He said he would – and he would. He belonged to her; they belonged together. Trust was too small a word for what they had between them.

She got slowly to her feet. The gardener was now piling the leaves into a kind of mesh-sided truck. It wasn't fair, really, to expect even Ma, let alone Ellie and Mags, to have the first idea of what she was feeling, or of what she and Wills felt for each other. Ma and Dad had had something pretty good going, for sure, but Mags was still a kid and Ellie didn't have a passionate bone in her body. She, Marianne, must remember that. She must go home and, while needing to remind them all that, with Wills absent, she was only half a person at all times, she must be forgiving and understanding about Elinor's limitations.

She began to walk back along the ridge towards the lane and the path down to Barton Cottage. She put a hand into her pocket to pull out her phone – and withdrew it. She would not torment herself by checking it for messages. She had switched it to silent for that very reason. He had said he would be in touch and explain everything, when whatever was the matter was sorted, and he would. She knew it. She knew him and he would do what he had promised. More likely, actually, she thought, scrambling down the bank to the lane where she had first seen his car, he would probably surprise her.

Half skipping down the path to the cottage, Marianne was aware that she felt almost light-hearted. It had been good to look at Allenham, good to remind herself of that magical day, good to reassure herself that exceptional people could not have anything other than equally exceptional relationships. And as she came round the corner of the cottage to the area of gravel Sir John had laid down for parking, she caught a gleam of silver, glossy silvery grey, exactly the colour and finish of Wills's car, and she began to run, stumbling and gasping, towards it, her arms outstretched and ready.

But it was a Ford Sierra on the gravel. A battered old Ford Sierra with a peeling speed stripe down the side. And Edward Ferrars was getting out of it, looking thin and tired, in the kind of sweatshirt that Wills would never have been seen dead in.

He gave her a half-hearted smile.

'Hello, M,' he said.

* * *

'Where've you been?' Margaret demanded.

They were sitting round the kitchen table with macaroni cheese and a bowl of salad that Margaret had positioned so that nobody could see she hadn't taken any.

Edward put down a forkful of pasta.

He said vaguely, 'Oh, here and there. Plymouth and stuff. The usual.'

Elinor wasn't looking at him. She wasn't, in fact, looking at anyone. She had arrived home, with Margaret, in the dusk, to find Edward and Marianne playing the guitar together, and Belle bustling in the kitchen – 'So lovely to have someone to cook for, *even* if it is only macaroni cheese' – and nobody had seemed particularly pleased to see her, let alone troubled to ask her how her day at work had been. All right, it had been her fourth day, not her first, but it was still her first *week*. And Ed – well, Ed might have managed to make some distinction between greeting her and greeting Mags. Mightn't he?

'Did you go to Norland?' Belle asked.

She'd had a glass of wine while she was cooking and her cheeks were pink. He said, still vaguely, 'About a month ago.'

Marianne leaned forward, her eyes shining.

'How was it? Oh, how *was* it?'

'Like everywhere else in autumn,' Elinor said shortly. 'Covered in dead leaves.'

'Ellie!'

Elinor jabbed her fork into her supper.

'Some things', she said, 'just aren't for sharing. Like you and your thing for dead leaves. Mags, you haven't had any salad.'

'What about these Middletons?' Edward said.

'I *hate* salad!' Margaret shrieked.

Marianne closed her eyes.

'They're awful. Beyond words.'

'No, they're not!' Elinor cried.

'Because of them,' Marianne said dramatically, 'I've had more to bear than I have ever been asked to bear in my life.'

Elinor pushed the salad towards Edward.

'Ignore her.'

'Darling!' Belle said reprovingly.

'It's a beautiful place, here,' Elinor said steadily. 'And this is a practical house. And the Middletons are kind.'

Belle looked at Edward. 'Talking of kind, Ed, how is your mother?'

He pulled a face.

'Don't.'

'Why not?' Marianne said.

Edward picked up a cherry tomato out of the salad and put it in his mouth. He said, round it, 'She simply *will* not get that I don't have ambition.'

'But you do,' Elinor said quietly.

He didn't look at her. He said, 'Not *her* kind.'

'Well, darling,' Belle said brightly, 'I expect she worries about you. I expect she wants to be sure you'll have enough to live on.'

Edward said gloomily, 'Money isn't everything.'

Elinor took a breath. Then she said, 'No. But it needs to be enough.'

'Enough,' Marianne said dreamily, 'to run a beautiful old house and be free to have all the adventures in the world.'

'I want to win the lottery,' Margaret announced. 'That'd solve everything.'

'Maybe—'

Elinor smiled at her younger sister. 'Oh, Mags!'

Edward said, smiling at her too, 'You could buy your own wheels then.'

'I'd buy paintings,' Marianne said. 'And clothes. And islands. And people to come and sing for me.'

Edward grinned at her.

'Romance for you. Cars for her. It's so nice that some things don't change.'

Marianne looked abruptly grave.

'But I *am* changed, Ed.'

There was a tiny silence. Then he said unhappily, 'Me too.'

Elinor said, too loudly, 'Well, I'm not.'

'No,' Belle said with relief. 'Nor you are.'

'I seem,' Elinor said, 'to be just as bad at reading people as I ever was. I think they're one thing and then they turn out to be something quite different. Probably I'm just stupid to believe what anyone says. I should stick to their behaviour, shouldn't I? I should just believe what I see and not what I hear. Don't you think?'

There was another silence, considerably more awkward. And then Mags reached across the table and seized Edward's hand.

'What's that?'

'What's what?'

'That ring! You're wearing a ring.'

Edward put his hand out of sight on his lap.

'It's nothing.'

'Show me!' Margaret insisted.

Edward hesitated. Belle leaned forward, smiling.

'Come on, darling. Show us.'

Reluctantly, Edward drew his right hand out of his lap, and

laid it on the table. On his third finger was a silver band with a small, flat blue stone set in it.

'You don't wear rings,' Marianne said. 'You are *so* not a jewellery man.'

Edward said self-consciously, 'It was a sort of present.'

'Who from?'

'Fanny', Margaret said, 'would never give anyone a ring like that.'

Edward looked miserable. He tugged the ring off and put it in the pocket of his jeans, tipping himself sideways to do it.

'Sort of,' he said again. 'Doesn't matter.'

'It's like Ellie's,' Margaret said, 'Ellie's got a ring like that.'

Elinor put her hands in the air.

'Not wearing it,' she said, 'look.'

Edward went on gazing at his lap. Margaret said, 'But it's like yours.'

'Is it?' Elinor said to Edward. '*Is* it like mine?'

He said nothing. Belle picked up the wine bottle.

'Refill anyone?'

Nobody spoke. She upended the bottle into her own glass.

'Well, I shall finish it. It was a present from Jonno. He's so kind, presents and parties all the time.' She glanced at Edward. 'He'll want to meet you. He'll want to have a party the minute he knows you're here.'

'I'm only going to another Barton party,' Margaret said, 'when Wills is back and I can go in his car.'

Edward looked round the table, his gaze suddenly focused. 'Who's Wills?'

'A friend of Marianne's,' Elinor said quickly.

Edward looked at Marianne. Her face was abruptly

illuminated, shining. He said teasingly, 'A friend with a significant car, then?'

She turned to look at him. She was almost crying with
eagerness.

'Oh, you'll really like him!'

'I – I'm sure I will. When can I meet him?'

Marianne gave him a wide, tearful smile.

'Soon,' she said. She looked round the table, nodding and
smiling. 'Soon!'

8

The house was very quiet. There wasn't even any wind, so that Belle knew she would be able to hear the sound of feet or wheels on the gravel to warn her of anyone arriving. She was, she told herself, perfectly safe. Mags was at school, Elinor was at work and Marianne had taken Edward out for a last walk (for him) and another longing, greedy look at Allenham (for her).

If it hadn't been Edward's final walk before he left, she would not be in Elinor's bedroom, hunting through her drawers. If he hadn't said that he really had to leave that day, even though he didn't want to and had no desire to be anywhere else, she wouldn't need to look for evidence in this decidedly underhand way. And if Edward was being incomprehensible, Elinor was just as bad. She had been perfectly civil to him all week but nobody could claim that she had shown him any special warmth or attention. And he'd plainly wanted it, needed it. No normal, natural woman, Belle thought, almost indignantly, could have resisted wanting to reassure a man so evidently in need of comfort and confidence as Edward Ferrars.

But not Elinor, apparently. Elinor found it not just acceptable but seemingly quite easy to behave towards Edward as if he were no more than a welcome but mildly irritating brother. And when Belle had said, slightly reproving, to her, 'I think he's depressed, poor darling,' Elinor had simply replied, 'Then that makes two of them. A soulmate for Marianne,' and turned the volume on the kitchen radio up louder.

And when Belle had tried to relay to Elinor a very significant conversation she had had with Edward about his family's ambitions being so very far from his own, and his despair at their ever coming round to his point of view, Elinor had waited politely till she had finished, and then said, 'I know all that, Ma. I know what they want. I know what he wants. And I know that his mother is completely dominating.'

'Then why aren't you nicer to him?'

'I am nice. I'm perfectly nice.'

Belle gave a little sigh of exasperation.

'Darling, you know what I mean. At Norland, you were both—'

'Norland was different,' Elinor said. 'We were different.'

'But I thought you loved him?'

'Ma,' Elinor said, glaring, 'I am not chasing after *anyone*. Right? And I am not discussing my most private feelings, or speculating about Edward's, with anyone. Ever. OK?'

Belle had blinked. In her head she could hear Henry saying, in the conciliating tone peculiar to him, 'Don't upset yourself, my darling. Don't be upset.' She swallowed.

'Very well, Ellie.'

Elinor had relaxed a little.

'Thank you.'

'I – just don't want *you* to be unhappy, too.'

Elinor had given her a quick kiss.

'I'm not.'

Well, she wasn't, not actively and visibly, like Marianne so much of the time. But there was something there, a shadow, a reticence, a holding in, that made Belle's heart ache for her oldest daughter, and drove her to search Elinor's bedroom for something, anything, that would prove that Edward Ferrars – were he free of that monster of a mother – was true of heart. It was too bad, really it was, to have two out of three daughters involved with men who seemed addicted to muddle and mystery.

Elinor's drawers were so unlike Marianne's or Margaret's. Both of them lived in persistent chaos: Marianne's a charming, bohemian clutter of colour and texture; Margaret's merely chaos. But Elinor's possessions had a system to them, and an order. She would know where to find a navy sweater, or something to write with, or her driving licence. There were even box files, Belle was chagrined to see, labelled 'Barton Cottage – Utilities', and 'Important Documents' as well as a small pile of invoices, weighted with a big smooth pebble, with 'Paid' written across them in red pen. On the chest of drawers were photographs of – gulp – Henry, and little Harry, and the three Dashwood girls dressed for Christmas in tinsel wreaths, and one of her, Belle, standing in the herbaceous border at Norland in a huge straw hat, her arms full of delphiniums. And in front of the photographs was a series of Indian lacquered bowls of various sizes, holding Elinor's necklaces and bracelets, jumbled up together and slightly dusty. Belle poked a finger into the smallest bowl, which held paper clips and a key or two and some rings, which she took out and laid on the chest of drawers. There was a ring made of turquoise Perspex and a brass ring – Indian? – inlaid with a domed reddish stone, veined like marble, and a plain, flat silver band. Belle picked it up and turned it round. It had a small blue stone set into one side. It was immediately familiar. It was exactly the same as the ring Margaret had noticed Edward wearing at supper, the first evening, which he'd been so embarrassed about, only smaller. Elinor and Edward had the same rings.

Carefully, Belle scooped up all three rings and stirred them back among the paper clips. They had the same rings, but they weren't wearing them. And, plainly, they didn't want to talk about why they possessed them and why they weren't wearing them. They couldn't have quarrelled, or Edward wouldn't have come in the first place, or stayed for a whole week in the second. And, as Elinor, said, she'd been perfectly nice to him. Perhaps they were waiting for something to happen. Perhaps it was something to do with Edward's mother, perhaps . . .There were feet on the gravel, just audible from Elinor's bedroom at the side of the house. Belle walked quickly out on to the landing and opened the cupboard where Elinor had put the linen when they had first arrived at Barton Cottage. Maybe she was, as Elinor had suggested, silly to worry. Elinor didn't look unhappy, and Edward was no unhappier than usual. The front door opened.

'Ma?' Marianne called out.

'Up here!' Belle cried. 'Just sorting the towels!'

Tony Musgrove, for whom Elinor worked, had found her a car. It belonged to his stepson, who was working in Bolivia for three years, and who had said it was fine for someone else to use it, in fact he'd rather have it used than have it sitting on blocks in Tony Musgrove's driveway. Tony said that the company would insure and tax it, if Elinor could pay for the petrol.

Elinor had hesitated. Tony, a blunt man in his forties, had stared at her.

'Don't you want it? Most people in your situation would jump at a chance like this.'

'Oh, I do.'

'Well, then.'

'It's just', Elinor said, 'that it's *so* kind. And you mightn't keep me on after three months. And then—'

'We will,' Tony Musgrove said. 'You're bloody good.' He held out the car keys. 'And bloody cheap. Now clear off.'

The car, Elinor thought, gingerly pushing the gears about before she started the engine, was hardly going to impress Margaret. It was, if anything, more dilapidated than Ed's – best, really, not to think about Ed – and had been sprayed a colour which was very nearly orange. It made her visible in a way that was anathema to her, but it was a car. It would get her from Barton to work and Margaret from Barton to school. It would mean that they weren't eternally dependent upon, and thus obliged to, Sir John. And it was truly kind of Tony Musgrove's stepson and truly kind of the company. She was very lucky and she would take as much care to be very grateful as she could to demonstrate to everyone, but especially to her family, that nothing had changed between her and Edward because there wasn't enough there, in the first place, *to* change, and also because nobody could do anything until he managed to break free of his mother.

Which, Elinor said to herself, carefully turning the car out of the car park and into the street, I am not going to have anything to do with. His mother is his problem, and not mine. And even if I wish that he would stand up to her, I know from personal

experience how incredibly hard it is to stand up to a member
of your own family who can make life unbelievably unpleas-
ant for ages for everyone, if crossed. He is stuck. I am also, in
consequence, stuck. But he was, for some reason that I was not
prepared to ask him, wearing a ring identical to the one he gave
me which he said he bought in a craft shop in Plymouth because
the girl who made it was local and called Eleanor. So I take heart
from that. I do. I *will*. It is very annoying to find that I haven't
got over him, at all – in fact, rather the reverse – but I am pretty
sure he hasn't got over me, either, so I won't keep asking myself
if I'm OK, like prodding at a sore tooth, because if I do, I will
drive myself quite *mad*.

She pulled the car to an uneven halt outside Margaret's
school. Margaret had been persuaded to join the school's homework club – 'It is so unfair, why do I have to, why, Thomas'd
always come and get me, he said he would, you are so, so *mean*'
– so that Elinor could collect her after work and they could
come home together. Margaret was standing on the pavement,
her skirt hitched unevenly high above her knees, scowling at
her phone. She goggled at the car. 'You're not telling me that
this is it?'

Elinor patted the passenger seat.

'Hop in.'

'It's a joke. It's completely *dire*. What if anyone sees me in it?'

'They'll think you're very lucky not to have to use public
transport. Good day?'

Margaret sighed and began to scrabble for her seat belt.

'Don't be ridic.'

'What?'

'You heard.'

'What', Elinor said patiently, 'is ridic?'

Margaret turned to face her sister and mouthed the word elaborately.

'Ridiculous.'

'Ah.'

Margaret held her phone out.

'Now look at this.'

'I can't, Mags. I'm driving.'

'We can't go straight home. We've got to go to the Park.'

'What?'

'Ma says. She texted. It's Jonno and Mrs J. and everyone. We've got to meet Mrs J.'s other daughter or something.'

Elinor gave a little groan.

'Why tonight?'

'Search me. It's bad enough Ed going, without this.' She sighed again. 'Nobody at school has a life like mine.'

Elinor patted her knee.

'Poor old you.'

'It's all very well for you,' Margaret said crossly. 'You don't mind.'

'What don't I mind?'

'Well,' Margaret said, 'it's all the same to you, isn't it? You're just fine, always.' She glanced sideways at Elinor's profile. 'Aren't you?'

'Awful wet day,' Sir John said exuberantly, kissing them all as they filed past him into the hall at Barton Park. 'Pissing down.' He gripped Marianne's arm. 'Far too wet for your usual walk to Allenham, eh?'

Marianne looked very grave and said nothing.

'But I've got a party here!' Sir John said. 'I've got people! I've got food and drink and a fire and people! Too bad poor old Bill's still stuck in London.'

There was a flurry in the doorway to the library and Mrs Jennings surged through, towing a very small, very pretty, very pregnant girl in her wake.

'My dears. Dashwoods all. This is – Charlotte.'

Sir John put an arm round his sister-in-law.

'She's a peach, what?'

Belle, seeing what was expected of her, stepped forward and kissed Charlotte's cheek.

'She is indeed.'

Charlotte looked delighted.

'Honestly. A peach! Look at the size of me, will you? I'm not due till after Christmas and I'm *huge*. Beached whales aren't in it.' She gave a peal of laughter. 'Except that's pretty insulting to whales, don't you think?'

Elinor smiled at her. She was so pretty and so merry. And so unlike her taller, thinner and equally pretty sister. Then Elinor glanced at Marianne. She was looking away from them all at a painting of a boy in blue silk breeches, his hand on the head of an elegant dog, and her expression was not helpful. Elinor said quietly, 'M?'

Marianne sighed, and moved a step further away.

'Leave her,' Sir John said in a stage whisper. 'Leave her to pine in peace.'

Charlotte Palmer stood on tiptoe, as if to try and attract Marianne's attention.

'You pine to your heart's content!' she called. 'He's a complete dish. Eat your heart out George Clooney, frankly. Wills is *gorgeous.* He's a neighbour of ours in London, of course.'

Marianne was still regarding the picture, but her expression had intensified to one of extreme alertness.

'No, he is not,' said a voice from the direction of the library.

They all turned. A youngish man in a business suit was standing in the doorway, studying the screen on his BlackBerry.

'He is too!' Charlotte said, smiling delightedly. 'He's practically round the corner.'

'John Willoughby', the man in the doorway said, still looking at his screen, 'lives the other end of the borough. King's Road.'

Charlotte gave a little smirk. She did not seem remotely abashed.

'Put that away,' Mrs Jennings commanded her son-in-law, indicating the BlackBerry. Sir John waved an arm at her.

'Come on, Mrs J., leave him be.'

The man in the doorway appeared to take no notice of either his mother-in-law or his brother-in-law, but instead put the BlackBerry to his ear and strolled back into the room, talking into it as he went.

'So rude!' Charlotte said happily. 'He's an absolute nightmare! Don't ask me what he does! I haven't a *clue.* It's all screens and figures and his BlackBerry is simply *welded* to him. He never tells me a *thing.* And it'll be a million times worse when he's an MP.'

'Goodness,' Belle said almost inaudibly. 'An MP.'

'I know!' Charlotte said. 'It's insane, isn't it? Especially when you consider Tommy. I mean, he *hates* people, simply *hates* them, doesn't he, Mummy?'

'Too true,' Mrs Jennings said, roaring with laughter. 'Simply *loathes* me, especially now he's saddled with Charlotte!'

Charlotte leaned slightly forward, her face alight with pleasure.

'And the funny thing is, isn't it, Mummy, that he's got to pretend he likes people if he wants them to vote for him! It's hilarious. Just imagine' – she held out a plump little hand as if writing in the air – 'Thomas Palmer, MP on the Houses of Commons writing paper. It's a scream, isn't it? But he says there won't be one single perk for me, not one. He's not letting me anywhere near the place. It's just too funny, don't you think?'

Elinor nodded, dumbly. Margaret was fidgeting beside her.

'Can I – Can I—'

'Can you what?' Sir John said jovially. 'Escape?'

Margaret nodded.

'Baggage,' he said, 'Complete baggage. Go on then, go upstairs and find the children. Good God, Belle, you're as hopeless with her as Mary is with ours. Now then, everyone. What d'you say to a spot of dinner?'

'Well,' Charlotte Palmer said to Elinor after supper, 'you drew the long straw, didn't you! Jonno on one side, Tommy on the other. Lucky you!'

'Oh,' Elinor said, slightly flustered. 'It was fine, he—'

'He's really taken a shine to you,' Charlotte said. 'Next thing is, he'll be asking you all for Christmas!'

'I don't think so, I wouldn't—'

'He adores having the right people. Adores it. I can't have you breaking his heart too, not with so many broken hearts already round here.'

Elinor leaned forward. She said, almost in a whisper, 'Do – do you know Wills?'

Charlotte beamed at her.

'*Everybody* knows Wills.'

'Do they?'

'But I know why you asked me, don't I! You didn't ask me just because he's the hottest—'

'I asked', Elinor said firmly, interrupting, 'because I'd like to know a bit more *about* him.'

'Of course you would,' Charlotte said, laughing. 'You'd want to know everything about anyone who's such an item with your sister!'

Elinor glanced across the table to where her mother was drinking coffee with the Middletons and Mrs Jennings.

'You don't want to pay too much attention to *them*, and what they say.'

'Oh, I don't!' Charlotte said airily. 'I've lived with my mother for nearly thirty years, don't forget! No, it wasn't them who told me first, it was Bill Brandon. You know Bill Brandon.'

Elinor was truly shocked.

'Bill Brandon told you . . .'

'Oh yes! In London. On Monday. I just happened to see him because I was picking up something in Bond Street and he was doing something pompous like going to the Royal Academy, and we were talking about Barton and all of you lot were mentioned and I said, Oh, Mummy says they're all so pretty and one of them has already got off seriously with Wills and he said—' She broke off abruptly.

'What? What did he say?'

Charlotte put her hand over her mouth as if to stifle a new burst of giggles.

'D'you know – I can't remember! Maybe he didn't speak! Maybe he didn't say anything, maybe he just sort of looked as if he knew it was true? Whatever. Does it matter? Course not! Well, only to him, of course, poor old thing.'

Elinor said, with difficulty, 'Why?'

'Well,' Charlotte said happily, 'Mummy says he's a bit gone on your sister too. He's such a romantic sweetie, even if he's a bit of an old stick.' She leaned forward herself now, as far as her belly would allow. 'Tell you what: Mummy and Jonno really tried to cook something up between me and Bill when Jonno married Mary until Mummy realised that being Mrs B. would be *less* than no fun for me! Yikes, just think of it!'

'Did you,' Elinor said, hardly able to utter the words by now, 'go out with him? With Bill?'

Charlotte stared at her for a moment and then fell back into her chair with squeals of laughter.

'Oh my God, no! He never even asked me to sit next to him! Though I bet he'd have liked me to. But I'm fine with Tommy. He's such a hoot. Even if he never tells me anything.'

Tommy Palmer materialised beside them, his BlackBerry still in his hand. He said to his wife, ignoring Elinor, 'If I did, you'd never listen to a word I said to you—'

'See?' Charlotte said delightedly to Elinor. 'See?'

'—so why bother, I ask myself. So I don't.' He held out an empty whisky tumbler. 'Get us a refill, Char. I didn't marry you for your brains. I married you for your body. As is evident.'

Charlotte heaved herself out of her chair and took the whisky glass. She gave Tommy a resounding kiss.

'See?' she said again to Elinor. 'Isn't he the absolute end?'

Tommy Palmer didn't look at his wife. Instead he glanced across at Elinor. His look was surprisingly kind.

'You OK?' he said.

She was startled.

'Yes,' she said. 'Thank you, yes, we—'

He smiled. He said, indicating his wife, 'They've got hearts of gold, these Jenningses, but as much sensitivity as hippos in season. It might not occur to any of them that jolly evenings at Barton Park aren't exactly up your alley.'

Elinor shot a look at Charlotte. She was gazing up at her husband and laughing, with every appearance of sheer delight. Elinor said, uncertainly, 'Thank you. Everyone's so kind, I mean ...' She stopped.

Tommy Palmer put the hand not holding his BlackBerry on his wife's head. He said, 'They do kind as naturally as breathing. But imagination wasn't what their fairy godmothers brought to their christenings.' He winked, very slightly and entirely unflir-tatiously, at Elinor. 'So I'm just saying that you've got an ally. Should you ever need one.'

She was stammering.

'Th-thank you.'

He took his hand off Charlotte's head and gestured airily with it.

'No thanks in order. Just remember. Now, Char, where's my drink?'

From her bedroom, where she was playing a Villa-Lobos Prelude – very haunting, very melancholy – on her guitar, Marianne could hear her mother on the telephone. She was probably talking to Jonno, who, despite having a business to run, rang most mornings to relay and pick up gossip. It was a habit Mari-anne herself found close to contemptible, and she couldn't help but remind herself that even if Wills did have a penchant for observations about other people — always redeemed, of course, by their being so funny — he more than counterbalanced it by his intense capacity to share all the cultural elements of life that mattered so much to her: the poetry and the landscape and the romance of history — and the music. Oh, the music! He'd picked her guitar up one day — he didn't play as well as Ed or as Bill Brandon, if she was honest, but he had such *feeling* for music — and said, 'D'you play the piano?'

She'd been startled.

'Well, I *can*. But I'd rather play the guitar.'

He'd looked straight at her, very seriously.

'I'm so glad.'

'Are you?'

'The piano seems so much more — more *distant*, to me. I love the way guitars are so passionate, so involved.' He'd bent towards her. 'Can you feel the vibration when you're playing?'

She'd nodded. She'd said softly, 'Of course I can. I can *feel* the tone.'

His face had been so close to hers. He'd said, almost in a whisper, 'So sensual. So sexy.'

Marianne gave a little gasp now, and checked herself. It was blissful and simultaneously agonising to remember such moments. Recalling them made her unable to sink into the music as she used to, because the only sinking she longed for these days was into Wills's arms. She stopped playing and bent her head over her guitar. Here came the tears again, a release but also accompanied by waves of misery, waves of memory, waves of—'Marianne!' Belle called up the stairs.

Marianne raised her head, sniffing.

'Coming.'

She laid the guitar on her bed, snatched a handful of tissues from the box on the floor and blew her nose. Then she rubbed the balled-up tissues across her eyes and crossed the room to open the door.

'Yes, Ma?'

Belle surveyed her woebegone face.

'Oh, darling . . .'

'I'm OK.'

'You've been crying again. You poor lamb.'

'Why doesn't he ring?' Marianne wailed. 'Why doesn't he answer my emails? Or my texts, even? Why doesn't he at least let me know he's alive?'

Belle came two steps up the staircase.

'He will, darling. I'm sure he will. It must be something very serious, something he wants to protect you from.'

Marianne sniffed again.

'Sorry. Sorry to go on about it.'

'I just wish I could help.'

'You do,' Marianne said. 'By being nice to me. Everyone's nice to me. Even those morons up at the Park who don't know when to stop teasing. I know they mean to be nice because they're too stupid to see how clumsy they are.'

'That was Jonno on the phone just now.'

Marianne sat down on the top step of the stairs. She said, wearily, 'Surprise, surprise.'

'He is inexhaustibly jolly. No sooner do the Palmers go – they left this morning – than he invites someone else to stay. Mrs J.'s late husband's goddaughter or something. And her sister. They are your sort of age, and Jonno wants us to go up for dinner, on Saturday.'

'No,' Marianne said.

Belle smiled.

'That's what I told him. I mean I didn't put it like that. I didn't say none of us could bear another meal at the Park. I said that we absolutely could *not* accept any more hospitality from them until we had repaid some of it here.'

'Oh, Ma . . .'

'So,' said Belle triumphantly, 'they are all coming to lunch on Saturday – minus the children, thank goodness – including these two girls.'

Marianne sighed.

'I can imagine them.'

'No, darling,' Belle said, 'you can't. You might love them. They might be just what you need to – to distract you. They are called Lucy and Nancy. Lucy and Nancy Steele.'

Margaret was going home with a new school friend and would not, she said with emphasis, need picking up by Elinor. There had been a good deal of telephoning and need for reassurance about this arrangement, but Elinor had finally prevailed over all Belle's anxieties by using her lunch break to visit the friend's mother and see for herself the absolute reliability of the situation: a semi-detached house in a suburban street, unmistakably inhabited by a family of unimpeachable orthodoxy. She had even felt impelled to half apologise to Margaret's friend's mother.

'It's just that we're a bit new to round here and Mags has only been at the school a few weeks and . . .'

The woman was laughing. She patted Elinor's hand.

'I get it, dear. No hard feelings.'

But even that confirmation of respectability didn't stop Belle from ringing Elinor's mobile several times during the afternoon, so that when it rang, yet again, Elinor snatched it up without glancing at the screen and said almost crossly into it, 'What now, Ma?'

'It's Jonno,' Sir John said.

'Help. Sorry. So sorry. Family stuff.'

'Tell me about it. Just tell me about it. That's why I'm ringing.'

Elinor felt an instant clutch of alarm.

'What, what—'

'I've been turned down,' Sir John said. 'By your mother.'

'Turned down?'

'I've got a brace of lovely girls here and your mother has declined to bring you all here to supper to meet them.'

Elinor swallowed.

'But you're too good to us. We were with you only—'

'Listen,' Sir John said, 'I'd have you to supper every night if I had my way, promise you. But I can't shift your mother. And it's dull for these lasses, stuck with us, although I have to say that they are brilliant with the kids, brilliant. They said they adored nippers and they really do seem to. Amazing. But look. I rang you because even if I can't shift your mother and Marianne, why don't you drop by on your way home?'

Elinor closed her eyes.

'That's sweet of you, but—'

'Don't but me. *Don't.*'

'Jonno,' Elinor said, opening her eyes, 'it's really nice of you, and I'd really like to meet them. But I'm tired. I—'

'It'll perk you up to come to supper!'

'No,' Elinor said, with more force than she intended. '*No.*'

There was a brief and startled pause. She could hear Sir John giving some instruction or other to his secretary. Then his voice boomed in her ear again.

'Just a drink, then.'

'Well . . .'

'Great,' he said. 'Splendid. Settled. We'll see you for a drink on your way home.'

Elinor sighed. He had already put the phone down. She laid hers down too, slowly, on the bottom rim of her drawing board.

Tony Musgrove looked at her over the top of his reading glasses.

'Boyfriend trouble?' he said.

Elinor made a face.

'I wish.'

The sitting room at Barton Park was in uproar. It seemed to Elinor to be too hot, too bright and too full of charging children, never mind the noise. There were two young women – dressed, Elinor couldn't help noticing, with elaborate modishness – on the floor, trying to field a child or two as it hurtled past, and, on a sofa at a slight distance, surveying the scene with every evidence of satisfaction, was Mary Middleton, placid in cream cashmere.

Sir John sprang forward to greet her, a glass in his hand.

'Hello, lovely girl. Welcome to the usual madness. G and T?'

'Actually,' Elinor said, 'could I have something soft?'

'No!' Sir John said. 'No! Don't be such a party pooper. Wine, at least, if you won't have any gin! I shall get you wine. Don't argue. You know I can't bear to be argued with.'

Elinor shrugged, resignedly.

'OK.'

'*Good* girl. That's more like it. Shan't be a tick.'

Elinor looked back at the riot in the room. One of the girls on the floor, with a sharp, pretty face and tumble of carefully arranged long glossy curls, caught her eye, got to her feet and came towards her, her hand out ready, and smiling. The hand, Elinor observed, was encircled with charm bracelets and carefully manicured.

'You have to be Elinor!'

'Yes.'

'I'm Lucy. Lucy Steele.' She turned and pointed towards the floor again. 'That's my sister. She was Mr J.'s goddaughter.'

Elinor nodded.

'We've come for the weekend,' Lucy said. 'Amazing house! You should see my bedroom. You could put our whole *flat* into my bedroom! And the children are so cute, really lively.'

'Certainly lively.'

'And she's just amazing, too,' Lucy said. 'Isn't she? I mean Lady M. Awesome clothes, and her figure! You'd never think she'd had *four* children, would you? Amazing.'

Elinor looked across the room. Mary Middleton was watching the two older boys pushing Lucy's sister down on to her back on the carpet, one of them using her hair to speed the process, with no sign that she was other than completely oblivious to the need for discipline.

Elinor said anxiously, 'Is your sister all right, d'you think?'

Lucy glanced across, almost casually.

'Oh, Nancy's fine. She can take care of herself.'

Nancy gave a faint but distinct cry of pain and put her hands to her head. Mary roused herself, without urgency, from her sofa. She said lovingly, 'Be careful, boys.'

'Get off!' Sir John roared at his children, returning with wine for Elinor in a glass as big as a small bucket. 'Get *off* the poor girl, this instant!'

'Jonno,' Mary said reproachfully, 'they're only playing, bless them.'

Nancy Steele struggled to her feet and adjusted her clothing. She smiled bravely, showing long, unnaturally white teeth.

'It's fine,' she said, 'I'm OK. Totes OK. Mos def.'

'Nancy,' Sir John said, 'come and meet Elinor. Elinor lives—'

'Oh,' Nancy said, advancing on Elinor and thrusting out a hand adorned with long, acrylic nails, 'I know about *you*! Don't we, Luce? You lived at Norland, didn't you? We know all about *Norland*.'

Elinor took her hand for as brief a moment as possible.

'Oh?'

Nancy looked significantly at Sir John. She said, nodding, 'Oh yeah. We know all about the F-word guy! Fo sho we do!'

'Nancy,' her sister said tensely.

Elinor looked steadfastly into her drink.

'We know it all!' Nancy said. She ran a hand through her visibly straightened hair, letting it fall back into exactly the same shape as it had been before she touched it. 'We know that your sister's made it with a really cute guy, and that you'll be next! Scream!' She gave Sir John a nudge with her elbow. 'We even *know* the F-word guy! Don't we, Luce?'

Lucy shifted slightly and examined her bracelets.

'Well, only slightly.'

'Luce! We do! At Uncle Peter's!'

There was a sudden squeal of pain and rage from across the room. They all swung round. Mary Middleton was holding her kicking three-year-old, Anna-Maria, and saying urgently, 'So sorry, darling, careless Mumma, silly Mumma, horrid Mumma's brooch to hurt poor baby Anna, sorry, sweetie, sorry, poppet.'

Sir John strode over.

'What's happened?'

'My pin caught her little arm, her poor little arm.'

Sir John seized his daughter's flailing arm and peered at it.

'Can't see a thing.'

'There!' Mary cried. '*There!*'

Anna-Maria wrenched her arm out of his grasp, flung her head back and screamed afresh.

'Totes adorable kids,' Nancy Steele said.

'Really cute,' Lucy echoed, without complete conviction.

Elinor regarded them both. She took a step back and put her almost untouched glass of wine down on the nearest surface.

'I think I'll just slip out,' she said. 'Quietly. Have a good evening.' She managed a smile. 'See you soon.'

At the end of Saturday lunch at Barton Cottage, throughout which Marianne had sat without speaking, gazing aloofly past the assembled company out of the window, Lucy Steele followed Elinor out to the kitchen. She said eagerly, 'I'll help you make coffee.'

Elinor put the pile of pudding plates she was carrying down, with difficulty, on the cluttered table.

'It's OK.'

'Let me help, do. Look at all this washing up!'

'I'm used to it.'

Lucy, taking no notice, began to run hot water into the sink. She said confidingly, 'I'm really sorry about Nance. All the endless, endless man talk. I'm afraid she's a bit one-track-minded and this guy in Exeter, Brian Rose, she was going on about, well, he's, um ... well, she's my sister but it's a bit much really. Kind of embarrassing. Are there any gloves?'

'Gloves?'

'Washing-up gloves. Rubber gloves. You know.'

Elinor shook her head, 'Sorry. We just have neglected hands.'

Lucy put her own hands behind her head, and twisted her hair into an artless knot.

'No matter. Anyway, poor old Nance. I'm afraid it's all boys and bags with her.'

'Bags?'

'Handbags,' Lucy said. She located a bottle of washing-up liquid and squirted some liberally into the sink. Then, appearing to concentrate very hard on swishing the soap into a foam, she said, almost carelessly, 'Have you ever met Mrs F.?'

Elinor stopped scraping scraps off plates into the bin.

'Who?'

'Mrs Ferrars. Ed's mum.'

'No,' Elinor said shortly. 'The scary mother. No, I'm glad to say.'

There was a short pause and then Lucy said, turning from the sink, 'That's a real pity. I wish you had. I – I so wanted you to advise me.'

Elinor put the scraped plate down on the nearest worktop.

'Sorry,' she said, 'I don't get ...'

Lucy looked down at her wet hands. She appeared to be deciding something. Then she looked up again, earnestly, at Elinor.

'Can you keep a secret?'

'Of course, but should you—'

Lucy held up one hand. She said solemnly, 'I knew I could

trust you. The minute you walked into the room at Barton Park, I just knew you were honour bright.'

'Well,' Elinor said, picking up the next plate, 'thank you, but I can't see how I can advise you about anything, nor where Ed's mum fits in.'

'Oh, not *now*,' Lucy said, 'She doesn't matter *now*. But she might, you see. Soon. Quite soon.'

She smiled to herself, shyly, as if she were relishing some secret. Elinor put the plate down and came round the table.

'Are − are you going out with Ed's brother or something? Is that what you're trying to tell me? You're going out with Robert and he hasn't told his mother?'

Lucy looked straight at Elinor. Her eyes were wide and guileless. She smiled again.

'Oh,' she said softly, 'not Robert. He's a complete muppet. I'm talking about Ed.' She let a fraction of a second pass and then she said, '*My* Ed.'

Elinor didn't move. She remained where she was, standing by the table. Everything seemed to have stopped, even her breathing. As she stood there, she was conscious, through the intensity of her own shock, that Lucy was watching her carefully. She made a supreme effort.

'Wow ...'

'I know,' Lucy said. 'It's so great, but it's so awful, having to keep it a secret. Are you OK?'

Elinor nodded. She could feel her body starting up again, tentatively, as if it was wondering whether it would work again.

'Ed wanted me to tell you,' Lucy said. 'He thinks the world of you and your family. You're like a sister to him.'

'Ed wanted you to tell me ...'

'Well, I know he *would* want me to tell you. You know how hopeless he is at expressing himself – it drives me mad some-times! But the thing is . . .' She stopped, significantly.

Elinor, concentrating on both breathing and giving nothing away, waited.

'Actually,' Lucy said, 'he is my Ed.' She looked away, as if privately communing with someone who wasn't there. 'I think you could actually say we were engaged, in a way. Enough for me to have this, anyway.'

She reached into the neck of her shirt and pulled out a chain, holding it bunched in her hand to indicate that it was private and personal.

'Wow,' Elinor said again, her voice sounding to herself as if it came from miles away, 'I didn't – know you even knew each other, let alone . . .'

'Oh yes,' Lucy said, moving to stand very close to her. 'Oh *yes*. My uncle Peter runs a crammers, in Plymouth. Ed was sent there. Didn't he tell you? And Nancy and I grew up in Plymouth. We were always round at Uncle Peter's. Peter Pratt. He was like a dad to Ed.'

Elinor recovered herself a little.

'Ed never said anything to me about—'

'No, he wouldn't. He's so shy. And there's his old witch of a mother so it had to be secret from *everyone*. But we saw each other again at a party the other day – mutual friends down here – and I just knew. The minute I saw him again, I knew. It was like we'd never been apart. Poor lamb, he was *so* drunk that night! Completely out of it. I expect it was the relief of seeing me, don't you? But honestly, Elinor, thank goodness I *was* there to look after him, he was in such a state.' She paused and gave Elinor

a wide smile. 'And the next day, I took him shopping.' She held
the chain out to Elinor. There was a ring on it, a flat silver band,
with a small green stone set into it.

'We got these,' Lucy said, 'both of us. He didn't really want
one but that's just a boy thing, isn't it, about having anything
that might be thought girly, so I made him have one too. And
now he texts me, like, all the time. Shall I show you how many?
I can't show you what they say, of course, but you'd understand
that, wouldn't you? I've told him that when I'm twenty-one –
any minute, so exciting! – we'll tell everyone, and between you
and me, Ellie – can I call you Ellie? – I'll be sick with relief. I
hate secrets, just hate them, and anyway it stresses me out, not
saying, and worrying that Nancy might, because she's so hopeless and blabs everything to everyone, and she's the only person
who knows. Oh God, it's been such a strain!'

Elinor regarded her. She said, as levelly as she could, 'Why
is it still a secret? Why don't you just marry?'

Lucy sighed. She picked up the nearest tea towel and held it
to her face, as if to wipe her eyes with it.

'Ed says he can't. He can't commit till he knows what he's
going to do. He says he can't expect me to live in a hole-and-
corner way on nothing.'

'Aren't you earning?'

Lucy raised her chin.

'I'm a therapist.'

'Oh.'

'Reflexology.'

'Oh.'

'I don't make enough money to support both of us. It's
heartbreaking.'

Elinor straightened her shoulders a little.

'I'm sure it is.'

'I just thought', Lucy said, her voice becoming little girlish, 'that if you knew Ed's mother, you could help me think of a way to get round her. Because we're so stressed about it all. Didn't you think Ed was stressed when he came to stay with you? He'd come straight from me, and we'd had such an awful time saying goodbye. Awful. We've got to take some action. We've *got to*. Don't you think?'

The kitchen door opened. Margaret stood there, holding the dish in which Belle had made an enormous apple crumble.

'What's going on?'

'Nothing,' Elinor said.

Lucy smiled at her and swooped forward to relieve her of the crumble dish.

'Your lovely sister', she said, 'is helping me to untangle a bit of a knot in my life. That's all.'

Margaret stared at her and let the dish go. She shrugged.

'Whatever,' she said.

Volume II

9

Elinor did not sleep that night. She heard the chime of Barton Church clock strike every remorseless hour, and at five in the morning, she got out of bed, pulled on her father's old cardigan and some socks and crept down to the kitchen.

It was quiet in there, apart from the low hum of the refrigerator, and even if not especially warm, warmer than anywhere else in the house. She switched on a lamp on the counter, and then the kettle, and found a mug and a box of tea bags, and a small dish of leftover roast potatoes, which oddly seemed to be the very thing to supply comfort and ballast.

It was a Sunday, after all. No one else in the family would be awake for hours. Elinor made her tea and settled with it, and a cold roast potato, at the kitchen table, hooking her socked toes over the stretcher of the chair she sat on, and pulling the sleeves of the cardigan far enough down to act as mittens. They concealed the knuckles on both her hands, but not her fingers, on one of which was the silver band that Ed had given her, at Norland. She had, after the encounter with Lucy the day before, extracted it from among the keys and paper clips on her dressing table and put it on.

Not at first, though. At first, last night, she had been in an agony of humiliation. The moment she could escape to her room, she had lain on her bed, face into the pillow, and agonised that she had been made a complete fool of by Edward, that he was a classic two-timer, and not to be trusted. But once that first rush of indignant misery was over, she could think about him more calmly, and possibly, she told herself, rolling over and staring at the ceiling, more justly. He had been a sixteen-year-old boy after all, expelled from school and sent in disgrace to a college in Plymouth to work for, and sit, his A levels. And there was Lucy, a knowing fourteen-year-old who was very, very sorry for him and who turned, in time, into a determined sixteen-year-old with a sharp awareness of exactly how much money Edward's father had made. There'd probably been sex – try not to think about that – and then some subsequent promises of loyalty, and a future, which Elinor, having spent several hours now in Lucy's company, could easily imagine being insisted upon.

She had got off her bed then, and crossed the bedroom to her chest of drawers and the Indian lacquer bowls. Edward, she told herself, hunting for her ring, was not actually a cheat, or a manipulator. He was sweet-natured, affectionate, good-hearted and an unquestioned fan of family life. His own family had rejected him, so he had done the classic adolescent turna-round thing of attaching himself to the next family, or families, who were kind to him – the Steeles, and the Pratts, in Plym-outh. Lucy came with that package – and no more. When she thought about how Ed had been when last staying, she could easily account for his gloom by explaining it to herself as being the result of Lucy's expectations of him, as well as his mother's.

She found her ring and slid it on to the third finger of her right hand – the finger he had chosen when he gave it to her. Edward was, she could now see, as stuck as he possibly could be. Everywhere he turned there was a woman demanding something of him which he could not possibly deliver.

Which makes me, Elinor thought now, holding her tea mug in her sleeved hands, the good guy, really, the one he has actually chosen of his own free will because – well, because he actually likes me. But he can't do anything about it, because he doesn't know what to do about Lucy, never mind his mother. And even if I can't actually admire him for not standing up to either of them, I can believe that he isn't a hypocrite and that I'm not a gullible dummy. And that's a vast relief, because when I think about him, my heart just turns right over with the longing to help him, and see him smile again, and be released into being the kind of person he is not just aching to be, but is designed to be.

The kitchen door opened. Belle came in, wearing a blanket round her shoulders like an immense shawl. She was blinking and rumpled.

'I looked in your room, Ellie, and you weren't there.'

'No, Ma. I was down here.'

'Obviously,' Belle said. She looked at the dish by Elinor's elbow. 'Eating potatoes.'

'Just the one.'

Belle advanced towards the table and peered at her daughter.

'Darling, are you all right? Is there anything you'd like to talk about?'

Elinor didn't move. She gave her mother a wide, untroubled smile.

'Nothing, Ma. Thank you.' She put her mug down. 'I am really fine. Really. Would you like some tea?'

'I'm such a softie,' Lucy Steele said, surveying the kitchen table at Barton Park, which was scattered with what appeared to be thousands of tiny fragments of pastel-coloured plastic. 'I said I'd mend it. Anna-Maria was in floods about it after her dad trod on it, and I told her mother I'd *mend* it, so . . .'

She paused. Elinor said nothing. It was a week since the lunch party at Barton Cottage, a week in which Elinor had had far too much time to doubt Edward once more, trust him again, hate Lucy, feel indifferent to Lucy, decide not to ring Edward, write him a text and then delete it, and then begin the whole cycle again in an endless, exhausting circle. So exhausting had it become, in fact, that Elinor had resolved to talk to Lucy once more, in order to try and discover a few more facts so that she could at best put some of her darker fears to rest, and at worst, know what she was actually confronting.

So here she was, in Barton Park's showpiece kitchen, contemplating the shattered pieces of Anna-Maria Middleton's Polly Pocket Princess Palace, a toy she never even played with, but which had become, after being accidentally trodden on by her absent-minded and substantial father, the most precious thing that she owned in the whole wide world.

'I don't know that you can do anything,' Mary Middleton had said, gathering up the broken pieces. 'Poor little sweetheart. She adored it so. I hate to have to tell her it's beyond repair.'

Lucy had knelt beside her, elaborately and equally concerned.

'I'm sure it isn't. I'm sure I can do something. I'm good with fiddly stuff. And Elinor's here. Elinor will help me.'

'And Marianne,' Mary Middleton said, pausing to put a hand-ful of plastic carefully into Lucy's outstretched palms.

Marianne, who had only been persuaded up to the Park with the assurance that it was for a polite cup of tea and no more, looked mutinous. She said, unhelpfully, 'I'm going to read.'

'Read!' Mary exclaimed. '*Read?* In *daylight?*' She got to her feet.

Marianne glanced at the ruined plastic palace. She moved towards the door.

'Well,' she said, 'I'm not wasting my time mending gimcrack rubbish.'

Mary gave a little gasp. She looked at Elinor as if the whole family were at fault.

'Your sister—'

'She's no good with her hands,' Elinor said hastily. 'Never has been.'

Mary looked frostily at Marianne's departing back.

'Good enough for the guitar, however!'

Elinor said, 'I'll help Lucy.'

'Oh, would you?'

Mary turned back to smile at them.

'That's so sweet of you both. And I've got people coming for bridge any minute. I really can't let them down.'

'Sorry,' Lucy said now, gazing at the table, 'but I'm hopeless when it comes to cute kids. I'm a complete pushover.'

Elinor began to pick up bits of plastic of similar colours.

'I don't mind.'

'Don't you? I've been thinking all week – can you believe we've been here a week! – that I'd upset you.'

Elinor gave her a steady glance.

'Upset me? By telling me a secret?'

'Well,' Lucy said, twisting her hair up again. 'That secret. That particular one, you know.'

Elinor picked up two pearlised pale green shards and turned them to fit together.

'I expect it was a relief.'

'A relief?'

'To tell someone. To tell someone else that you are engaged to a guy who can't move a muscle without asking his mother. Is this worth mending?'

Lucy said carefully, 'What are you saying?'

'That the Middletons can afford a hundred Polly Pocket Palace replacements.'

'No—'

'Well,' Elinor said, putting down the green pieces, 'you must be really mad about each other to have been together all this time, and still not have told his mother or made any real progress, mustn't you?'

There was a short silence. Lucy extracted a new tube of glue from the plastic bubble of its packaging and unscrewed the cap, with great attention.

Then she said, primly, 'I can't ask him to give everything up for me. I can't. She might disinherit him completely and it wouldn't be fair to ask him to watch Fanny and Robert get loads while he gets nothing, because of me.'

Elinor found a broken pink turret and examined it.

'Why does it have to be about family money? Why don't you earn some, you and him?'

Lucy sighed.

'You know why. He's such a sweetie, I adore him, but he's a

bit of a dreamer, isn't he? I don't think he knows what he wants to do, more's the pity.'

Elinor said nothing. She watched Lucy pick up some random shards of plastic and deftly glue them back together into a miniature drawbridge.

Then Lucy said, apparently intent on her mending, 'I know there's no one else, at least. Not for Ed. He's such a one-girl guy and I'd know the minute there was anyone else. I'm the jealous type, at the best of times, so I wouldn't give anyone else a second chance, I promise you that. The trouble is, you see, he's so dependent on me, he really is. I can't let him down by not going along with all this, but I'm really scared of what will happen when his mother finds out.'

'Perhaps,' Elinor said, thinking that this was what Margaret would say, 'she'll die?'

Lucy gave a little gasp, and then a giggle.

'Not much hope of that. She's only in her sixties.'

Elinor held her turret closer, as if examining it.

Lucy said, 'I don't even know your sister-in-law.'

'And I don't know Robert.'

Lucy smiled. She said, 'He is a complete idiot. I mean, loads of fun, but so shallow, all parties and tweeting. A million miles from Ed.'

Elinor said calmly, 'Why don't you just break off the engagement?'

Lucy put down the glue tube. She said, almost dangerously, 'Are you telling me to?'

'No,' Elinor said.

'Are you sure?'

'I couldn't tell you to do anything you didn't want to do

anyway. You wouldn't take any notice.'

'Then why', Lucy said, 'mention it?'

'You asked for advice. Unbiased advice. Last weekend.'

'Unbiased?'

'Yes.'

'Well, so you are,' Lucy said. 'You don't care one way or the other, of course you don't. Why should you?'

Elinor shrugged.

'Exactly.'

Lucy leaned forward. The ring on its chain swung out of the neck of her top, and she touched it lightly.

Elinor glanced at her own ringless hands. What instinct – what instinct on *earth* – had made her take it off again that morning and put it back in the lacquer bowl of paper clips? Lucy was smiling down at her own ring.

'I'll win Mrs Ferrars round,' she said. 'You'll see. When I go up to London.'

'Are you going to London?'

'Yes,' Lucy said. She let a beat fall and then she said, with a tiny but unmistakable note of triumph, 'To see Edward.'

'Are you awake?' Marianne whispered.

Elinor opened her eyes into the darkness of her bedroom, and shut them again.

'No.'

'Please, Ellie.'

Elinor moved slightly across her bed, towards the wall. She felt Marianne slip in beside her, and pull the duvet across.

'Ow! Horrible cold feet.'

'Ellie?'

'What?'

'Will you come to London with me?'

Elinor turned over on to her back.

'London! What are you talking about?'

'Today,' Marianne said, 'at the Park. While you were in the kitchen with Lucy. Mrs J. cornered me and said would we like to go and stay with her in London because she thought it was very boring for us stuck out here with nothing to do and no shopping.'

'Don't be daft.'

'What's daft about it?'

'Well,' Elinor said, 'for starters, you can't stand Mrs J.'

'I can.'

Elinor glanced sideways. Marianne's profile was clear, even in the dim room, outlined against the glow from Elinor's bedside radio.

'M, you tell everyone that she's ghastly. Tactless and noisy and uncultured.'

'Well,' Marianne said calmly, 'maybe I've been a bit mean. She's got a flat in Portman Square.'

Elinor waited a moment and then she said, 'Have you told Ma?'

'She's all for it.'

'She's all for you going up to London in the hopes of bump-ing into Wills?'

Marianne shifted a bit.

'Not so crudely.'

'But accurately,' Elinor said. 'Mrs J. and a flat off Oxford Street suddenly stop being vulgar and unbearable and become intensely desirable because Portman Square isn't a million miles from the King's Road?'

Marianne said, as if she'd thought about this with immense care, 'It would be much easier for him, if I took the initiative. He trusts me, like I trust him, and sometimes a really strong man like him is just longing for a helping hand.'

'Which you, with your vast experience of men, would know all about?'

Marianne turned on her side to face Elinor. She said, much more urgently, 'Ellie, I've got to. I am going mad here; it's like a kind of prison, a prison of boredom and nothingness. I've got to know what's happening to him.'

Elinor said, 'Have you looked on Facebook?'

'He hasn't been on it. He hasn't been on it since he left here. He hasn't even changed his status from "single".'

Elinor sighed.

'M, it's such a risk.'

'I don't mind risks. I like risks; at least risks are taking *action*.'

'And Ma—'

'She's all for it,' Marianne said again. 'She says I need to get away, I need something to do, to occupy my mind.'

Elinor turned to face her sister. She said, soberly, 'What would occupy your mind would be thinking about your future. Are you going to study music further, are you going to teach music, are you going to uni—'

'Ellie, I can't.'

'Of course you can!'

Marianne began to cry.

'Don't bully me, please don't bully me.'

'I'm not bullying, I'm just trying to make you see that your future happiness depends upon what you do for yourself and not on what some guy you hardly know—'

'Don't say that!'

'It's true.'

Marianne sniffed and rolled away from her sister again.

'It might be true for you,' she said, 'but it isn't true for me.'

Elinor sighed again.

'OK.'

'Ellie. Come with me.'

'Where to?'

'London.'

'M, I can't come to London! I've got a job!'

Marianne turned to stretch her arms up into the dimness and interlace her fingers. She said, 'Come at weekends, then.'

'But Ma—'

'Ma won't mind. She'd rather we were together.'

'I – might. Why are you talking about weekends, anyway? How long are you planning on going for?'

'As long as it takes.'

'As long as what takes?'

'As long', Marianne said, and her voice was full of hope, 'as it takes to find Wills. And talk to him.' She turned her head sideways and smiled. 'So I know where I am, with him and our future. And then I'll think about all the dull stuff you want me to think about.'

She lowered her arms and put the back of one hand against Elinor's cheek.

'Promise,' she said. 'I promise.'

10

'**N**onsense,' Mrs Jennings said, 'you've got time for a cup of coffee.'

Bill Brandon looked at his watch.

'Well, I—'

Mrs Jennings took his arm.

'We don't see you for weeks, dear, weeks, and then I just run into you like this, coming out of the Underground...' She paused and looked at him. 'Bond Street Underground, Central Line. Where have you been?'

Bill Brandon sighed, as if courtesy compelled him to give information he would have preferred to keep private. 'Mile End,' he said.

'Mile End? What on earth were you doing at Mile End?'

'Visiting the hospital,' Bill Brandon said patiently. 'The specialist addiction unit.'

'Ah!' Mrs Jennings cried, as if a penny had dropped. 'Ah! For your Delaford people!'

Bill Brandon gave a non-committal smile. He tried to extract his arm. He said, 'And now I've got to get back.'

'Where?'

'To Delaford.'

'But not before', Mrs Jennings said firmly, 'you've had a cup of coffee with me.' She leaned closer. 'I have a lot to tell you.'

He glanced down at her, as if seeing her for the first time.

'Oh?' he said.

She smiled and nodded.

'Yes, dear,' she said, 'I have. Guess who I've got staying with me?'

'I can't—'

She let his arm go at last, and then she said, in a tone that implied she knew she'd finally caught his full attention, 'Marianne!' she said.

Settled in Dolly's café in Selfridges, Mrs Jennings was very disappointed by Bill Brandon's choice of only a cup of black coffee.

'Have some carrot cake, dear,' she said. 'It isn't called heavenly for nothing. Or the walnut and coffee. Come on, Bill, you're too thin and too thin isn't good on a man, trust me.'

He closed his eyes, briefly.

'Just coffee, thank you.'

'But—'

'Just *coffee.*'

'Jonno would get you to eat cake.'

'Jonno isn't here.'

'Bill,' Mrs Jennings said, suddenly picking up a spoon to stir her large chocolate-dusted cappuccino, 'you're quite right. Let's get down to business. I have Marianne Dashwood moping in my spare bedroom and she's quite a worry to me.'

Bill said quietly, not looking at her, 'I heard she was in London.'

'From whom? Oh, Jonno, I suppose.'

'Yes.'

'Then why', Abigail Jennings demanded, putting her spoon down decisively, 'haven't you been to see us? You know you're always welcome, you know.'

'I've been a bit tied up.'

'With what?'

Bill Brandon glanced up at her. He smiled tiredly.

'None of your business, Abigail.'

'Delaford?'

'Maybe.'

'*Or* this mystery daughter of yours?'

Bill picked up his coffee cup.

'She doesn't exist.'

'Now then—'

'Abigail,' Bill Brandon said, 'can we get back to Marianne?'

'Aha! I knew you'd take my bait!'

'Well, I have,' he said patiently. 'And I want to know how she is.'

'Pathetic,' Mrs Jennings said, 'unhappy. Just – oh, Bill dear, you know, moody and miserable. I thought I'd take her shopping, to cheer her up, and so we headed for Bond Street – show me a girl on this *planet*, Bill, who isn't cheered up by Bond Street – and at first I thought she had actually perked up a little and then I realised – I think we were in Fenwick's – that she wasn't looking at the bags and the jewellery like any *normal* girl, she was just examining all the *people*, as if Wills might suddenly materialise out of a cosmetic counter. It was so sad, and absolutely exasperating at the same time. She found a missed call from him on her mobile the other day, and was wild to ring him back, and when she did, was told that the number had been cancelled. So he can't have rung her, it can't have been him, perhaps he isn't even in London—'

'He's in London,' Bill said shortly.

Mrs Jennings put down the cup she had just picked up, with a small bang.

'My dear! You don't *tell* me!'

Bill said slowly, 'John Willoughby is in London. He's in London because he has just done a deal. For him, a big deal.'

Mrs Jennings leaned forward. Her gaze was intensely focused.

'Bill—'

'There's no reason not to tell you,' Bill said. 'It's been in the press.'

'Not in *my* paper!'

Bill gave her a small grin.

'No, Abigail. Not in your paper. Property deals only interest your paper when they're shady. And this, as far as one can tell, isn't shady, just substantial. John Willoughby has brokered the sale of a very expensive flat in one of those new towers in Knightsbridge to a wealthy Greek getting some of his euro millions out of Athens.'

Abigail Jennings threw herself back in her chair.

'I am flabbergasted. I didn't think that boy knew how to put one business foot in front of another. What was the commission?'

Bill laughed.

'Dear Abigail, I have no idea.'

'Well, then – who is the Greek? Is he in shipping?'

Bill shrugged.

'He's a Greek, Mrs J., a Goulandris or a Chandris or a Niarchos: all the same to me. I know nothing about him except that he has bought a high-end flat through John Willoughby, which has kept the latter very firmly in London.'

Mrs Jennings looked suddenly sober. She said, 'But nowhere near Marianne.'

'Thank the Lord.'

'Bill dear, that's not how she sees it. He's a rogue.'

'I think', Bill Brandon said quietly, 'that he's worse than that.'

'And Marianne, poor dear, has got all the looks a girl could want, but no money.'

Bill Brandon said nothing. He finished his coffee and pushed the cup away. Then he said, 'How's her sister? How's Elinor?'

'Oh, my dear. So sensible. Really making something of that job you found her. I gather they're so pleased with her and of course, unlike the rest of her family, she has a proper work ethic. In fact, dear, she's coming up this weekend to see her sister. Frankly, I'm thankful. It's quite a strain trying to cheer Marianne up on my own. I'm sending them both to a wedding – Charlotte's old friend Suzy Martineau, remember? It should be fun. All the old crowd. I made Charlotte get them invited and as Jonno and Mary are coming up from Barton for it – Suzy was at school with my girls – there'll be plenty of people to look after them.'

She stopped and looked directly across the table, as if abruptly struck by something.

'Bill dear . . .'

He roused himself from whatever thoughts he had been plunged in. He said, affectionately, 'I'd be glad to see Elinor.'

'Bill,' Mrs Jennings said. '*Bill.* Has this Greek got a daughter?'

In the car going home from work and school Margaret wasn't speaking. She had climbed into the car – which she now required

Elinor to park round the corner so that none of her school friends would see her actually having to get into it – and immediately launched into a diatribe about how unfair it was that she had never had a ride in the Aston, as had been promised, and Elinor, strained from a week of worry about Marianne, tension about Lucy Steele and silence from Edward Ferrars, had snapped at her to say nothing more unless she could say something pleasant. So Margaret had goggled at her and shrugged and made her dissing 'whatever' hand gestures, and was now slumped beside her sister with her earphones in and a faint, maddening beat emanating from the iPod in her lap.

Elinor drove with fierce concentration. Marianne had not initiated a phone call or a text for days, and whenever Elinor rang her, sounded remote and inert or else worryingly wound up. Elinor had heard the story of the missed phone call a dozen times, as well as an endless litany of reasons why Wills wasn't in touch, followed by hysterical assertions of certainty that he would be. She knew that Marianne had walked the residential streets off the King's Road day after day, and although she had never seen the right Aston Martin parked by any kerb, was still insistent that one day she would, and that Wills would be there, with a perfect explanation, and that she, Marianne, would not only be restored to ecstasy, but also justified in her complete faith in his feelings for her being as hers were for him.

'How's Mrs J.?' Elinor said, keenly aware of the consequences of living with Marianne's intensity.

'Fine,' Marianne said carelessly. 'You know. Jolly and insensitive. Thinks all ills can be cured with chocolate. And parties.'

'Parties!'

'I go,' Marianne said, 'and I stand there with a glass in my hand. And then I go home again. The *inanity* of all those people is beyond anything.'

Elinor had said, during the last call, and unhappily, 'Oh, M, I do hope you are being at least a bit grateful—' and had immediately regretted it.

'Grateful?' Marianne had almost screamed. '*Grateful!* When she only has me here because she's obsessed with romantic gossip and I'm providing her with an on-going story? Would she even *have* me in London if both her daughters weren't already married?'

'M, I only meant out of politeness—'

'Politeness,' Marianne said witheringly. 'Politeness! It's all you care about, isn't it, manners and decorum and – and *respectability*. You wouldn't know real feeling, real passion if it hit you on the head with a hammer. You are so completely buttoned up, Ellie, that you can't even *begin* to understand someone like me who is *open*. About *everything*.'

Then she had ended the call, bang. Elinor texted her, to say sorry. Silence. There had been silence since, too, a silence as uneasy and troubled as the one now reigning between her and Margaret in the car.

Without looking sideways, Margaret suddenly took out her earphones and laid them in her lap. The beat from the iPod grew louder and Elinor was about to say, exasperatedly, 'Oh, turn that thing off!' when Margaret said, in quite a different tone to the one she had used earlier, 'Ellie . . .'

'What?'

Margaret glanced out of the window for a moment, and then she looked back at her lap. She said, almost inaudibly, 'Sorry.'

Elinor shot out her left hand and grasped her sister's nearest one.

'Mags. What for?'

Margaret sighed.

'Just – being a pain.'

'Well,' Elinor said warmly, 'you were promised.'

Margaret gripped Elinor's hand.

'I – kind of insisted I was. But he never said. Not really. Not in so many words.' She sighed again, and then she said, 'Is he really just a tosser?'

Elinor gave Margaret's hand a squeeze and let it go.

'Well, he's not behaving very well to Marianne.'

'Is – is she overdoing it a bit?'

Elinor hesitated.

'Not according to how she sees things, Mags.'

They turned in through the gates to Barton Park's drive, Elinor's headlights picking up ghostly tree trunks. Margaret spun the dial on her iPod to silence it. Then she said, 'Do we *have* to have boyfriends?'

'Who?'

'Us. Us girls.'

Elinor said, half laughing, 'Of course we don't *have* to. But we seem to want to, to need to, don't we?'

'But we don't need to make them our whole *world*, do we, like Marianne?'

'Not', Elinor said carefully, 'if it doesn't suit us to.'

She pulled the car up on the gravel in front of the cottage. Belle had all the lights on, as usual, and although it made the house look wonderfully welcoming, Elinor could not help thinking anxiously about the consequent electricity bill. Which she, as usual, would have to deal with.

She turned off the engine. Margaret gathered up her iPod and earphone cables and hauled her school bag from the floor into her arms. She nudged the car door open. She said, 'Sorry again, Ellie.'

'Thank you, Mags, but there's nothing to be sorry for. Really.'

Margaret got out clumsily, trailing cables, and Elinor was about to follow her, when her phone rang. She called after Margaret, 'I'll just take this.'

She looked at her screen. Not a number she recognised. She put the phone to her ear.

'Hello?' she said cautiously.

'It's Bill Brandon.'

She smiled broadly into the darkness beyond her windscreen.

'Bill!'

'Am I interrupting?'

'No, no, not at all. How *are* you?'

'I'm fine. Fine. But it's Marianne—'

'Oh my God,' Elinor said, sitting up straighter. 'What's happened?'

'Nothing,' Bill said. 'That's the trouble.'

'No word still?'

'No. I saw Mrs J.'

'I'm coming up to London.'

'I know. That's why I'm ringing. How are you getting to London?'

'Oh, Bill,' Elinor said, 'how do you think? National Express bus from Exeter.'

'Are you sure?'

'Very sure.'

'I'll meet you. I'll meet you at Victoria Station.'

She said, smiling, 'You don't have to.'

'I'd like to.'

'Bill,' Elinor said gently, 'she still thinks the sun rises and sets with him.'

'I know.'

'It isn't a question of merit . . .'

'There isn't', Bill Brandon said, 'a man less deserving of your sister on this *earth* than John Willoughby.'

Elinor was silent. Belle appeared in the lit doorway of Barton Cottage and began to gesticulate to her daughter to come in.

'Bill,' Elinor said, 'I've got to go. I'll see you Friday. I'll ring you en route. I'll put your number in my phone, if that's OK. Thank you.'

She dropped her phone into her bag and climbed out of the car.

'Who were you talking to?' Belle called from the doorway. 'Was it Ed?'

Elinor locked the car doors and then turned towards her mother.

'No,' she said flatly. 'It wasn't.'

Marianne would not wash her hair before going to the wedding. Nor would she even look at the cream silk dress Mrs Jennings produced from Charlotte's old wardrobe and which, Elinor could see at a glance, was probably the best-cut, best-made garment either of them had ever been offered. Instead, Marianne pulled on – crossly – her old gypsy skirt and piled her hair randomly on top of her head, and added her usual hoop earrings and looked – well, Elinor had to admit it – sulky but wonderful.

'You could put that girl in a bin liner,' Mrs Jennings said, 'and she'd still eclipse every other female in the room. Maddening.'

In the taxi on the way to the church, for the wedding, Marianne sat staring mutely out of the window, her phone gripped, as usual, in one hand. The taxi went via Conduit Street, to collect the Middletons from their flat, and even with Jonno in the cab – resplendent in a gold brocade waistcoat from Favourbrook's under his black morning coat – Marianne seemed entirely indifferent to the occasion and to the company.

Mary Middleton made an elaborate face at Elinor, nodding in Marianne's direction. Elinor merely shook her head. Marianne said clearly, without turning from the window, 'I'm not *ill*. Or *deaf*.'

Sir John looked at Elinor. He winked.

'She's a party in herself, don't you think?'

In the church in Chelsea, Marianne did not even bother to look about her. Both Dashwood girls had been squeezed into the same pew as the Middletons and the Palmers – Charlotte in a hat whose immensity almost extinguished her – and Elinor could not help noticing that they were the only two bare-headed women in the congregation. The service was conducted by a camp and sophisticated priest who managed to imbue the whole occasion with irony, and then it was out into the winter dusk and a further taxi ride, back to the Cavalry and Guards Club, where Elinor and Marianne found themselves propelled up an immense staircase, past a spectacular cup awarded, said the attached brass label, for valour in pig-sticking, and into a roaring room full of people clutching glasses of champagne and kissing each other round their hats.

'Oh Christ,' Elinor said to Marianne, in dismay.

Tommy Palmer appeared beside them.

'Shed the old bag, have you?' he shouted above the din.

They stared at him.

'Nice to see you!' he shouted. He waved his champagne glass. 'Thought you'd got stuck in Devon!'

'No, we—'

He waved his glass again.

'Good-oh!' he shouted and vanished into the crowd.

Marianne looked after him. Then she glanced down into her drink. She said conversationally to Elinor, 'Shall we get drunk?'

Elinor was looking past her, her gaze following Tommy Palmer's back into the crowd ahead of them. Just past the point he had now got to, about ten feet away, was someone unmistakeable, someone she had not perceived in church, someone with his arm around the shoulders of a tall and handsome girl, her loudly blonde hair piled on top of her head in an elaborate arrangement. And as she realised who she was looking at, Wills turned his head and looked full at her, and then at Marianne – and turned back, quite deliberately, to talk to the girl within his arm.

Elinor spun round to Marianne, her heart leaping with a sudden prayer that Marianne had not yet seen him. But she was, in that instant, already too late. Marianne, her face instantly illuminated with relief and joy, had thrust her champagne glass into her sister's hand, and was plunging through the crowd, crying out Wills's name as if he could not possibly be anything other than enraptured to see her.

But he wasn't. She reached him in seconds, the crowd falling away around her violent passage in amazement and, in complete disregard of the girl he held against him, flung her arms around his neck and held her shining face up to his, completely and utterly certain of her welcome.

'Wills,' she was saying. 'Oh Wills, at last, at last, I *knew* we'd find each other again!'

He did not move. His expression, staring down at Marianne, was wooden. The girl beside him tried to disengage herself, but he clamped her closer. Then he bent, very slightly, towards Marianne and hissed at her, 'Get *off* me.'

There was a gasp from everyone around them, so loud that it obscured Marianne's own cries. Elinor saw, to her horror, that Marianne was trying to cling to Wills, that she had manoeuvred her hands further round his neck and that she was trying to say something urgently, her face close to his. A man standing next to them laid a restraining hand on Marianne's shoulder, and Elinor, thrusting both glasses in her hands at a conveniently passing waiter, found herself pushing forward, battling to get to her sister, before any of the guests attempted physically to defuse the situation themselves.

She took Marianne's nearest arm and tried to prise it from Wills's neck.

'M, M, *please...*'

'Thank God,' Wills said, seeing her, his voice strangled by Marianne's grip. 'Someone with some sense. Please, Ellie, get her off me.'

'Marianne,' Elinor said loudly in her sister's ear, 'let him go. Drop your arms. Let him go.'

'You should call a doctor,' the blonde girl said. Her voice was richly, exotically foreign. 'She needs help. She is a crazy person.'

'You didn't answer my calls!' Marianne shrieked. 'You didn't text me! I've heard nothing, nothing, for weeks!'

Elinor had by now got her hands on both Marianne's arms. 'Let him go now.'

'Please,' Wills said, 'just get her away from me.'

'And fetch a doctor,' the blonde girl said again. 'This is crazy.'

Tommy Palmer was suddenly beside them again, both hands empty. He gave Elinor a quick pat.

'Let me.'

'But—'

'No,' he said. His voice was quite steady. 'No. Leave her to me.'

Elinor let her hands slip from Marianne's shoulders. Tommy Palmer took hold of Marianne's arms, gently and inexorably pulled them from around Wills's neck. Then, his own arms still round her, he turned her and guided her steadily through the crowd, out on to the landing by the great staircase, and to a group of empty chairs. Elinor, dazed and horrified, followed them.

'There,' Tommy Palmer said. He pushed Marianne down into one of the chairs. She was sobbing and shaking, her hair in a tangle over her face and shoulders. 'I'll get you some water.'

'Get *him*,' Marianne wept. 'Get him to come to me, get him to come and tell me what's going on . . .'

Elinor threw Tommy a grateful glance. She sank into the chair next to Marianne's and took her nearest hand.

'We can't do that, M. We can't make him come.'

'Why was he like that? Why was he so horrible? Why did he behave as if he didn't know me?'

'I don't know, babe. I don't know any more than you do.'

Marianne took her hand back and put both over her face, beginning to rock backwards and forwards. Her breath was coming in little gasps. Elinor leaned closer.

'M, have you got your inhaler?'

Marianne took no notice but went on rocking and sobbing. Elinor put a helpless hand on her back and, raising her eyes above her sister's heaving shoulders, saw Wills and the blonde girl coming hastily out of the reception room, hand in hand, and then begin to race down the staircase, him tugging her behind him as fast as her towering heels would allow. Elinor bent towards Marianne. She said urgently, 'He's gone.'

Marianne's head flew up. She said hoarsely, 'What?'

'He's gone. Wills has just gone. With—' She stopped.

Marianne looked wildly at Elinor.

'Who was *she*?'

'M, I don't know—'

'But he had his *arm* round her! Who *was* she?'

'Here,' Tommy Palmer said. He was holding out a tumbler of water. 'Drink this, and I'll get you a taxi.'

'Thank you,' Elinor said.

Marianne leaped to her feet and rushed towards the staircase. Tommy, in a flash, was beside her and in front of her. He held out his arms to stop her flying down the stairs.

She glared at him.

'Who', she screamed again, '*was* she?'

Late that night, after the doctor had gone, and the fear of having to admit Marianne to hospital had abated, Elinor went quietly into Mrs Jennings's kitchen to make tea. The doctor had given Marianne a thorough check and a sleeping pill, and it was the first moment since the awful events of the afternoon that Elinor had been free to collect her breath and her thoughts.

The episode in the Cavalry Club had only been the beginning. It had been followed by a terrible taxi journey back to Mrs

Jennings's flat with Marianne alternately ranting and gasping, followed by an ill-timed and unintentionally tactless call from Belle asking cheerfully if they had seen Wills at the wedding – 'Mrs J. was sure he'd be there!' – and then a full-blown asthma attack which initially looked as if it would end nowhere but in hospital. But Mrs Jennings, entirely practical in an emergency, tracked down her own doctor peacefully choosing a new sofa on a Saturday afternoon, with his wife, in Tottenham Court Road, and had him at Marianne's side within half an hour. He had closed the spare bedroom door firmly, on both Elinor and Mrs Jennings.

'P and q are what we need in here, thank you both very much.'

They had fidgeted about in Mrs Jennings's over-stuffed sitting room.

'You poor dear,' Abigail had said to Elinor. 'It always comes back to you, doesn't it? The price of having your head screwed on the right way.'

Elinor was standing by the window, swinging the wooden acorn at the end of a blind cord against the glass. She said tensely, 'As long as she's OK.'

'She'll be fine, dear. Gordon's so experienced. He's been in practice for over forty years, I should think. Long enough, anyway, to have seen hundreds of asthma attacks.' She looked across the room at Elinor. 'I was so hoping it wasn't true. I just kept telling myself that the moment he saw her again, he'd remember what he felt for her in Devon. He'd realise that there's no substitute for true love, however big your bills.'

Elinor turned round. She said sharply,

'What d'you mean?'

Mrs Jennings spread her hands. She was sitting balanced on the edge of one of her huge sofas, as if she couldn't quite settle to sitting properly. She said, 'Wills.'

'What about Wills?'

'That girl, dear. The Greek girl.'

Elinor came away from the window. She said loudly, 'Tall? Blonde?'

'Dyed blonde,' Abigail Jennings said. She looked at the carpet. 'Rich as Croesus. Aglaia Callianos. Aglaia means splendid or beautiful or something, in Greek. Their family comes from Cephalonia. Shipping.'

Elinor shouted, 'I don't care where they come from.'

Abigail gave a little jump.

'Don't shout, dear. It's not my fault he's followed the money.'

'*What?*'

'He brokered a deal about a flat. Her father. That girl's father. Wills met that girl when he managed to get her father to buy this wildly expensive flat. There's talk of it costing over a hundred million, would you believe.'

Elinor sat down hard next to Mrs Jennings. She said, 'You're telling me that Wills has dumped Marianne for the daughter of a rich Greek he hardly knows?'

Mrs Jennings sighed gustily.

'Yes, dear.'

'I can't *believe* it.'

Mrs Jennings looked at her.

'That's life, dear. That's men.'

'Not *all* men!'

'Well, men like John Willoughby with fancy tastes.'

'But he's going to inherit money from Jane Smith at Allenham.'

'I don't think so, dear.'

'But—'

'He's upset her. I don't know the details, but Mary tells me that she's very angry, and it takes a lot to make Jane Smith angry, especially when it comes to that boy.'

Elinor said, in a whisper, 'Poor, poor Marianne.'

'I know, dear.'

'I want to *kill* him.'

'You won't be the first, dear.'

'He just led her on ...'

'Typical, I'm afraid.'

Elinor stood up, abruptly.

'I'll have to tell Ma.'

'Leave it till the morning, dear.'

'No, I ought—'

'Leave it, dear,' Abigail said firmly. 'Leave it till you're all calmer. Leave it till tomorrow.'

Elinor closed her eyes briefly. She said, 'I saw all her texts. I saw all her messages to him. It was heartbreaking; she never doubted him, she never—' She broke off and gave something like a sob.

Mrs Jennings got up and put an arm round her.

'I know, dear. It's all wrong. He's all wrong. It's a bad, bad business. That Callianos girl has her car shipped into London for the winters, I'm told. A Porsche, with her own number plates. No change out of twenty grand for that sort of nonsense.'

The door opened. Mrs Jennings's doctor, in his weekend cords and urban waxed jacket, leaned into the room.

'All quiet,' he said, smiling. 'Good as gold. Fast asleep and breathing like a baby. I'll be back in the morning to check on her and you're to ring me any time if you're worried.'

* * *

And now, Elinor thought, filling the kettle as quietly as she could, in Mrs Jennings's kitchen, I would like to think that sleep is possible for me, too. I would like to think that when I lie down, after this unspeakable day, I won't be so filled with fury at Wills and despair for Marianne that I just lie there and toss and turn and fret and rage and *worry*. What will she be like when she wakes up? What can I say to her? How do I tell her that that vile, *vile* complete *shit* of a man has thrown her over for money? You couldn't make it up. You couldn't. Not in this day and age. I have never wanted just to *eliminate* anyone before but I do him. And I want him to *suffer* while I do it. I want him—In her cardigan pocket – her father's reassuringly familiar old cardigan – her phone began to vibrate. It would be Belle, from Barton, still in ignorance of Wills's terrible conduct; and needing to be told, as calmly as Elinor could, what had happened, not just today, but to all Marianne's most passionate hopes and desires for the future. She pulled her phone out and looked at the screen. 'Bill Brandon', it said. Elinor felt a sudden rush of pure relief that she couldn't at all account for. She said, thankfully, into her phone, 'Oh, Bill . . .'

'Are you all right? You sound—'

'I'm fine, I'm fine. And so is she, so is Marianne, now. I mean, she's OK. It's OK.'

'Elinor,' Bill said, his voice suddenly alarmed, 'what's happened? I was ringing to see how the wedding went, whether—'

'I can't tell you over the phone.'

'Why not, what's—'

'It's all right now,' Elinor said. 'It really is. She's fine. She's sleeping. But I wonder . . .'

'What?' he said. His voice was sharp with anxiety. 'What?'

She swallowed. She could feel more tears thickening in her throat. She said, 'Can – can you come?'

'What, now?'

'Yes.'

'Dear girl, I'm down at Delaford. But of course, if it's really urgent—'

'No. No, of course not. Not now. Just – just soon, Bill. Please. I'll be in London for a few days.'

'I'll come tomorrow. Are you sure she's—'

'Yes,' Elinor said, tears now sliding down her face. 'Yes. She's fine. Thank you. Thank you. See you tomorrow.'

11

'You wouldn't *believe*,' Charlotte Palmer said, 'but it's all over YouTube already! Someone must have been filming, on their phone, at the wedding. Aren't people just the *end?*'

She was standing in her mother's sitting room, as round as a robin, her mobile in her hand.

'I mean, I wasn't going to look at it, I really wasn't, even though absolutely *everybody* was sending me the link, but then I thought, Well, I can't defend poor Marianne if I don't know what I'm defending, can I?' She glanced at Elinor. 'Have you seen it?'

'No,' Elinor said. 'And I don't want to.'

'It really isn't too bad,' Charlotte said. 'I mean Marianne looks really pretty even if she is crying and you can't see Wills's face that well—'

Elinor put her hands over her ears.

'Please stop.'

Charlotte gave a little shrug. She said, 'Of course, everyone's siding with Marianne. I mean, they're all sick of girls like Aggy Cally just *buying* up our hottest men like this.'

'Charlotte dear,' her mother said, not raising her eyes from her Sunday newspaper, 'enough, don't you think? However riveting?'

Charlotte looked intently at her phone, as if deaf to any implied reprimand. She said brightly, 'Tommy was a bit of a star, wasn't he? I just adore it when he gets all masterful like that and strides about knowing what to do!'

Elinor said faintly, 'He was great.'

'God,' Charlotte said, stabbing at the keys on her phone, 'he *loved* it. He thinks you are just *fantastic*. He adores brainy girls even if he couldn't be married to one for a minute. Hey, Mummy?'

'Yes,' Mrs Jennings said, still not looking up.

'Did you say Bill was coming?'

Mrs Jennings raised her head and looked knowingly at Elinor. 'So I gather.'

Charlotte beamed at Elinor.

'So adorable. He's got a sporting chance now Wills is out of the picture.'

'She's very frail,' Elinor said. 'And broken-hearted. Completely.'

'Fabby Delaford,' Charlotte said to her mother. 'I know it's full of all Bill's crazies, but he's got that separate house that could be *so* gorgeous if it was done up, and of course the landscape's divine.'

'And', Mrs Jennings said, taking her reading glasses off, 'he has money and he's sensible with it. He's the only ex-soldier I've ever known who has a cool head about money.' She looked directly at Elinor. 'He's doing the usual idiot man thing round your sister, of course he is, they all seem to need to, but he's clearly got a very soft spot for *you*.'

Elinor felt herself glow unwillingly pink. She said irritably, 'He's just nice to me.'

'Nicer, dear,' Abigail Jennings said, 'than that useless Ferrars boy of yours is.'

'He's not useless.'

'No?'

Elinor said, more indignantly than she intended, 'He may be a bit weak but he isn't cruel, like Wills. He isn't selfish and – and *venal...*'

Charlotte and her mother rolled their eyes at one another.

'Oooh!'

Elinor said more calmly, 'And he's not *mine*! He's nobody's. He's his own person. Like – like Bill is. And – and I am.'

Charlotte moved sideways and poked Elinor in the ribs.

'Every cloud has a silver lining, Ellie!'

'Oh, my dear,' Mrs Jennings said, laughing, 'almost *platinum*, in his case!'

'Please,' Elinor said, in sudden, real distress. '*Please.* Marianne's *ill.*'

'But she'll get better. Of course she will! A bit more sleep, Gordon said, and a quiet life—'

The bell from the street door storeys below rang loudly. Without reference to her mother, Charlotte ran to the intercom on the wall and snatched up the receiver. She said excitedly into it, 'Bill? Bill! We're expecting you! Kettle on! Come on up, top floor, welcome mat out!' She put the handset back in its cradle and turned to face the room again. 'D'you suppose', she said, 'anyone at Delaford showed him the YouTube clip?'

* * *

'I had to get you out of there,' Bill Brandon said. 'You looked as if you were about to commit murder.'

Elinor looked across the cold, sunny spaces of Hyde Park. She hunched her shoulders inside Mrs Jennings's borrowed fur-collared padded jacket. She said, 'Mrs J. has been so wonderful, really, so supportive and generous. But she has a complete tin ear for anything sensitive. And Charlotte has two.'

Bill said, slightly self-consciously, 'Marianne looked so lovely, didn't she, lying there asleep.'

'I'm so thankful she's asleep.'

'Was – was she desperately upset?'

Elinor put her hands in the pockets of her jacket.

'She woke at three. And cried till five. It's coming to terms with what he really is that's going to be so hard. If she could believe him to be basically decent, it would be different, but there is nothing to be said for him, *nothing*. And she's got to face the fact that she fell utterly for someone like that.'

Bill let a small silence fall and then he said, 'It's the "utterly" quality in her that I can't resist.'

Elinor darted a quick look at him.

'I know. It's always been like that with her. Absolutely all or absolutely nothing. And you risk humiliating yourself if you're like that.'

Bill paused by a bench at the edge of the path they were following. He said, 'Will you freeze if we sit down?'

Elinor indicated her jacket.

'Not in my Mrs Jennings insulation.'

He waited courteously for her to sit first. He had driven from Somerset that morning and he looked as clean and organised as if he had started the day ten minutes ago. Elinor said, 'You're so nice to come.'

He sat down beside her and put his elbows on his knees. He said, 'I wanted to. I had to. The very thought—'

'Better sooner than later, maybe,' Elinor said. She looked down at the toes of her boots. 'I mean, with hindsight you could see this disaster coming, you could see it had hopeless written all over it, but Marianne was so sure, so sure . . .'

'Elinor.'

'Yes?'

'I've got something to tell you.' He half turned and looked at her. 'Not a nice story. But you need to know. You need to know she's well out of it.'

Elinor stared at him.

'What?'

Bill looked away from her again, across the cold, bleached winter grass.

'I don't know where to start.'

'At the beginning?'

There was a silence, and then Bill said, 'His father knew my father. And Jonno's.'

Elinor let another small pause elapse, and then she said, 'Is that the beginning?'

'No,' he said. 'No. Sorry. The beginning was – was a girl.'

'Yes.'

He linked his hands and stared on, into the distance.

'A sort of cousin. My father had a soft spot for her mother, I suspect, and when her mother died of cancer, very young, Eliza came to live with us.'

'Us?' Elinor said.

'My family. My parents and my brother, and me. She grew up

with us. She was fair, not dark, but ... but she was so like Marianne. Just – just the same eagerness and passion and energy. Just the same – carelessness about what people thought.'

Elinor waited.

Bill said slowly, 'We – we all adored her. Me especially. I'm afraid my brother just adored being adored. And he was such a daredevil and she was sort of mesmerised by him. She really liked me, trusted me, maybe loved me, even, but my brother was such an exciting challenge. To do her justice, my mother never thought they should marry, but my father was all for it. Thought it would tame him and that her money would mend Delaford. I was a basket case on their wedding day. Thank God for the army, frankly; it gave me somewhere to go, something to do. I didn't actually want to be in touch after they were married, but our parents both dying soon after – they were heavy smokers, the pair of them – meant that I couldn't avoid knowing that the marriage was catastrophic from the get-go, and then, of course, she left him.'

He stopped and looked down at the path between his feet. Elinor said awkwardly, 'Did – did you ...' And couldn't finish her sentence.

He sat up straighter and put one arm along the back of the seat behind her.

'I didn't go and find her, if that's what you mean. I should have, and I didn't. I was so involved in what to do about Delaford, which was now my brother's, and he was pretty well an alcoholic by then.'

'Was?'

'He was killed,' Bill said, 'in a car crash. In fog. About four times over the limit. That's why I've got Delaford.'

Elinor glanced at him. It came to her that Bill Brandon, sitting beside her in the cold, bright winter sunshine, looked very much more satisfactory as older-brother material than John Dashwood. She said gently, 'And then?'

'And then,' Bill said, 'after George's death, I went to look for Eliza.'

'And?'

He sighed.

'It was hideous. I can't tell you. She'd run through her money, gone from man to man, had a baby by her first dealer—'

'Dealer?' Elinor exclaimed in horror.

'Oh yes,' Bill said. 'I found her at last in a crack house, in east Birmingham. The baby – well, she wasn't a baby any more, she was three – was in care. Eliza was, literally, a wreck.'

Elinor said nothing. She slid one hand out of her pocket and touched Bill's arm. He gave her a faint smile. He said, 'I'm afraid that's not the end. Can you stand any more?'

She nodded.

He gripped her hand for a second with his free one, and let it go. He said, 'I got her into hospital, before she died. It was days only. Her heart just gave out. Years of chaos, of rackety living. And then I spent the best part of the next three years persuading social services to let me at least educate little Eliza, even if she had to live with a foster family because I was deemed some unfit old pervert for even suggesting bringing her up myself.' He gave a short, wry bark of laughter. 'I came out of the Army about then, and set up Delaford. As a kind of memorial to Eliza, if you like. I never thought—' He broke off.

'What?'

'I never thought it would serve for little Eliza, too.'

Elinor gasped. Bill leaned a little towards her.

'Sorry about this part. Really sorry. But you have to know.'

'OK,' she said.

'Little Eliza knew how and why her mother had died. She had lovely foster parents and we made a real effort that she should be under no illusions about addictions. Christ, Elinor, I even took her to the street where I'd found her mother, and even though the house wasn't a crack den any more, it wasn't fit for dogs to live in. And she was fine. Really fine. For years. Even with her mother's temperament and sense of adventure, she was OK. I *know* it. And then she fell for someone. She met him at a club, a club in South Kensington. And he gave her her first hit. And, Elinor, you – you know him.'

Elinor felt her mouth dry, suddenly and completely, as if her tongue were being glued to the roof of her mouth. She said, hoarsely, 'Wills?'

Bill Brandon sighed again.

'He knew about her, because of our Somerset and Devon connections, because of all the awful stories swirling round my family. I couldn't truthfully say he set out to corrupt her, but I would guess he thought he might have a bit of fun. Like mother, like daughter. Party girls. Up for anything. The last few years have been a repeat nightmare of what happened to Eliza. One crisis after another.'

He looked directly at Elinor.

'That's why I had to dash off, that day at Barton. The police had smashed down a lavatory door in a pub in Camden the night before, because little Eliza was inside, injecting into her feet.'

Elinor gave a small cry and put both hands over her mouth.

'I'm so sorry,' Bill said, 'I really am. The details are so horrible, and for poor little Eliza too. She'd had an abortion, you see, and I think it drove her back on to the hard stuff. I wish you didn't need to know. But you can see . . .'

Elinor nodded vehemently, unable to speak.

'Your sister,' Bill said, 'your sweet, impulsive, whole-hearted sister – I couldn't bear to see another girl sacrificed just because she wasn't worldly wise. I didn't want to rain on anyone's parade but I just could not stand to see that bastard making your sister believe he was worth a minute of her time. I thought, when I first saw them at Barton together, that he *might* be redeemable, with someone like her, but then all the Eliza business blew up, and I heard about the Callianos girl and I thought, No, sorry, same dangerous old Wills, and that you should know.' He paused and then he said, in a lower voice, 'I've been such a failure in looking out for either of them. Haven't I?'

Elinor took her hands away from her mouth and regarded him. She looked grave, but no longer horrified. He tried to smile at her. He said, 'So you see why I'm such a . . . such a sad old stick.'

She shook her head, and then she leaned forward and kissed him on the cheek.

'You are *so* not,' she said. 'You are a lovely, principled man.'

'You can look if you like,' Marianne said. She was lying on her side in bed, in her plaid and rosebud pyjamas, facing away from her sister. At the end of the bed, balanced against the foot-board, was a stiff green department-store carrier bag. 'It's got everything I ever gave him in it,' she said. 'CDs and books and stuff. And a photo in a frame. And his ring.'

Elinor picked up the carrier bag and peered inside. The contents were in a jumble.

'Oh, M.'

'The ring is inside a plastic bag,' Marianne said, not turning. 'Just an old plastic ziplock thing, the kind you put sandwiches in. Just – dumped in there.'

Elinor put the bag down again. She said, 'Was there a note?'

'No.'

'Nothing?'

'Nothing,' Marianne said. 'It was delivered on a bike. There was a boy on a bike who needed a signature from Mrs J. The bag didn't even have a handwritten name and address on it. It was a typed label.'

Elinor sat down on the side of the bed. She put her hand on Marianne's hip.

'Where's *your* ring?'

Marianne fumbled inside her pyjama jacket.

'Here.'

'Wouldn't you like to take it off? Especially now you know what Bill Brandon told me, and this bag has come?'

Slowly Marianne turned on to her back and sat up. There were violet smudges under her eyes, but she was breathing normally, and her skin, though pale, was no longer grey-white with lack of oxygen. She put her hands up into her hair, behind her neck.

'I can't undo it.'

Elinor bent forward, arms outstretched.

'M, did you take in what I told you about Wills, and Bill's ward?'

'Yes,' Marianne said. 'I'll be glad to get this off.'

Elinor found the ring bolt on the chain and released it. She held it up.

'In the bag?'

'In the bin,' Marianne said. 'With everything else. Put it all in the bin.'

Elinor dropped the ring and the chain into the carrier bag, and then put the bag on the floor. She said, 'Have you told Ma?'

Marianne looked away.

'She was on the phone almost all the time you were out. She says I shouldn't go home. She thinks that if I'm at home I'll only start remembering, that I'll be reminded all the time—' She broke off and said, in a whisper, 'Ellie, how could he?'

'How could he behave to you as he has?'

Marianne shook her head slowly.

'How could he do what he's done – to everyone? How *could* he?'

'M, I don't know.'

Marianne slid down in the bed again.

'Ellie, you've been so great. But I can't talk about it. I can't. I don't know what I'm going to do, but I can't think or speak just now, I can't.'

'No, no...'

'Are you staying?'

'I've got to go back to work.'

'Will you come back next weekend?'

'Marianne, you can't just stay in bed, in Mrs J.'s spare room.'

Marianne turned away once more.

'I may have to. What's that?'

'What's what?'

'That noise.'

'Oh, somebody coming to see Mrs J., or something. M, Bill was so lovely, telling me, so *straight*.'

'He is straight,' Marianne said. 'He's not the one who gives men a bad name.'

The noise from down the corridor beyond the closed bedroom door was growing louder. Marianne said, 'You'd better go.'

'Will you be OK?'

'Yes. Yes. Just get that bag out of the room, would you? And could you ring Ma again for me? Poor Ma. You'd think it had all happened to her.'

Elinor bent and kissed her sister's cheek. Marianne's hand came up and held Elinor's hair, compelling her to stay close.

'Thank you,' Marianne whispered. 'Thank you.'

'Surprise!' Mrs Jennings cried as Elinor came into the room. She made an extravagant and theatrical gesture, flapping the scarf she was wearing round her shoulders for emphasis.

Lucy and Nancy Steele were side by side on the sofa, holding cups of tea. Nancy, impeded by being on a very low sofa while wearing very high heels, made no attempt to get up, but Lucy sprang to her feet and rushed at Elinor as if they were bosom friends whom fate had recently cruelly prevented from seeing one another. Carefully holding her teacup away from her body with her left hand, Lucy put her right arm entirely round Elinor and pressed her cheek to the side of Elinor's head.

'Ellie.'

'Hello.'

'God, I'm so thankful to see you. I thought you'd never make it to London, what with work and everything, I thought it was useless, hoping I'd see you!'

Elinor extricated herself.

'I'm – just here for the weekend.'

'And *these* girls', Mrs Jennings said, 'came up to London in some style, isn't that right?'

'Totes amaze,' Nancy Steele said, tossing her hair. 'Couldn't *believe* it! He just said, Look, two seats in the plane going begging! Hilar!'

Mrs Jennings nodded, knowingly.

'*So* useful to have a top-flight plastic surgeon in hot pursuit—'

'Oh, not *pursuit*,' Nancy said, tossing her hair again. 'I mean, the plane makes all my girlfriends wel jeal, but not the paunch, *please!*' She threw her head back and gave a little scream.

'Sorry,' Lucy said *sotto voce* to Elinor. She looked round. 'Where's Marianne?'

'Not well, I'm afraid.'

Lucy made a face of intense sympathy. She put her teacup down.

'Oh, the poor love. It's so utterly ghastly, being trolled online like that.'

Elinor moved a few steps away. Lucy said, 'I mean, she's so well out of it and he's just so blatant, isn't he? God, it's been such a day, hasn't it? First all that horrible, tacky *rubbish* about your sister on YouTube, and then all the stuff about Robert Ferrars—'

'She doesn't know, dear,' Mrs Jennings said, rustling across the room with her Sunday paper in her hands. 'She's been so caught up with poor Marianne that she won't have seen this.' She thrust a double-page spread under Elinor's nose. 'Look at this, dear. The original party boy. He couldn't be less like his gloomy brother if he tried!'

'And of course,' Lucy said, moving to stand very close to Elinor once more, '*that's* all over the social media too. But in a good way. Or at least that's what Robert will think!'

Elinor gazed at the newspaper held out to her. Under the headline *King Robert – Britain's Party Royalty* was an enormous picture of a good-looking, slightly feminine young man in a tight-fitting grey shirt and trousers, with a fur coat slung over his shoulders, a large silver cross on a chain round his neck, and his arms around two identical girls in cocktail dresses.

'Read on!' Mrs Jennings commanded.

Elinor said weakly, 'I'm not sure I need to ...'

'One hundred parties in the last year!' Mrs Jennings said. 'Incredible. That's one party every three nights that wouldn't have happened without him!'

'Too silly,' Lucy said, looking straight at Elinor. 'Brainless. My poor Ed must be *cringing*.'

'Amaze,' Nancy said from the sofa. 'Amazeballs.'

Elinor took a step back.

'Well, I suppose it's good to be good at something.'

'Only if it's worthwhile,' Lucy said. 'Or genuine. Like *poor* Marianne.'

'She's much better ...'

'Can we see her?'

'Well, I think she's still fairly—'

'Of *course*,' Lucy said earnestly. 'Oh, of *course*. I was just going to sit on her bed and have a bit of a girly chat but if you think ...'

'I do,' Elinor said. 'And' – glancing at her watch – 'I've got to get the bus, a bus back to Exeter.'

From the sofa, Nancy Steele erupted into giggles.

'A bus!'

'Good news, dear,' Mrs Jennings said, folding up her paper. 'Your brother rang, asking how Marianne was. Of course, your sister-in-law had seen everything on this YouTube thing, everything. Never mind her little brother in the papers! How do you have a private life these days, I *ask* you! But your brother John said he and Fanny happened to be in London for something or other, and he wanted to do something to help, so I said he could come and take you to the bus tonight and have a chat.' She beamed at Elinor. 'Wasn't that sweet?'

'My goodness,' John Dashwood said, the moment he had Elinor in the car, 'you *have* made a useful friend there!'

Elinor, busy with her seat belt, affected not to understand.

'Abigail Jennings,' John said. 'She clearly has a lot of time for you and Marianne, and that's quite a flat, isn't it! Penthouse in Portman Square? Not much change out of five or six, I'd say. And charming, I thought her, really charming.'

'She's very generous,' Elinor said primly.

'Well,' John said, turning the car towards Park Lane, 'for girls in your situation, it never hurts to have someone like her on your side. A sort of patroness, I suppose. What luck, Ellie. You really did fall on your feet, didn't you, going down to Devon. Lovely cottage, by all accounts, and the Middletons sound delightful. And so supportive of you all. Fanny would really appreciate an introduction to Mary Middleton, you know, both of them with young kids and huge houses to do up and keep up. Could you do something about that?'

'Well, I—'

'The thing is, Ellie, we could do with a tip or two. It's wonderful at Norland, of course it is, but I can't *describe* to you what it's costing me.' He beat the steering wheel lightly with one hand. 'I'm telling you, it's just insatiable. I had to buy old Gibson out

– remember him? East Kingham Farm? – and of course he knew I needed the land because it always was Norland's, in the past, so he had me over an absolute *barrel*. And what with rewiring and replumbing the whole house, never mind this amazing new reed bed sewage system that Fanny was quite right to insist on – the Prince of Wales has one at Highgrove, you know, state-of-the-art eco everything – it's been non-stop cheque-writing, I don't mind telling you.'

Elinor cleared her throat. She said, 'How is Harry?'

'Oh, on top form. Absolutely jet-propelled. We took him to the zoo and then he had a day with Granny. Well, we all had a day with Granny because he's a bit of a handful on his own, and if you hadn't been going back tonight – what *is* this job thing you've got in Exeter, anyway? – I'd have asked you to give Fanny a bit of a break from Harry because she is simply exhausted, being such a completely hands-on, conscientious mum.'

'I'd love to see him.'

'Talking of seeing people,' John said, swerving round Hyde Park Corner, 'I hear *you* are very definitely seeing someone!'

Elinor tensed.

'No, I'm not.'

'Not what I hear!' John said triumphantly. 'I hear that not only have you and Marianne – I do wish she hadn't made an ass of herself over that Willoughby boy – managed to get your knees *very* well under Abigail Jennings's table but that you've hooked an extremely satisfactory fish. Big estate in Somerset, never been married, solid business going, good age—'

'No, John,' Elinor said firmly.

'Now, I know your modesty . . .'

To Elinor's relief, they were now approaching Buckingham Palace Road. John looked fretfully ahead.

'Do you *have* to travel by bus?'

'Yes,' Elinor said, 'I do.'

He slowed the car to a gradual standstill under some plane trees. Then he switched off the engine and turned to look sternly and directly straight at her. He said, almost threateningly, 'Elinor.'

'Yes?'

'I want to say something very seriously to you. You may have got very lucky in Devon with all your new connections, but do *not* be an idiot. If this Brandon fellow comes good, take him. Because it's *no* good hoping for Fanny's brother. None at all. Ever. Do you hear me? Just please use the good sense you at least were born with and put Ed *right* out of your mind. He is *not* for you, or the likes of you, most definitely. OK?'

12

Belle Dashwood had resolved, as one of many New Year resolutions, that while she had the cottage to herself during the day, she would not turn on the central heating, but would instead light the fire – logs generously supplied by Sir John, and replenished by Thomas – in the sitting room, and add extra sweaters. It was not only, as she pointed out to Elinor, a material contribution to their situation, but was also, she felt, an almost spiritual acknowledgement of Marianne's suffering and Elinor's quiet stoicism. It seemed to her that it was somehow fitting to be cold, and that she was acknowledging a need for mild sacrifice that the whole family appeared to feel, even Margaret, who was currently astonishingly biddable and amenable and had, that morning, actually thanked her mother for breakfast, and put her cereal bowl in the sink without being reminded at least four times.

Kneeling in front of the fireplace – and noticing in what immaculate order Thomas laid the logs for her; well, for Marianne, really, even in her absence – Belle made an effort not to remember Wills standing on that very spot, so magnificent, so gallant, in his damp clothes, towelling his hair. How excited they'd all been, how trusting, how full of hope and expectation, and now all of it was over, dashed to the ground, trampled on. Wills had, quite simply, broken Marianne's heart, not just by throwing her over – and so brutally! In *public*! – but also by turning out to be such a worthless person. Belle turned the word over in her mouth. Worthless. Without worth. No worth of any kind, beyond his beauty, and that turned out to be part of the wickedness of him, because it was a deception, wasn't it, to look so good and to be so bad?

And he was bad. Elinor had told her something of his badness when she got back from London, about the Greek girl and the money, and she had hinted that there was more, which she might divulge later, but Belle wasn't sure she wanted to hear any more. She had, as she told Elinor, heard quite enough to convince her that Wills's beauty was, as she'd always hinted – hadn't she? – only skin deep. Elinor had looked at her with the kind of affectionate scepticism she'd sometimes caught on Henry's face, a sort of fond tolerance, which had made her most indignant and extra determined to assert her mistrust of Wills from the very beginning. She was equally assertive in her conviction that Marianne must stay away from everything that might remind her of happier and more hopeful times.

'I'm glad you think that, Ma,' Elinor had said that morning before she went to work, 'because I don't think I could persuade Marianne to move just now, whatever I did. It's probably shock, the effect of shock. There's so much for her to come to terms with.'

'Exactly,' Belle said. 'Just what I said to her. Poor darling. But she wouldn't be warned.'

She twisted newspaper pages into spirals, now, and laid them in the fireplace; then she added kindling, which Thomas had left arranged as carefully as breadsticks in a wicker basket. Marianne was impulsive to the point of wilfulness, entirely certain that what had captured her imagination needed no other justification for providing the obvious, indeed the *only*, course of action. It was wonderful and terrible to see the consequences of Marianne's predilection for allowing emotion to prevail over everything, and it was also alarmingly familiar. Belle leaned forward to place a few small, split logs on to her wigwam of paper and wood. Marianne was just as she had been, and, if she was truthful with herself, was still very capable of being. She sat back on her heels and dusted her hands off against one another. But admitting that, she assured herself stoutly, did not in any way diminish the fact that she had been suspicious of Wills from the start. Who wouldn't be, faced with such utter male glory? It wasn't natural, it really wasn't, for a man to be as good-looking as that.

The landline telephone began to ring from the kitchen. Belle scrambled to her feet and hurried to answer it.

'It's Mary,' Mary Middleton said in her unengaged way.

'Oh, Mary.'

'Awful day.'

'Well, I suppose—'

'I hate this time of year in the country. Thank goodness the boys are all at day school now, and Anna-Maria's doing three days at nursery. It means Baby and I can keep scooting up to London. A lifesaver.'

Belle leaned against the kitchen table. Outside the window, the rain fell noisily into the small paved yard in which the rotary clothesline was planted, and dripping.

'Yes, I'm sure.'

'I thought I'd better ring you,' Mary said. 'To let you know that I've met your sister-in-law, in London.'

'Fanny!'

'Yes,' Mary said. 'Her Harry and my William are about the same age. And of course, she's got Norland.'

Belle straightened a little. She said crisply, 'Indeed she has.'

'It sounds lovely.'

'It is.'

'Well,' Mary said, in the tone of one who had been instructed to pass on information which they, personally, saw no need to share, 'we've all been asked to dinner at Fanny's, next weekend. Jonno thought you should know, for some reason. Perhaps because the girls have been asked too.'

'The girls?'

'Elinor,' Mary said, 'and Marianne. And Lucy and Nancy. We'll be swamped with girls. At least Bill's coming too. It's so great he can be relied on not to mind being the universal man.'

Belle closed her eyes. She took a deep breath. She said, 'I'm not sure Marianne will be well enough.'

'Oh?' Mary said. 'Won't she? Isn't the best remedy for a broken heart to accept every invitation going?'

'It's not her heart, Mary, it's her asthma.'

'I don't think the Dashwoods have any dogs in London. It's a house somewhere near Harley Street.'

'I know perfectly well where my stepson and his wife live in London, Mary, thank you. And dogs are not, this time, the problem.'

'Oh, I thought—'

'Mary,' Belle demanded, 'have you any idea of the complete waste of space that John Willoughby has turned out to be?'

There was short a silence on the other end of the line, and then Mary said, 'Jonno says he'll never speak to him again, and he never says that about anyone.'

'Good. And you?'

Mary said, with more energy, 'He never took *any* notice of the children when he was here. He paid more attention to the *dogs* than my children, for heaven's sake.'

'There you are then.'

'Will you tell Elinor?'

'Tell her what?'

'Will you tell Elinor', Mary said, 'that John and Fanny expect her for dinner, in London, on Saturday? But you'd better not tell her that Edward won't be there.'

'Mary—'

'Lucy told me that he won't. I don't know why she should know where he is, but she seems to. He can't stand his mother, or something.'

'His mother!' Belle exclaimed.

'It's weird, when her house is the only home he's got, according to everyone. But I expect it's to do with her wanting to marry him off to some heiress or other, so he won't be pounced on by a gold-digger. She sounds quite something, Mrs Ferrars.'

'But why', Belle said, bewildered by Mary's stream of consciousness, 'does it matter where Ed's mother is?'

'Oh,' Mary said, 'Fanny said her mother would be there at dinner. Won't that be interesting? The dragon who guards the cave to the Ferrarses' millions. Mrs F., and Fanny's other brother. The one who was in the paper. Belle, I've got to dash. Baby wake-up time and we do *not* like it if the first thing we see when we open our eyes isn't Mumma.'

'Of course,' Belle said faintly.

'And you'll tell Ellie? Smart casual, Saturday night.'

'Yes,' Belle said. 'Yes. Goodbye.'

She put the handset back into its cradle with elaborate care in order not to slam it. No Edward, but instead, Edward's mother, Fanny, John, those gruesome Steele girls, smart casual . . . Poor Elinor. Poor, poor Marianne. Why was the world so intent on pretending that nothing had happened?

The phone rang again. She snatched it up. Before she could utter a word, Mary said, 'Completely forgot to say that Wills is getting married, or something.'

'What?'

'Don't know the details, just heard that he's gone to Athens. Must fly, really, *really* loud baby noises from on high now!'

And she was gone.

From her sitting room, Abigail Jennings could hear the sounds of Marianne's guitar. It was, she had said to Charlotte on the telephone that morning – Charlotte's baby was late now, by five days, and therefore constant encouraging telephoning was required, on both sides – such a relief to hear. Even the dirgeful, gloomy things she seemed to want to play were better than all that sighing or silence. Thank goodness, she'd said to Charlotte, for Bill Brandon's besottedness. He'd said he'd bring the guitar up to London on his next trip from Delaford, and she was sure he'd made a special journey to collect it, but who cared, really, as long as Marianne had the thing in her hands and could play some of her misery *out*, at least.

'I never cease to be thankful, dear,' Abigail said to her younger daughter, 'that you never went in for having your heart broken.'

Charlotte gave a squeal of laughter.

'No fear!'

'These Dashwood girls, Char, such sweeties, but really hope-less. So *emotional*. I suppose you only have to look at their mother, don't you?'

'Now, now, Mummy.'

'Well,' Abigail said, 'she was all over Wills like a rash. And now the Ferrars boy, for Elinor . . .'

'Don't think so, Mummy.'

'Char dear, he went to stay; there's all that mystery about him just coming and going—'

Charlotte's voice dropped to confidential. She said quietly but emphatically, 'He'll do as he's told.'

'What?'

'Mummy, there's *squillions* in that family. Just loadsa money. His father made an absolute *pile*, you know that, and Mrs F. will be *very* picky about the girls those boys end up with. They won't be allowed to *choose*, Mummy, or if they do, there'll be awful consequences. Ellie can moon about after Ed till she's blue in the face but he's got to marry where he's told, which is Tassy Morton.'

'Tassy?'

'Of course!' Charlotte exclaimed. 'It makes absolute sense. Property prince marries scaffolding heiress, it's perfect! And she's really sweet. She'll do anything Daddy tells her, so if he says marry Ed Ferrars, she'll do it. I don't suppose she's ever had an opinion of her own in her life!'

'My dear,' Abigail said with satisfaction, 'you do know everything, don't you?'

'Chip off the old block!' Charlotte said gaily.

'Just think . . .' Abigail said musingly. 'Just think how very, very fascinating this supper party of Fanny Dashwood's is going to be . . .'

'Is it on Saturday?'

'It is, dear.'

'If this baby hasn't come by Saturday,' Charlotte said, 'I shall just come with you and have it right in front of everyone. Do you think I'm going to be pregnant for *ever*?'

'He's not here,' Lucy hissed to Elinor as they got out of the taxi on Saturday night, 'because of *me*.'

Elinor, focusing on managing the descent from a taxi in unaccustomed high heels, said nothing.

Lucy put a hand under Elinor's elbow to steady her. She said, close to Elinor's ear, 'I mean, it would completely give the game away. You know Ed. He simply can't hide his feelings. One look at me and it would be completely evident to everyone.'

Elinor removed her elbow. She said, straightening up and trying not to sound cross, 'Would it matter?'

'Oh, Ellie,' Lucy said reproachfully, 'you know we've got to play the long game!' She looked up at the façade of the house they were outside. 'I thought it was all doctors and stuff in Harley Street.'

'Ooh,' Nancy squealed from her other side, 'totes inappropes to talk about doctors in front of *moi*!'

Lucy went on staring at the house. She said, dismissively, 'It's all *you* talk about, Nance.'

'You can be such a cow, Luce.'

'Better than boring.'

'Boring, is it, to have a boyf with a *plane*, rather than one with a wrecked Sierra?'

'Something has to compensate for a beer belly and no hair.'

'You make me vom—'

'Stop it,' Elinor said. '*Stop* it. This house belongs to the family. Well, to John now. He rents out all of it except their flat.'

Lucy took her arm again.

'Nice little earner. For your brother, I mean.'

Elinor made no reply. She glanced down the street, to the second taxi, from which Bill Brandon and Sir John Middleton, watched by Marianne and Mary Middleton, were endeavouring to extract Mrs Jennings. Lucy pressed the arm she held to retrieve Elinor's attention. She whispered, 'Help me, Ellie.'

'What d'you mean?'

Lucy pushed her face so close to Elinor's that their skin was almost touching.

'I feel so sick. I can't *tell* you. I'm about to meet Ed's mum and he isn't here to support me and our whole future depends upon what she thinks of me. Honestly, if you weren't here, I couldn't face it, I simply couldn't. I know you've got to look after your sister a bit, but *please* don't leave me, *please*.' Her fingers dug into Elinor's arm. 'After all, Ellie, you're the only sensible person here who *knows*.'

'Hello,' Mrs Ferrars said, not looking at Elinor, 'I don't know which of you girls is which. I told Fanny there'd be too many of you, and I'd never remember. So don't expect me to.'

'I won't,' Marianne said loudly from beside her sister.

Mrs Ferrars did not appear to hear her. She was a small scowling woman in an expensive dark dress with gnarled little hands knobbly with diamonds.

'We are Fanny's sisters-in-law,' Elinor said helpfully.

Mrs Ferrars sniffed.

Elinor shot out a hand and gripped Marianne's nearest one warningly. She said, 'We were brought up at Norland. We know Harry.'

Mrs Ferrars looked past them both.

'Harry is my grandson.'

'Yes, we know that.'

Mrs Ferrars's eyes, as small and dark as currants, shifted their focus to anything but the Dashwood girls in front of her. She said, as if making an announcement, 'Harry will inherit Norland.'

'Yes, we know that too.'

'And we don't care,' Marianne said. 'If that's what you mean.'

Mrs Ferrars stiffened slightly.

'Where's Fanny?' she demanded.

'Here, Mother,' Fanny said, materialising beside her. She flashed a perfunctory smile at Elinor and Marianne. 'Lovely you could come.' She took her mother's nearest arm with a hand, Elinor couldn't help noticing, that it was identical to Mrs Ferrars's, only younger. 'Mother, I'm sure Ellie and Marianne will forgive us, but I want you to meet some adorable new friends of ours. The sweetest girls. Harry adores them.'

'Girls?' Mrs Ferrars said with a little grimace.

Fanny gave another mirthless smile in Elinor and Marianne's direction.

'Yes, girls, Mother. Divine girls. Mary and I are just mad about them and you know how you love young people!'

Mrs Ferrars regarded her daughter. She sniffed again.

'Do I?' she said.

Fanny gave a playful little laugh.

'Oh, these ones you will!' She threw a fleeting glance towards her sisters-in-law. 'Supper soon,' she said, as if food was plainly all that they had come for. 'A buffet, as we're so many, but all Ottolenghi. Don't you just adore their cooking?'

'That', Marianne said, hardly lowering her voice, 'was absolutely awful. The longest, dullest supper of my life. And the food – well, it's pure exhibitionism to serve food like that, for just standing about with plates and forks. And can you believe that a roomful of supposedly educated people could be just so banal and boring?'

'Sh,' Elinor said automatically.

'Cars and right-wing politics from the men. Nothing worth the breath it was uttered with from the women.'

Elinor bent towards her sister.

'M, someone will hear you.'

Marianne raised her chin a little.

'I don't care if they do. Why are we here? Why did we get ourselves mixed up in—'

'John and Fanny', Elinor said firmly, 'are *family*. We had to come.'

'And why is Fanny all over those Steele girls? Look at her and her mother and your friend Lucy.'

'She's not my friend.'

Marianne gave her sister a quick, mischievous smile. She said, '*She* thinks she is.'

Elinor said sadly, 'That's the sort of thing Mags would say.'

'Don't. *Don't*. I miss Mags, I miss—'

The door opened suddenly and revealed Harry on the threshold in his pyjamas, wearing an expression of ferocious defiance.

'Oh!' Mary Middleton cried at once. 'Spider-Man! Look, Spider-Man! My William just adores his Spider-Man PJs!'

Fanny, not to be outdone in the maternal rapture stakes, rushed forward and knelt by Harry.

'Now, poppet—'

Harry shouted, 'I don't like being in bed!'

Fanny tried to put soothing arms around her son. He wrestled himself free immediately.

'Don't! Don't!'

'Now, Harrykins, Mummy's *big* boy . . .'

Mary Middleton said, to no one in particular, 'Such a big boy! But not quite as tall as William.'

Fanny twisted round. She was wearing a tight, small smile.

'Oh, I think you'll find he's taller.'

Harry caught sight of his aunts. He shouted, 'Ellie! Ellie, Ellie, Ellie . . .'

She came forward, smiling, and knelt on the floor beside him.

'Hello, Harry.'

He said, 'I don't want to be in this bed. I want my *proper* bed.'

'Perhaps I could come and read to you?'

'I think you'll find', Mary said to Fanny, 'that William is in the top percentile of height for his age and that Harry—'

'—is a *much* bigger boy!' Fanny said brightly to her son.

Mary was in no hurry. She indicated Elinor, kneeling beside Harry. She said calmly, 'She'll know. Elinor knows both boys. She sees William at least every week.'

Fanny turned to fix her hard, demanding gaze on Elinor.

'Well?'

There was a pause. Elinor took Harry's hand and, for once, he didn't snatch it back. They looked at one another. From the edge of the group, Lucy Steele, whose opinion had not been sought, said loudly that she thought both boys were enormous and that she'd have thought them years older than they actually were, if she hadn't known their ages. No one took any notice, not even Mrs Ferrars, who had now come to stand on Harry's other side, as if to defend him from all slights.

'*Well?*' Fanny said again to Elinor, remorselessly.

Elinor squeezed Harry's hand.

'You are my nephew,' she said to him, 'and I love you, and I think that by next year you will be as tall as William, and by the time you are both grown up, you will probably be the taller because your daddy is taller than his daddy. So you just have to eat all the good stuff, and not the rubbish, and wait.'

Harry nodded. He did not seem unduly upset by the verdict.

'Thank *you*,' Fanny said sarcastically to Elinor.

'It's a pity', Mrs Ferrars said, 'that she can't show loyalty even to her own family, don't you think?'

'You asked me', Elinor said, 'for my opinion, and I gave it.'

She got stiffly to her feet. Looking up at her, Harry said, unexpectedly, 'I don't mind. I'm gooder at football, anyway.'

'Thank you.'

He said, still holding her hand, 'Will you come and do drawing for me?'

Fanny gave a little snort.

'Drawing?' she said, witheringly.

Mrs Ferrars gave Elinor a hostile stare.

'You *draw?*' she said accusingly.

'Yes,' Elinor said. 'Sort of. I – I'm doing architecture.'

Mrs Ferrars and her daughter exchanged glances.

'Oh, *architecture.*'

'So,' Fanny said to her mother, 'nothing *artistic*. Terribly neat and clean. She's very good at neat and clean.'

Mrs Ferrars gave a tiny, chilly smile.

'Not like Tassy Morton, then?'

'Oh, no, Mother, nothing like. Those divine flower paintings—'

'And the dragonfly—'

'Oh, the dragonfly! And those darling autumn berries, bryony or something.'

'I regard Tassy', Mrs Ferrars said, 'as a true artist, with a real gift.'

From the other side of the room, Marianne called, 'So has Elinor.'

There was sudden silence. Everyone turned and looked at her.

'What?' Fanny said dangerously.

'I don't know who this Tassy person is,' Marianne said, 'and I don't care. Nor do I care for the utter inhibition of botanical watercolours, actually. But Ellie draws like a dream. She can draw anything. Harry's right to ask her to draw for him. You'd be amazed at what she can draw.'

Elinor, gripping Harry's hand, stared at the floor. How had the evening come to this?

'Who is that?' Mrs Ferrars enquired of Fanny.

'Mother, you met her earlier. She's John's half-sister, one of the three.'

'Oh,' Mrs Ferrars said contemptuously, '*them.*' She gave another deliberate sniff. 'No money and plainly no common sense either.'

There was a distinct exclamation of anger, and Marianne

plunged forward and flung her arms round her startled sister.

'Don't listen to them, Ellie. Don't pay any attention. They're just small-minded, money-obsessed—'

'Sh,' Elinor said desperately, struggling to stay upright and, at the same time, to put her free hand over Marianne's mouth. 'It's OK, I'm OK.'

'Is she crying?' Harry said.

Marianne nodded vehemently, taking both hands away from grasping Elinor and covering her face with them.

Elinor said, slightly desperately, 'Yes, I think she is.'

'Why don't *you*', Fanny said crisply, 'take Harry back to bed and see if you can't calm Marianne down at the same time? What a ghastly scene, totally unnecessary, John always said she was hysterical.'

Elinor put her free hand out to take Marianne's.

'Come on, M.'

Bill Brandon was suddenly beside them. He looked at Marianne with an expression that betrayed everything he felt.

'Can – can I help you? Can I—?'

Elinor smiled weakly at him.

'I'll just try to get her quiet with Harry.'

'*I'm* not crying,' Harry said.

'No, nor you are.'

'Will you tell me if there's anything . . .'

Elinor turned, holding Harry still in one hand and Marianne in the other. As she turned, she caught a glimpse, across the room, of Sir John and Lucy Steele talking animatedly together, their eyes fixed on the group in the doorway. She said to Bill Brandon, 'Well, you could murder a few people for me, if you like,' and then, as she saw him struggling to take in what she had said through his own distress, added with as much lightness as she could muster, 'only joking.'

'Sorry, dear,' Mrs Jennings said, peering into the bathroom, 'but Lucy's here.'

Elinor stopped wiping her face. She stared at Mrs Jennings's reflection in the bathroom mirror over the edge of her washcloth.

'*What?*'

'Lucy's here, dear. No, I didn't ask her. I didn't. She's just turned up, all bright and breezy, without so much as a phone call, saying she just has to see you. How's Marianne?'

'Asleep. She slept quite well, considering.'

'I'm glad to hear it. Poor girl, so emotional.'

Elinor dropped the washcloth.

'She was defending me.'

'I know, dear. It was adorable. Even if it ruined the evening. Now, what am I to do about Lucy?'

Elinor sighed. She pulled her hair off her face into a rough ponytail and secured it with a clip.

'I suppose I'll see her.'

Mrs Jennings gestured towards Elinor's pyjama bottoms and grey T-shirt.

'Like that?'

'Well, Mrs J., I'm not dressing up for *Lucy*.'

Mrs Jennings gave a conspiratorial smile.

'No, dear, I quite see that. I'll get you both some coffee.'

Elinor turned round to face her.

'You're lovely, but I don't want to encourage her to stay, exactly.'

'Like that, is it?'

'Mrs J., I've got to get back to Devon and I—'

Mrs Jennings held up a hand.

'You can't go anywhere in pyjamas with no breakfast inside you. You're as pale as a ghost. Talking of pale, did you see Bill's face last night when Marianne—'

'Yes,' Elinor said shortly.

'Right,' Mrs Jennings said. 'Right. I'm not one to butt in where I'm not wanted. Charlotte's always telling me to mind my own business. Fine one to talk, she is. Well, Elinor dear, *your* current business is sitting on my sofa in full make-up and ridiculous shoes. So run along and deal with it, would you?'

'Ellie!' Lucy cried, leaping up from the sofa.

She was wearing skinny jeans and stilettos, and her hair had been tonged into long, soft curls which hung well below her shoulders.

She caught Elinor by her upper arms.

'Wasn't that amazing?'

'Amazing?'

'Last night! Wasn't it fabby? She was so lovely to me. Gosh, Ellie, are you OK? You look, you look . . .'

'Awful?'

'Well, I wouldn't – I didn't want – Were you up all night with your sister?'

Elinor detached herself.

'Marianne was fine, thank you.'

'I just thought—' Lucy began.

Elinor glared at her.

'She's *fine*,' she said. 'She's asleep.'

Lucy took a long, elaborate breath and said, with deliberate politeness, 'I'm so glad.'

'Yes. Well.'

'Ellie?'

'What?'

'Wasn't she just lovely to me last night?'

Elinor was in no mood to be helpful.

'Who?' she said.

Lucy sat down on Mrs Jennings's sofa again with a little bounce.

'Ed's mum, of course.'

'Edward's *mother*?'

Lucy bent her head so that her hair swung forward becomingly.

'She was so sweet. She made such a fuss of me and Nance. So did your sister-in-law. I just *loved* your sister-in-law. Did you see her shoes?'

Elinor lowered herself into an armchair opposite the sofa. She leaned forward.

'Lucy . . .'

'Yes?'

'Lucy,' Elinor said, 'they weren't sweet to you for anything particular. I mean, I don't know why you're so happy, because they don't know about you and Ed, do they, so they weren't pleased for that reason.'

Lucy tossed her hair back.

'I knew you'd say that!'

Elinor said resignedly, 'Well, it's obvious.'

Lucy leaned forward.

'Ellie. Listen. I can't expect you not to be a bit jealous of everything looking so rosy for me, but they liked me. They really did. I won't let you rain on my parade; I know they liked me. And I adored them. Why didn't you say how amazing your sister-in-law was?'

Elinor said nothing. Lucy peered at her.

'Ellie, have you got a hangover?'

'No,' Elinor said between gritted teeth.

Lucy slipped off the sofa and knelt beside her. She tried to take Elinor's hand.

'You're a fantastic friend, Ellie. I don't know what I've done to deserve a brand-new, lovely best friend like you. Next to Ed, you mean the world to me, you really do, even though we've only known each other a few months.'

'Please get up.'

Lucy put up a hand, as if to try and stroke Elinor's forehead.

'Don't,' Elinor said. '*Don't.*'

Lucy sighed. She got to her feet, with difficulty, in her heels.

'Poor you,' she said. 'You carry *so* much, and all alone. It must be awful seeing someone like me with all this lovely future rolling ahead of them, and new friends like Fanny. I hope you'll tell Fanny that I thought she was awesome.'

Elinor stared at the rug under her bare feet in silence.

'I *know* she liked me,' Lucy repeated, still standing over Elinor. 'You couldn't mistake it. Nor Ed's mother. I was expecting her to be really frosty with me because I know she's got a killer reputation—' She broke off. 'Was that the doorbell?'

'Maybe.'

'Who could it be?'

Elinor roused herself slightly. She said, 'I have no idea. Some friend of Mrs J.'s. Bill, maybe.'

'Oh, of course,' Lucy said with emphasis, 'Bill coming to ask after Marianne.'

The sitting-room door opened, revealing Mrs Jennings holding a tray of mugs and behind her, slightly dishevelled and looking as short of sleep as Elinor felt, was Edward Ferrars.

'There!' Mrs Jennings said loudly. 'One dressed girl, one undressed girl, one young man, and three mugs of coffee!'

She advanced into the room and put the tray down on the low glass table by the television. Neither girl said a word. Edward stood frozen in the doorway, his gaze directed at the ceiling.

Mrs Jennings straightened up. She looked round at them.

'What on earth's the matter? Don't you three know each other?'

Elinor swallowed. She said, 'Yes, of course, it's just that I was not expecting – We weren't—' She stopped and glanced at Lucy. Lucy was staring out of the window, holding the absurd pose of a fashion model, her lips slightly parted. Elinor looked, cornered as she was, at Edward.

'Hello, Ed.'

He croaked something in reply, hardly intelligible. Mrs Jennings marched back towards the door.

'I don't know what's going on. With a daughter like Charlotte, tongue-tied isn't a problem I ever have to face, thank goodness. I'll be in my bedroom, telephoning, if you want me. Or,' she added to Elinor, 'you need an interpreter?'

Elinor said faintly, 'Thank you for the coffee.'

Mrs Jennings pushed Edward a little further into the room and then bustled out, closing the door resoundingly behind her.

Elinor picked up a mug of coffee and held it out to Lucy.

'Coffee?'

Lucy gave a little smirk, but didn't speak. She accepted the coffee and resumed her seat on the sofa, staring into her mug. Elinor looked at Edward.

'Coffee, Ed?'

'Thanks,' he said, not moving.

She held a mug out, offering him the handle so that their fingers need not touch. Lucy lifted her head and regarded them both and, although her pose didn't alter, her eyes were watchful.

'How are you?' Elinor said to him, into the silence.

He took the mug and held it in both hands.

'Fine. Thanks.'

Elinor waited. The awkwardness in the room was as thick as smoke and she was suddenly conscious of being barefoot in pyjamas with unbrushed hair. She was also seized with a flash of irritation at Edward's inability to help with any conversation and Lucy's deliberate refusal. She said, too loudly, 'Well, before you trouble to ask, Mum is fine, Mags is fine, Marianne is doing OK, and I am about to go back to Devon. When I've dressed, that is.'

Edward took a swallow of coffee. He seemed unable to look at either girl. He then said, hesitantly, 'I'm – I'm so glad if Marianne's OK.'

'She's down,' Elinor said, 'but not out. Definitely not out.'

He gave a ghost of a smile.

'Brilliant.'

Elinor looked at Lucy. Lucy seemed perfectly composed now, but in no hurry to help with the conversation. Elinor said to her, 'You OK?'

Lucy nodded, smiling.

'Perfectly, thank you.'

'Well,' Elinor said, putting her mug down, 'you two haven't seen each other for ages. I'll – I'll just go and see if Marianne has woken up.'

'Please . . .' Edward said.

'Please what?'

He sidled behind an armchair. Lucy watched him, still smiling.

'Please see if she's awake,' Edward said. 'I'd – I'd love to see her.'

Elinor moved towards the door. Lucy didn't take her eyes from Edward's face.

'Me too,' she said.

'Ed's here?' Marianne cried, starting up in bed. '*Here*? In Mrs J.'s flat?'

'Yes. He wants to see you.'

Marianne began to rummage about, hanging over the edge of her bed, for her slippers.

'How fantastic. God, how cheering. A human being after weeks of monsters. Can you see the other one?'

'You don't need slippers,' Elinor said. 'And – and Lucy's here.'

Marianne flipped upright and pushed her hair off her face.

'*Lucy?*'

'Yes.'

'What is *she* doing here?'

'I – I don't know. She just came.'

Marianne climbed off the bed and stood up. She said, grinning, 'You mean thing, Ellie, leaving him to have to talk to her.'

'Well, I thought that as they know each other a bit—'

'*Nobody* should have to talk to anyone from the Steele family unless at gunpoint. I'm going straight along.'

'Aren't you going to brush your hair?'

Marianne looked at her.

'You haven't brushed yours.'

'Mrs J. pounced before I could.'

'And you', said Marianne, 'pounced before *I* could. Poor Ed.'

She wrenched the bedroom door open and went racing along the corridor towards the sitting room, with Elinor stumbling in her wake.

'Ed!' she cried, flinging her arms round his neck. 'Oh, Ed, I am so pleased to see you!'

Edward, who had hardly moved from his position behind the armchair, returned her embrace as enthusiastically as he could whilst encumbered with a coffee mug.

'Hi, M, oh, hi, hi.'

'We've been longing to see you! Ellie especially, of course, but me too, to see someone *normal*, someone from home.'

He held her away from him a little.

'You're terribly thin, M.'

'Oh,' she said, tossing her hair, 'that doesn't matter. I'm fine, I really am. But Ellie's great. Don't you think she looks great? As long as Ellie's OK!'

Elinor caught Lucy's instant change of expression to one of unmistakable fury. She tried to say something conciliatory, and failed.

Edward said to Marianne, 'Are you OK here? In London?'

She shook her head. She said quietly, 'You know what happened?'

'Yes,' he said sadly, 'I heard.'

247

'And then', Marianne said, brightening at the recollection of how dreadful the previous evening had been, 'we had this family gathering thing, organised – sorry about this, Ed – by your sister, which was *beyond* awful. Why didn't you come? It would have made it bearable.'

He shifted slightly. He said, mumbling, 'I – couldn't.'

'Why not?'

'Well, I'd kind of promised someone—'

'And Edward', Lucy said, suddenly and sharply, 'isn't like the kind of guys *you* know, Marianne. Edward keeps his word. Don't you, Ed?'

Marianne stared at her. She said in surprise, 'I know he does. I know if he says he'll do something, he will. I *know* that. What are you on about?'

Elinor turned away, clenching her fists. It was one thing not to like or trust Lucy Steele especially; it was quite another to be on the point of hitting her.

Edward put his mug down on a side table. He said to Marianne, with real affection, 'I'm so sorry, M, but I've got to run.'

She laughed at him.

'But you've only just come!'

'Just – just wanted to see how you were.'

'I'm fine. I *will* be fine. And she' – gesturing towards Elinor – 'is the most fantastic sister and person. As you know.' She leaned forward until her mouth was against his ear. 'Lucy'll be gone in a minute, I'm sure she will,' she whispered. 'Stay and talk to us.'

He shook his head, even though he was smiling at her.

'Sorry, M. Got to go.'

He glanced up, his gaze sliding rapidly over Lucy and Elinor.

'Sorry,' he said again.

Elinor didn't speak. Anger at Lucy and disappointment in Edward formed a lump in her throat she didn't seem able to swallow past. She looked steadfastly ahead, aware of Edward leaving the room, having some brief encounter with Mrs Jennings in the hall and then hearing the slam of the front door behind him. From what seemed like far away, Lucy's voice said, primly, 'I ought to be going too.'

Elinor jerked into full consciousness. Marianne had walked past Lucy and flung herself on the sofa, where she was examining her fingernails with fierce concentration.

'Oh,' Elinor said.

Lucy moved towards the door. She put her mug down on the side table, close to Edward's.

'Busy day,' she said, and gave a little laugh, '*and* after a really late night!' She looked at Elinor. 'You are', she said with theatrical emphasis, '*such* a trustworthy person. And I do *so* value that!'

When the front door had slammed for the second time, Marianne uncoiled herself from the sofa.

'OK, Ellie. Why was she here?'

'I have no idea.'

'Why was she here, Ellie? Her *and* Ed?'

Elinor looked out of the window. She said, 'They've known each other for yonks.'

'And?'

'No and.'

Marianne marched to the door.

'OK, Ellie, don't tell me. But don't expect me to play games with you either. You hardly give him the time of day, and then *she's* here, whatever that means.'

Elinor started to speak but Marianne held up a hand to silence her.

'Don't fob me off, Ellie. Something's going on that's not good for you, and if you won't tell me, then you won't. But don't expect me, either, Elinor Dashwood, not to smell a rat.'

And then she strode out of the room and left Elinor staring out of the window at the sky.

13

Sir John thumped a heavy bottle down on Belle Dash-wood's kitchen table. Belle, who had not been expecting him and was not prepared for visitors, looked at the bottle in amazement.

'Champagne!'

He beamed at her.

'Champagne, indeed! To celebrate.'

'But', Belle said, 'it's just a Tuesday . . .'

Sir John put his hands flat on the table, either side of the bottle, and leaned towards her.

'We're going to drink to Charlotte. She's had the baby. Tommy Palmer's got a son and heir!'

Belle smiled broadly back.

'I'm so glad.'

'A whopper,' Sir John said happily, 'over nine pounds. Bigger than any of ours. Mary's gone flying up to London and I imagine the monster-in-law is already barking orders in the hospital. Isn't it great?'

'Wonderful! Wonderful. I'd get the girls but they're not back yet, from Exeter. Margaret had some after-school club.'

'Then', Sir John said, grasping the bottle, 'we'll have to swig the lot, you and me. Get the glasses!'

'I haven't lit a fire yet.'

'I'll do that. Come on, come on, Belle, if we've got to make a party on our own, then we'll *do* it. Abi said to me on the phone that Tommy was all over the place while Char was in labour, and then the moment the baby's here, he reverts to type and is making out that he can't tell one end from another and that the poor little blighter looks like Churchill. Abi said he was as exasperating as ever and the baby looks exactly like him, poor little sod.'

He began to march round the kitchen, opening cupboards.

'Glasses? Glasses?'

'Here,' Belle said. 'But not proper flutes.'

Sir John made an exclamation of false annoyance.

'No flutes? No *flutes?*' He nudged her jovially. 'Between you and me, Belle, I'd be happy to drink it out of jam jars.'

'I can't,' Elinor said.

She was sitting up in bed, the sleeves of her father's cardigan pulled down over her knuckles, drinking a mug of tea. On the end of the bed her mother sat, still dressed and still slightly flushed from a quantity of champagne drunk at astonishing speed. She had tried to make Sir John stay for supper, but he had declared that he was off to Portugal in the morning, to visit his factory, and that he needed to sort himself out for an early start. He had roared off into the dark in his Range Rover, and left Belle slightly dazed and with a mild attack of hiccups, to await Elinor and Margaret's return from Exeter.

She sighed, now, regarding Elinor.

'Darling, I know it's exhausting, all this toing and froing to London. But John – and Fanny, I suppose – have asked you to this concert, and Marianne won't go without you. And you could go and see Charlotte's baby. Couldn't you?'

Elinor drooped over her tea mug.

'I've been every weekend, for ages.'

'I know you have.'

'And that bus journey is so long. And grim on Sunday nights.'

'Darling Ellie. Could you just go one more time? Because I think it's time Marianne came home.'

Elinor's head jerked up.

'You *what?*'

'Well,' Belle said carefully, 'she's got to face life again, some-time, hasn't she? You may think I didn't notice anything but I *am* aware that we've been here more than six months, and she has just drifted about and not really focused on what she's going to do.'

Elinor said shortly, 'I've tried.'

'Oh, darling, I'm sure you have . . .'

Elinor put her mug down on the pile of books beside her bed. She said, 'So you think getting her back here will focus her? On *anything?*'

'It would be a start,' Belle said. 'She can't go on taking Abi's hospitality—'

'Mrs J. loves it. She's using Marianne as a substitute daughter.'

'All the same . . .'

Elinor rubbed her eyes. She yawned.

'So you want me to drag up to London again for some concert—'

'I think', Belle said, interrupting, 'that John wants to – well, make amends. For Fanny, I mean. He wouldn't say so, in so many words, but I think he feels that they weren't very supportive over Marianne, and he'd probably like to offer you a bed in Harley Street. At least, that's what he was implying on the phone.'

'I would hate to stay in Harley Street.'

'Ellie darling, John is family.'

'And I', Elinor said, sliding down under her duvet, 'am exhausted.'

Belle leaned forward. She patted the duvet roughly in the region of Elinor's stomach.

'One more weekend, darling. Be nice to John and persuade Marianne to come home. You can see your friend Lucy—'

'I detest Lucy,' Elinor said.

'Oh, I thought—'

Elinor twisted over on to her side, facing the wall.

'That's what everyone does,' she said. 'They think what suits them. And one of the things that suits *you* is to have me make things nice with John and Fanny, and persuade Marianne that she's got to stop making an opera out of a broken heart and think seriously about the future.'

There was silence. Belle stood up. Elinor waited for her to cross the room to the door, but she didn't. Instead she said, in a voice that was not entirely steady, 'I do appreciate you, darling.'

Elinor stared at the wall. Was it worth saying that she was no longer going to do anything for anyone since it seemed to her that the more generous she was, the more she herself seemed to get punished? Or was she going to be sensible, reliable, patient Elinor who never put her own feelings first because – let's face it – she didn't have any worth considering in the first place, did she?

She rolled back and peered at her mother. Belle was standing with her hands clasped together, almost in an attitude of supplication.

'One more London weekend,' Elinor said severely. 'And that's *it*.'

The concert was in a grandly converted church in Chelsea. The audience, Elinor guessed – uniformly well fed and well dressed – could be divided into those who really liked music and those who liked to be thought to like music. Fanny, she was sure, was in the latter category, and spent a good deal of her time swivelling in her seat to see whom she knew and might make a beeline for in the interval. Only Marianne sat quietly studying her programme, pausing just long enough to say to Elinor, 'Rachmaninov Two. I don't care how often I hear it. Bliss.'

Fanny gave a little screech.

'Oh my God, there's Robert! What on earth is he doing here? Classical music is *so* not his thing!' She leaped up and began brandishing her programme.

'Robbie! Robbie! Over here!'

A slender young man in a suit of exaggerated cut, halfway down the aisle from their seats, began to gaze about distractedly.

'Robbie!' Fanny shouted. 'Here! Up here!'

The young man, Elinor saw, was the one she had seen in the double-page spread in Mrs Jennings's Sunday newspaper. He came swooping up the aisle and gave his sister a theatrical kiss.

'Lovely to see you, big, *big* sis!'

'And this is Elinor,' Fanny said without enthusiasm. 'You know. Johnnie's half-sister. Or rather, one of them.'

'Ooh,' Robert Ferrars said, rolling his eyes at Elinor, 'so we're nearly related!'

'Well, sort of.'

'And *you*', Robert said with emphasis, 'know our bad black sheep brother, Ed, don't you?'

'A little,' Fanny said crisply.

'Well,' Robert said, shooting his shirt cuffs, 'I always say – don't I, Fan – that if Mother and Father had done the sensible thing with Ed, and sent him to Westminster, like me, we'd have had none of this nonsense. Would we, Fan? It was being sent in disgrace to that crammer in Portsmouth—'

'Plymouth,' Fanny said.

'Well, that's what did for him, wherever it was. He just ran wild. And he hasn't stopped since, has he? Such a naughty boy.'

John Dashwood, noticing his brother-in-law for the first time, got to his feet and moved into the aisle to greet him. Marianne glanced up from her programme, took in someone – yet again – of no interest to her, and returned to her reading.

'Hello, old boy,' John Dashwood said heartily. 'Didn't expect to see you *here*.'

Robert Ferrars winked at Elinor.

'Not really my thing, I have to admit. Why sit in silence, listening, when you could be talking, I say!' He looked at his sister. 'Remember Sissy Elliot? Or, *Lady* Elliot, darling, as she now is since *he* got booted into the coronet department. Such a hoot! Well, I was supposed to be there tonight, helping her with a party. Robbie, she said, there's no way we can get two hundred people into a room the size of a small fridge, and I said to her, Darling, easy peasy, leave it to me, sofas out on the balcony, under plastic, open the double doors to the dining room and hey presto, party space with somewhere even for the smokers to sit, outside. She was thrilled. But *so* cross I wouldn't be there, after all.'

Elinor was equally fascinated and repelled by him. She said, almost without meaning to speak, 'Why aren't you?'

He touched her hand.

'*Entre nous*, Elinor my nearly sister-in-law, I had a better invitation. The Elliots are life peers, ducky, and I' – he glanced down the aisle – 'was asked here by a *duchess*. Who wants me – yes, *me* – to organise her daughter's wedding.'

'Oh,' Elinor said blankly.

'You are so naughty,' Fanny said with real affection.

He leaned forward and kissed her cheek. Then he laid two fingers against Elinor's.

'Kisses next time, sweetie pie.' He looked past her, at Marianne. 'Is that *the* famous—'

'Shh,' Fanny said, mock scolding, 'you are awful. So awful.'

He grinned at her.

'And I'm gone,' he said and darted back to his seat.

'Such a sweetheart,' Fanny said to Elinor. 'We adore him. He's welcome any time, isn't he, Johnnie?'

John Dashwood looked at Elinor. He said in a rush, as if he were greatly daring something, 'As *you* are, of course, Elinor. Any time.'

'Thank you,' Elinor said awkwardly.

Fanny cleared her throat. She said to her husband, in measured tones, 'We talked about that, sweetness.'

'I know we did,' John Dashwood said. 'But I didn't want Elinor to think—'

Fanny turned to look at Elinor.

'I don't suppose Elinor thought anything. Did you, Ellie? Why should Elinor mind if I offer a bed to the Steele girls while they're in London?'

'Oh, I don't. I didn't know, I—'

'After all,' Fanny said smoothly, 'my family rather owes Lucy's uncle for coping with Ed during those difficult years, don't we? I've never had a chance to say thank you for all they did, before, have I?'

'No,' John Dashwood said uncertainly, 'I suppose you haven't.'

'And I', Elinor said, hardly caring if she sounded rude, 'don't mind, either way. It's lovely, anyway, staying with Mrs J.'

There was a small pause, in which Fanny regarded Elinor, and Elinor looked at the carpet. Then Fanny said, without any warmth, 'Come another time,' and, after a further pause, 'Harry just loves having Lucy around.' She looked at her husband. 'Doesn't he?'

John Dashwood gulped a breath. He did not catch Elinor's eye.

'Look!' he said with relief. 'Look. The lights are going down!'

Volume III

14

'We're going out for coffee,' Elinor said firmly to Marianne the next morning, 'and you are going to listen to me. I mean *listen*. Not just gaze at me while you think about something quite different.'

Marianne was in front of the bathroom mirror, fixing her earrings. Her eyes met Elinor's in the mirror, wide with innocence.

'OK. But I don't want to be lectured.'

'You mean you don't want to hear any point of view but your own.'

'No, I mean I don't want to be talked down to, and told — what's that noise?'

'Mrs J. on the phone. As usual.'

Marianne was suddenly very still. She said, 'She's screaming.'

'She's always loud.'

'No, but—'

The voice down the passage to the sitting room stopped abruptly and there was the sound of heavy feet, almost running, towards them, instead. Seconds later, Abigail Jennings appeared in the bathroom doorway, her mobile phone clutched to her tremendous bosom.

'Girls,' she said. She sounded as if she could hardly catch her breath. 'Girls—'

They stepped forward, towards her. Elinor put out an arm as if to support her.

'Goodness, Mrs J., are you OK? Are you—'

Abigail pressed her phone into the folds of the cashmere scarf draped around her neck.

'My dears . . .'

'What? What — it is something awful?'

Mrs Jennings looked at the ceiling as if for divine sustenance.

'Not exactly awful . . .'

Elinor and Marianne now both put steadying hands on their hostess and guided her solicitously across the bathroom to sit on the closed lid of the lavatory. She said, gasping slightly, 'I just rang Charlotte . . .'

'Yes! Yes?'

'Because, you know, she was in such a state about the baby crying, and I said, Well, it'll be colic, it's *so* common and you need this divine Donovan man, the osteopath, to do a little cranial massage on the baby, and you'll be *amazed* at the effect. It's astonishing how many people simply do not understand how the plates of the brain get squashed on that *grim* journey down the birth canal, and then *that* compresses the nerve endings at the base of the skull, and hey presto, colic, poor little—'

'Is that', Marianne said, interrupting, from her kneeling position on the bathroom floor beside Mrs Jennings, 'why you were screaming? Because of the baby and—'

Mrs Jennings gazed at her, round-eyed.

'Oh *no*. No, dear. That was why I rang Charlotte. To tell her—'

'Then why—?'

'Why what?'

'Why were you screaming?'

Mrs Jennings took a huge breath, lifted her plump hands and let them fall dramatically into her lap, still holding her telephone.

'My dear, you will *not* believe what Charlotte told me. *Such* dramas. It's like something out of a novel.'

Elinor knelt too. She said, 'Please tell us!'

Mrs Jennings bent forward, as if to impart something confidential.

'There's been the most ghastly row. In Harley Street. Just this morning. Apparently Nancy Steele thought that everyone there was getting on so famously that it would be perfectly acceptable to tell your brother and sister-in-law that Lucy and the Ferrars boy – your sister-in-law's brother, dear, the F-word boy, God help us – have been engaged for more than a year, and never told a soul because Mrs Ferrars senior has such fixed ideas about who her boys should marry, being so terrified, as she is, of fortune-hunters. Your sister-in-law went completely ballistic, Charlotte said, and rushed to wake Lucy up and tell her she was sick of cheap little gold-diggers sniffing round her family, and next thing we know, Lucy and Nancy are out on the pavement and round they go to Charlotte's, straight away, and Tommy found his kitchen was absolutely full of crying women and a screaming baby and Charlotte says he just went straight off to the office, even though it's Sunday.'

Marianne was ashen. She sat back on her heels, her hand over her mouth. From behind it, muffled, she said, 'Not Ed. Not—'

Mrs Jennings patted her.

'Come on, now, dear. It's lovely he's stood by Lucy, isn't it? I think to defy those money-obsessed Ferrarses takes some doing,

I really do. I rather applaud him; I can't bear people who think money is all that matters.'

Marianne's gaze swung round to Elinor. She whispered, dropping her hand, 'Did you know?'

Elinor nodded mutely.

'When?' Marianne said.

'Weeks ago. Months.'

'And you didn't *tell* me?'

Elinor said, looking at the floor, 'I didn't tell anyone.'

Mrs Jennings heaved herself to her feet. She said, cheerfully, 'It's quite a story, don't you think?'

'Yes,' they both said politely, not moving.

She stepped clumsily over them.

'I know she's your sister-in-law, dears, but really, what a reaction! Poor Lucy. Sweet girl. It's such a lovely story, especially in this day and age, don't you think? Now, I'm going across to Charlotte's, to see what I can do to help. Will you girls just help yourselves to breakfast? Croissants in the cupboard.'

'Thank you.'

Mrs Jennings paused in the doorway.

'You know,' she said, 'they might make a go of it. They really might. Love on a shoestring and all that. I'm sure I could help with some furniture.' She glanced back at the Dashwood girls, still crouched on the floor. 'I wonder what will happen when Ed's mother knows! Fireworks won't be in it and, I'm telling you, I don't want to miss a moment!'

Elinor looked up at her. She managed a tired smile.

'Give Charlotte our love,' she said.

When her footsteps had retreated, Marianne said hoarsely to her sister, 'You have known all along, Elinor Dashwood, that Ed and Lucy were engaged, all the time I've been like I've been?'

Elinor nodded reluctantly.

'So,' Marianne said, leaning forward to grip Elinor's nearest wrist, 'Ed is as much of a complete scumbag as Wills is?'

'No,' Elinor said, with vehemence. '*No.*'

'Two-timing, choosing a complete little cow like—'

'It's different,' Elinor said. 'He's different. He was neglected and bullied when he was little, and then all those people in Plymouth were kind to him, and Lucy was in the mix, and he felt this obligation . . .'

'Huh,' Marianne said.

'She's not a bad person.'

'She's a witch.'

'And he', Elinor said with an effort, 'isn't bad either.'

'He's pathetic.'

Elinor gave a little gasp, as if she was choking down a sob.

'Ellie?'

'What?'

'Did you love him?'

Elinor writhed a little, on the floor.

'I don't know. Yes. No. I – I love quite a lot of people.'

'Not *men.*'

'Even some men.'

'But not Ed!'

Elinor looked at her. She said seriously, 'M, I don't believe in a one and only love, like you do. But yes, I do have feelings for Ed, I do. And before you rubbish him any more, I just want to say that he's never promised me anything, he's never made me hope or believe in anything he couldn't deliver. In fact, I think he likes me. I'll go further. I *know* he likes me. But he's trapped. By his mother and now by all these circumstances, and he's got to assert his independence and he's got trapped in how he does that, too. I don't know if he wants to be with Lucy or not, but he's not going to let her down because he's been let down himself by so many people all his life that he can't bring himself to do it to someone else, whatever the cost to him is. Don't you see?'

There was a long silence. Then Marianne got slowly to her feet. Looking down at her sister, she said quietly,

'You love him. Don't you.'

Elinor sighed. She gave an imperceptible nod.

Marianne said fiercely, 'All this time while I've been banging on about Wills and weeping and wailing and being a general diva pain to everyone, you knew about Lucy and Ed, and you never said a word to me.'

Elinor got to her knees, and then awkwardly to her feet. She didn't look at Marianne. She shook her head. 'No.'

'I feel awful.'

'Please—'

'Ellie,' Marianne said, her voice breaking, 'I've been such a bitch. So selfish. I got so obsessed that I never even looked to see if you might be suffering.' She reached out and took Elinor's nearest hand. 'I'm so sorry. Ellie, I really am. I'm so, so sorry.'

Elinor gave a little bark of half-laughter.

'Doesn't matter.'

'It does. It *does*.' Marianne dropped Elinor's hand and put her arms round her instead. 'God, Ellie. I feel terrible about how I've been to you, I could kill myself!'

'Don't do that. Please, don't...'

'What can I do? Ellie, what can I do to try and make it up to you in even the most minuscule degree?'

Elinor gently disengaged herself. She put her hands on her sister's shoulders and regarded her gravely.

'There is something.'

'What? Anything, anything!'

'M,' Elinor said, 'I want you to behave as if neither of us gives a stuff about any of this.'

'What?'

'I mean it. I want you to be nice to Lucy and like you always are to Ed. I want no one ever, *ever*, to suspect that I have any axe to grind. Lucy and Ed are just another happy couple we happen to be vaguely connected to, and no more. OK?'

Marianne said sadly, 'But I want to murder her.'

'It's not about you. It's not about her. It's about *me*. I want you to promise to help save my face. I want you to do this for me. Me, Elinor. Do you get it?'

Marianne sighed. Then she smiled wanly.

'I get it. Promise.'

In Elinor's cardigan pocket, her phone began to ring. She pulled it out and peered at the screen.

'Gosh,' she said, 'it's John!'

'Answer it,' Marianne said. 'Quick.'

Elinor put the phone to her ear.

'Hello?' she said. 'John?'

'Elinor?' he said. 'Elinor. Do you have a moment?'

'Of course.'

She motioned to Marianne to resume sitting on the floor beside her, their backs against the panels of the bathtub.

'Something very – *grave* has happened,' John said. 'Fanny is really upset, terribly hurt, you know how trusting she is—'

Elinor said quickly, 'John, we do know, if you mean—'

'It's appalling,' he said, interrupting, his voice high with indignation. 'It's like wildfire these days. There's a private family upset and the world knows about it in seconds. Fanny feels completely betrayed, of course, and who wouldn't, after all she's done for those worthless girls.'

'Yes.'

'Elinor, she took them in because she felt that her family owed their family for looking after Edward during his teens. She was behaving beautifully, and generously, as she always does, and then she finds that Lucy has got her claws into Edward and plans to marry him and when confronted with this – honestly, Elinor, you would not believe his sheer *brazenness* to his sister and mother – Edward has the utter *nerve* to say it's all quite true and that they *are* going to marry.'

'Oh,' Elinor said. She was staring straight ahead. Marianne had taken the hand not holding the phone and was gripping it. 'So – so Ed's mother knows?'

'She was distraught,' John said. 'Absolutely distraught. And you know what a wonderful woman she is – you met her. She only wants what is best for her children, that's all she's interested in, but when she pointed out to Edward what a lovely match Tassy Morton would be for him, and how happy she'd be to give them the family house in Norfolk, he just laughed. Can you believe it? He simply laughed.'

'Good for him!' Marianne called.

'Who was that?' John demanded.

'It's Marianne, John. She's next to me.'

'What did she say?'

'She said, "Good heavens",' Elinor said, not looking at her

sister. Marianne put her face into Elinor's nearest shoulder, shaking with giggles.

'I should say so,' John said. 'It's appalling conduct. Disgraceful. I'm not surprised that she reacted as she did. Not another penny his way, ever. Not one. He's burnt every boat.'

Elinor said quietly, 'What did he say?'

'Nothing much, actually. Odd really, but I suppose silence is part of his defiance. Even when Fanny's mother said – perfectly understandably, in my view – that she would do everything to stand in his way in the future, he didn't really react. He just said he'd promised.'

'He probably did.'

'But come on, now. Promises to a girl like that?'

Elinor took a breath.

'Mrs J. is very fond of Lucy, John. And Mrs J. has been really kind to us.'

'Well,' John said, beginning to bluster, 'I know Lucy is some sort of connection of Mrs Jennings, and I'm sure she was never any trouble before, but it really isn't *on*, is it, to make a boy you know is worth a fortune promise to marry you, when you don't yourself come from much of a background. I mean, you can't avoid thinking eye-to-the-main-chance, love-me-love-your-wallet kind of thing, can you? It's no fault of Mrs Jennings that her late husband's goddaughter or whatever behaves in a disappointing way, now, is it? I'd be the last person to think that. Just as I'm the last person to think Fanny's mother has been other than exemplary – so fair, so generous. She offered him a six-bedroom house in Norfolk, Elinor, never mind the farm that goes with it! And he just threw it all back at her. Just like that. Well, he has made his bed, stupid boy, and he must lie on it.'

Marianne leaned closer to the phone. She called, 'John, how did it end?'

'How did what end?'

'All this. This row.'

'Well,' John said, 'Edward slammed out of the flat, and we have no idea where he is. Fanny just said to me, "Oh, John, get a taxi for those girls and get rid of them. Even put a cab on our account, *anything* to get them to go." So I did. So generous of her, you know – and when you think of the circumstances! But where Lucy is now, I have no idea. I know she and her sister went straight round to the Palmers but I think Tommy threw them out again, sensible fellow. So we are just picking up the pieces here. Poor Fanny. She's so cut up; you know how sensitive she is. She even said she wished she'd had you two to stay, not the Steele girls.'

'Really ...'

'And, of course, Fanny's mother is going straight to her lawyer in the morning. There's no holding her, once she gets going; she'll have her will changed by lunchtime. She'll just stand over them till they've done it. Lucky old Robert. He'll get Edward's share now. And of course, there'll be some for Fanny, not that she's in the least interested in money.' He paused, and then he said, 'So Mrs Jennings knows all this?'

'Yes,' Elinor said. 'She told us.'

'And what do you think her reaction will be?'

Elinor smiled into the phone. 'Oh, I expect she'll be all for it, John. She's very fond of Lucy, and she'll hate to see someone like Edward thrown out of his family. She's very family-minded, you know.'

There was a short pause. Then John said, stiffly, 'I'm sure

Fanny would love to speak to you, if she weren't so upset.'

Elinor smiled more broadly.

'Give her our love.'

'She's really so hurt. And of course you feel humiliated as well as hurt when someone you've been so kind to lets you down like this.'

Elinor suppressed a laugh.

'Yes, you do, John,' she said. 'You really do. It's so tough when people close to you turn out not to be what you thought they were,' and then she clicked her phone off and turned to her sister.

'You're a star,' Marianne said, laughing back. 'You're an absolute star.'

15

'What are you doing?' Margaret said.

She and Elinor were seated either side of the kitchen table in Barton Cottage with their laptops open. Margaret was supposed to be doing a biology project on hers – the digestive system, complete with diagrams and analyses of all the chemical interactions of the various digestive fluids, but was in fact having a Facebook conversation with a girl in her class who had a cool – and coolly remote – older brother.

Elinor said shortly, and without looking up, 'My emails.'

'Can I see?'

'No.'

'Why? Are they private?'

'No.'

'Are they from Ed?'

'No.'

'If they're not private,' Margaret said, 'and they're not from Ed, why can't I see them?'

Elinor sighed. She turned her laptop round so that Margaret could see the screen.

'They won't interest you.'

Margaret lurched forward across the table, screwing up her eyes to see better.

'Who's Fancynancy?'

'Nancy Steele.'

'Yuck. Gross. Why's she writing to you?'

'To show off.'

'She's written *pages*. Is it all about the plastic surgeon?'

'How do you know about him?'

'I know', Margaret said, 'because she's *always* on Twitter. She tweets about how he said this and how he said that and how he liked her pink handbag and all that gross stuff. Sad isn't the *word*.'

'No,' Elinor said, 'it's not about him.'

Margaret wriggled back to her seat. She said, 'Jonno says she has the attention span of a midge.'

'He's right.'

'Well, why are you emailing her?'

'I'm not,' Elinor said patiently. 'She's emailed me. To tell me all over again about Lucy and Ed. And to make sure I get the message, Lucy has emailed me as well.'

Margaret put the end of a pen in her mouth. Round it, she said, 'What message?'

'That they are getting married.'

'We know that.'

Elinor sighed again. She said, looking at the screen and not at Margaret, 'Well, they want to rub it in. That Lucy felt she should offer to let Ed go if it meant a breach with his family and no inheritance, and that he wouldn't hear of it and told her she was an angel.'

'I bet he never said that.'

'No,' Elinor said. 'That was me. In my crossness.'

'Why are you cross?'

'Because Ed is behaving so well. And because Nancy Steele is such an airhead and because Lucy only writes to me like this so that I will forward the email to Mrs J. and Mary and everyone, and they'll think: Ah bless, what a lovely person Lucy is and how horrible the Ferrarses are.'

Margaret took the pen out of her mouth. She said, 'Well, aren't they?'

'Some of them.'

Margaret began to roll the pen back and forth across the table.

'Ellie ...'

'What?'

'Does it matter about money? Does it matter whether Ed and Lucy have any?'

'Well,' Elinor said carefully, 'they have to live.'

'He hasn't really got a job, though, has he? And she kind of faffs about doing courses and stuff. Not earning, really.'

Elinor looked back at her screen.

'Lucy asks me to see if Jonno would give Ed a job. Or Tommy even.'

'Crikey,' Margaret said unexpectedly.

'Yes.'

'Would they?'

'I doubt it.'

'Would Jonno or Tommy Palmer *really* give Ed a job?'

Elinor looked at her sister.

'Well, what do you think?'

Margaret picked her pen up again.

'I think', she said, 'that money is even more boring than love. But not quite as utterly boring as biology.'

In the bath above the kitchen – she could hear her daughters' voices through the floor, even if she couldn't make out what they were saying – Belle Dashwood lay in the hot water, her face stiffly blanked out by a face mask. Mary Middleton had been seized with an urge for clearance, and had emptied out the contents of her lavishly appointed bathroom cupboards, sending down to Barton Cottage a carrier bag full of expensive half-used pots of this and that, including a face mask which promised to leave your skin not just unlined, but dewy. Margaret had been very contemptuous of the idea of dewy.

'They just mean wet. Who wants to look wet, unless they're a fish or something?'

Belle had no desire to look like a fish. But she had discovered, in the last few weeks, she did have a desire not to look only like the mother of three grown daughters. She had begun to be anxious not to be seen only relatively, indeed to be acknowledged as a woman who amazed people by revealing how old her daughters were, a woman who was admired for what she still had, rather than was pitied for what she now lacked. Lying in the bath and feeling her skin tightening under the cracking shield of the mask, Belle reflected that although Henry was, and always would be, the love of her life, the heart was a muscle as well as an organ, and required exercise.

She had tried to suggest something of the kind on the telephone to Abigail Jennings. The conversation had started with Belle's gratitude for all the kindness shown to Marianne for so long, and had then proceeded, on Belle's part, to hint at that kindness being possibly extended to Marianne's mother.

'It's wonderful here,' Belle said, gazing out of the window
at the rain falling as straight as stair rods on to the paved patio
outside the kitchen window. 'So beautiful. And Jonno's so kind.
And Mary. Everyone's adorable. But it is – it is rather *remote*,
you know.'

Abigail, no doubt surveying a very different view and prospect from her London window, chose not to get the hint.

'Don't worry, dear. I've no intention of forgetting Margaret.
It'll be her turn next, I promise you. Charlotte has persuaded
Marianne down to her weekend place, with the baby, and I can't
make her return with me here afterwards, so I'll be all bereft,
won't I?'

Belle threaded her fingers into the coil of the telephone cable.

'I just wondered, Abi, whether *I* might...'

'*You*, dear? What would you want with London, living where
you do? Send me Margaret, in the holidays, and then there won't
be any jealousy, will there, between the sisters.'

Belle had taken a deep breath.

'Abigail,' she said, 'you've been so kind, and so hospitable.
But my daughters are *my* daughters. They aren't library books.
They're not there just for anyone to borrow on a whim, you know.'

And then she had put the phone down. Abigail did not ring
back. That was three days ago, Belle reflected, lying there in a
no longer quite hot enough bath, and there had been absolute silence. Trying to communicate with Marianne – she was
better, Elinor said, but very bruised still – was hardly easy and
now Elinor was eluding her, too, declining, as she put it, to be a
go-between any longer.

'You'll have to sort it yourself, Ma. I can't do any more with

Marianne. I can't make things smooth with John and Fanny. I can't always be the one who does all the bits of life you don't want to be bothered with. I have got a job to do, which pays a lot of our bills, and keeping that going and getting Margaret to school is all I can manage right now. *All.* OK?'

Belle groped along the side of the bath for a face flannel, soaked it, wrung it out and began to wipe it across her masked face. The relief was indescribable. Was half the effect of beauty treatments the sheer deliverance when they stopped? She heaved herself up out of the bath and climbed dripping on to the mat beside it, reaching for a towel. What a mess it all was, suddenly – or had it been a mess, in fact, since Henry died? No money, John and Fanny's behaviour, this cottage which they had to be so grateful for, Willoughby, Ed – Ed! Belle wrapped the towel round herself tightly, like a sarong. Was it Ed? Was that why Elinor was so distinctly unhelpful? Was Elinor, in truth, deeply upset about Ed and the Steele girl, even though she swore she wasn't?

She crossed the bathroom and rubbed a circular space in the steam on the mirror. She leaned forward and peered at her post-face-mask complexion. Did she look dewy? Or did she just look – red?

Bill Brandon was waiting for Elinor in an Exeter coffee shop. He had rung in the morning to say that he was in Exeter that day, and could he give her lunch.

'I don't really eat lunch.'

'You've got to eat something!'

'I bring something. In a plastic box, from home.'

'Sounds depressing.'

'It is.'

'Well, at least let me buy you a non-depressing sandwich you haven't had to make yourself, then.'

'Thank you,' Elinor said, sounding suddenly grateful, even thankful, 'I'd – I'd really like that.'

Now, Bill put a plate down on the table between them.

'Crayfish and cream cheese and rocket. Smoked salmon. Chicken and salad, all on granary bread. Now, eat.'

Elinor said, sincerely, 'Thank you. Really, thank you.'

Bill pulled out the chair opposite to hers and sat down.

'And I ordered two cappuccinos with chocolate on yours. *Yes.* I hate cappuccino but I knew if I didn't drink it, you wouldn't drink yours, either.'

'Am I being a pain?'

He smiled at her, holding out the plate of sandwiches. He said, 'You're allowed to be fed up, you know.'

'I've always felt that it was fine to be fed up as long as you didn't take it out on other people. And I'm not being very nice to Ma.'

Bill took a sandwich himself and regarded it.

'She's a lovely woman, your mum, but she exploits you.'

'No, she—'

'*Yes,*' Bill said with another emphasis. He took a bite of sandwich. 'Eat up,' he said and then, chewing and grinning, 'What would Mrs J. make of us now, eating lunch together in a public place?'

Elinor had bolted her first sandwich. Steadying herself with a second, she said, 'Why would she make anything?'

'Because she has it in her gossipy head that I'd come on to you if I dared.'

Elinor stopped eating. She said, 'But . . .' and paused.

He smiled at her. He said, 'I do think you are wonderful.'

She smiled back.

'And I think the same of you.'

'But not . . .'

'No. Not.'

He held out the plate of sandwiches again. He said, 'Do you think you and I are the sort of people who are doomed to want what we can't have?'

Elinor looked away.

'I don't know.'

'Elinor?'

'Yes?'

'Ed Ferrars. And Lucy. What do you really feel about that?'

Elinor looked back and directly at him.

'Fine,' she said.

'Really fine? Really?'

'Bill,' Elinor said, 'I am determined − absolutely determined − not to waste my emotional energy in yearning. I don't even entirely understand what's going on, and yet I do see how he's got himself into this place. It's all to do with family, his family. And his mother. They are crashing snobs, his family, and he hates that. He's defending Lucy; he's being kind of old-fashioned, and honourable.'

'But he can't condemn himself—'

Elinor leaned forward.

'Bill, I think he'd rather live, not particularly happily, in a way he thought was right, and not − not purely materialistically, like his family, than in a way that didn't sit well with his conscience. I know it isn't how people think now, but I think he's got to do it his way.'

A waitress came over from behind the counter and put two huge thick white cups of coffee down in front of them.

'Enjoy,' she said, without enthusiasm.

When she had gone, Bill said, 'And you?'

Elinor looked at the fat cushion of foam on top of her coffee. She said, without complete conviction, 'He's never promised me anything. And he's got to do what seems right for him to do. I'd be the same, in his place. You're stuck with yourself, so you might as well try and be someone you can stand to live with.'

Bill said gently, 'You must be honest with me. Would you mind if I tried to help him?'

Elinor's head jerked up.

'Help him!'

'I've got a vacancy at Delaford. It's a managerial job, but more people-orientated than admin- or finance-based. We've tried several people with fantastic social-science qualifications, but they all seem a bit theory based, a bit academic, for what we need. So many of the people at Delaford are truly chaotic and we need someone who doesn't expect either order or miracles. Someone for the staff to turn to, really. Do – do you think that might appeal to him?'

Elinor felt herself growing pink. She put a hand out and grasped Bill's nearest one.

'His family sound so grim,' Bill said, 'and – and what you say about his conscience really hits home with me. I'd like to help, if I can, even though I don't know him very well. There'd be accommodation, too, of course. A flat. Nothing special. But I wouldn't even suggest it, if you – if he—'

Elinor gave Bill's hand a little shake. She said, fervently, 'You – you are *fantastic*.'

'But you—'

'I'm fine,' Elinor said resolutely. '*Fine*. Promise.'

'As long as you really are?'

Elinor leaned back. She smiled at him. She said, 'You know, Bill, that I think you can get used to anything as long as you know exactly what you are getting used *to*. And if I know what lies ahead for Ed, then I can get on with my own future.'

He laughed.

'I wish Mrs J. was right. About you and me.'

'But she isn't.'

He sighed. He said, 'I must try and copy your supreme good sense. I wish I wasn't such a hopeless old romantic.'

Elinor picked up her coffee cup. She said, 'I ought to be more of one.'

'Never wish that. Will you do something for me?'

'Of course.'

'Will you tell Ed to call me?'

She looked straight at him again. She said, 'You should do that directly.'

'Elinor, I hardly know him. I know *of* him, thanks to you, and I have a strong instinct that he's right for Delaford, but I can't call him out of the blue. It would seem weird.'

Elinor looked down into her coffee.

'I'll text him. I'll text him your number and tell him to ring you.'

'And Mrs J.?'

'What about Mrs J.?'

'Will you tell her that even if I haven't proposed to you, I have made a proposal that might benefit her goddaughter?'

Elinor smiled broadly at him.

'Yes,' she said, 'yes. I'd like to do that.'

'It's Ed,' Edward Ferrars said Elinor, sitting in the orange car waiting for Margaret to come out of school, her phone clamped to her ear, stared straight ahead.

'Hello,' she said flatly.

'I got your text.'

'Yes.'

'Something – something about ringing Bill Brandon?'

Elinor tried not to sound too wooden.

'Yes. He asked me to give you his number. He asked me to ask you to call him.'

Edward said diffidently, 'Do – do you know why?'

She let a small pause fall, and then she said, 'Yes.'

'Elinor?' he said. 'Elinor, can you tell me why?'

She closed her eyes briefly. Then she opened them and made herself smile, so that he would hear the warmth in her voice.

'He wants to offer you a job.'

There was a stunned silence.

Then Edward said, incredulously, 'He wants to offer *me a job?*'

'Yes. At Delaford.'

Edward said, with real feeling, 'I would adore to work at Delaford.'

'Yes,' Elinor said, 'I know.'

'But I – I'm not really qualified.'

'I think he's looking for qualities not qualifications.'

'Oh, wow,' Edward said. His voice was shaking. 'Oh, wow. Did he say—'

'Ring him. Ring him and ask.'

'Ellie?'

She put a hand up to her mouth. He'd called her 'Ellie'. 'Ellie,' Edward said again, 'did – did Bill talk to you about this?'

She took her hand away.

'Yes.'

'Did he ask you if – if you thought I'd like it?'

'Yes.'

'And he knew, and so did you, that I don't have a job and nor does Lucy, really?'

'Yes.'

'And – and you – you didn't stand in my way? You said you'd pass his number on?'

'Of course.'

'Oh my God,' Edward said. His voice was now really unsteady. 'Oh, Ellie.'

She could see Margaret now, dawdling out of the school gates, fifty yards away, bent sideways by the weight of her bag.

'You'd have done the same,' Elinor said. 'Get on and ring him.'

'He's so generous. He's amazing. So – so are you.'

'Get on and thank *him*, Edward.'

'Ellie—'

'I've got to go. Margaret's here, I'm picking her up.'

'Mags?' Edward said, almost longingly.

The car door opened.

'Bye,' Elinor said. 'Bye. Good luck,' and clicked her phone off.

Margaret crashed into the passenger seat.

'I hate this car.'

'I know.'

'Who were you talking to?'

Elinor leaned across to drop her phone into her bag in the well by Margaret's feet.

'Someone who I won't see again, till he's married,' she said. 'And I do not, *not*, want to talk about it.'

Margaret put her seat belt on. She gave a theatrical shrug.

'Whatever,' she said.

'Now,' Belle said, folding her arms. 'Now. What is going on?'

Elinor busied herself with the kettle, her back to her mother.

'And don't say nothing,' Belle said.

'I wasn't going to.'

'I have Abi on the phone saying Bill is fantastic and Lucy is so happy, and then John saying Fanny is too upset still to be happy about anything, and they think Bill's offer is very strange, to say the least, and then Jonno rings to say Mary saw Robert Ferrars having a very cosy dinner with the Morton girl Ed was supposed to marry, and then *you* come in, cool as a cucumber, and won't tell me anything!'

Elinor began to look for mugs. She said steadily, 'I *will* tell you. I was going to. I just need tea.'

'*I'll* make tea,' Belle said. 'You talk. Where's Mags?'

'She went up to her room.'

'Is she all right?'

'She got seventy per cent for her biology.'

'But that's *wonderful!*'

'Ma—'

'Sit down. Tell me. Tea tea or a herbal?'

Elinor sat down by the kitchen table and leaned on it. She said, 'Ma, Bill's offered Ed a job at Delaford.'

Belle swung round from the kettle, her mouth agape.

'Darling! He never! How wonderful. Or is it?'

'Oh, I think it is. It's the kind of human, helpful job he might be just brilliant at.'

'And Miss Lucy?'

'Well,' Elinor said, 'I don't imagine either human or helpful is exactly on her wish list, do you? But she'd like the status of the house and Bill's connections and all that.'

Belle poured boiling water into Elinor's mug.

'And you, darling?'

'I'm fine with it, Ma. I told you I am OK and I am not discussing it further.'

'But it's so sad for you. We all thought—'

'Ma!'

Belle put Elinor's mug on the table in front of her. She said, 'That explains John.'

'What does?'

'Bill offering Ed a job. It completely explains John. I couldn't think why he was ringing – he never rings – and then I couldn't think what he was on about, Fanny this, Fanny that, Fanny so hurt and betrayed, and her mother such a marvellous mother, and them both being so brave when they heard about Ed and how we ought to know how brave they were even though we mustn't even mention the subject because it is so painful for both of them. And d'you know what?'

'No,' Elinor said. She blew into her tea.

'D'you know what John said? What he had the nerve to say?'

'Nothing', Elinor said, 'would surprise me.'

'He said,' Belle said, 'he said that Fanny was so appalled by his choosing the Steele girl that she would have even preferred it to be you! Can you believe it? He said that of course it was all too late for that now, but if she were given the option, Fanny would rather have had you for a sister-in-law. I could hardly believe my ears. I said, "John, you have an absolute *nerve* to say any such thing after the way you and Fanny behaved to Elinor and me," but you know what he's like, he just swept on telling me how brave and wonderful Fanny was, and then said that the only consolation she had was Robert, who finds the whole situation hilarious and did a send-up imitation of Edward dealing with all Bill's loonies and made her laugh. I suppose he must be very amusing.'

Elinor took a gulp of tea.

'He's idiotic.'

'John said he really took to *you*!'

'Maybe.'

'But he said that Robert didn't think Ed could cope with Delaford, he'd be completely out of his depth, and in Robert's view, Lucy is deeply, deeply ordinary.'

'Ma, I really don't want to know.'

Belle took the chair next to Elinor's.

'And Fanny has invited us all to Norland!'

Elinor turned to stare at her mother.

'I don't believe it.'

'Not very warmly. In fact, I would describe her invitation as very faint. But she did say it. She did! What an afternoon!'

Elinor said reflectively, 'I suppose Lucy will run rings round Bill Brandon.'

'He'll get wise to her. He's not a fool. Darling...'

'What?'

'Do you – do you think he still carries a bit of a torch for Marianne?'

'Yes,' Elinor said shortly.

'Of course,' Belle said, 'I've always liked him.'

'Have you?'

'Just as I always was a bit wary of Wills. He might have been a god, but there was something about his eyes that I didn't like. I always said so, didn't I?'

'Ma,' Elinor said, 'on the subject of Marianne—'

'I wish she could think of someone like Bill. A good person, a good man, like Bill.'

'Ma,' Elinor said again, 'she *is* leaving London.'

'What?'

'She's leaving Mrs J.'s. Charlotte's persuaded her to go to their weekend place. Near Bath or Bristol or something. It – it'll kind of break her in to coming home.'

Belle regarded her daughter, suddenly sober.

'Ellie, is that progress?'

'I hope so.'

'Poor little Marianne.'

Elinor took one hand away from her mug and put it on her mother's.

'She's changed, Ma. She's different.'

'Is she?'

Elinor leaned forward and kissed her mother's cheek.

'She's doing things her own way, in her own time. But she's trying very hard to grow up. You'll see.'

16

Marianne stood very, very still in the middle of the bedroom at Cleveland that Charlotte had assigned her. It was a pretty room with two beds in it and two windows facing west, through which the April sun was now streaming in all its clear mercilessness: spring light was, in Marianne's opinion, brilliant but cruel. And it was almost cruel, too, to have to look west out of those windows, west towards Devon, where Barton was, where Allenham was, and where Wills had been born, he'd told her, in a place called Combe Magna.

She crossed the room slowly and stood by one of the windows. She could feel a weight of depression settling on her again, despite the sunshine, and the spring garden below her window, and the domestic sounds of Charlotte and her mother and her baby coming from other parts of the house. It wasn't really the depression of a broken heart any more, but more the recollection of what she had felt like, what she had been, before she went to London, the memory of that violently happy girl who had been possessed of a complete, untarnished inno-cence of heart, and who would never be recaptured. The girl who had last looked at the West Country with such rapture did not exist any more, and the one who looked at it now was not just sobered, but somehow diminished, reduced as if a huge emotional lung had been removed and replaced by a grim little nugget of disillusion.

The window was open, a high sash window between white linen curtains striped in grey and pink. Marianne folded her arms on the sill and leaned out. The gardens below her were extensive, and even if Cleveland Cottage called itself a cottage, it was an affectation, really, because it was a house. A considerable house, with stands of mature trees round it, and a gravel sweep, and a prospect of hills to the south-east with even a little folly as a focal point, some distance away, a faux Greek temple, which Tommy said some ancestor of his had put up when the house was built.

'In 1808, 1810, thereabouts,' he said. 'We Palmers may never win a Nobel Prize, but we have a knack with money.' He'd glanced at Marianne. 'I s'pose you think I shouldn't mention money, let alone boast about it.'

Marianne had given him a small smile by way of reply. As the chief witness of her public humiliation, she could never quite forgive him, nor see in him the good heart and good sense that Elinor insisted were there. It had been a relief to her that Tommy was not coming down to Cleveland until later, bringing, apparently, Bill Brandon as another weekend guest, and by the time they both got there, Elinor would have arrived too, from Barton, and would, as usual, take responsibility for both herself and Marianne, leaving Marianne free to read, or go for a walk, or generally absent herself from the well-fed, deep-drinking jollity that Charlotte was plainly planning.

Marianne turned to face the room again. She would let Elinor choose the bed she preferred; she would let Elinor take the lead, dictate the pace. She was trying very hard – hard enough for Elinor not to fail to see – to adjust herself, to be less self-absorbed, less wilful, more mindful of what other people (Elinor in particular) were bearing with a stoicism she had to acknowledge, even if she didn't want to imitate it just yet. She was striving to change, she *was*, but it was hard, all the same, to let go of the glory of her past certainties, of her belief in passion, and surrender, and the seductive power of giving in to inclination. But she was trying, and she would go on trying, and agreeing to a weekend in Charlotte and Tommy's country house was proof of her real intention to be different. Wasn't it? She sneezed suddenly, shivering, and looked for a box of tissues. They'd be somewhere. Charlotte was the kind of hostess who, even with a new baby, would never overlook the details.

The tissues were there, of course, hidden in a white wicker cube in the bathroom, beside a graded pile of snowy towels and a new cake of pink soap shaped like an egg. Marianne snatched a handful from the box and blew hard. Maybe it wasn't depression she was feeling but something altogether simpler. Maybe the aches in her joints and head were not psychological at all, but merely the physical portent of a heavy approaching cold. She blew again and then put her palm against her forehead. Did she, she wondered, have a temperature?

Elinor, driving the seventy miles from Exeter to Cleveland after work, watched the evening deteriorate. She had left Exeter in late-afternoon sunshine, but as she drove up towards Bristol, the clouds ahead darkened and lowered, piling up into great bruised masses until, ten miles from her destination, the rain suddenly crashed down on to the motorway as if a bath had been tipped sideways, and she found herself battling both to keep the car steady, and to see. She had Heart FM on the radio – Margaret's preferred choice – but even that was drowned out by the drumming of rain on the car roof. She leaned forward in an effort to see better, and, not for the first time, wondered what it was in Marianne that made her requests so difficult – even impossible – to refuse.

'Just a weekend at Cleveland,' Marianne had said. 'Two nights. *Please*. Don't make me go alone.'

'But I don't see why you want to go at *all*. Why don't you just come straight home?'

Marianne said, sadly, weakly, 'I can't quite do that...'

'But what's the difference between coming straight home on Friday or, via a weekend you don't want to do, on Sunday afternoon?'

There was a pause. Marianne was silent and Elinor, at her desk in Exeter, was in no mood to help her. Then Marianne said, in an even smaller voice, 'It's a kind of test.'

'What? What is?'

'Going to Charlotte's. I've got to make myself be normal again. I've got to – to train myself to be more ordinary. I've got to go to Charlotte's and be a good guest and take notice of the baby and be appreciative.'

'If I were Charlotte,' Elinor said, 'I'd be pretty insulted by an attitude like that. Luckily for you, she's too nice and cheerful to care, even if she notices.'

Marianne said, 'It came out wrong.'

'Did it?'

'I didn't mean to sound superior. I don't think I'm superior. I think *you* are superior. I just meant that – that I was trying. Not – to be like I was being.'

Elinor relented a little.

'OK.'

'If it's a big deal when I get home, Ellie, I'll know it's because I *made* it a big deal. I really don't want melodrama, or even drama drama. I want to get home and plan my future and be – well, something like I should have been. But I would so ... *value* it, if you came to Cleveland.'

So here she was, battling up the motorway in a spring storm with a weekend ahead among people who were all, with the exception of Charlotte's baby and Marianne, not only older than she was, but who had a completely different take on life. Life, she thought suddenly, and almost bitterly. Is life what I'm having? Even if I fairly powerfully do not want pubs and clubs and getting wasted, surely life for someone of my age should be just slightly more *fun?*

'She got soaked,' Charlotte said. 'I mean, *drowned.* She wanted to walk up to the temple and I said, Oh, do wait for Tommy to show it to you, it's his pride and joy, he's even had a Wi-Fi connection put in there, but she wouldn't, she said she *had* to have some exercise after all those weeks in London, and next thing we knew was this absolutely *deafening* crash of thunder and the heavens opened and Marianne, of course, was *drenched*, and then I *could* not make her take off her jeans and put on something dry, and nor could Mummy, and really, honestly, Ellie, it's no wonder she feels ghastly. Aren't these little pea shoots just adorable? I'm going to put them in the salad. I put nasturtium flowers in salad in the summer, and it's *completely* worth it, just to see Tommy go ballistic. He can't *bear* savoury food with fruit or flowers in. Too funny.'

Elinor was leaning against one of Charlotte's artfully distressed painted cupboards, nursing a mug of tea. She said, 'I'll go and see her. Did she go to bed?'

'Well, I hope so. I told her to, and so did Mummy, but she waved away Lemsip and Nurofen and, quite frankly, I didn't want her sneezing all over poor little Tomkins, so I said go to bed and stay there.'

Elinor glanced across the kitchen. Inside a playpen on the carefully flagged floor, little Tom Palmer, dressed in bibbed dungarees and a miniature check shirt, was lying in a bouncing chair, feebly waving his arms and legs like a stranded insect. She said, 'I do *hope* she hasn't given him anything.'

'Never fear,' Charlotte said, competently slicing a fennel bulb, 'I didn't give her the chance. Bundled her upstairs at the double.' She looked across at her son. 'Didn't we, baby buster? And won't Daddy go apeshit when he sees you dressed up like that? It's so funny, but Tommy thinks all babies should be in white nighties for months. So we'll just hide the new cashmere baby cardi from Daddy, shall we? Ellie, you must be exhausted. Go and have a bath. The men won't be here till nine and Mummy's glued to the telly news, as ever. I keep saying to her, Isn't it better not to know, when it's all so ghastly, but she says not knowing makes her feel worse. Ellie, what *am* I going to do with her in London without your sister to fuss over?'

Marianne was lying on her side, on her bed, not in it, with her knees drawn up and her eyes closed. Elinor bent over her. 'M?'

'Oh,' she said, not stirring. 'Oh, Ellie. I'm so glad you've come.'

Elinor put a hand on her sister's leg. Her jeans were damp, almost wet, and the strands of her hair snaking across the pillow were clearly not dry, either.

She said, almost crossly, 'What *are* you doing?'

Marianne said, gritting her teeth against her shivering, 'I don't feel too great.'

'No,' Elinor said, 'of course you don't. You look awful. Have you got a temperature?'

'Probably.'

'And you are an asthmatic. And you lie there in wet clothes with a fever. You are not a *baby*, Marianne.'

Marianne said weakly, 'Please don't be cross. I just suddenly felt so awful, and then a bit caged, and I got caught in the rain—'

'Sit up,' Elinor said.

'I can't...'

'Sit *up!*'

Marianne, her eyes still closed, struggled into a sitting position.

Elinor grasped the hem of her sweater and began to pull it over her head. She said, 'Help me.'

'I'm trying...'

'Now your shirt.'

'Ellie, I'm sorry, I'm sorry, I just can't—'

'Jeans,' Elinor said. 'Socks. Everything. God, you are so clueless.'

'I didn't want it to be like this.'

'Have you got your inhaler?'

'Yes.'

'Where?'

'In my bag,' Marianne said. She crouched on the edge of the bed in her underwear, shaking. Elinor dug her own pyjamas out of her case and held them out.

'Put these on. I'll get your puffer.'

'I don't need—'

'M,' Elinor almost shouted, 'if you have a cold and it's anywhere near your chest, what will happen? What? *What?*'

'I didn't want it to be a drama—'

'There's *always* a drama round you!'

'I'm really sorry,' Marianne said. 'I am, I am. I needed you to come, I wanted you to come, but I didn't mean this to happen.'

'I'll get you a hot-water bottle.'

'Ellie?'

'What?'

'Have Bill and Tommy come?'

Elinor paused by the door.

'Why should that make any difference?'

'I don't know. It's – it just seems to be a bit reassuring when Bill's around, doesn't it . . .?'

'Heavens,' Elinor said tartly, '*there's* a change of tune. I thought you thought he was old and boring.'

Marianne said, with as much dignity as she could muster struggling into Ellie's pyjamas, 'I'm – trying to think differently. I was trying to *be* different. I don't want to have a cold. I'm sorry, Ellie. I'm sorry.'

Elinor looked across at her. The pyjamas were very old, made of brushed cotton and patterned with teapots. They had always been too big. But even dressed in them, with her hair in damp ropes on her shoulders, and her eyes circled with fatigue, Marianne looked, well, outstanding. Elinor sighed.

'Get into bed,' she said. 'Right in. Properly. I'm going to get a hot-water bottle and some paracetamol and you are going to swallow it.'

Marianne attempted a smile.

'Of course,' she said.

Bill Brandon tried to make Elinor have some whisky.

'Just a weak one. Medicinal. You look worn out.'

'I don't really like it.'

'Even if I add ginger ale?'

'Even then.'

'I suppose I couldn't take some up to Marianne ...'

Elinor smiled at him. She said, 'I hope she's asleep.'

Bill Brandon said, 'I don't want to fuss but shouldn't we get a doctor? Or ring NHS Direct or something?'

'She's got a cold,' Charlotte called from the other side of the kitchen, where she was feeding the baby, a cream pashmina shawl draped decorously over the child and one shoulder. 'She's not dying, you old fusspot.'

'She's asthmatic.'

Tommy came across the room, put a glass of wine into Elinor's hand and clumped Bill Brandon on the shoulder.

'Don't be an old woman, Bill. She's got a cold. Listen to the sister lady.'

Elinor took a sip. She said to Bill, 'I've lived with asthmatics all my life. Honestly. She's got a cold because I expect her immune system's a bit shot after everything this winter, and she just needs to sleep. She'll be fine in the morning.'

'I still think—'

'Too awful,' Mrs Jennings said, sweeping into the room. 'Why do I watch the news when it just makes me despair? I'm sure the Greeks hate austerity but your father, Charlotte, always maintained that if you haven't got it, you shouldn't borrow to spend it. I'm with Mrs Merkel, all the way. Now, Tommy, it's a Friday night so I think something serious is called for.'

'Gin and serious?'

She gave him a wide smile.

'Lovely. Just go easy on the serious. Elinor dear, you look a wreck. How is that sister of yours?'

'I want them to get a doctor,' Bill said. 'She's asthmatic.'

'She's OK,' Elinor said. 'She's asleep. She'll be fine by the morning.'

Mrs Jennings nodded towards her grandson.

'Let's hope she hasn't given *him* her lurgy, poor mite.'

'Not while I'm feeding him, Mummy. He's immune to everything. Tommy, is that glass just neat gin, really?'

'Pretty well.'

'Perfect,' Abigail Jennings said with satisfaction. She raised the glass towards the assembled company. 'Chin chin dears. Happy weekend to us and happy futures all round.' A thought suddenly struck her. 'Bill,' she said. 'Bill. Wonderful of you to give that boy a job. Wonderful.'

'And a flat,' Charlotte called.

'Which I'm doing up,' Bill said, smiling. 'I couldn't ask any girl to put up with it as it is. I was going ask Elinor to help me, as it happens.'

'Oh—'

'Perfect,' Abigail said again, swinging round to beam at her.

'The perfect person. Our tame architect! Ideal. And the more you
two see of each other, the happier I shall be.'

'Abi—'

'Mrs J.—'

She waved a plump hand at them.

'Oh, get on with you both. We need cheering up in the romantic department after all we've been through.'

Elinor put her wine glass down on the nearest kitchen counter. Tommy Palmer, she noticed, was holding his son's tiny feet
and smiling down at what the cream pashmina hid from view.
She said, 'I'll just go and check on Marianne.'

Bill touched her arm.

'Can I help? Can I do anything?'

She shook her head.

'No. But thank you.'

'Just call me. If you need anything . . .'

'Of course.'

He looked at her, suddenly intent.

'Give her my love,' he said.

Across the room, Charlotte and Mrs Jennings rolled their eyes
at one another.

'Not a hope,' Charlotte mouthed at her mother.

Tommy Palmer turned his gaze from his son's shrouded head
to his wife's face. His expression was reproving.

'Don't you, either of you,' he said clearly, 'be so sure.'

Someone, somewhere in the cloudy confusion of Bill Brandon's
dreams, was knocking. He couldn't tell where the knocking was
coming from, or what it was made by, but it was persistent, on
and on, and then somebody was calling as well as knocking,

calling him by name and suddenly his eyes were open and he was abruptly awake, staring into the darkness of the single bedroom at Cleveland Cottage where Tommy Palmer kept his weekend clothes.

He was, as a soldier, alert and out of bed in a second, grateful to have remembered – being in someone else's house – to have put on at least pyjama bottoms the night before. The knocking was on his bedroom door, and the voice was Elinor's. He flung it open and said, in a voice that was not quite as steady and purposeful as he had intended, 'Marianne?'

Elinor was dressed in an oversized T-shirt and her eyes were enormous with distress.

'Oh, Bill, thank goodness, so sorry to wake you, but she's awful, *awful*, can't really speak, all blue round her mouth, like Dad was, like—'

He put a hand out and gripped her shoulder.

'We need an ambulance.'

'Her nebuliser doesn't seem to be working. We've tried and tried. I think she needs oxygen, like – like Dad did. And that beta agonist stuff. Bill, I'm frightened—'

He stepped forward and, oblivious to his naked chest, put his arms round her. He said, as reassuringly as he could, 'I'm going to ring the B.R.I. – the hospital in Bristol. I'm going to do it right now. Is she wheezing?'

'Hardly at all.'

He let her go.

'Then it's severe.'

She gazed at him.

'How do you know that?'

He gave her the ghost of a smile. He said, 'I've learned a lot about asthma since I met your sister. I – I made it my business to. Now scoot back to her. I'll come in the minute I know an ambulance is on the way.'

The far end of the landing, another door opened. Mrs Jennings, upholstered in a quilted dressing gown patterned with peonies, her hair endearingly on end, emerged into the dim light Charlotte now left burning all night as there was a baby in the house.

'Elinor?'

Elinor swung round.

'Is it Marianne?'

Elinor nodded, unable to speak. Mrs Jennings came quickly down the landing. She put her arms round Elinor as Bill Brandon vanished back into his bedroom to find his phone. She said, 'You poor child.'

'It's Marianne that's poor—'

'It depends', Abigail said, patting Elinor's back, 'on who you think has really borne most.'

Elinor relaxed a little against the comfort of the peony quilting.

'Oh, Mrs J. . . .'

'I know, dear,' Abigail Jennings said, still patting, 'I know.'

'I'm going to cry.'

'Why don't you?'

'It's just – just like Dad, hardly speaking, battling for breath...'

'There, there, dear.'

From the bedroom, Tommy Palmer's Madras bathrobe now added to his pyjamas, Bill Brandon emerged, his phone in his hand. He looked at Mrs Jennings with approval. He said, 'Ambulance is on the way.'

Elinor tried to speak, and nothing happened. Her throat seemed to be full of something that obstructed her muscles, and tears were pouring out of her eyes and soaking into Mrs Jennings's shoulder.

'There, there,' Mrs Jennings said again, patting. 'There, there. Poor girl.'

Bill Brandon put his phone in the bathrobe pocket.

'Fifteen minutes,' he said. 'Let's go back to the patient, shall we?'

'Oh my God,' Charlotte Palmer said to her mother. 'Intensive care! I can't *believe* it! One minute she's got a cold coming, and she gets wet in the rain, the next it's ambulances at dawn. Mummy, I didn't hear a *thing*. Not one *thing*. Isn't that awful? But when Tomkins sleeps through, which is practically never, we all sleep like the proverbial. But honestly. All that drama and we hear not a dicky bird.'

Mrs Jennings, still in her peony dressing gown, but with her hair combed into its customary bouffant, and her pearl earrings added for dignity, was cradling her grandson.

'There was nothing you could do, Char. Nothing. Elinor sensibly alerted Bill and there was an ambulance here in seventeen minutes – I timed it – and she got whisked off. Elinor and Bill went with her, thank goodness, Elinor looking simply terrible, poor lamb. I don't think she'd even brushed her hair.'

Tommy Palmer was absorbed in reading the weekend edition of the *Financial Times* on his iPad. He said, without looking up, 'And who would have noticed or cared if she had?'

Mrs Jennings continued to look down at her grandson. She said imperturbably, 'She never thinks of herself, that girl. It's time she did. Do too much for other people and all they do is take you for utter granted. At least Bill sees what a darling she is.'

'Mummy,' Charlotte said, hunting for coffee in her well-stocked cupboard. '*Mummy*, just give over on that topic, would you? Bill Brandon only has eyes for Marianne.'

'Nonsense.'

'He thinks Ellie is wonderful, Mummy. Which she is. But he doesn't *fancy* her.'

Mrs Jennings said firmly to her grandson, 'It isn't *all* about sex.'

'It mostly is,' Tommy said, his eyes still on his screen. 'And if it isn't, it should be.'

'Ignore him,' Charlotte said. She put a new packet of coffee down beside the kettle. 'It's all he thinks about. When he isn't thinking about money.'

'You're a lucky girl,' Abigail said. 'What else d'you want in a man? Or expect, for that matter. I always said to your father—'

'Listen,' Tommy Palmer said suddenly. He was staring at his BlackBerry. 'Text from Bill.'

Charlotte turned to look at him, the empty kettle in her hand. Mrs Jennings raised her eyes from the baby.

'"High-flow oxygen,"' Tommy read. '"Nebulised salbutamol and..." something or other, can't read it, "... bromide, systemic steroids, all ongoing. Not responding so far. Collecting Belle from Barton soonest. Elinor staying put. More anon. B."'

He stopped reading. There was a shocked and complete silence. Charlotte put the kettle down and crossed the kitchen to take her baby from her mother. She bent over him, her face against his.

'Poor little Marianne,' Abigail Jennings said softly.

Tommy Palmer stared out of the window.

'Poor buggers,' he said, 'the whole bloody lot of them. What a nightmare.'

There was a small visitors' room where Elinor was told she could wait. It was furnished with unwelcoming vinyl-covered armchairs, a low plywood table bearing a scattering of outdated and well-thumbed magazines, and its walls were meagrely hung with small sentimental watercolours of generic country views and clusters of cottages. The air of the room held the same density of accumulated tension and apprehension that she remembered from a similar room at Haywards Heath Hospital less than two years before, and she knew that, whatever privacy the room might offer, a chair in the corridor, or the hospital coffee shop, would actually be a great deal more bearable as places to pass the time.

And bearing was what she had now to do. In there – in that little, dramatic, concentrated ward – Marianne was being given everything she remembered as necessary to be given in the case of a severe asthma attack. A young consultant – he looked to her only student age – had explained punctiliously that the maximum inhaled beta 2 agonists might need supplementation with IV aminophylline, and if there was respiratory arrest, some adrenalin as well, and she had gazed at him and nodded and been absolutely unable to say please don't list all these drugs for me but please, please just tell me if she's going to die? She had felt sick with panic, looking at his young, pale, serious face, sick with helplessness, sick with a terrible, engulfing loneliness that had nothing to do with being by herself in a strange hospital and everything to do with the unendurable possibility of a future life without Marianne. This last prospect was so truly crushing that, for the moment, it left no room for remorse, even though she knew it was just waiting to swallow her up, reminding her of her irritation with Marianne, her lack of sympathy and empathy, her exasperation with her sister's intensity, her resentments, her impatience – the list was endless. But it was not for now. Now was just a kind of terrible paralysis, on a plastic chair in a hospital corridor, picturing Bill Brandon speeding down to Devon like a man possessed to collect her mother and Margaret.

He'd been wonderful. He'd masterminded the ambulance and the hospital arrival, somehow forcing immediate attention in A and E, never raising his voice or taking no for an answer. He'd been like that for the first turbulent half-hour, and then, suddenly, had turned to Elinor with a face of utter anguish, and said, 'I'd stay with you, I really would, but I'll go round the bend if I don't *do* something. So would it be OK by you if I go and get your mother?'

Elinor had swallowed, nodding violently. She said, 'I'd be so glad, so grateful, I'd—'

'Have you rung her?'

'Not yet. I haven't rung anyone.'

'Ring her,' Bill said. 'Ring her now. Tell her I'll be there in a couple of hours. If—'

'Don't!'

He flinched and put his hand briefly to his face. He said indistinctly, 'They do wonders, now . . .'

'Go,' Elinor said.

'Will you be all right?'

'We're neither of us all right. Go and get Ma. Please. Thank you.'

'Text me. Ring your mother—'

'Go!'

He'd whirled round and started running. Somebody stopped him, almost at once, a nurse somebody in a dark blue uniform, and Elinor had seen him pause for a second, and then race on towards the lifts, leaving the nurse watching him, shaking her head. And then Elinor had taken her phone out of her pocket and rung her mother, standing in the corridor looking down at an asphalted space between the buildings, dotted with concrete tubs of tired, serviceable shrubs, and had a conversation of a kind that seemed as surreal as if it were happening in a hideous dream, and not on a Saturday morning in real-life April.

'Bill's coming,' she kept saying through Belle's tears. 'He's on his way. Bill's coming.'

Then Margaret had taken the phone from her mother, and Elinor had had to say everything all over again and Margaret – oh, bless her, really bless her – had sounded calm and together, and reassured Elinor that they would be ready for Bill, whenever he came, and only at the end had said, suddenly and desperately, 'Will we be too late?'

'No,' Elinor said, crossing her fingers automatically, idiotically. 'No. Of course you won't.'

She looked at her watch now. Her wrist was bare. She hadn't had time to put her watch on, hadn't thought about it, hadn't brushed her teeth even! She should do that. She should go and buy a toothbrush and a comb and some coffee, and go through the inevitably reassuring rituals of starting the day. An abrupt pang of agony about Marianne hit her so hard that she gasped and bent over, her head hanging, staring at the grey and shining vinyl floor, muttering to herself, 'Please, M, don't die, don't leave me, fight, M, please fight, please, just for me, I'll do anything,

I will, I will—'

'Are you Marianne's sister?'

On the shiny grey floor, right in her field of vision, were a pair of large white medical clogs. She took a second or two to absorb the sight; then she straightened up, her gaze travelling up a pair of jeaned legs to a checked shirt and a white medical coat. Above that was a face, Elinor thought distractedly, possibly an Iraqi face or an Iranian face or even a Syrian face or a Turkish face, but Middle Eastern anyway, wonderful hair, so dark it almost had a blue sheen to it, navy blue—'Marianne's sister?' the doctor repeated.

He was smiling. Smiling! Elinor shot to her feet.

'Yes! Yes? Is she—'

'She's responding,' he said. 'She's breathing. Bronchodilation weak still, but it's happening.'

Elinor goggled at him. 'You mean—'

He held up two crossed fingers. He nodded.

'I mean', he said, 'not out of the woods, but on her way. You did right to bring her in.'

'Can – oh, can I see her?'

'Not yet. Later, maybe. When we're sure we've stabilised her.' He looked at her. He was older than she'd first realised, older than the other, earlier doctor, maybe a father even, someone who might understand about families, understand that even if you sometimes wanted to murder them, you couldn't do without them, couldn't imagine life without – 'Why don't you', the doctor said, 'go and get yourself something to eat?'

Half an hour later, fortified by a blueberry muffin, a mug of coffee and ten minutes in a discouraging hospital washroom,

Elinor was back on her chair in the corridor. That corridor, which had looked to her, earlier, like some sort of living tomb, now appeared almost cheerful, with sunlight slanting in through the dusty windows and casting sharp shadow stripes on the grey floor. The row of blue plastic chairs was still empty, although there was a middle-aged man in the visitors' room leafing restlessly through the magazines, and, rather than join him and feel an obligation to talk to him, Elinor thought she would turn one of the chairs to face the window and the sun and merely sit there, with her eyes closed, and bask in the unspeakable joy of sheer, pure, unfathomable relief.

She had texted everyone as she ate her muffin. It was the dullest of muffins, studded here and there with synthetic blueberries tasting of nothing but an indefinable bland sweetness, but nothing Elinor could immediately recollect had ever tasted so wonderful. She ate and drank with her left hand and texted furiously with her right, texts to her mother and Margaret, and Bill, to Mrs Jennings and the Palmers. 'It's OK,' she wrote, 'OK!!! She's breathing! She's breathing!' She lay back in her chair now, eyes shut, her hands on her own ribs, feeling them rising and falling, rising and falling, letting her mind bob gently like a boat on little waves in the sunshine, over the miracle of her relief, the extravagant immensity of her gratitude, the intense and marvellous sense of being alive, herself, and able to relish that because Marianne was still alive, Marianne was breathing, breathing—

'Elinor,' someone said.

She opened her eyes, and looked up.

There was a man standing beside her, a vaguely familiar, dishevelled-looking man in a suede jacket with too long hair. She stared at him.

He sat down beside her. He was holding a showy modern car ignition key, the kind where you press a button—'It's Wills,' Wills said. He tried a smile. 'Don't you recognise me?'

'God,' Elinor said, instinctively drawing back. 'God, how *dare* you—'

He put a hand out.

'Please,' he said. '*Please.*'

'How did you know?'

'Charlotte.'

'*Charlotte?*'

'She rang me. At seven o'clock this morning. She said it was an emergency.' He looked down at the key in his hand. He said, with quiet emphasis, 'She knows how I feel.'

Elinor edged on to the next chair, away from him. She said, 'I don't want to talk to you.'

'*Please*, Elinor. I won't stay long, I promise. But I have to know, I have to know ... Is – is she going to be OK?'

Elinor looked out of the window.

'Yes,' she said shortly.

He gave a kind of shuddering sigh, a gasp of thankfulness.

'Thank God. Thank *God*. I couldn't have borne it. I couldn't—' He stopped. He glanced at Elinor, and then he said, 'D'you think I'm a shit?'

She continued to look out of the window. She said, 'Are you drunk or something?'

He sighed. He said, 'I got in the car at seven ten this morning and drove here like the clappers. I haven't even had a coffee.'

She turned to glare at him.

'I don't know what the hell you think you're doing. I don't care if you drove from – from *Aberdeen*. You have no business to be here. Charlotte had no business to ring you.'

He let a moment or two pass before saying, 'Will – will you give me five minutes, just five minutes?'

'I don't see why I should. I can't think why you should imagine I'd give you a second's thought, let alone any time.'

He leaned forward. He said, with naked earnestness, 'I did behave like a shit, Elinor. I did. I'll never forgive myself. But can I just try and explain, can I just . . .' He stopped again. Then he said, almost in a whisper, 'I want to say sorry.'

Elinor said nothing.

He said, 'I can't hope that she'd ever forgive me—'

Elinor said quietly, 'She already has. That's another reason why you never deserved her.'

He almost sprang to his feet.

'She *has*? She's forgiven me?'

Elinor looked away again.

'Long ago.'

He said fervently, 'She's amazing. I've never known anyone like her. And I never will.' He said, almost desperately, 'You must believe me. Your sister is the most wonderful person I have ever known, or ever will.'

Elinor turned her head again and looked at him, stonily. He was still beautiful, but he looked disreputable today, slightly jowly, unshaven, with his hair straggling over his collar and bloodshot eyes. She said coldly, 'What about the others?'

'Others?'

'Little Eliza,' Elinor said, enunciating with deliberation. 'And I bet she wasn't the only one.'

He said with difficulty, 'No.'

'Busted by the police, in a pub lavatory.'

'I didn't know that, till after it happened.'

'Which absolves you?'

'No. No, of course it doesn't. But it doesn't make me culpable—'

'You started it. You gave her drugs, in the beginning.'

He winced. He said, 'You sound like Aunt Jane.'

'Good,' Elinor said, 'I mean to. And she was pregnant.'

'Not by me.'

'Huh!'

He said sadly, 'Would it satisfy you to know that that's why Aunt Jane threw me out and changed her will? I always thought Bill Brandon had—'

'Leave him out of it!'

Wills licked his lips. He said, 'I was in such debt. Utterly maxed. Every card.'

Elinor said tartly, 'Well, you aren't now, are you. You dug for gold, and' – she glanced pointedly at his wedding ring – 'you found it.'

'I was in real trouble. I had to.'

'Like you had to publicly humiliate my sister? Like you had to send back everything she had given you as if it was the contents of a – of a waste-paper basket?'

He said, in a low voice, 'That was Ally.'

'So none of this is your fault really. Your godmother, your wife – your poor wife – they're all instruments of your great *misfortune*, are they?'

He raised his head and looked at her. He said, 'I've only been in love, truly in love, once, and that was with M – with your sister.'

Elinor said nothing.

He said pleadingly, 'Will you tell her that? Will you tell her, when she's better, that I came and that – that she wasn't wrong. I did care. I do care. And Ally knows that. Ally knows why I married her.' He stood up and looked down at Elinor. 'Will you tell her that?'

'I might.'

'Do – do you still think I'm a shit?'

Elinor sighed.

'I think you're a car crash. A destructive car crash.'

'I'll take that as one degree more approving than a complete shit.'

She shrugged. He bent over her. He said, 'Can I ask you one more thing?'

'One more.'

'Is – is there anyone else in Marianne's life? Anyone else will be bad enough, but there's a particular person—'

Elinor stood too.

'Get out,' she said.

He said, persisting, 'You know I'll never forgive myself, don't you? You know I'll be punished all my life—'

Elinor looked at him. She said, 'If your worst punishment is Marianne never giving you another thought, as long as she lives, then yes, you will,' and then she turned on her heel, marched down the corridor to the visitors' room and shut the door of it behind her with a bang.

17

Belle Dashwood came out of Marianne's bedroom and closed the door quietly behind her. Elinor was halfway down the stairs. She turned. 'Is she—?'

Belle put her finger to her lips.

'Sleeping. Or on the verge of it. D'you know, she nearly has pink cheeks?'

Elinor smiled. They had been back at Barton for a week now, and, after an initially tearful response to being home among everything that was familiar – and painful, for the very reason of being familiar – Marianne had set herself to recover with a purposefulness that astonished all of them. She had even, Elinor discovered, been online, researching a guitar foundation course at the Bristol branch of the Brighton Institute for Modern Music.

'I could even apply for a scholarship, Ellie. Your family income has to be below forty thousand pounds, and ours easily is.'

Belle came down the stairs towards Elinor.

'I still can't believe it.'

'Nor me.'

'That drive. That ghastly drive to the hospital – till your text came, of course. And the waiting for Bill, before, and feeling I shouldn't ring you again, because I'd only howl. Mags was so brave. Every time I looked at her, she smiled even though her poor face was a *mask* of tragedy. Thank God she isn't asthmatic. Or you, darling.'

'Ma?'

'Yes, darling?'

'Can we talk?'

'Of course! But maybe not on the stairs. Shall we even open some wine? Jonno's sent enough to float a ship. He thinks red wine is an absolute cure-all and I haven't the heart to tell him that Marianne doesn't really like it.'

'But Bill sent some white, didn't he?'

Belle smiled fondly at the thought.

'Darling Bill. I've never met a man so thoughtful.'

In the kitchen, Margaret had left her school bag on the table. She herself was nowhere to be seen, and was no doubt in her Thomas-made tree house, messaging her friends. Since Marianne's recovery, her relief had manifested itself in a permanent state of contempt for her family, and every time she was asked not to do something – play her music at anti-social volume, monopolise the bathroom for hours, stare mutely and moodily at whatever was on her plate at mealtimes – was inclined to shout, 'Ruin my life, why don't you?' and stamp out of the room.

'Ought she to be doing her homework?' Belle said now.

'Probably.'

'Shall we – not make her, just for the moment?'

Elinor subsided into a kitchen chair.

'Oh, please yes,' she said tiredly.

Belle opened the fridge and took out a bottle of white wine. She put it on the table and glanced at Elinor.

'Are you all right, darling?'

'Yes. I'm fine. I just wanted to tell you that – Wills came to the hospital. Just before you did.'

Belle seemed neither surprised nor especially interested to hear this. She inserted a corkscrew into the neck of the bottle. She said, non-committally, 'Did he now.'

'Yes, Ma. He drove down from London because Charlotte alerted him to Marianne's asthma attack.'

Belle wound the screw in with great concentration. She said, 'That was very silly of her.'

'I know. I've told her so. But she says he's still mad about Marianne, and always was, and never stopped being, and she thought he ought to be allowed to say that in such a crisis, and even more that Marianne ought to know it.'

Belle drew the cork out very slowly. She said, almost dismissively, 'Water under the bridge, darling.'

'Ma. Should I tell Marianne?'

'Why bother?'

'Well,' Elinor said, pushing the two glasses Belle had put on the table towards her mother, 'might it not be a bit consoling for M to know that he did mean it, and that she was right to insist that he did?'

Belle began to pour the wine carefully into the glasses.

'Lovely colour. Look at that! We're so lucky that Bill knows about wine. D'you know, darling, I don't think we need bother Marianne about Wills any more. That's history. He's history. She's got far better fish to fry now.' She stopped pouring and pushed a glass back towards Elinor. 'I didn't tell you . . .'

'Didn't tell me what?'

Belle sat down on the opposite side of the table. She took a deep and appreciative swallow of wine.

'My journey with Bill. We were all in such a state at the beginning, of course we were, and I thought he was just being grim and silent because he was respecting how upset we were, but then your text came, and I suddenly saw that he was fighting back tears, real tears, and I didn't actually mean to say anything specific but before I could help myself, I said, Oh, Bill dear, are you more than just relieved for the girls and me? And he nodded and couldn't speak and then he suddenly swerved the car on to the hard shoulder and put his arms on the steering wheel and his head on his arms and honestly, Ellie, he just wept like a baby. And Mags and I patted him a bit, like you do, and then he gave a kind of gasp and said it was hopeless, he was so boring and why would anyone like Marianne ever even think of an old fossil like him, and we said, There, there, nothing ventured, nothing gained, and he said we weren't to mention it to anyone, ever, and blew his nose, and off we went again. But wouldn't it be wonderful?'

'He's the nicest man.'

'I know. And very attractive.'

'You mean well-off.'

'No, darling. Of course, it's lovely he's got money and a house and a business and all that, but it's beside the point. The point is that when you look at him, you think, Oh, very attractive. A very, very attractive man. What does Marianne think?'

Elinor ran a finger round the rim of her glass.

'I don't think she's thinking about men just now—'

The door to the hall opened.

'I might be,' Marianne said.

'Darling!'

She came into the room in her rosebud and plaid pyjamas, pulled out a chair and sat down. She looked at the wine.

'Can I have some of that?'

Elinor said, 'Were you listening at the door?'

Marianne smiled at her.

'Yes, I was.'

'For how long?'

'To hear enough,' Marianne said. She looked at the wine again. 'No sharing?'

Elinor regarded her. She said coolly, 'Get a glass.'

'Darling,' Belle said, 'I don't want to get anyone's hopes up. Especially Bill's.'

Marianne got up and went round behind Elinor's chair to the cupboard where the glasses were kept. She said casually, 'He's a lovely man. A really lovely man. And you're quite right, he's attractive.'

'And', Elinor demanded, 'Wills? Is he attractive?'

Marianne went back to her seat and put the wine glass on the table.

'I – I can't answer that,' she said quietly. 'Not yet. You shouldn't ask me.'

There was silence. Belle pushed the wine bottle towards Marianne. She picked it up, poured, and put it down again. Then she said, more hesitantly, 'What would make a difference to how I think about all that is just to know that I wasn't duped, that I didn't imagine it all, that I didn't make something up because I so wanted it to be true. I would love to know he wasn't cynical, on top of everything else.'

She stopped. Belle looked at Elinor. Elinor leaned towards her sister.

'You didn't overhear that bit, then. He wasn't cynical.'

Marianne took a sip of her wine.

'How d'you know?'

'Because he came to the hospital.'

Marianne put her glass down with a small bang. Her cheeks suddenly flamed and she put her hands up against them.

'He – he *what*?'

'He dashed down from London, the day you were in hospital.'

'But – but how did he know?'

'Charlotte rang him. She thought he deserved to know because he's still crazy about you. Always has been. He asked me to tell you.'

Marianne took her hands away from her face and laid them on the table. She sighed. She said simply, 'Oh.'

Belle leaned forward. She said, 'It's what I always said, darling. That he wasn't to be trusted.'

'Ellie,' Marianne said, as if her mother hadn't spoken, 'why didn't you tell me he'd been?'

'I was going to—'

'Did you think it would start me up again?'

Elinor said hesitantly, 'Well, I did wonder.'

Marianne smiled at her a little sadly. She said, 'So you could say, like Mags, that he is just a shagbandit?'

Belle gave a little jump.

'Where does she *get* such language?'

'School, Ma.'

Belle looked round.

'I suppose I should summon her out of her tree . . .'

'In a minute,' Elinor said. She leaned towards her sister.

'M. M – are you OK?'

Marianne nodded vehemently.

'I am. I *am*. I'm – *going* to be.'

'Don't force yourself,' Elinor said.

Marianne said a little desperately, 'Believing in a bastard takes a bit of getting over.'

'Of course.'

'But I'll do it, Ellie. I'll get there. It just – just shakes your self-belief a bit, doesn't it?'

There was a flash of someone running past the kitchen window.

'She's coming.'

The door flew open. Margaret stood on the threshold, panting, her school tie, with its carefully uneven ends, under one ear.

'You'll never guess ...'

'What, Mags?'

'I just saw Thomas,' Margaret said. 'He came to put that other plank in, so I've got more floor space, and he said he'd seen Lucy in Exeter today, all dolled up and stuff, and she flashed a ring at him, a wedding ring.' She paused, and then looked at Elinor, and her expression was one of intense distress. 'Ellie,' she said, 'Ellie, I'm so sorry. I really am – but they're married.'

Elinor lay wakefully in the dark. Marianne had wanted to stay with her and be comforting, but Elinor had said that she needed to be alone, quite alone, and Marianne hadn't persisted but had simply slipped back to her own room without saying anything further, just squeezing Elinor's shoulder as she left.

So, Elinor thought, here I am, here we are, all of us, roughly where we were when we left Norland, except that Marianne has survived an adventure – or, you could say, had an amazingly lucky escape – and I have had my hopes raised and lowered so many times that now that they are finally dashed, I'm so battered by the seesaw that I hardly know what I feel. Except I do. If I'm honest, I know that I went on hoping, hoping and hoping, that Edward's good conduct would finally see a bit of good sense too, and he wouldn't actually *marry* her. Of course, she'd want to marry *him*, as fast as possible, in case he got away, but I really thought – no, I really *hoped* – that he would realise that if he went through with it, he was committing an act of utterly idiotic nobility, and the end result would be misery all round. A gigantic pratfall, and the biggest prat would be him.

I don't want him, Elinor thought, twisting restlessly on to her side, to look a prat. I don't want him to be miserable. I don't want him and Lucy all mixed up with Bill and Delaford and everything, so that I can't avoid them, and have to go on pretending I'm OK. I'm not OK. Even Ma saw I wasn't OK tonight and made a very un-Ma-like speech about taking me for granted and how sorry she was. I don't think I was very graceful about what she said. I think I just grunted. I shouldn't have, but I couldn't quite summon up the energy to behave as I ought to have done. Poor Ma. I'll say sorry tomorrow. I'll do a lot of things tomorrow, like starting to emulate Marianne in putting loving a waste-of-space man behind me. It's so – so disappointing. Disappointment is so hard to bear – why don't we make more allowance for it? Dashed hopes, resigning oneself, learning to bear, to endure – why is there so much of it, all the time?

Sleep was clearly out of the question. She got out of bed and went to the window. It was completely dark at Barton at night-time, and the only lights she could see now were the security ones in the stable yard down at the Park, no doubt triggered by a passing fox. They'd been so concerned, everyone at the Park, about Marianne, sending flowers, and a basket of mini muffins, and the children had drawn pictures for her, and signed them with hearts and smiley faces. And when Elinor had gone to find Thomas at suppertime to ask him the details of meeting Lucy in Exeter, he'd looked so grave and sorry, and told her what had happened with the most profound reluctance.

'I didn't want you to know,' he said. He was holding the high-pressure hose he used to wash mud off Sir John's Range Rover. 'But I didn't want you not to know, either.'

Elinor looked away. She said, with difficulty, 'Did you see him?'

'No,' Thomas said. 'To be honest, I was glad not to. She said he was waiting in the car. I don't know where they were going. I didn't ask. I didn't want to know.'

Elinor wrapped her arms round herself for consolation. She said sadly, 'Thank you for telling me.'

He sighed. He yanked out a length of hose and let it slap on to the garage floor.

'I wouldn't have,' he said, 'if she hadn't shown me her ring. I wouldn't have believed her. But there was the ring, and her saying – laughing, she was – that she was Lucy Ferrars now.' He'd glanced up at Elinor. 'Pardon my French, but he's a bloody idiot.'

And that, Elinor thought, will be the general opinion. That gormless Ferrars boy, captured by a gold-digger. Those silly Dashwood girls, blighted by a universally hopeless taste in men. No wonder they're single. Their poor mother. The lights in the stable yard went out suddenly and the whole valley below vanished into darkness. Elinor shivered. It might be almost early summer, but the night air was still quite sharp. Was it easier to detach yourself emotionally from a real bastard, like Wills, or from a basically lovely man who'd got so screwed up by his childhood that he persisted in doing the wonderfully right thing in the totally wrong way? Whichever, it hurt. It hurt and hurt. And she was going to have to get used to living with that hurt because she was not the kind of person who gave her heart away at all easily. Damn him. Damn them all. Instead of lecturing Marianne about facing herself rather than seeking a rescuing soulmate, she was going to have to eat her own patronising words, syllable by syllable.

She ran back across the room and leaped into bed, whirling the duvet over her head and letting it settle softly round her.

'Serve you right,' she said to herself in the shrouded darkness. 'Serve you *completely* right, stupid, *stupid* Miss Sensible.'

One of the advantages of Barton Cottage was its position. Not only were there spectacular views, but you could see anyone approaching: in fact, nobody could get to the cottage by one of Sir John's estate roads without being visible for the last mile at least. But that visibility, Belle had decided, after nine months of living without neighbours, noise or light pollution, also served to remind her how astonishingly isolated she was. She remembered once reading an interview with a man who had retreated to live on a remote Hebridean island and who, when asked if he wasn't lonely, replied robustly that luckily he wasn't afraid of the inside of his own head. It wasn't that Belle was exactly *afraid* of what was inside her head, but more that she was rather bored by it. Life at Norland had always been busy with all those rooms and people to look after. There wasn't a day, she reflected, without more people to feed than just the family, and if it wasn't guests, it was the garden. The garden at Norland had been insatiable. The garden here at Barton Cottage was negligible, being laid out with holiday lets in mind, and whatever trimming or mowing needed doing was done by Thomas with a kind of park-keeper's competence that was not at all to Belle's taste. Sometimes – and even with a convalescent Marianne in the house – Belle would stand at her sitting-room window, between the old damask curtains brought from Norland, and gaze at Sir John's well-maintained and virtually empty roads laid out below her in the valley, and feel an isolation so intense that she wondered that a booming voice didn't issue from the clouds above the hills and ask her if she was all right?

'I can't spend all summer doing nothing,' she said to Marianne. 'And nor can you.'

Marianne was in a chair by the sitting-room window with her laptop balanced on her knee.

'I'm not,' she said, without looking up. 'I'm checking courses.'

'Oh, good,' Belle said. 'Not—' She stopped.

'Not checking Facebook to see what Wills is up to, you mean?'

'Well, I—'

'Ma,' Marianne said, 'I think I am pretty well over John Willoughby.'

'Really, darling? Really?'

Marianne raised her head to look at her mother.

'I'm over him enough to see I had quite a lucky escape, and that just fancying someone isn't enough, especially if you can't trust them or respect them. I can't say I don't still fancy him a bit, if I'm completely honest, but I do see that he was bad for me, and bad to me, and made me far more miserable than he ever made me happy. So I've come a long way, Ma, don't you think? And don't start crying. *Don't.* Just tell me something nice – like what plans have you been making?'

'Darling, I never—'

'Yes, you do, all the time. You're always planning something. What have you got in your little Ma mind now?'

Belle said, sniffing slightly but with an elaborate air of casualness, 'I thought we could ask some people to stay.'

'Like?'

'Well ...'

'Not like Fanny and John, please, Ma.'

'No,' Belle said. 'Certainly not Fanny and John. More like – Bill, actually.'

'Bill,' Marianne echoed, without emphasis.

'He'd be a lovely guest.'

'He usually stays at the Park, Ma.'

'He's been so sweet, ringing to ask how you are. He was horrified when you came out of hospital, you were so pale and drawn. It was pitiful to see.'

Marianne looked up, smiling.

'Who was, Ma? Me or him?'

Belle took no notice.

'Well, I've asked him to come and stay, and he hasn't said he won't.'

Marianne went on smiling.

'Good,' she said.

'Will you be nice to him, darling?'

'Of course. As long as you don't watch us.'

'Darling! Would I?'

'Yes,' Marianne said. She looked back at her screen.

Belle went on staring down the valley. Then she said, 'That *could*, of course, be his car.'

Marianne refused to look up.

'What a surprise.'

'I thought he drove a Range Rover.'

'He does,' Marianne said.

'Well,' Belle said, peering, 'this car coming isn't a Range Rover, but it's quite big, bigger than—'

'Ma,' Marianne said, 'I think you knew he was coming all along. He can sleep in Ellie's room and she can move in with me.'

'It isn't a Range Rover,' Belle said. 'It's quite big and dark, one of those four-wheel-drive things.'

'Maybe it isn't coming here. Or it's one of Jonno's estate people, a surveyor or something.'

'It *is* coming here,' Belle said. 'It's coming up the hill, quite fast. It won't be a woman driving; women don't drive like that – have you noticed? – they don't sort of *gun* the engine.'

Marianne put her laptop on the floor and rose to stand by her mother, peering too. After a few moments she gave a little gasp.

'Ma!'

'What, darling?'

'I – I think it's Edward!'

'It can't be ...'

'I think it is. It's his hair. And the way he's sitting. He's – he's coming here!'

'Ellie's not back from work!'

Marianne drew a huge breath and stared down the valley again.

'Ed,' she said, almost to herself. 'Ed. How *dare* he?'

Edward Ferrars pulled up in front of the cottage and got slowly out of the car. He looked terrible, thinner than ever and as pale as if he'd been under a stone for a month.

Belle said at once, 'I must go and greet him. Poor boy.'

Marianne tried to clutch her.

'Ma, don't—'

But Belle had gone, running out of the room, out of the front door. Marianne saw her go up to Ed and put her hands on his upper arms and look up at him. She was probably, being Ma, saying something sweet, something welcoming. He just stood there and stared down at her, looking wretched. Had he, in a typical, clumsy, good-hearted, wrong-footed Ed way, come to say sorry? If he had, what the hell good would he think it would do, with a ring firmly on Lucy's finger and Elinor's heart in pieces on the floor? What was he doing there, what was he thinking, if indeed he was thinking anything at all, having made such a massive mess of so many lives?

A flash of colour caught her eye. Down the valley below the cottage, making its lurid way across the park, was Elinor's car. Elinor and Margaret were on their way back, would be up the hill and at the cottage within minutes.

Marianne hurried out on to the drive. Ed was still standing gazing distractedly down at Belle, who was saying, in a way that made Marianne briefly despair, 'Of course we hope you'll be happy, Ed, of course we don't wish you anything but a happy future—'

Marianne shouted, 'Elinor's coming!'

Ed's head jerked up. He said, almost gasping, 'She's who I came to see.'

Marianne looked at him, unsmiling. She said grimly, 'I bet you did.'

'No, I—'

Belle gave him a little pat.

'I'm sure she won't be cross with you.'

'And *I'm* sure', Marianne said, 'that she should be.'

The orange car was climbing up the hill.

'Just listen to that poor old engine!' Belle said with determined gaiety.

'Shush,' Marianne said. 'I vote we none of us say anything till Ellie gets here.'

'But, darling...'

Marianne folded her arms and stared down the hill. Ed glanced at her, stepped away from Belle and looked at his feet. Belle retreated a step or two and put her hands in her trouser pockets. Slowly, unevenly, the orange car toiled up the hill and crunched to a halt beside Ed's car. Immediately, the passenger door opened and Margaret climbed out, scattering her possessions. She glared at Ed.

'Where's the Sierra?' she demanded.

'I – I haven't got it any more.'

'New car?' Margaret said. 'New wife?'

'No,' he said distractedly. 'No. I – The car's Bill's. Bill lent me the car. It's a Delaford car.'

Elinor had emerged slowly from her side of the car, and now stood with one foot still inside it, looking at Ed across its roof. She said, wonderingly, 'Ed?'

'Yes.'

'What – what are you doing here?'

He shifted a little on the gravel. He said unhappily, 'All this stupid Twitter stuff . . .'

'What of it?'

'I came . . .'

'Yes?'

He took a step forward, and then another, and then, in a stumbling rush, got as far as the orange car and leaned on the roof, stretching out towards Elinor. He said, almost shouting, 'Ellie, it isn't me who got married!'

Elinor gave a little cry. She put a hand over her mouth.

'What?' Margaret said.

Edward said, 'I was worried you'd think from Lucy's tweets that it was me she'd married. It's not me. It – it was Robert.'

Elinor's face was as white as paper.

She whispered, 'But I thought Robert was – is . . .'

'He is,' Ed said. 'He wanted a beard, or whatever you call it, for some reason. No, not for some reason. Because – because, oh, I'll tell you. Another time. And Lucy doesn't care. Lucy wanted money. They just did it, on impulse, like – like celebrity kids do. For a sort of laugh.'

'Oh, Ed . . .'

He put his foot on the sill of the passenger door and stepped up, so that he could almost touch Elinor across the car roof.

He said, 'I'm so relieved. I was in such a state in case you thought—'

Elinor stretched a hand out to meet his. She said, shakily, 'So – so you aren't with Lucy, you aren't married—'

'No,' he said, and his face broke into a wide smile. He made a kind of dive across the car roof so that he could grasp both her hands. 'No. Thank all the gods. But, Ellie – Ellie, I really would like to be. Please?'

18

Margaret stood in the landing window of Barton Cottage, looking out into the dark garden. She was supposed to be in bed – she was wearing the T-shirt and American flannel pull-on trousers she slept in – and had done a lot of door-banging and lavatory-flushing and shouting, in order to convince everyone downstairs that she was on her way to bed, but had actually crept out on to the landing again, so that she could look out at her tree house for a bit longer.

It was softly illuminated by several candles in old jam jars, illuminated enough, anyway, for her to see Ed and Elinor up there, huddled together under a blanket. She couldn't quite see their faces, but sometimes she caught the gleam of Elinor's hair, or the shine of the wine glasses they had taken up there, and if she leaned out of the window, she could hear the murmur of their voices and occasional little bursts of laughter. They sounded very happy.

Margaret felt rather proud of their happiness. They had been absolutely glowing with it at supper – Ed was like a different man: he said he'd been so sure Elinor would send him away with a flea in his ear that he'd felt extremely sick when he first arrived

– and Margaret had found herself wanting somehow to augment all this joy and so she'd said, out of the blue, 'Why don't you two go up to my tree house? There's masses of space now.'

Elinor had beamed at her.

'Oh, Mags! Could we?'

And Ed had looked as if she'd given him a present or something, and had got up, and come round the table to hug her, and said, 'You're a complete star, Mags Dashwood. D'you know that?'

Margaret had felt not only a glow of satisfaction, but also a novel sense of having done something both good and useful. She'd got up from the table then and found a basket, and Belle had put a bottle of wine in it, and glasses, and a new packet of chocolate biscuits, and some apples, and a piece of cheese, and they had all processed out into the dusky garden and helped the two of them climb up the ladder Thomas had made. It was Marianne who put the candles in the jars, and Belle who produced the old rug from the back of the sofa, and then they'd left them there, on the platform in the tree, with each other and their future and the ring Ed had actually had, all along, in his pocket.

It wasn't a diamond, Margaret was told, it was an aquamarine. Same difference, Margaret thought, except it was sort of blue, not white, but it sparkled, and it made Elinor cry, even if in a way Margaret could see was very different from the kind of crying they usually went in for. Elinor kept looking at it, on her hand, kissing Ed, and then laughing. Ed had talked more at supper than Margaret had ever heard him, describing how he'd kept going back to Lucy's family when he was a teenager, because they were cosy and welcoming, and didn't make him feel an utter failure, like his mother and sister did, and he'd thought Lucy was quite pretty, then, because he didn't know any better – 'Only a moron would think that,' Margaret interrupted, and he'd laughed and said, 'Moron's the word, Mags!' – and how he'd got so defeated by his mother insisting on him training to be things he couldn't bear to be that he'd got himself in a hopeless state, on the very edge of doing something that would cause him the keenest regret all the rest of his life.

Margaret strained her eyes to see them both in her tree. She thought she could make out that Ed had his arm round Elinor, and that their heads were very close together, probably touching. It was so great, it really was. Not just because it was what Ellie had wanted all along, but because Edward would be very susceptible to her, Margaret's, nagging him to teach her to drive. After all, if he was part of the family, he'd have no escape.

'Are you cold?' Edward said.

'I'm too happy to be cold.'

'Me too. It's like paradise here, in Mags's tree, with you. I can't believe it, I can't believe my luck, I can't believe you said yes.'

'You knew I'd say yes.'

'I didn't, I was terrified.'

'You had the ring in your pocket.'

'I wanted you to know I meant it; I wanted to prove to you that you were it. For me. If you'd have me.'

'I'll have you,' Elinor said.

'That's what I can't believe.'

Elinor shifted a little, so that her left shoulder was tucked right under Edward's arm.

'What I can't believe', she said, 'is Lucy.'

'Do we have to talk about her?'

'Only enough to satisfy my curiosity.'

'About what?'

'About', Elinor said, 'what she was doing, marrying your brother Robert, who is—' She stopped.

He kissed her nose.

'Gay,' he said.

'Yes.'

'He knew he was gay when he was tiny. I remember him coming down to breakfast once, when he was about seven, in a necklace of Fanny's and a huge hat with a feather. And my parents didn't blink. Did not blink. They used to describe him to other people as being very much his own person. That was their phrase. Very much his own person.'

'So – your mother doesn't know?'

Edward captured Elinor's left hand and held it out to see the ring glinting by the light of the nearest candle.

'I have no idea if she knows. But she won't acknowledge it if she does. She won't discuss it. She just says he's unusual.'

'So – he can't talk about it, with her?'

Edward raised her hand to kiss it.

'You can't talk to her about anything. Except money. Stocks and shares and house prices.'

'Poor Robert.'

'He doesn't care. He lives his own life and milks her for money when he needs it.'

'But Lucy,' Elinor said, 'Lucy must know he's gay, she must have known all along.'

'She won't care, either,' Edward said.

'She must, she can't not mind that her husband is just using her as a shield—'

Edward said flatly, 'She'll be fine with it.'

Elinor turned to look at his shadowed face.

'But—'

'Ellie,' Edward said, 'don't judge everyone else by your lovely and right standards. Lucy is only out for Lucy. If there isn't trouble, she makes it, like snowballing me with texts threatening to tell my mother we were an item, as she put it, so that I had to text her back saying please don't, please, please don't. God, Ellie, I was so drunk that night, and of course that played right into her hands. She's got exactly what she set out to get, even if not with the brother she first thought of. Don't waste an iota of concern on her. Lucy's got her hands on a pile of money, and Robert's got a cover as far as my mother is concerned to do whatever he wants. They've done a deal. It suits them both. They're as selfish as each other. They'll live their own lives and probably enjoy the joke of being married. And I – lucky, lucky me – have got you.'

'But—'

'I want to kiss you, Ellie, I want to just—'

'One more thing,' Elinor said.

'What?'

'How did you know you were off the hook with Lucy?'

Edward gave a bark of laughter. He said, 'You'll never believe it. An email.'

'An email?'

'Yes.' He looked back down at her, and bent so that he could kiss her on the mouth. 'She wrote me an email,' he said, his face almost touching Elinor's, 'saying that she couldn't marry me when she was in love, actually, with someone else. Who just happened to be my gay brother. Who, I wonder, did she think she had a vestige of a hope of fooling?'

'Perhaps she didn't care?'

He put his hand under her chin and tilted her face up to his.

'I don't care,' he said. 'I don't care about her or Robert or my family or anybody. I can't tell you how much I don't care about them. All I care about, lovely Elinor with my ring on your finger, is you.'

'What?' Mrs Ferrars said. She held the telephone a little distance from her ear, as if it might scorch her.

Fanny Dashwood, ringing her mother from her new sitting room cum office at Norland Park, raised her voice even further.

'It's not good news, Mother. Are you sitting down?'

'I hear better if I'm standing up,' Mrs Ferrars said, as if explaining something to someone extremely stupid. 'You know that.'

'Mother,' Fanny said, 'it's about Robert.'

'What?' Mrs Ferrars demanded, suddenly alert. 'Is he ill?'

'No, Mother,' Fanny said. 'No. He's perfectly fine. But – but he's got married, would you believe ...'

There was a pause. Mrs Ferrars adjusted something in her mind. Then she said, 'Nonsense.'

'It's not nonsense, Mother.'

'If Robert were married,' Mrs Ferrars said firmly, 'he or the Mortons would have told me. He tells me everything.'

'Mother,' Fanny said, raising her voice again, 'he hasn't married Tassy Morton.'

'He must have.'

'He hasn't, he hasn't, he's married – oh God, Mother – Robert has married Lucy Steele.'

There was a further pause. Then Mrs Ferrars said, 'Who?'

'Lucy Steele. The girl with the teeth and the sister. You know, Mother. She was going to marry Edward.'

Mrs Ferrars gave a little scream.

'You're making it up!'

'I'm not, Mother. I'm not. They got married in Devon or something, from Lucy's home, on an impulse.'

'Why?' Mrs Ferrars wailed. 'Why?'

'Oh, Mother, who knows? He's always been a law unto himself.'

'How could he do this to me?' Mrs Ferrars cried. 'How could he treat his own mother like this?'

'It's not about you, Mother,' Fanny said crossly. 'It's about the family. And Father's money.'

Mrs Ferrars seemed to pull herself together.

'Well,' she said in a much more decided tone, 'they won't get a penny of that.'

Fanny said wearily, 'You don't mean that, Mother.'

'I do, I certainly do!'

'No, you don't. You adore Robert. You always forgive Robert.'

Mrs Ferrars said, unexpectedly, 'Why isn't that girl marrying Edward? After all the fuss?'

Fanny said sharply, 'Because she knows which side her bread is buttered, Mother. And she knows Robert is your favourite.'

'She's right,' Mrs Ferrars said, her voice somewhat softened, 'I have always found Robert much easier to deal with. A sweeter nature, you know.'

'So you'll forgive him—'

'I didn't say that, Fanny.'

'But you will. You'll let Lucy worm her way in, with Robert's help, and before you know it, she'll have carte blanche to do up the house in Norfolk—'

'Don't be so jealous, Fanny,' Mrs Ferrars said. 'I've never liked sibling rivalry: you knew that. And you've had your fair share, and more. I don't care for someone with a house like Norland begrudging her brother having a mere farmhouse in Norfolk.'

'Mother, I never said, I never meant—'

'In any case,' Mrs Ferrars said, interrupting, 'that house needs renovating. I would say, actually, that renovation is long overdue.'

Fanny gave a little shriek, and threw her phone across the room. Mrs Ferrars took her own phone away from her ear and shook it a little, as if in puzzlement, and then, with determined precision, began to dial Robert's number.

Sir John Middleton was in his element. The weather was better, the house was full – both Bill Brandon and Abigail Jennings had returned to occupy their old bedrooms for at least a long weekend – that poor girl up at the cottage was on the mend, and there was also a full-blown romance going on up there between her sister and the F-word boy. Add to that the news that his son and heir had gained a place at his father's old school – Mary was making an immense fuss about the boy boarding, at his age, but he had yet to silence her with reminders of pipes and tunes – and the signing of a satisfactory new contract with a clothing distributor in northern India, and Sir John could feel that all was pretty well in his good-natured if not over-sensitive world.

He was especially pleased to see old Bill back at Barton Park. It seemed months since he had been there, months in which Bill had been preoccupied with all the halfwits he seemed so devoted to, never mind that mad bad daughter of the girl he'd once been so keen on. Sir John shook his head. He had a shocking propensity to try and sort the wrecks, poor old Bill, and seemed never happier than when knee deep in other people's problems and trouble. And it had had an effect, of course it had, ageing the poor fellow before his time, stiffening his morals, fossilising his sense of fun. But he seemed different this visit, very different, improved even. In fact, Sir John would go as far as to say that Bill was very nearly relaxed.

Last night, when they were all at dinner – nine of them round the table, and Sir John would ideally have liked double that number – and those girls were telling Bill what had happened to Robert Ferrars and Lucy Steele, Bill was laughing with the best of them. Mind you, Marianne was a brilliant mimic, and by the time she'd taken off Lucy Steele and old Mrs Ferrars, and Fanny Dashwood having the vapours, they were all of them sobbing with laughter. It had been a riot, an absolute riot. With many more riots to come, Sir John sincerely hoped. Not only was fun right up his street, but it livened Mary up nicely. She'd been, well, quite amenable later that night, even – dare he say it – a bit frisky. He beamed to himself and leaned forward to read something that had just popped up on his screen.

There was a knock on his office door.

'Come!' he called.

The door opened on to a familiar billow of scarves.

'Jonno?'

'Abi, my dear.'

'Am I interrupting?'

'Yes, Abi. You always are. I am a busy man.'

'Two minutes, Jonno.'

He waved a hand towards a chair the other side of the desk.

'Sit, you. No coffee, because I don't want you staying.'

Abigail subsided into the chair.

'I must have a little sound-off.'

'Go ahead.'

Mrs Jennings settled her scarves. Then she leaned forward slightly.

'Last night, dear. Huge fun. Enormous fun. And those girls are a joy, aren't they? Bill looked a decade younger, even though there is no point in him gazing at Marianne. She could have her pick, the form she's in right now, she has no need—'

'Abi,' Sir John said warningly.

Abigail collected herself.

'Sorry, dear. Sorry. Well, what I wanted to say was that I'm afraid I just don't care how rude they are about that little minx, Lucy Steele. I tell you, Jonno, she was in my sitting room, plead-ing poverty and true love for Edward, ten minutes before she runs off with his brother! And then, no sooner has she gone, than her sister tips up, having lent Lucy whatever she could spare, in a panic that Mrs Ferrars would have their guts for garters, and also distraught because she now couldn't afford the plane fare to join her plastic surgeon at a villa party he's having in Ibiza, or somewhere. So, me being as silly as I'm soft-hearted—'

'Abi,' Sir John said, 'you could tell me all this any time. I may look as if I'm hardly ever working—'

Mrs Jennings shook her head.

'I'm hopeless, dear. Really I am. But I'll get to the point. And the point is – is that Ferrars boy really in love with Elinor?'

Sir John gawped at her.

'Several hundred per cent, I'd say.'

'Well,' Abigail said, 'I need to know because you see, he utterly adored Lucy.'

'No, he didn't.'

'My dear Jonno, she broke his heart!'

Sir John stood up, for emphasis.

'Rubbish,' he said.

She stood too, uncertainly.

'He was trying to do the right thing,' Sir John said. 'He felt obliged to her family, having a mother like he's got. That's all.'

'But she said—'

Sir John strode over to his office door and opened it.

'Out, Abi.'

'Yes, dear.'

She trotted over, and paused in front of him. She said, defensively, 'I like to think the best of people, Jonno.'

He bent towards her. He said firmly, 'Then don't waste your time on the worst ones, Abi,' and pushed her out of the room.

Edward was lying on the sofa at Barton Cottage. He had spent the day at Delaford with Bill Brandon, being shown round the place and meeting the people, and had come back to Barton with the contented and slightly disbelieving feeling that he had at last found a work environment that chimed amazingly with his own temperament and beliefs. He was waiting now, his head on a cushion and his feet dangling over the arm at the end of the sofa, for Elinor to come home from work in Exeter.

He could not believe the depth of his contentment, nor the height of his optimism. He wasn't sure he had ever felt either, before, and certainly never to such a degree. Everywhere he looked seemed bathed in light, and every time he thought of Elinor, something inside him felt as if it was simply dissolving in rapture. He lay there, looking at a faint crack in the ceiling and watching a very small spider venturing out along its length, and thought that if this was happiness, then it ought to be bottled and fed intravenously to every single patient of the National Health Service.

'Gosh, you look down,' Marianne said, approvingly, from the doorway.

He turned his head and waved at her.

'Never been more miserable,' he said. 'Can't you see?'

She held out the phone in her hand. She said, smiling, 'Call for you.'

He swung himself upright.

'For me? On your phone?'

Marianne made a slight face.

'It's brother John. He wants to talk to you.'

'Yikes.'

Marianne put the phone to her ear. She said, 'I've found him, John. Hard at work on the sofa. I'll hand you over.'

Edward took the phone and held it gingerly against his head. 'John?'

The other end of the line, John Dashwood sounded very grave.

'I imagine, Edward, it's a bit late for recriminations—'

'Much too late,' Edward said cheerfully, 'and completely pointless, as I have never, ever, in my whole life been so—'

'Edward,' John Dashwood said majestically.

'What?'

'Your mother is heartbroken. Your sister is feeling, naturally, completely betrayed. It is, in fact, astonishing that either of them are still functioning, let alone as well as they are.'

Edward looked back at the spider.

'Oh,' he said.

'I would have hoped, Edward, for a much more concerned response. Your mother, your sister—'

'Sorry, John,' Edward said, 'but you should be ringing Robert, not me.'

John Dashwood took a steadying breath. He said, 'Do you realise, Edward, that your mother has not actually mentioned your name since this whole disgraceful business began?'

Edward aimed an imaginary gun at the spider and fired. He said, with one eye shut, 'No change there, then.'

John Dashwood sounded outraged.

'Edward!'

Edward said nothing. He got up and stood looking out of the window. Soon, Elinor's car would come into view.

'Are you still there?' John Dashwood said.

'I am.'

'Will you please listen to me?'

'Of course.'

'Your sister and I – Fanny and I – think you could very easily do something to ease the situation. Your own, as well as your mother's.'

'Which is?' Edward said guardedly.

'You should write to her. You should write and say how sorry you are for upsetting her.'

'Why?' Edward demanded.

'Because she wants nothing so much as for her children to be happy. Because she has been badly wounded by her sons' conduct just recently.'

Edward ran his hand through his hair. He said incredulously, 'Are you saying I should write to my mother and say sorry for Robert?'

'Well, it would be very much to your advantage—'

'No.'

'Edward—'

'No. Absolutely not. Never. I wish I hadn't had all that nonsense with Lucy, but I am so certain, so certain about Elinor that I don't give one single stuff about what any of you think. I'm not sorry. I'm not humble. I might talk to Mother about all this, one day, if she'll ever listen, but I absolutely refuse to write a letter that I don't mean and for something I haven't done. Right?'

John said stiffly, 'You are making a big mistake.'

'Not as big as my mother's!' Edward shouted.

There was silence. Then John said, with elaborate dignity, 'I shall go and convey this to your sister.'

'You do that,' Edward said rudely. 'How does it feel to be pussy-whipped by two women in your life?'

There was shocked silence at the other end of the line. An orange car was creeping along the valley floor, and Edward felt his heart lift in his chest, like a bird.

'Bye,' he said, into the phone, carelessly, 'bye,' and tossed it on to the dented cushions of the sofa.

Marianne was sitting on the ridge above the valley where Allenham lay. She was sitting upright, her hands round her knees, and a yard away, Bill Brandon lay on his elbow in the grass and watched her. Her hair was loose down her back and, every so often, a breath of breeze lifted a strand or two and he watched them float and then settle again.

She was not, he observed, looking tense or strained. She was gazing down at the old house, at its eccentric Tudor chimneys and neat hedge-partitioned gardens, and her expression was one of dreamy half-interest, rather than one of any intensity. It was strangely comfortable, being up there with her, in silence, and he found he was in no hurry to break it, or to know what she was thinking as she looked down, not just on a place she knew, but a place she had hoped to know so much better.

It had, after all, been astonishing to him that she should ask him to walk with her at all. Of course, Belle didn't want her going anywhere alone for the moment, and he had been conveniently lounging about in the garden, ostensibly waiting for Edward, when Marianne had come right up to him, and looked straight at him, and said she needed to go and have a look at Allenham, and would he go with her?

They'd climbed up, companionably enough, through the woods, across the lane and he'd made her, without fuss, stop to catch her breath before they set out across the ridge itself. He'd offered to carry the sweater she'd taken off, and she'd said, 'No,' and he'd calmly said, 'Don't be silly,' and taken it, and she'd turned to him, laughing, and let him. And now here they were, on the rough, tussocky grass high above Allenham, in easy silence, a yard apart. Only a yard, Bill thought, but it's a distance. And I've made it, because I am desperate not to push her. And, actually, it's more than enough, it's wonderful to lie here and watch her able to look down at that house without it distressing her. She's not indifferent – that would be too much to hope for – but she's not yearning, either.

As if she'd read his thoughts. Marianne turned and smiled at him.

She said, 'It's OK.'

'Is it?'

She nodded.

He said, 'Was it a test? To come back here?'

She nodded again.

'Sort of.'

'And you passed?'

She turned to look at him properly. Then she dropped her gaze to the turf. She said softly, 'First love . . .'

He let a beat fall, then he said, 'Tell me about it.'

She gave him a quick smile.

'I don't suppose there'll ever be anything quite like it.'

'No,' he said hesitantly, 'but that doesn't mean it's the best. Only that it's unique in its own way.'

'Because it's the first—'

'And one doesn't know enough not to surrender oneself completely.'

She said, not in a melancholy way, 'I liked that quality.'

'Me too.'

She glanced at him.

'Did you?'

He plucked a buttercup and twirled it. He said ruefully, 'I wanted to drown in what I was feeling.'

'Really?'

'I didn't want to know what she was like. In fact, I wanted not to know. I just wanted what I believed, and to feel.'

'Wow,' Marianne said respectfully.

He smiled at her.

'And you?'

'Just like you,' she said.

'So perhaps,' he said gently, 'we didn't get it so wrong. We didn't deliberately choose the wrong people, because almost anyone would have done, to feed the passion.' He looked across at her and winked. 'At least we chose beautiful people.'

She edged a bit closer to him across the turf. She said, 'Elinor told me that Wills said I didn't mistake him. He did mean it. He does.'

Bill looked at her. He said steadily, 'Eliza knew she'd have been a different person with a better life with me.'

Marianne said, 'Could you have lived with her?'

'I'd have tried.'

'Me too. And it would have half killed me.'

'Yes. Sacrifice is only exciting at the beginning.'

She reached forward and took the buttercup out of his hand. She said, 'I think I'm only beginning.'

'In what way?'

'To learn that there is more to a good life than ... I can't say it.'

'A good life,' he said, stating it.

'Yes. You live a good life.'

He looked at her seriously. He said, 'It could be.'

She looked away. She said, 'I know.'

He got to his feet and held a hand down to her.

'Up you get. Time to go home.'

'Bill—'

'No,' he said. 'No more. Not now.'

She leaned forward and threaded the buttercup into the top buttonhole of his shirt. Then she reached up and kissed him, quickly and lightly.

'I've been so happy with you today,' she said.

19

Mrs Ferrars's flat in Mayfair had not been touched, decoratively speaking, for thirty years. Climbing up the building's common staircase, Edward was transported back to his eight-year-old self, trudging up those same stairs on the same green trellis-patterned carpet between walls dotted with the same dim little flower prints in gilt frames, and feeling an apprehension and a reluctance that time had done nothing to diminish. When he pressed the brass doorbell outside the flat, he couldn't help sighing. He had spent a great deal of his childhood sighing, one way or another. But the last few weeks had introduced him to a completely new kind of sighing, that resulting from an excess of incredulous happiness, which was the kind, he thought, listening to his mother's heels tapping their way along the parquet floor inside the flat, he must arm himself with now.

'Edward,' his mother said without inflection, opening the door. She held up her powdery cheek for a kiss.

He bent obediently. He was aware that she had instantly observed and judged his clothes, and found them to fall short of the standard set by her formal day dress and expensive jewellery.

'Hello, Mother.'

'I imagine you've had lunch?'

'Well, I—'

'I'll make coffee, then. Or you could make yourself useful, and make it for us?'

He said truthfully, 'It's never right for you when I make it.'

She surveyed him again, without, somehow, looking at him in the face. It struck him for the first time how alike she and Fanny were. In a few years' time, they would be indistinguishable: tiny, immaculate, forceful and hard.

In her drawing room, with its elaborate curtains and draped tables bearing rafts of china boxes and silver frames, Mrs Ferrars wasted no time.

'I have had a terrible time recently,' she informed Edward. 'As the mother of a family, I have suffered acutely. I feel, I don't mind telling you, as if I have had no sons at all.'

Edward cleared his throat. He was holding the small bone-china mug she had handed him, a puddle of lukewarm coffee at the bottom.

'Mother,' he said, 'I am here. I have come to see you.'

'And what do you mean by that?'

He made an effort, remembering what Elinor had urged him to do.

'I mean', he said, 'that whatever either of us has done, or not done, I am your son and I don't want to be estranged from you.'

Mrs Ferrars considered this. She was perched on the edge of one of her upright sofas, her patent-clad feet neatly together. She didn't look across at him. She said, 'I hear you aren't going to marry that girl.'

'Not Lucy—'

'Well, what was all that about then?'

'It was a mistake, Mother. I'm just amazingly lucky that it wasn't a worse one.'

She raised her chin. She said disapprovingly, 'A fortune-hunter.'

Edward ignored her. He had no wish to discuss Lucy, or to go anywhere near the topic of his brother. He said, instead, 'But you should know something, Mother. You should know that I am getting married.'

Mrs Ferrars turned to scowl at him.

'Sensibly, I do hope.'

'I've never done anything more sensible in my life.'

'The Mortons are nice people,' Mrs Ferrars said. 'Scaffolding has proved—'

'I'm not marrying a Morton,' Edward said, 'I hardly know them. I have no interest in them. I am marrying Elinor Dashwood. I have asked her, and she has said yes. I absolutely cannot believe that she said yes.'

There was a prolonged silence. Mrs Ferrars looked into the middle distance and Edward looked at his feet. Then she said, 'Even you, with your over-developed sentimental side, must see the sheer folly of doing that. Tassy Morton is worth seven figures now, and will be worth many times that in the future. The Dashwood girl hasn't a penny.'

Edward raised his eyes and looked steadily at his mother. He said, 'I love her.'

Mrs Ferrars made an impatient gesture and clicked her tongue.

'Don't be ridiculous.'

'I am not being ridiculous,' Edward said. 'I have never been less ridiculous. Elinor is the most wonderful person I have ever come across, and it will be your loss if you don't try and get to know her. I wouldn't be here, if it wasn't for her. She told me that I must make things up with you because, to be honest with you, Mother, three days ago I didn't care if I never saw you again.'

Mrs Ferrars gave a little jump. She fished about in her sleeve and brought out a small lawn handkerchief, which she pressed to the skin under her eyes. She said unsteadily, 'You must see the force of what I say. About the discrepancy in their wealth.'

'I do,' Edward said. 'Of course I do. But the thing is, I don't care. I only care about living with the best person I've ever met, for the rest of my life. I'll be earning at Delaford. Elinor will earn more when she's qualified. We get a flat thrown in. It's perfect.'

Mrs Ferrars sniffed. She appeared, if no warmer, at least not to be rallying for further attack. After another pause, she said, 'You know what I gave Fanny ...'

'When she married John?'

'Yes. Well, of course you will have the same.'

'Wow,' Edward said, with genuine appreciation.

'But no more.'

'I don't want more, I didn't even expect—'

'There's no one on the planet who doesn't always want more.'

'Not me, Mother.'

Mrs Ferrars plainly decided to let this idiocy pass. She said, 'I never wanted to fall out with my boys.'

'No, Mother.'

'I never want to stand in the way of your – happiness.'

'Good, Mother.'

'You can't, of course, go back to where you once were in my

352

estimation, but I am relieved to feel I have at least one of my boys back again.'

Edward said nothing. He put the little mug down among the nearest scattering of china boxes and leaned forward.

'Come to Delaford, Mother.'

She looked mildly startled.

'What?'

'This weekend. Everyone's coming this weekend, to see our flat. Come too. Come and meet Bill.'

Mrs Ferrars shifted slightly and blew her nose. She said cautiously, 'Everyone?'

'Elinor's family. The Middletons. Mrs J. John and Fanny and Harry.' He paused and then he said, 'Ellie's going to ring Lucy. Lucy and Robert might be there. We're going to have a sort of picnic. In the grounds if it's fine; in our flat if it's not.'

'A picnic,' Mrs Ferrars said indistinctly.

'Yes, Mother. I know you hate picnics, but it'll be fun. I'll find you a chair.'

'I suppose', Mrs Ferrars said with difficulty, 'that you leave me no option.'

'Is that a yes?'

She looked at him, quickly, for the first time since he had arrived. She gave him a gracious little nod.

'I suppose so,' she said. 'I must just get used to it, mustn't I?'

'My goodness,' John Dashwood said, swinging the Mercedes four-wheel drive through the gates of Delaford, 'Elinor must be insane.'

Fanny, tapping out a text on her smartphone, wasn't paying attention. She said distractedly, 'Why, sweetheart?'

'Well, fancy accepting your brother – no offence, my angel – when she might have had all this!'

Fanny looked vaguely about her. Then, realising what she was looking at, her gaze sharpened. She said, 'It seems very well maintained, I must say.'

'Wonderful trees.'

'Not better than Norland, sweetness.'

'No,' John said hastily. 'No, of course not. I was just thinking that it all might have been Elinor's.'

Fanny gave a little trill of laughter. She said, 'Well, the fact that she bagged Ed leaves the field open for Marianne.'

'D'you really think so? My goodness, look at the house!'

Fanny peered. She said, 'What a pity to use such a gorgeous house for rehabilitation. Such a waste. Yes, I do think if Marianne is waved under Bill Brandon's nose often enough, he'll bite. He's a pushover as far as daffy girls are concerned. You can see that a mile off.' She twisted round in her seat to give the new au pair girl (Czech, this time) the benefit of a dazzling smile directed at Harry, strapped in his car seat. 'OK, Harrykins?'

Harry, who was staring out of the window, took no notice. The Czech nanny didn't lift her eyes from her own phone screen. Fanny twisted back.

'Let's hope everyone behaves,' she said. 'I simply dread seeing Lucy, I don't mind telling you. And if she starts smarming all over Mother—'

'She wouldn't dare, dearest.'

Fanny took a lipstick out of her handbag and flipped the sun visor down to see in the mirror on the back.

'There is no limit to her effrontery, Johnnie,' she said, applying her lipstick. 'And Mother has no resistance to Robert.'

The car ground on to the gravel in front of the house. It was slightly shabbier close to than it had appeared from a distance, but it was still supremely impressive.

'It's a stunner,' John Dashwood said regretfully, 'a real stunner.' He slowed the car to a halt and wrenched on the brake. 'And I'm telling you, my angel, that I wouldn't have minded coming here as Bill's brother-in-law. Think of that! Norland and Delaford.' He gave a sentimental sigh. 'My poor old dad would have been so proud of that!'

'Elinor can't possibly cook in here,' Mrs Jennings said to Belle.

They were, on account of Mrs Jennings's amplitude, almost wedged together into a narrow galley kitchen, whose end was entirely taken up with a window looking out towards the park.

'Oh, I think Bill's going to completely redo it for them,' Belle said. She had drunk a celebratory glass of champagne she had been handed by Sir John, rather fast, and it had made her feel expansive and confident. 'I think he's going to knock walls down and everything. Elinor says we won't recognise the flat in three months' time.'

Abigail gestured towards the window.

'Lovely view.'

'Lovely place,' Belle said. 'Lovely people.'

'Well, dear,' Mrs Jennings said, 'I wouldn't say all of them were.'

'Today,' Belle said, 'everyone seems rather lovely to me. And seeing Ellie so happy, and her and Ed with such a future. And even Marianne—'

'She could do worse', Mrs Jennings said, peering into the sink, 'than set her cap at Bill Brandon—'

'My girls', Belle said, 'never set their caps at anyone. Edward found Elinor in just the way that I hope Bill might find Marianne.'

Mrs Jennings straightened up.

'Point taken, dear.'

'He's the kind of man, Abi, who needs someone to cherish. Like my Henry was.'

'If you say so, dear.'

'But I do have hopes.'

'Well founded, I'd say.'

'She's so young yet—'

'Talking of young,' Mrs Jennings said suddenly, 'what about Margaret?'

Belle focused abruptly.

'Margaret?'

'Hasn't she got a boyfriend yet? She's old enough.'

'She's fourteen. Honestly, Abi, it's all you ever think about. You're like those nineteenth-century novels where marriage is the only career option for a middle-class girl.'

'Just like you, then, dear. You and me both. People pretend things have changed, but have they, really? Look at Charlotte. No brains, I admit, but plenty of capability, and how does she use it? Running houses for Tommy and inventing schedules for that baby. Which reminds me. Or rather the mention of Charlotte reminds me. She told me something about Wills—'

Belle said loftily, interrupting, 'I don't wish to hear his name, let alone anything about him.'

'Yes, you do,' Abigail said. 'Of course you do. Especially if it reflects well on Marianne.'

Belle gave a little shrug.

'In that case ...'

Abigail Jennings wedged herself into the narrow space between the cooker and the wall. She said, 'He went to see Jane Smith.'

Belle tried to look indifferent.

'So?'

'He told Charlotte, dear. Charlotte has a bit of a soft spot for him because she knows he still adores Marianne. Well, he went to see Jane Smith, thinking she might refuse to see him. But she didn't, and she let him speak, and tell her why he'd married the Greek girl, and how he felt about Marianne, and all about that awful drama with Marianne in hospital. Everything. And when he'd finished, she let a silence fall, and then she said – quite affectionately, he told Charlotte – that she forgave him. And of course, he could hardly believe what he was hearing, and he was about to cast himself at her feet and tell her how wonderful she was when she stopped him, and said that if he'd done the right thing by Marianne, he could have had hers – Jane's – money as well as her forgiveness, but as it was, he'd have to make do with just the latter! Charlotte said she expected him to be furiously angry, but she said he was more rueful than angry. He said it was a gamble that hadn't paid off, but that he wasn't sorry he'd taken the risk. And . . .'

She paused and looked at Belle with significance.

'And', she went on, 'he said to Charlotte that although he didn't love his wife, he didn't think his life would be all dark, either, that he'd probably salvage something out of it one way or another. But that he'd never feel about anyone the way he felt about Marianne, and if he heard that she'd married Bill Brandon, he'd be gutted. That was the word he used to Charlotte, dear. Gutted.'

Belle took a deep breath and edged herself past Abigail to the doorway.

'I never trusted him, you know,' she said. 'It was something about his eyes.'

'Holy smoke,' Sir John Middleton said to his wife, 'will you look at those two?'

Across the lawn, to the south of Delaford House, came Mr and Mrs Robert Ferrars. They were dressed alike, in cream cutaway coats over skinny jeans and cowboy boots. Lucy's hair was in long ringlets down her back, and Robert's was crowned with a cream trilby hat. They wore sunglasses, and they were holding hands.

'It's jaw-dropping,' Sir John said.

Mary Middleton put her own sunglasses on so that she could scrutinise them less conspicuously. She said, 'What do they think they're doing?'

Sir John took her arm.

'Watch,' he said.

Halfway across the lawn, Bill Brandon had set up tables, under sun umbrellas, laden with food and drinks. People had gathered there, in companionable groups, among them Edward and Elinor. He had his arm firmly around her shoulders and they looked, as Mary had pointed out to her husband, as delighted with themselves and their situation as a newly engaged couple ought to be.

They were not, plainly, aware of Lucy and Robert advancing towards them, but were instead talking to John Dashwood, who, since he was facing the direction of the house, saw the newly married couple before Edward and Elinor did. He not only saw them, but was utterly astonished by what he saw, and broke off what he was saying to stand there, his mouth half open, and his arm, clutching a tumbler of Pimm's, outstretched in a gesture of amazement.

'Ellie!' Lucy Ferrars cried, loud enough to be heard across the lawn. 'This is so fab!'

She flung her arms out wide, and then swooped forward and wrapped them round Elinor.

'Big brother!' Robert exclaimed to Edward, who was standing stunned by what had happened to Elinor, and did the same.

'They planned it!' Mary Middleton exclaimed to her husband.

'She's a baggage, that girl,' Sir John said.

'You didn't think so once.'

'Neither of us did, my duck. We were completely taken in.'

'Well,' Mary said, 'that's not happening now! Look at Ellie!'

Elinor had stepped smartly back out of Lucy's embrace, and taken Edward's hand to help him do the same. Lucy and Robert exchanged glances and took another step forward. Elinor held up a hand.

'No!' she said warningly.

Sir John shook his wife's arm.

'Good girl,' he said approvingly. 'Good for Elinor.'

There was a small stir in another group across the lawn, and from it emerged Mrs Ferrars, diminutive and upright in a linen coat dress, her handbag over her arm. She marched determinedly across the grass until she was standing beside Elinor.

'It might be', she said to Elinor in carrying tones, 'how you go on in your family. But it's not the case in ours. Family is family. Blood is thicker than water. This party is, I believe, to celebrate your engagement to my son. It was at your instigation that my younger son and his wife were invited. So I think it hardly behoves you not to welcome them when they do come, do you?'

There was an appalled silence. Edward and Elinor stared at his mother, mute with surprise. And then Lucy Ferrars, tearing off her sunglasses and uttering a theatrical sob, tottered forward and put her arms round her new mother-in-law instead.

'Oh, thank you!' she said tremulously. 'Thank you, thank you.'

The sun was setting. From the window of the room that would be their future sitting room, Edward and Elinor watched the shadow of the house inch its way over the grass to where the trees began, on the edge of the park. Elinor said, 'It makes me think of Norland.'

He put an arm round her. He said, 'If it wasn't for Norland...'

'I know.'

He kissed the side of her head. He said, 'We pulled it off today, you know.'

'Even your mother's little moment?'

'Even that. Lucy won't get very far. My mother will do almost anything for Robert, but she won't let anyone else have first call on him. It might have looked like a little triumph for Lucy today, but it won't last. Mother has a hair-trigger response to exploitation.'

'And Fanny—'

Edward laughed.

'Fanny won't forgive Lucy.'

'She was quite nice to me today.'

He kissed her again. He said, 'No one can resist being nice to you. In the end.'

Elinor leaned against him. She said, 'D'you think Ma means it, about moving into Exeter?'

Edward said, 'At least she's got the good sense not to try and move here.'

'It would be better for Mags, in Exeter,' Elinor said. 'Barton Cottage will be unbearable for Mags if I'm not there, and Marianne's in Bristol much of the time. And if Ma actually gets this little teaching job she's after—'

'Hey,' Edward said suddenly, 'look at that!'

Along the edge of the trees, in and out of the dappled sunlight, came a couple walking together, her long skirt catching picturesquely on the clumps of tall grasses as she passed. Elinor bent forward to see better. She said, 'They're not holding hands.'

'No. But they look pretty comfortable together.'

'She's holding flowers instead. She's always done that. When we were little, we had to keep stopping on walks so she could pick something, and then she'd just leave them somewhere, on the doorstep or the table or in her gumboot, and they'd die.'

Edward said softly, 'They actually look pretty happy, don't you think?'

Elinor smiled.

'Nine months ago she said he was old and boring and wore scarves to protect his throat in winter.'

'What would she say now, d'you suppose?'

Elinor glanced up at him. She laughed.

She said, 'I think she'd say that she was mistaken!'

Edward looked out across the lawn again. He said, 'What d'you reckon his chances are?'

Elinor turned to face him, so that she could put her arms around him and lay her cheek against his chest.

'I reckon', she said, her voice faintly muffled, 'that his chances are pretty good. Marianne can't do anything by halves, and certainly not loving.'

'All or nothing.'

'Yes.'

Edward put his own arms around her and laid his cheek on the top of her head.

'All,' he said contentedly. 'All. I'll settle for that.'